Praise for

America W...

"Sprawling but absorbing. . . . Amb... descriptions of small and often deva... ...dividual experience within those larger histories. . . . The reader experiences the era's social upheavals and contests of values at their most intimate register."

—*The New York Times Book Review*

"Sixties radicalism and the space program are set in fruitful juxtaposition in this ambitious novel. . . . Displays a sure-handed lyricism . . . its energy lies in its skepticism about the American century and the parallels the author finds between contradictory currents."   —*The New Yorker*

"Ms. Alcott is an impressionistic stylist capable of lovely, luminous effects on the brushstroke level of the sentence. . . . Such writing seems well suited to fantasy, and because nothing is more like a fairy tale than space travel, it makes sense that Ms. Alcott is at her best in zero gravity."

—*The Wall Street Journal*

"Ms. Alcott's tale of the late twentieth century and its discontents mirrors and contextualizes our current times. . . . Readers who value elegant style will savor Alcott's musical sentences and dreamlike pacing. . . . Readers who enjoy literary fiction have a golden opportunity to not just look, but also to really see. Highly recommended."   —*Pittsburgh Post-Gazette*

"[Alcott's] prose has a way of finding the cinematic in the personal. . . . What hooks the reader are Alcott's darts of wisdom and finely tuned observations. . . . Alcott's narration is penetrating and elegant, but she gives her characters some of the wittiest and most screen-ready dialogue in contemporary fiction."   —*The Paris Review*

"Kathleen Alcott writes with pulsating, intense prose, delivering an account of how lives can be meshed and torn apart. . . . Powerful. . . . *America Was Hard to Find* leaves readers wanting more of this story and everything else Alcott has written."   —*BookPage*

"Alcott offers her own antiwar observation of Cold War America. . . . The elegance of Alcott's writing poses an interesting contrast to her heroine's inner life. . . . Alcott brings her full aesthetic gifts to bear." —*Longreads*

"Like Franzen or DeLillo, Alcott brings awe-inspiring exactitude and lyricism to her dive into three of America's most iconic moments. . . . In her exquisite and poignant reimagining of historic events, Alcott dissects their impacts in a sweeping yet intimate saga that challenges assumptions and assesses the depths of human frustration." —*Booklist* (starred review)

"This richly ruminative novel refracts thirty years of American culture and history through the lives of [its] characters. . . . A sharp and moving reminder of the human dimension of even the most outsize historical events." —*Publishers Weekly*

"[Alcott's] empathy for troubled souls, rendered in haunting, impressionistic prose, makes a powerful emotional impact, giving the novel a staying power. . . . Impressively ambitious and extremely well written."
—*Kirkus Reviews*

"Every sentence of this novel is charged with the electricity of an intellect sharp and awake; and every instant of this story reverberates in us with the insistency of a deep longing. Amidst the noise of the world we live in, Alcott's voice is the one I want to always hear. Having access to her mind and sensibility is a rare privilege."
—Valeria Luiselli, author of *Lost Children Archive* and *Tell Me How It Ends*

"*America Was Hard to Find* beats with the culturally savvy heart of a Rachel Kushner novel, extends the moral reach of a Philip Roth novel. . . . Alcott is a master of many tricks, and her novel is a marvel of style, information, intelligence, and humanity."
—Heidi Julavits, author of *The Folded Clock* and *The Vanishers*

"A story of mismatched lovers shocked by their bond, a chronicle of an adored but neglected son, and a passionate meditation on the ways in which we as both individuals and a collective subject others to the destructiveness we believe we deplore. Kathleen Alcott writes with a fierce tenderness." —Jim Shepard, author of *The Book of Aron*

"*America Was Hard to Find* moved me on every single page. Kathleen Alcott's prose sings and stings as she crafts a wrenching countermyth of America's vaunt into the space age. This book tells the truth: the cost of conquest is always disintegration at home." —Smith Henderson, author of *Fourth of July Creek*

AMERICA WAS HARD TO FIND

ALSO BY KATHLEEN ALCOTT

Infinite Home
The Dangers of Proximal Alphabets

AMERICA WAS HARD TO FIND

A Novel

Kathleen Alcott

An Imprint of HarperCollinsPublishers

HarperCollins books may be purchased for educational, business, or sales promotional use. For information, please email the Special Markets Department at SPsales@harpercollins.com.

A hardcover edition of this book was published in 2019 by Ecco, an imprint of HarperCollins Publishers.

FIRST ECCO PAPERBACK EDITION PUBLISHED 2020

Designed by Michelle Crowe

Library of Congress Cataloging-in-Publication Data

Names: Alcott, Kathleen, author.
Title: America was hard to find : a novel / Kathleen Alcott.
Description: New York : Ecco, [2019]
Identifiers: LCCN 2018036321 (print) | LCCN 2018037862 (ebook) | ISBN 9780062662545 (ebook) | ISBN 9780062662521 (hardcover)
Subjects: LCSH: Families--Fiction.
Classification: LCC PS3601.L344 (ebook) | LCC PS3601.L344 A82 2019 (print) | DDC 813/.6--dc23
LC record available at https://lccn.loc.gov/2018036321

ISBN 978-0-06-266253-8 (pbk.)

20 21 22 23 24   LSC   10 9 8 7 6 5 4 3 2 1

This book is for Virgil "Gus" Grissom
and Diana Oughton,
Americans lost in the smoke

remember me I am
    free at large untamable not nearly
as hard to find as America

—Father Daniel Berrigan

1969

It is possible they are the only Americans not to watch Vincent Kahn walk on the moon—despite the proximity of a black-and-white television, a Panasonic rolled out for the occasion, despite the gasping and weeping around it. She and her son remain where they sit in the unnamed restaurant. Its floor is dirt, its tables are plastic, the fourth wall at their backs a retractable fence. The family in charge ferries rice and juice and deep-fried plantains from the back rooms where they live, pushing aside a half-parted wood curtain. Behind this sits an unmade bed on the tile, at the foot a toddler's discarded sock.

What is said about her, not often with warmth, is that her dress is poor but her teeth are rich. Her son is nine years old, and he might be the only American child who does not know Vincent Kahn's name. He has swum that day, in the middle of July, in a tributary of the Amazon, in the Morona-Santiago province of Ecuador. He wears saddle shoes, tan and white, and so does his mother. If his chin drifts over his shoulder toward the noise, she snaps it back with her voice. On the table between them lie small squares of paper, adjectives and verbs in tight cursive, and the things he has insisted she buy him, decks of cards and glass beads. The major events in his life have been the violence of new molars in his mouth, the loud chirp of pale geckos in the windows at night.

As the room becomes the applause, she speaks his name, Wright Fern, and touches his face. Because she has the posture of a dancer, a center of gravity that draws all to it, in the second after it seems his cheek has come to her palm, and not the other way around.

The sounds now are minor, the clicks of saliva in open mouths, sentences that only get started. Back in the country they left, boys about to be deployed, already in uniform, lean on the floral arms of childhood couches to see Vincent Kahn cross the virgin surface. Nurses snap on the wall-mounted TVs and usher the dying awake.

His mother is the only person he has ever really known, and he will grow up largely without any photos of her, at least who she was before this. In the second-to-last letter Fay writes to her parents, three years from now, she'll ask that they destroy these images, and they will, along with the request.

BOOK ONE

1957–1964

1.

In under a year she had lost touch with all of her friends, girls whose hair she had braided into hers, whose naked bodies she had watched more closely than her own, and so she would tell no one about the first day he took her up in a plane.

They had disappeared into their new lives, those Cindys and Judys, at Scripps and Mills and Bryn Mawr, and she into hers: the gin cut with lime, the desert cut with wind. Her forearms and deltoids were toned from lifting the chrome canisters above her and shaking. The sounds of the planes from the base a mile away ceased by five, a quiet that always seemed to register with the men as a failure. It was as if, when the noises stopped, they began looking for someone to blame. When someone called her a cunt the first time, she made his ten-dollar change in pennies. There was not a second, at least that she heard. Her stationery had been lilac, embossed in gold, a gift from her parents, and the day she met him she had just thrown it out, watched the color take on oil in the trash under the register.

Vincent and Fay were the only people who did not step outside the bar to watch, but they could hear the hooves shifting on the buckling metal slide and the pilots' hands slapping at the shallow pool. The horse was Lloyd, astride him Fay's sister, Charlie. If Charlie's palomino could make it down the slide without slipping, walk the chlorinated circle, and leap over the stand of coral and olive cacti that bordered the far edge of the pool, five of the men had vowed to make their next flight without pants. If Lloyd failed or his passenger fell, Charlie owed all sixteen present a steak dinner. On the wall a fractured Coca-Cola clock said five after seven.

The wager's conception had left the stools along the bar pulled far from their original line, some bunched in groups where men had made bets on the bet, one on its side in the middle of the room. Atop it had stood Rusty, a pilot famous among them for a flawless record with carrier landings and for once having drawn, on the sleeping face of the first man to break the speed of sound, a permanent-markered monocle. He had pushed back his feather-fine blond hair as he composed an impromptu limerick: *There was an old horsey named Lloyd, who never did see too much . . . Freude.*

Vincent sat closest to the screen door, where a desert wind came through, warm and pointed. It was his first time at the Doctor's, as it was unofficially called. *I was at the Doctor's until very late,* they would say, *the Doctor demanded to see me.* Fay leaned on the warped wood of the bar, her sight fixed on the window above the piano. Through it a green-barked tree with yellow flowers leaned at an angle that suggested remorse somehow, pleading.

She poured from high, the liquor catching the strata of dusky light before reaching his tumbler.

"Fay."

"Vincent."

He spoke his name without meeting her face, which she had turned toward him and opened somehow, a stern way she had of holding it released.

"Not in the gambling mood tonight?"

He sat with shoulders gnarled forward, shook his jaw left and right.

"There are monkeys better behaved than some of these fucks after eight," she said.

"Would you call them . . . flying fucks?"

She raised her glass, gin, just ice, no soda.

"You're not the only one thinking a monkey might do a better job," he said.

"God bless us and God bless the Russians. I personally derive no small bit of happiness from the thought of those chimps in flight suits. Imagine the underwear. Imagine the shoes."

He straightened to look at her, the remaining light showing the difference between his eyes, one green and glacial, the other flinty, lightless as an ashtray. He was thirty-three but retained the sandiness of a boy's complexion, a face the sun loved but hadn't punished.

Outside they chanted her sister's name, the horse's, the different cries mutating into one unrecognizable slogan of drunken menace. Someone stepped into their car to turn the radio on, and the headlights sailed through the mesh door, beating down on the tilted portraits of aviators and Hollywood cowboys, the pale Lucite beads that necklaced the beer taps. *Ain't a-gonna need this house no longer, ain't a-gonna need this house no more,* came the music.

His eyes fell down the rag slipped between two of her fingers, the pinched area where her shirt stole into her shorts. Coating the floor were peanut shells and cellophane cigarette packages. He pointed at the book she had open on the bar.

"What are you feeding yourself there?"

It was Whitman, part of a transcendentalist program she was wandering through, and she read him a few lines. *For these States tend inland and toward the Western sea, and I will also.* He told her she looked like a cowboy when she read, something in how she turned out her feet. She replied that he looked like a horse, the way his mouth was open.

"How many teeth do you have, besides too many," she said, and turned around.

Into the bar then came a different set of sounds, the bet-upon event itself: water battering the pavement and Charlie's yell, a mean joy that sputtered, then vanished. They heard the thump of a body stopped, the percussion of the men's feet as they all began to run.

Fay was past Vincent and out the door in four seconds, searching for her sister. The inn's twelve doors, arranged in a U around the pool, were painted a cheap blue, the color of ocean mixed with bleach. Across the road and into the dust, four men moved through the stands of yucca, the lone spindles leaning into the wind. A sound made her look down. Charlie was sprawled on her back, gurgling in shock. Fay reached her and crouched, swiped the bar cloth along the round of her sister's face and over her chest, which was hauling breath erratically, short, reedy inhalations followed by groaning releases.

"She's okay," someone said from above them. "Just lost her wind."

"And her horse," another mentioned.

"Might have cracked a rib."

Charlie opened one eye, the sharp green of it a sad dare.

"Oh, Fay. I have to tell you something, baby."

"Listening."

"Can you make these motherfuckers steak?"

HE DID NOT, SHE WOULD learn, much believe in valedictions. All conversations he had were part of the same long talk he had with his life, and this rendered goodbye unnecessary. As she removed the slabs of meat from the industrial fridge out back, returned to the kitchen to rub salt and pepper into them, oiled and warmed the skillets on the stove, Vincent had gone.

The men's conversation moved from the events of the afternoon into a language she only partially absorbed. With great solemnity they mouthed the phrase X-15 to each other and nodded, people in love and shocked by it. It was the plane, they believed, that would reach space. The mood turned over when someone grumbled a certain word, *NACA,* and then sweaty money emerged, raised index fingers made tight circles to indicate more, right now. She served fifth and sixth rounds. "National Advisory Committee for Aeronautics," she heard someone say through his nose. Vincent was part of this subset, three hundred men working among the two thousand others.

A howl came from the bathroom. Someone had spread industrial glue on the toilet seat, and she spent ten minutes chipping at it with her pocketknife as she smoked, crouching on the mouth, listening to the conversation come in through the propped door.

"Do you think that—simulator, do you think it's anything at all like the real thing?"

She had heard this vein of speculation so often she knew how they would be sitting. Elbows meeting on the bar, they murmured to each other, their eyes never fixed on any one thing so as to better convey the smallness, the placidity, of the question. For appearances' sake they might have been reciting state capitals to combat boredom.

Although they could not listen well to each other, the one not speaking was always nodding, biting at the inside of his mouth as though to extract some vital information from it, calling the other by his name so that he could hear the regard there.

"It's not as though they can take the X-Series from us. It belongs to the Air Force, they're just doing some checks, maybe publishing a paper or two on what we've done. It's us who will take it, space."

"The control stick a fucking broom handle. What else? Ironing boards for wings? I'll be sure to ask Arlene whether she's got any to spare. For progress, honey, you understand."

"Not going up there with one hand on my cock, the other out the window, for the joy of it, without a care in the world for the mechanisms."

There were the pilots she hated, but she was moved by their

lives. In the main they believed in intuition, theirs, and this impressed her, the voice that was quiet until they were airborne, where it spoke in stark, lucid imperatives. It was a law she'd bought into without realizing, that the only apology a man needed offer the world was his talent.

2.

Even the clouds the next day seemed immutable. The roar of planes woke her, sounds receding and coming into volume again, a kind of pulse that pinned down the hours. She read on her cot, under the photographs of childhood friends still taped there and places she vaguely meant to travel, redheaded girls posing by their fathers' cars and European cities rendered gray by war, until the heat became too great. Then she passed through the curtain that separated her room from the bar. She ground coffee beans and swept, the screen door kept open with an old iron. When the floor was clean she passed into the light and weather, wiped mauve dust from the windows of the rented rooms. In the outdoor shower she sung halves of songs she'd always known, *Mares eat oats and does eat oats and little lambs eat ivy.* Her overalls were filthy, her undershirt was fresh. The afternoon shadows moved across the tawny landscape in spills, and she looked at the print they made with a kind of jealousy, knowing how long she would be inside.

Perched on the counter she ate the stale peanuts and downed her first drink. Men filtered in, some with blue eyes that winked when she slid a glass across the bar, some who smoked silently as though it were a job. By eight o'clock Charlie was liquor-smeared enough to prank-call their parents, not speaking but holding up the receiver to the noise of the room, something Fay couldn't watch. She vanished by ten, and at dawn Fay woke to the sound of her crossing the courtyard, walking the bundle of her sheets to the washing machine behind the main building. Her sister's unhappiness had become the avoidable disasters of her body. A week passed, surly and indifferent to what Fay might have wished from it.

He appeared on her day off in a low-slung Ford truck, driving with one arm, the other tanned and dangling out the window, something white and angular held in his clean fingers.

From her room she could hear the tires working, shifting from the dust onto the gravel that Charlie periodically threw onto the entrance of the lot, and she cursed. There was always one who showed up, disappointed, then bellicose, forgetting the sandwich board always placed there on Tuesdays. SOMEWHERE ELSE, it said, loopy blue on splintered pine.

She stepped into the fulvous decay of the afternoon, her lips and eyes posed to communicate an intractable position. Vincent kept his head down as he approached, but she didn't match his gesture of modesty and appraised him anyway, the creased blue flight suit and the diagonal zippers that highlighted his chest.

In his hand was an elaborate paper airplane, multitiered, slim isosceles triangles that could have been knives, and she pointed at it loosely, her index a little curved.

"We're closed, and, judging by the size of that thing, my condolences on your demotion, sir."

He didn't answer, just blinked, as if to acknowledge that some moment he wasn't a part of had passed.

"For you," he said.

He raised a finger then, gauging the wind or making a point. They stood with their backs to the pool, the U of rooms around it, almost always empty. The pilots never recommended their families stay at Charlie's inn, and the few stragglers that followed the sign on the highway—crooked, three exclamation points—never lasted more than a night. Rising in the air was the overwhelming smell of chlorine, under it layers of vice, a can someone had peed in and hidden under the porch, butts of Camel Wides dug into the dirt of potted plants. The wind was manic, licking at the exposed skin of her neck and arms. She wore work boots and the silk shorts she had slept in, a mechanic's shirt whose patch said BOBO. Her clothing came almost exclusively secondhand, an insult to her parents' wealth she relished.

She held it limply, hardly gripping it.

"No, you have to—"

He stopped himself from speaking. She watched him roll his shoulders back and stuff his fists in his deep pockets, pained not to expound.

"May I?"

"You may."

Without a strategic thought she launched it. Even thrown clumsily, it seemed determined, protected, and the memory she had was of a cat, leaping. When its nose hit the speckled dust too soon, he nodded as though receiving some disappointing news, unfortunate but not unexpected.

"A drive?" He looked at his truck as he asked, perhaps imagining her into it.

IT WAS THE TIME IN the hour before dusk when all the colors, imperiled, flare up in protest, and Fay was aware of how she smelled, onions and salt, an aspect of her time in the kitchen that would not leave her. He moved to open the door but she depressed the searing button of the truck's silver handle and leapt up into it. Already most of her upbringing had fallen away, though it could be seen still in how she held a fork, heard in how she answered a phone. In the cab her legs fell against a brown sack filled with more planes.

They sped under low-hanging telephone wires, through flats of brown where barely verdant tufts appeared, brief and nagging. Not long into their drive he patted his front pocket, reached across her to check the glove box.

"See any sunglasses down there?" he asked, pointing floorward. "Tan case. Might be under the seat." Instead of bending she wriggled straight down into the wide space there, crouching as she slipped a hand under, her cheek resting on the seat where her thighs had been. When she rose she arranged them on his face.

"Hey now. That looked a little too easy for you. Rosebud, was you done born in the belly of a truck?"

It was the first time she laughed, bright, quick, a bird as stunning and red as it was swiftly gone. He looked at her long enough that she gestured to the road—he should watch it.

A teal convertible pulling alongside of them turned the moment over, Rusty gesturing in a tight twirl, Vincent sighing as he acceded and rolled the window down.

"How about a race, finally? You missed out on a good one last night, nearly to Vegas. Rick switched between my car and Chip's at eighty on the freeway."

"I like my bones very much as they are."

"Come on, Kahn. You say that every—"

"I like my bones. I have a few things I'd like to do with them."

He shouted slowly over the wind from the deep cab of his truck, every syllable doled out evenly onto the conversation. When Rusty pulled in front of them and sped away, his hand floated out the passenger side, fingers clapping twice to the palm.

A silence passed, more comfortable than it should have been to two people new to each other, as they climbed into the San Gabriel Mountains. She removed her boots and pressed her heels into the dash. He said what he did next as the view fell open, the fact that diminished their options against the sky that seemed to increase them.

"You should know I've got a wife."

"No ring."

"It's uncomfortable to fly with."

"Oh, I'll bet it's a real encumbrance."

"For maximum control you want to be able to feel absolutely everything."

"You haven't done anything wrong."

"I haven't, but I'd very much like to."

"That seems like an excuse I could just-almost buy if I were your wife. Maximum control."

To this he did not reply, a way of cutting the remark from existence, and they parked soon after. On the mountain the seven o'clock light could barely provide for them, but they spent the last of it pitching the planes he had folded. She was underdressed for the altitude and he stood behind her arranging her arms and fingers, crouched to correct the dig and splay of her bare feet. The first thing he ever kissed was her ankle, briefly, a small and eager threat. A sliver of moon appeared, tactful above the scabrous bushes that ran the cliff.

"There's a German scientist, arguably he was a Nazi, who says we can put a person on the moon by 1978."

"I'll be forty by then," she said. "Speaking of other planets and the completely unknown."

The remark was irrelevant—she felt it die. There was nothing inherently compelling about her being young, but it was the reigning god in her life, the thing from which came all permission and unhappiness.

"Where did you come from," he said, both hands back in his pockets.

"Not far from here geographically, but very·far from here. Do you know about my sister? About Charlie?"

"She was—is?—an aviator. Broke an Earhart record. If you don't mind my saying, a raiser, manufacturer even, of hell."

"Truly, she seized the means of production on hell. She wasn't, in fact, raised naked in an outhouse. We come from people who care deeply about the appropriate silverware. My grandfather invented the question mark, was the town joke. What he actually did was, the second Sutter's foreman had his lucky morning, before Polk had even made his announcement, he went up and down California, buying out all the shovels and trowels and importing more. And then he sold them for twenty times the cost. Some saloons, too, where the people who made money lost it."

He nodded. She should go on.

"No," she said. "What about you?"

Ohio, was all he would say. Son of Andrea and Frederich, brother of Sophie. Boy Scout Troop 46. Cabin in the mountains, quieter than the base though not the done thing. He acted as though he knew nothing about his life except what could be seen.

There was no discussion of leaving—he simply got into the car. Had she upset him, she wondered, as they coasted down the canyon, but then he placed two fingers on her earlobe and kept them there the whole drive back, a slight pressure that made her delirious, all of who they might be to each other imagined by that gesture.

3.

Listening to the ticks of the car shutting down, Vincent stood looking up at the crowd of stars. Ash-colored scrubs grew rabidly along the cabin, atop their widening tangles small ruby blooms that seemed like concessions to ugly beginnings. Inside he removed his boots and set them on a high driftwood shelf near a canvas bedroll, a worn pair of binoculars, and a fishing rod. His steps and adjustments were all economical, considered so as not to wake the woman on the couch. Squatting now he felt the things around her, the pale mug inside of a glass on the floor and the heels of her brocade slippers under the coffee table, trying to infer the shape of her day by the temperature of the things she had touched. He retrieved the blue-and-white quilt from where it had bunched at her toes and he spread it over her.

HIS WIFE HAD BEGUN TO complain about the dust as soon as they arrived. Elise had spoken of it without a name, like a domestic menace so familiar to the inhabitants it needed none. *It sneaks in and changes things,* she said.

While he was diving and spinning one Thursday—nailed to

his seat by the negative gravity, the force of it tugging the skin of his jaw to his ears, calling on his calves and torso to make even the slightest adjustment to the controls, reaching the speed brake and watching the plates of metal bloom before the windshield— she was moving through their apartment on the base with a roll of duct tape around her wrist. She bit off stretches as long as her torso, applying them along the walls of the house with her head tilted.

He had leaned on the door, all the lightness he felt after flying replaced with an intestinal roil. The unclean ripping sound as the seal gave way, the jerks of its opening as the last bits of glue detached, were a warning he could not ignore. In moments like these he saw his father's ossified pointer finger, the spill he had not cleaned, the grade that would not do. The open hand, the leather belt. Like his father, he saw things in two ways, acceptable and not.

Elise was silent, very much a piece of the dark, still room, upright at the dining table, fingering the silver roll she wore as a bracelet. Tape bordered the windows, the crack that grew up the bare east wall.

It did keep the dust out, she said, as though remarking on the finer aspects of a mediocre meal. He sat down across from her and pressed his palms together, waiting a minute to speak.

This won't do.

The next day he'd entered the housing office, a box of three bowls and their framed wedding photo balanced on his hip, and told a version of the truth, alluding to health issues, mentioning the mountain air. He slid two bare keys across the grain of the desk. There was no protocol, no form to fill—no one ever chose not to live on the base, the name of which pilots across the country spoke very slowly—so the kid with the reddish crew cut just nodded, stunned. Elise, in the idling car, turned the radio knob every three seconds. On the dried-up lake beds shadows of planes appeared and vanished. They had driven through the blue day inside a silence that was calm but not happy. It had been six months.

BAREFOOT NOW, DONE LOOKING AT her, he killed the light and passed through the small, dark kitchen. In the bedroom the air was stiff, made up of her nail polishes and removers and perfumes, so he shoved open a window and went straight to sleep.

4.

Someone pulled the plug on the patio lights, a string of fat bulbs that fell from the eaves, to see the satellite better. From the frequent flare of matches the smell of sulfur had gathered and stuck, and glass bottles hung empty between the middle and index fingers. Lloyd moved behind the rough line they formed, placing his fifteen-pound head on various shoulders, licking sweat from the backsides of sunburned ears.

Standing with her thumbs hooked into the waist of her overalls, Fay imagined Vincent behind some hulking telescope on a neat patch of sand, an olive cardigan pushed up to his elbows, the men around him sober and well equipped.

The feeling couldn't have been more feverish outside Charlie's, the men less certain. A ladder leaned against the far side of the building for reasons immediately forgotten, abandoned tumblers sat in clusters on the porch railings. Although it would signify a failure and a threat and the obsolescence of an era over which they had reigned, when it came it was easy to love, particularly under the desert's primitive covering of beige, where nothing could truly glow. Like debris raised up by a gathering wave, they lifted an inch off their heels as Sputnik gave its last detectable winks.

Inside, after, the mood was hot and finicky, the course of it hard to determine, and Charlie, smelling the money that might slump out her door, announced half off the next two rounds.

"And anyone," she said, her torso swaying to reach different parts of the room, "who can tell me the exact percentage of piss in the ocean gets a free kiss on the ass."

She always spoke this way, around these men, an outsized simulacrum of the bravado that had made her. Alone with Fay she would be monosyllabic, eaten by her own performance, upset by the smallest sound, but now she was on the piano, her elbows in flight. It was a song they all knew and that hardly needed playing, so engraved was it in the collective memory. *Someone's sneakin' 'round the corner—is the someone Mack the Knife?*

At the register, a pen behind her ear, Fay followed suit, doing her own part in massaging the collective morale, speaking like an auctioneer. "Nineteen forty-five. Bud's got a shiny silver 1945. Who can go lower? Have I got a 1944, 1943?" With the pads of their fingers, the men scraped their coins around on the bar, creating piles, squinting.

"'Thirty-nine!" someone yelled from the far end.

"'Eight."

"'Thirty-fuckin'-two."

"'Thirty-two, we've got 'thirty-two. Can anyone here top Tom's lustrous, golden 'thirty-two penny?"

Tom was squat and silent with long eyelashes, a man who seemed unnecessary even to himself. He held the coin in his closed fist, grinning in a way that seemed private. There was the scratching sound of twenty of them double-checking, then a lull through which Charlie's singing voice stabbed—*a cement bag's drooping down.*

From the center of the bar Rusty shot a hand up and held it there until all eyes had climbed up to meet it. He would not say the number, she realized. He would make her go to him, touch his scorched fingers to retrieve the dime.

"Nineteen eleven," Fay said, knowing he would be there the next six days, redeeming his free shot of whiskey, memorizing the length of her fingernails, the placket of buttons on her shirt, for some use of his own.

The rest of the night passed easily, rearranged by the familiar models of contest and loss. "You're my fireworks girl," Charlie said, kissing Fay on an ear on her way out. Fay played gardener to the last few men, taking from them what they didn't need, presenting them water. She stacked pint glasses fifteen high, twenty, until the last customer had gone. An hour poured in around her as she mopped. Only in killing the lights of the bar did she understand the lamp in her room was on.

Atop her unmade bed Rusty was as pink and naked as the just born, far into sleep and a peace that seemed real. She looked at her things as he must have, the Mexican candles Charlie had brought her, deep red and blue, melted onto the floor, the cotton panties she had kicked off in the night crumpled like rotting blossoms. The feeling in her body was some crucial omission, an organ she'd been born without, a place where bone should be but was not. She was gone in ten seconds, waiting out the time he would leave from a room across the way, watching the pink and silver come vicious to the sky. It was the first morning of the space age, and her life most resembled an accident.

FAY DIDN'T KNOW WHY SHE told her sister the lie she did, that the wooden handle on the older chopping knife had splintered, that they needed to order a new one from the puckered Sears catalog Charlie kept in her personal bathroom. It was in fine condition where she'd slipped it between her cot and the floor, handle side out.

She worked her shift with the lump under her bed not far from her mind, waiting for Rusty to return and redeem his prize. He would leave money on the table for her, she imagined, a large tip that was a substitute for an apology, and she would take it. She listened to the president's address as she mopped, in his promise that America would not fall behind the implicit admission that it already had. Brawls broke out without their customary circling, the rising bridge of insults. What she heard instead was the hollow note of a toppled chair, the liquid thud of a gut against a wall. She saw the tallest of them spitting blood from his mouth, as he floated out the door, so casually she believed, at first, it was a nutshell or a seed.

5.

He took her flying on her birthday, three hours she swallowed. After it happened Fay thought of the friend most likely to forgive and indulge her—*a married man*—and she imagined Rebecca Fuller into the room, Rebecca Fuller who had worked afternoons at the pet store and smelled indelibly of it, the shredded newspaper stained with chick urine, the warped salt lick that was the dominion of the ancient parrot. *Never Becky,* she had begun to say, one transformative summer after a factual lifetime of Becky. Fay could imagine how she would phrase it, circle her thumb and finger around a friend's wrist, say, *Oh Ms. Fuller, can I trouble you for a spell?* Standing by the wood birdcages where Rebecca lazily ran a cloth, or shoeless but lipsticked in the orchards behind Fay's house, they had addressed each other formally when talking about the things that were private. It was a way of rising to the occasion, of imagining themselves into the women they would be. Pinkies linked, they swore to keep their own names. Like many of the worst lies, it felt marvelous to tell.

She had decided not to mention it, October 17. It was a way, one of many she'd devised with Vincent Kahn, of avoiding disappointment. Certainly he had never asked, never sat up naked over her some afternoon in bed and demanded to know. Her middle name, her first word or memory. He had picked up her datebook while she was in the bathroom, plucked it from the pile of beads and cards and matches.

"What's 'crowning achievement'?"

"Oh, that's my birthday. It's something Charlie and I say to each other."

He waited.

"As in then I crowned. As I emerged from the birth canal."

He put two palms out as though weighing each and let them drop and rise in rotation.

"Clever, disgusting. Disgusting, clever."

Two days later, her birthday began quietly. Charlie took her shift. Fay marked the occasion only by a new bar of soap, rose hip that she'd dog-eared and mail-ordered, unwrapped in the outdoor shower while the morning was still purple. He showed up at nine, two hands spread on her window, and tapped on the glass, her name in Morse code he said when asked, learned it the summer he was eight, and drove them away from the base, an hour, two, landscape that didn't change from a long blink to the next. She was shocked by what she missed of her childhood, the sounds of a four-way intersection, radios on in mechanics' garages, unseen children running piano scales. As a girl she had been entrepreneurial, inspired by her family's wealth and defensive about it, had put her allowance into bonds. Some of her teachers rented from one of the buildings her father owned, and she mentioned to them how he wrote Christmas bonuses to the tenant farmers of his orchards. Her feelings about money changed when her body did, when she began to feel watched.

THEY PULLED UP TO THE tiny landing strip, a stretch of corroded asphalt that didn't last a mile, the hangar a squat tin box with two walls that rolled up. On a door-mounted clipboard he scrawled his name. He tried a series of pale dented lockers until he found one that opened, and from it he took a bulky headset and a key that glowed in the noon flowing in.

He didn't ask her to, but she followed him around the plane while he did his checks. Vincent dipped a knuckle into the fuel tank and sniffed, then pushed the whole thing back a foot, leaning into his grip on the wings as it rolled and he examined the tread of the tires. He didn't ask if she was afraid, if she'd ever been in a plane, how old she was turning. She was nineteen. She felt she was entering an interstitial year, a string of months in which she would not be culpable for what her life enacted upon her. It was before her like a painting, something she could be alone with to consider but not to change.

Inside of it the instruments, the dials she could guess at by the way her sister had once talked of planes, gave the air of waiting.

"Put your hands on the controls," he said.

"What?"

"Just enough that you can feel them. The plane is incredibly reactive, all-seeing and -knowing, though less like a god and more like a nun. You can't sneak anything past her. She'll punish you. Feet on those pedals there. Those are the rudders, and they coordinate your turns. Think of them as your colleagues. Respect them. Think of these"—he pointed to the raised handles of the steering column—"as being the assistant to the rudders, never the other way around. You can tell a bad pilot because he forgets he has feet. Remember your feet."

He had buckled her in and was gesturing for her to lean forward, raising the cold metal teeth to loosen the tawny slip of strap, and she felt his fascination with her was representative of the world's in general, an endorsement of her future.

"I'll be helping you up. The propeller turns left, so you're always up against a bias. The right rudder needs more from you."

This was the last thing he said before slipping the headset over her and turning the plane on. Sound became something she could see and feel, the trembling altimeter alive with it, her body made smaller by the roar. In her ear on the radio his speech was clipped, only every third word and even that flattened.

—*Rudders,* was all she heard him say, spoken like an invective, so she put her feet down, mimicking the alternating pressure he had demonstrated with his hands, and she kept the fat of her palm on the throttle where he had arranged it, pulling it when he pointed. Soon the blades of the propeller were not separate and then she could see, the way she could the color of her own hair—the very edge of what one could know for certain—that the ailerons on the wings were down. They were two thousand feet up before she looked to him and saw that his knees were loose, his boots far from the ridged pedals. She had been flying alone. To keep from laughing he had a knuckle in his mouth. He threw a raised thumb in her general direction.

—*To the asylum, then?* she said. —*Lunatic,* she said, pulling the column back. In the half-second delay it took for what she'd barked to reach him in his headset, she surveyed what was spread below her. Everything was the color of fruit about to turn, the light, the two-room folk houses the size of buttons.

—*Your first takeoff. Knew you could do it. Feather for your cap. Rudders.*

He took over soon after and flew the rest of the way, keeping them in turns for longer than was necessary. —*Birthday swim,* he asked, when they kissed the coastline, yawning, unmoved by the total blue.

She would have told Rebecca Fuller about the two different colors of his eyes, then how much sense he made in a plane. How what she had noticed before—the slightness of his movements, how he drank a beer without tipping a glass a millimeter more than was necessary—was part and parcel of how he moved the control column, barely, the nose rising or dipping without her noticing, the change in altitude something she only sensed after.

She imagined relating this to Rebecca Fuller, how she would throw her open palms up by her ears, equally aghast, *I know, I know,* when Rebecca, pink with jealousy, upbraided her. They'd be sitting cross-legged, mirrors of each other in posture, devouring the last of something, rice pudding, applesauce, sharing a spoon. In girlhood you pretended you were part of the same body, the same itches and cravings. It was how you dealt with the pain of having to inhabit one.

Even in her imagined confession, there were things Fay could not tell Rebecca Fuller. It would be necessary to frame the transgression in romance, something filmic and orchestral, so she would exclude what happened after in the bed of his truck. There were the women men loved, Fay was coming to understand, those whose voices in the kitchen over running water were familiar, whose handwriting they could forge if pressed, and there were women like her. Reclassification, she suspected, was impossible. There was no door between those rooms, though you could hear each from the other.

He put down a sleeping bag and directed her so that she was on all fours, her overalls tugged down around her calves, twisting her back onto him like she was some stubborn part of a machine, necessary but prone to glitch. When she threw her head back to see his changed face, she saw that the legs against his, the waist he encircled with his trim fingernails—her legs, her waist—could have belonged to anybody.

6.

He recognized her unhappiness as he would an aging relative, all its expressions familiar, and tried to keep his impatience with it a secret. As his wife was, and his mother though she'd never say it, Fay was hurt by the few words he used to sum up his life, certain experiences she might have assumed had carved something away, fashioned him inalterably. What did they imagine? It was no one edict booming from a uniformed chest, no one edifying fluke, a carrier landing on little fuel, the rear hook of his plane barely snapping into the taut steel and preventing his roll into ocean. Even if he wanted to, he could not tell the story of his life.

It was the sum of these hours, eating at other ways he might have gone. It was the model glue, fibrous and salty if you tasted it, left behind on his mother's stiff embroidered doilies, on fat mugs and tall glasses, on the knobs on the radio and the rubber horn on his bike, in five points on the mesh screen door that led to the backyard. It was the models of planes, flawless, assemblies that took full weeks, which he hung from his ceiling. He watched them as he tried to sleep, how they twirled when a wind came across the flat town of small houses. It was the year he stopped buying them, twelve, so that he could save his dull pennies for flying lessons, and how it starved him to walk past the storefront downtown, the boxes stacked in a tantalizing stagger, inside them the concise instructions, a world explained. It was the job he worked to pay for the lessons, the trembling of his alarm before it was light out, the necessary extension of the wrist as he hurled the bundles, the newsprint now the thing on his fingers, impossible to truly excoriate. Even the bathroom soap bar turned ashy, and at dinner his father cursed this. *Your own money, your own damned soap.*

It was the veterans who gave him the lessons, men whose sleep never fully left their faces, looking out the thick glass, muttering clipped directions. It was all purchases thought of in terms of the instruction they cut into—an egg cream one-seventh the cost of an hour in the sky, a Jules Verne paperback one-fifth—and almost nothing worth it. He was fourteen, then fifteen, and he lived like a monk, an early bedtime so he'd be rested for his dawn lesson. He had only the most glancing interest in food. Television did nothing for him. He was unmoved by the pinups his peers kept in their lockers.

It was his first solo, announced to him only by the unbuckling of the other man's belt, a clap on the shoulder, all the air in the cockpit suddenly just his to breathe. No chance to call home first. Pilot's license, age sixteen. A drunk friend of his father's spread out in the living room, feet high on an ottoman, swiping at his wet eyes and howling: *But he can't drive my* Ford *five blocks to the drugstore?* He had little interest in the automobile, where it could go and how it got there. He wanted the blue that was spotless and matchless.

It was the package from the Navy, propped up on his mother's dining table when he came home from school: four years of university, paid, cut in half by three years of service. It was the chalky air he breathed in the low-ceilinged college classrooms where the courses in engineering began at seven, right where they'd left off, so he learned to arrive with the coffee already angry in his system. Tight capitals in graphite, headings and subheadings, scatter diagrams he made to pop with colored pencils, one red and one blue. The other classes he attended like some errant father, squinting to grasp their return on his future, turning away from the heart of the conversation. Friends were a hobby other people had. It was each day closer to the time he would be flying again.

And then he was in training in Pensacola, in the company of other boys who were also always looking up to identify planes, spitting out makes and models, good news and bad. The air in Florida was alarming, thick to an extent that breathing felt like a choice you might forget to make. Add the suit, an inner inch of fluff like what kids wore to career down snowy hills, the outer shell like tractor tire.

It was his first solo in the Navy, six hundred horsepower, and the difference was an occasion. He wrote in ink in his journal: *like the difference between an out-of-tune fiddle and an orchestra pit.* When he flew, so far from his Ohio boyhood, he was no longer aware of where his house was, the roof under which his mother was making meals go further with the liberal use of bread crumbs, or his younger sister's school, where she might be stationed on the blacktop, peering up, hoping to signal to him, moving her arms in elaborate formations, the meaning of them known only in her little-girl mind.

Alone in the SNJ for the first time, his first monoplane, he heard the gruff strictures of his superiors. He'd made their voices a part of his thinking. *Kahn, if you treat a change of altitude like an emergency, then it will become an emergency.* When he landed, parking the thing without so much as a bump, disrobing did little to cool him. His whole body was a source of heat, pride bigger for knowing fear. In the cafeteria later, giggling like the children they'd recently been, all the other pilots in his class came at once, drooling to perform this act of tradition. He didn't protest, didn't say the tie had been a gift from his Scout leader, a man who had taught him to read stars and carve a tent from snow. He just grinned as the blades of the scissors came in, coruscating, and felt the lightness, the small shift in his weight, as they waved the bottom half of his tie around like just-killed dinner. In his bunk at night in the lined composition notebook he taped it in with two strips he'd borrowed from the office. *FIRST SOLO USNAF, WITH APOLOGIES TO ERNIE,* it said.

How could he have written that for anyone else? And Korea? He couldn't have told Elise, who needed the radio on the whole time she slept, what it was to suddenly get your funeral suit cleaned ahead of time, to make a practice of imagining your bunk the one made in the morning and never returned to. That it actually came recommended, from the few older men who would speak about it— that you envision yourself ejecting too late, a soaring, newly soulless thing on fire, practice thinking out the morbid possibilities while on god's earth so that when the choice came, when the awful moment knocked high over a country not your own, it was not these images you saw but your training that you felt.

If he had told Fay that he once flew over a squadron of Korean officers exercising, that any of his colleagues would have shot or bombed, that he watched the perfect synchronicity of their jumping jacks and couldn't—if he had revealed this to her, would it have explained anything?

He took from her only what she gave so freely, he told himself, along with certain lies about her youth. She was fourteen years his junior. Experiences only passed over women that young, he thought. Whatever went on between them was something she could afford. He'd be a blip in time, something as small as a dress she'd once worn and only vaguely remembered. A color, a shape. He wasn't in the way of anything, he thought. All her life was open.

7.

What James Fern wanted, in the weeks movers packed up the Spanish Colonial where he had raised her, was to corner the precise moment Fay had ceased to identify as his daughter. The closer to the minute he could pinpoint it, the further from blame he would feel. He spent this obsession physically, walking often, behaving as though it were a visible imperfection he was going to locate somewhere on the estate, a fissure in the peach stone courtyard. With Christine—he had refused to call her Charlie—the reasons had been much easier to see, a girl from school in her room too late too many times, the two of them caught naked in the orchard by a farmhand sent to check on a busted valve in the water line.

As a Christian I won't tolerate it, he had said to Christine, fingers steepled, speaking to her in a part of the house that was never used, a sitting room where velvet teal shell chairs surrounded a low glass table. She had been sixteen, brawny but not heavy yet, the pride of the local equestrian chapter, always a little sunburned, a delight to his friends who called her the Wabash Cannonball. *A reg'lar combination.*

As a Christian I will not tolerate it.

As a goddamn person, she had said, splayed far out on the edge of the chair, her baby fat gone though he couldn't say when, *I cannot help it.*

For her last competition the month before, he had given her a six-piece luggage set, monogrammed Peruvian calfskin with brushed nickel padlocks. It was no small irony. He heard her say goodbye to the cat.

It began when Fay was fifteen and Charlie was already six years gone: what came first with her were questions, posed at lunch at the country club, where her food went mostly untouched, watercress fallen, pink ice cream melted. She wanted to know how much her nanny was paid. The maid, the groundskeeper, the gardener, the men who picked their oranges. James caught Fay in town wearing clothing from a box in the attic, his own old Army-issued thermal chopped at the sleeves. Their daughter refused, her last two Christmases at home, to compose a wish list.

In her senior year—she was sixteen then seventeen, had skipped the third grade—the packages from all the Seven Sisters colleges had come like holiday visitors, bringing news from different places, their arrivals staggered until the table was full of them. She asked to borrow his letter opener and brought each to a place outside, a reclining patio chair she liked to drag from among the potted ferns and into the sun on the lawn. He had spied on her with some pride, watching how carefully she held the blade, the glossy brochures she touched lightly so as not to smudge them.

She waited until the last had arrived to cry. They found the congratulatory letters and embossed pamphlets in the waste bin, images of books spread under centuried oaks, lecture halls lit only by sun, stairwells where bobbed girls in pearls linked arms. At first they could not understand the word she was repeating into her pillow in her bedroom, still painted the eggshell lilac she'd chosen as a girl. *Scholarship,* they mouthed to each other, *scholarship?* And then when they had heard it clearly there was a kind of dumb relief, a leap to a conclusion about her plans that excluded who she had become. *Honey, you didn't have to apply for a scholarship.* They were laughing, clutching at each other's elbows as she turned over onto her back, *why would you apply for, only a thousand a term,* her face setting around the hard line of her mouth that was its organizing principle. Everything else about their daughter, the rest of her body on the bed, was flushed, boneless.

The next weeks had been like a deathbed vigil, each of them taking their turns growing simpering and then apoplectic by her locked door. The few times she chose to respond she did so calmly, with the same perfectly turned phrases about the injustice of wealth, and for as many times as he yelled, furious, about how many people dreamed about being in a position like hers, there were twice as many occasions when he stood begging, knocking with one curled finger, bargaining, calling her names he hadn't since she'd been a giggling figure in tulle on the piano bench at their cocktail parties, *peaches,* gripping a stick of celery all night like a wand for reasons unknown, *daisy,* entreating guests to visit her room and collection of abalone shells, *my sweet bird.* He started to believe that there was a smell coming from his daughter's room, from her, and this unnerved him beyond all else, that the change in Fay had entered other parts of the physical world. As many times as he asked her to, Claudette could not agree. It was like yeast and also like sap, he told her. Sniff again. One of these evenings he pinned Claudette under him and was rougher than he meant to be. He wanted to make things move, to make her breasts fight their way up to hit her chin. She was in the bath after for a long time.

After a week their daughter emerged for dinner, looking somewhat recognizable, her hair combed, half of it pushed back with a blue headband the width of a pencil. She dabbed at the corners of her mouth with a napkin and thanked Libett for the posole and looked, again, like a young woman who knew the art of being with people, could recite the relevant Milton or fox-trot across the room.

Claudette's chignon flashed high as he began to speak, chin

sewn to her neck, a hint about her unhappiness he ignored. Had she considered what they talked about, had she decided on a school.

Fay cleared her throat, a womanly noise he couldn't remember her adopting, and put an elbow on the table and a palm to her jaw, a transgression in etiquette he once would have corrected immediately. Daughter daughter strong and able, take your elbows off the table.

Libett, she called, a name she had known before all others, one she had screamed the summer she'd fallen from the roof, where she'd been going in secret. Her first kiss, eight years old in the pantry, had been Libett's son Joaquin who did beautiful impressions of birds and trains. He had taught her how to put two fingers in her mouth and whistle.

Libett was at her side in a minute. *Libett, how is Joaquin,* she said. *I haven't seen him in a year I think.*

They all knew the answer and Libett tried to leapfrog her confusion at this being spoken, head it off at the pass by saying only, *He is well,* taking a table brush and sweeping it in a practiced arc to remove any crumbs.

Where is he now, for instance.

There was Brahms on the phonograph, the last light of the day filling the wineglasses. Through the open balcony doors they could smell the ocean, warm and amenable and ignorant of what happened in houses like these. Flanking the dining room, hallways led to rooms that were confections, tasseled bed skirts and oil paintings of mountains, perfect and empty and useless.

She looked like she had the autumn she mastered backgammon, a game he had taught her in the study he forbade anyone else to enter. He remembered her lunula on the felt, white as milk, her fingertips tapping to imagine her next move, her posture, every part of her curved toward the chips and dice and darted fabric. When she finally beat him she did not look surprised.

Where is he now, for instance.

Libett had stopped looking for a task to hide inside of and answered the girl's question. *Resting, I think. He worked today.*

Worked? Worked where? She was feigning ignorance like a true criminal, he remembered thinking at the time. She was admitting nothing of what she knew into her eyes.

That's enough, he said. He was holding his fork with every muscle in his hand, he noticed, maybe every muscle in his body.

For your father. Picking fruit.

I see. And where's he going to university?

You can clear the plates now, Claudette said. *Please. No dessert tonight.*

Where's he going to university?

Not.

He's not? She looked back and forth to each of her parents. *But he's so bright.*

The plates.

I'll tell you what, Daddy. You can send me to college if you send him, too.

Their border collie, red and white, got up and padded away, taking with it all the shine and warmth of the room. Libett was finally gone. Claudette was a shape on the balcony. He made a fist around his daughter's right hand, obscuring it completely, tightening it until he could feel it seizing.

What is this? What exactly do you think this is? Are you very proud of yourself for taking this little political soapbox? It doesn't suit you. You look like a fool. You look like someone who needs to be let out into the world and ruined some.

He was speaking low enough that only Fay could hear him. They looked almost like lovers, his hand keeping hers, his neck locked in the angle that put his mouth near her ear. She stayed there until he released his grip, her last obedient act as a daughter.

He found Libett still in the kitchen late that night and let her go, waiting until her head was hidden in the cupboard where she was putting things away to actually say the words. She had worked for the family nineteen years.

FAY HAD SPENT THE WINTER writing letters they didn't understand, eating only almonds from the dry pantry, behaving in general like a kind of rodent, her light always on, her face never at rest, her old happy industriousness changed into something leaner and unbecoming. She was at the library every day, doing what they didn't know, walking the three miles there, insisting on it. Though she was careful about always giving her outgoing mail to the postman, Lou, whom she called by first name and with whose ailments and hobbies she was familiar—an embarrassment to James that presaged the rest—there was a day she left a letter to be sent wedged into the flag of the mailbox that sat at the head of the long, curving driveway. He removed it without fully stopping the car.

She was posing as—what? A scholar, a journalist, somebody documenting the education of women. The note was at least the third in a series of letters, and he skimmed it looking for the thing she wanted, his wicked and resourceful daughter, which he knew was hidden in the language of her perfect cursive. *Any syllabi you could enclose would be most appreciated,* it said, *as I assemble the compendium that will capture this unique pedagogical moment in our country, a time when the minds of girls are being nurtured as never before.*

If she could not go to college on her terms, she would make it come to her. He read the letter in the parking lot of the bank and punched his horn.

The books listed on the papers returned by professors she sent away for in droves, and they arrived tied in cruciform and wrapped in brown paper, so many that in the rare glimpse of her room they could see the texts becoming pillars before her closet. At Easter, Claudette bought Fay a dress and hung it on her bedroom door, which was where it stayed.

Deep in the summer, the fallen purple of the jacaranda trees already thick underfoot, the vendors on the side of the road selling sculpted mango dipped in chili powder, there was a visit from her sister. The artifice in these returns of Christine's confused him. Arriving with souvenirs and descriptions of exotic birds, a telegram the day before if they were lucky, she never acknowledged that her departure had been something less than a choice. They did not notify anyone of Christine's presence and were careful to keep it from the papers. Claudette accepted the brash, woodsy perfumes Christine brought in boxes of taffeta and wore them, for the few days her older daughter was back, to the table.

He had seen what would happen before it did, woke up the third morning she was there and heard it in how they laughed, a sound that had too many parts and was everywhere in the house whose design he had so carefully overseen, spilling down the tile of the arcaded covered porches, from the top of the rounded stairwell, where they sat with Fay's bare feet threaded between her sister's. By the fountain in the rear courtyard at midnight, he caught them before an audience of lilac bushes, tossing a log of ham like it was a football. *She's going to leave with her sister,* he told Claudette, removing his cuff links from a velvet drawer in their bureau. His wife, a mannequin in the half hour before she had her coffee, sitting up against four tasseled pillows in the canopied bed, did not or would not hear him.

THE WEEK BEFORE HE AND Claudette left, a house where they had lived thirty-odd years, a part of the state where their lives were written up in the society pages, he pinched the bridge of his nose and whispered at the woman they'd finally hired to pack up Fay's room. *Was there a thought in your mind,* he said.

She had put the church dresses with the ski jackets and summer camp pinafores, and there was no way, when his daughter needed something, she would be able to find it.

8.

They lasted two and a half years, existing to each other only on Tuesdays they made outings, hikes that she took in old oversized boots of Charlie's until he brought her a new pair, mail-ordered to his office, the length of her feet guessed perfectly by how he remembered them on his dash. She told him what she was reading, what it made her think and feel, and he gave her the names of things. Cirrus, ponderosa, osprey. He was working on a paper, alternatives to parachutes, a frame not unlike a bicycle. Once she mentioned that she loved him and he nodded as one does at a child who has made an understandable mistake.

In the Angeles National Forest they ate sandwiches she'd made up high on granite ridges, or down in view of the pool of a waterfall, everything they could see coated in moss that ranged from olive to sylvan, everything they could touch changed by water. As though his vision could cut through the covering of green to the flat, dry places where he might press her down and unbutton her ill-fitting clothing, he had a strong sense of where to deviate from the trail. He had been a Boy Scout, he never let her forget, and seemed almost to wish for the minor disaster that he might cope with in a programmatic way. When she took a deep, crooked step into a sudden concavity in their path and cried out a little, he insisted on a series of tests that would diagnose any sprain or fracture. It was almost, she thought, like he wanted to see her compromised, but then she ignored it, that beginning of hatred, banished it.

There was a line from a poem she wanted to understand, and on a day her life felt possible she repeated it aloud as they passed from shade to sun. *"'Except for us the total past felt nothing when destroyed.'"* "Total nonsense," he said, laughing. "I wouldn't buy a used bike from your friend Wallace Stevens." Their infatuation was not with what they made together but an astonishment at their differences, how far each had to travel even to reach the other's thinking. On the drive back he was silent except to point out a circling eagle. There was no one on the road, serpentine curves dictated by mountains, and he was already, she refused to see, halfway gone.

IN THEIR SECOND NOVEMBER SHE violated their terms, unspoken rules he'd made her suss out like the inclinations of an animal, where not to scratch or press. Fay had called him at home, and he was punishing her, and she was not going to be punished. It was remarkable how easy it was to decide. It made her whistle, songs she'd known long before him, in the shower and out riding Lloyd, bright, vicious.

Her crime had transpired in thirty seconds, less. A slow shift, few orders of liquor, no one on the piano, everything already wiped down twice. She was in a mood, or a mood was in her. It was a change other people could notice. Her sentences were faster, or they took three ways to the same point, and her usual six o'clock gin, no ice, no tonic, had no effect. There was a story she wanted to tell him, a pilot who had used the word *gargoyle* when he meant *argyle*. *You wouldn't believe her in this gargoyle sweater,* he had said. It was as if the alcohol couldn't find purchase in the channels of her body. She was more interested in mirrors than usual, the pocket of hip visible at the crook of her overalls. When her mind felt sharpest was when she most wanted it obliterated: the thoughts rendered null by his body behind her, the mouth that would speak them stuffed with a pillow.

She called him at home.

The sense she had, the sense he'd given her, was that his wife did not exist, and so she had actually not considered the possibility of her voice, her *good evening*. Somehow she asked for him, whether he was in. Immediately she wanted to sever the connection to that room where his wife stood—she imagined it as yellow, she imagined a wedding ring on a dish-soaped finger—and never think of it again. The babel of the bar behind her, she followed the first idea that came to her and didn't wait for an answer. *Are you happy with the overall condition of your appliances,* she had said, and then she hung up.

He had not come in on her day off, no call since then, no letter taped to her window predawn that began *Dear Bess Rainy* or *To Whom It May Concern, Pertaining to the Matter of the Hole in Your Bucket.* Charlie took her shift when Fay asked, the first request of this kind, and slid the car keys down the bar. "All I require is that you don't die," she said. "If you die, I'll kill you." Fay kissed her goodbye on the mouth and slid the metal loop onto her ring finger.

She would not be punished; his absence was not that if she failed to note it. Los Angeles appeared through the windshield sooner than it should have, buildings with rounded corners of milky glass windows, neon arrows that curved, an hour and fifteen flat. She'd gone ninety most of the way, smoking her sister's Luckies.

Under an eight-foot-wide donut mounted on a twenty-foot pole she parked, the truck at a sharp angle in the painted lines, its wheels still fixed in a turn. Nobody knows where I am, she thought, walking into the diner, and it was a sharp, chamfered kind of thrill. After two cups of coffee she switched to liquor. She was wearing one of two dresses she owned, sleeveless dark green linen with buttons down the middle and a tie belt she knotted.

He looked at her first but she returned it three times over.

His name was Raymond and he was closer to her age, not hand-some or charming but clearly observant of people who were, their habits and gifts, and he came over when she smiled. A comb in his back pocket, Korea tags down his chest, dark blue felt jacket buttoned once at the neck. She could smell the starch coming off his shirt and it was a taste in her mouth alongside the rye. Remov-ing his pocketknife was a nervous habit and he showed her all the different parts, describing the benefits of a blade's shape, testing the point on his index finger. She had little to say, only his face to watch. He suggested his apartment, and on this point she remained noncommittal.

"I'd love to see your car," she said.

But the quickness of her feeling, the competing voices of the coffee and whiskey, had caught up with her, and the whole time in his front seat she felt like her mouth was a loan, a borrowed thing whose limits and quirks she didn't know yet. Even as it occurred she was forgetting it, the hairy knees, the moth-eaten military blanket, the eight-ball gearshift in her spine. She cried once but covered it with a sound that meant the opposite.

It was the first time someone put a hand on her throat, and also the last. "I thought I was paying," he explained after. "I apologize," she said, buttoning her dress, not knowing for what. His car was out of the lot before hers was unlocked.

9.

Vincent's interest in the program had not begun as a little dream, but occurred to him like an injury does, sudden, impossible to ignore.

It was a quarter after ten on a morning that had begun at four thirty, and he edged an X-15 with a violent jerk onto a patch of sand, the voices in his ear going whoa-ho and joking again.

—*I'm not saying you have to act like a ballerina, Kahn, but maybe not like a toasted hillbilly throwing a punch, either.*

They tended to treat his stoicism like an invitation, the fact that he would almost never respond an encouragement to continue.

He climbed out, squinting, waiting for the truck that would take him back to the base, listening as the life went from the engine. He'd lost his follow plane, probably on purpose. The pinch of morning was gone from the weather already, and he was forty miles south of where he had meant to land. He was tired of Edwards, of the broad-backed Air Force monkeys who hated him and the pencil he carried, of the commute back up the mountains to his listless wife, and he was going to apply to become an astronaut, a title that was sweet on the tongue of the American public before they even knew what it would become. The organization that employed him had quietly changed its acronym, subbing an *S* for a *C,* the National Advisory Committee on Aeronautics transmuted into the National Aeronautics and Space Administration, and he was going to follow it up the rest of his life.

They radioed to say there was a delay in retrieving him, a flat on the way out, and he said no problem and there wasn't one. He wasn't eager to explain why he'd overshot by so much, why he'd failed to lower the nose when it was crucial that he do so, where his mind had been when he'd roared past the landing site at two thousand miles an hour.

Elise had been stunned into grief when she lost the baby, it was true, but it wasn't as though before that they were happy, spending the mornings in bed making long plans, taking road trips documented in Kodachrome. They had never hosted a dinner party and told stories in unison, the ends of his sentences courting the beginnings of hers. She had become pregnant on one of the few times they had come together in that way, and it was a shock, some cosmic slap on the wrist that said there were consequences for feigning love. They had begun to curate that waiting life together, pinky-sized yellow socks and wooden rattles, and then it was gone, then it was a great deal of blood, in the bathroom of the rented house, that he scrubbed and bleached. The smell of ammonia became a taste in his mouth, then a clawed pain at his temples.

It was not long after that the offer from the High-Speed Flight Station at Edwards had come, and he had sold it to her as a new start. The word *California* had seemed to reach her, if briefly, seemed to make a tender swipe at the lines around her mouth. He could already imagine how she would age, which tics of despair would become permanent. She didn't sleep or smile enough, and that was going to come through.

The whole long state was a mistake, he thought now, for them and in general. Elise was not the type of person who did well when left with her own head, not a girl who found peace in the bigness of the natural world. She needed a parked row of polished cars on the main drag, a town where people watched her run errands, friends who dropped by to remind her of who she was. An annotated calendar, a telephone that woke you ringing.

He considered this as he waited, walking the periphery of the plane, surveying the damage one more time. It would be weeks before it flew again. In truth he had already come so far from the first machines he loved, the propellers, a comprehensive taxonomy of jerks and shudders whose meaning he knew. The X-15s hardly gave a shiver. Through the windshield you couldn't see any part of the machine, only sky, as though the goal were to make a pilot forget that the thing he flew, by extension himself inside, was separate from it at all.

By the time the truck pulled up his decision was made, and in his head he was already making the necessary phone calls and coughing for the doctor during one of many examinations and packing, again, the mementos he brought with him everywhere. A photo of his grandmother, a young wife in a new country. Postcards from Ernie, who had become a widower and set out to camp in all fifty states. A violet sock that belonged to the baby they didn't have. It had somehow evaded the box of donations he'd put together, and it was a thing he hated and needed to keep, its precious, evil irrelevance.

He thought of the two of them as though he'd known them in different times of his life, Fay and Elise. To meet Fay he arrived with a head full of facts and anecdotes, with plans for an ideal viewing of the eclipse or a rock-polishing kit for the limestone and citrine they'd found hiking. To come home to his wife was to drop into another kind of attention, passive, absolute. In the trunk by their bed were the wool blankets he had folded, in the kitchen window the lemon jam he'd jarred. He solved, he arranged, he repaired.

Sometimes he believed he had become better with Elise for the hours he spent with Fay. It was as though the exuberance he gave to Fay—the pressure he put on the gas pedal to see the thrill on her face, the sweat-dampened time he spent licking her and trying to break her porcelain look—abraded him of his oldest wish, a life that was always becoming bigger. He came home softer, carved out of ardor. For the first time in their marriage, he was the man his wife needed. She built a trellis and he brought her grapes as she painted it, telling her it was beautiful, touching the back of her neck.

He knew it was not a long-term solution, that if he made the cut for the next class of astronauts, extrication would be delicate. The break with Fay would have to be firm and certain: he would do it just before he left.

Vincent thought he could pull it off, two women, for the little bit longer that was required, and in the truck back to the base that day the resolution of it made him cheerful, amenable to the banter of his escort. As they pulled up he slapped the exterior door.

It was not the first time he had underestimated Elise, what she could gather from small changes in him, where she was driving at that moment in her car.

10.

He had never described his wife, but Fay knew who Elise was the moment she folded her hands on the bar. Something essential changed about a person, Fay thought, when they belonged fully to someone else, as particular as a color. A certain softness in the shoulders, a diminished curiosity that came from no longer performing for potential futures. She was disgusted by it, she was envious.

It was early on in the evening, the bar still partially lit by sliding sun, and though two men had recognized Elise from her brief residency on the base and tipped their chins and raised spread hands, her eyes stayed ahead. She was a person without periphery.

Elise was the most beautiful woman she had ever seen, even the most beautiful animal, shaming the cougars Fay had caught flashes of in the mountains, though the green eyes recalled them. Her posture sharpening, she was immune to the piano becoming louder, the report of shot glasses slamming the bar in unison.

Fay told herself that the moment Elise made eye contact, or turned even an inch in Fay's direction, or indicated with a raised hand that she required help, she would go to her, every part the professional. Five minutes passed, ten, and she couldn't pretend any longer she had not noticed the exception Elise was in that room, her shell-pink manicure on the warped wood. Inhales and exhales transpired in hyperclarity. Her body was just a map of pulse points now, all of them angry. Finally Fay went to her, her face arranged in amenable servitude, and waited.

"Seltzer," she said, her eyes still not meeting Fay's.

Fay made a quick scan, searching for the cleanest glass on the rack, and she filled it and set it on a cardboard coaster. In a sidelong glance she saw the floral brocade of the dress as through the carbonation, and then she was imagining Elise underwater, taking great breaststrokes, surfacing to breathe and laugh and call to her nearby husband. The fantasy came to her unbidden, already fully formed.

"Ice," Elise said. She hadn't appraised Fay as she ordered, only as Fay filled the glass and then scooped the ice, and this was not lost on Fay, who knew how she was being seen—in her lowly position, the dirty demands of it. The fans mounted on the ceiling went at full force; the vinyl curtain to her bedroom trembled. It was a reminder of the privacy she no longer deserved, had destroyed by taking what she shouldn't. Elise planned, it was already clear, to stay awhile.

Over the next hour and fifteen minutes she ordered a basket of french fries, a Coca-Cola, extra napkins, a Seagram's and 7 Up, the rib-eye steak, the Cobb salad, a martini up. The things remained exactly where Fay had set them down, the grease on the paper fixing, the glasses dripping condensation. Elise would not so much as stir a drink with a straw.

Sitting up incrementally straighter, the men at the bar became a divided audience. Some grabbed Fay's hand and patted it, offered their handkerchiefs and made benign gestures toward the cover of sweat on her face. They cooed softly as she struggled to keep up with the string of orders, called *there now, you got it,* as she oiled the griddle for the fourth time in twenty minutes. Others hooted, two ordered popcorn. They tipped their stools back so deep they had to hold on to the bar, and they bit down on their cheeks as they watched Elise, then Fay, then Elise. One, a man she had watched Rusty kiss on both cheeks, asked Fay to send Elise a drink on his tab. He chose a Mudslide, the most complicated cocktail on offer, and he breathed with his mouth open as he watched her dole out all the liquors, pour out the Kahlua and take down the blender.

It was not a secret, the time she spent with Vincent. They knew it in the way one knows of someone's addiction, an embarrassment it is best not to mention. But because Fay was the person who handed them what they needed at the end of the day, the gossip had not come to taunt her beyond a look that lasted too long. This was, she knew, the end of that era, the end of evenings in which she tended the bar and felt alone in her thinking. It was the end of any invisibility, the beginning of the feeling that would consume her until she left the desert. She would come to believe that every private thought was written explicitly on her face, that every time she smiled or didn't it was proof to them of the foolish mistake she continued to make.

In the bar that night Fay imagined her sister walking through the door, disarming the spectators of her sister's poor judgment, slipping the guitar from around her back and opening the room with a long, bright C. But Charlie wasn't scheduled to come in for another two hours, was hauling back a delivery of booze and meat in her unreliable truck. Fay was alone with the row of faces.

Elise never asked for the check. When she finally stood to leave, she placed a bill on the table that amounted to three times what she owed, and left without change. Fay couldn't bring herself to collect it, and it stayed there until closing, when someone—Fay never knew who—put it out of its misery and into his pocket.

THAT WEEK SHE WAS MOST conversations at the bar, Elise, a distraction from the standard talk of explosions twenty thousand feet up and those who might jump the Air Force ship for NASA's second round. She showed up most nights, stately in silk, gold brooches in the shape of coral. Dark with focus, she sat once and played Debussy, as private and purposeful as some nun seen walking alone, removed from her institution only in geography. Fay prepared the gin and tonics, the waffle fries, and continued to refuse the money, which sat as limp and oily as the things uneaten. At the close of the third day, Tom taped a mason jar with a label that read GOOD LUCK FUND, and at the end of every night he placed Elise's money in it. It was the only thing left on the bar when Fay turned out the lights.

Charlie confronted Fay during an afternoon windstorm, the mean streak of weather a part of her voice. She came through the door pointing, the hour before the bar opened, at the back booth where they would talk. Around them were the smells of orange wood cleaner and pine mopping solution.

"Are you going to tell me who that belle of the ball is coming in most nights, or do I have to ask her?"

Fay was quiet, pressing her spine against the torn red vinyl. Between the pristine salt and pepper shakers, the menus stood at a slight lean, and she straightened them.

"Honey, do I have to ask her? Are you going to make me ask her who she is?"

"There are things on here we've been out of for months. Did we ever have a tomato pie?"

"I'm guessing not a starlet on her way to a premiere at Grauman's."

"Why does it say all whites are also available by the bottle? No one has ever even ordered a glass. Doesn't really go with the taste of our nineteenth-century peanuts. Who was president when that jar was new, or did we even have one?"

"Not a friend of yours trying to lure you back to society life."

"That is Vincent's wife."

"Vincent the Midwesterner of few words?"

"Astonishingly few."

"And how much money you estimate is in that jar and not in the fucking till?"

Fay rolled one of her shoulders forward, tilted a palm up.

Unlike the transparency of her red joy, the maudlin play of her little tragedies, Charlie's rage did not show easily. There were few tells, but Fay could see them now, a new one every few seconds. Charlie was erect, her surroundings no longer resembling a personal arrangement of pillows, without a cigarette, not reaching for one, the soft pack she always carried not on the table or in her hand.

"Okay, Fay. We have a couple options. The first being that I leave you here to burn the place down, and I take that money and go to college, become somebody's aging typist."

Fay looked up with a grin, but the look on her sister's face dismantled it. Charlie's words were as few, then, as they were in all else excessive. She would take over nights until Elise had gone. Fay would make herself scarce. Did she understand. Fay nodded, the bob of her head deep with the relief of a decision made for her. She slid a hand across the table to Charlie, who squeezed it once.

They switched rooms for three days, Fay in Charlie's. She touched the cracked aviator's helmet that hung over the bed, she sang through her baths, she smoked. There was no way to know how his wife reacted to her absence, and Charlie, when she delivered to Fay what Elise would not eat, refused to speak of it.

11.

The next Tuesday his truck pulled up, she was back in her own bed and wouldn't get out. Around her were candles she had burned way down, books she'd barely started. He was calling from the car, a laugh in his throat, "Git in this gole-dang car, rose-buddy!" She knew how he would look, the stubble on his jaw a blink short of a genuine lilac, how he would smell, metal and dairy. He was whistling now, the theme from *Oklahoma!*, something he knew she found obnoxious. She had assumed that the first she had seen of his wife would be the last she had seen of him, and had accepted that sentence. What could another hour with him do, besides describe to her the reckless person she was? Ten minutes passed and she could still hear the engine. When she emerged, barefoot on the filthy porch, she could see him using the surface of his horn to scribble something, a note for her he'd tape facing in to her window. He called her Bess Rainy in these notes, she didn't know why, something that made him laugh. *A rainy look to you sometimes* is all he would say when asked. *Dear Bess Rainy,* he had written once. *I smelled you on the back of my hand in a room full of people today and it was so painful I had to excuse myself.* His tenderness was stunning because it was rare.

In just the way he leapt down from the cab, a hop onto one boot and a boyish stomp with the other, she could tell he didn't know. It made her furious, that she should have to be all parts of the crime, the cause, the victim, the messenger. As he saw her face his gait slowed, and he set down the things he had brought her, a book on trees, some lemons he'd preserved with rosemary. He always came with gifts, a protection against the things he wouldn't talk about. On the uneven planks he sat two steps below her, his arms around her calves. She spent a foggy minute waiting for him to ask, then another, rage-smeared, realizing he would not.

"Your lovely wife didn't mention her visit?"

His arms returned to their place at his sides. He looked at his boots and then his truck, as if hoping the things in his life were the life itself.

"What did she do?" His voice was light, his bottom lip pushed out. She was standing now. It felt like she had to use her body or it would use her.

"What did she do? Why do you ask it like that? Is it so hard to believe she could have done something?"

He hopped up, raising himself from his seated position without the use of his hands. The vim of it infuriated her. She would not turn to face him. She was aware of every part of her that did not belong to him, her feet in perfect line with her hips, her hips with her shoulders, her chin with her navel.

"She doesn't do a lot of leaving, is why. So my thought process seems to stop before her even—"

"Let me give your thought process the kick it needs. She came here dressed to be painted for a portrait and she ordered everything on the menu, one by one over the course of the longest two hours of my life, looking at me like I was a broom."

"I can't always get her to the front porch for some sunshine."

"Your thought process in general seems to rely on convenient omissions."

"Car I bought her I have to turn over the engine to make sure, sometimes."

"I wonder why she's been so unhappy."

Vincent stared at her then, trying, she thought, to calculate how total her anger was, where he could find the break in the fence. She could feel her face was ruined with color. He tried to take her hand, but her fingers wouldn't curl around his, so he slipped an arm behind her back, another under the joint of her knees. Carrying her, pacing the porch, he raised and lowered and raised her.

"Sir, I'm going to guess that one thousand one hundred twenty-two beans are in this jar. I'm just a simple hog farmer, but I believe in this like I believe Jesus Christ gave some damn good speeches. If that doesn't win me a prize, I don't know what." She snorted against the thin cotton of his shirt, hated herself for it, all in the same second. They were inside in under a minute, her feet never touching the ground.

In her bedroom the noon light was invasive, highlighting the clutter made by her sunken week, the western shirt of his she'd slept in and left balled in her sheets, a plate still holding two wilted fries at the foot of her cot. Pint glasses of water at different levels lined the length of her room. The reminder of it separated her from him again, and she insisted he put her down, pushed the flat of her feet against his stomach.

"Who's the lowlife done been living in here, rosebud?"

She climbed onto her narrow cot and he followed, mirroring the shape of her body, pressing the points of his knees into the backs of hers. When he spoke it was into her neck, the words coming into her body before they came into her mind.

"I couldn't have known, Fay. Babe, I could not have known. I deserved that, not you. I did."

That was as much of an apology as he gave her, no sorry inside it, but still she felt the breadth of her ribs pushing back into his chest, his leather belt digging against her hips. It was the first but not the last time that she wondered what it was about a woman truly distraught, disarmed by crisis, that planted the idea of sex in a man's mind. It was perverse, she was thinking, disturbed, and soon after the thought arrived it disintegrated. She began to hear very clearly. The pop of a jet gone sonic, the snort of Lloyd's nose in the pool. She couldn't explain it to herself, but then she was pressing against him, too.

He liked to arrange her and she let him. She was pliable under his wishes, to put her thighs just so, to slide a doubled pillow under her hips as he lowered his mouth. When she looked up it seemed the colors in the room wanted to become each other, the blues of the sky through the windows braided into the gold of his hair where it moved a little between her legs. He came up with his eyes open and she turned over, her forearms crossed in a point where she rested her head. She didn't want to see him.

When it was over she knew that nothing had been resolved, but the fact of this seemed less urgent, an unpleasant appointment she would endure after many more warm and gentle hours. There was nothing in her body to alert her to what had changed, the switch that had been pulled on, the microscopic reactions beginning. Whether it happened then or in that parking lot on La Cienega, it made sense, she thought later—it could not have been a daughter.

12.

He knew that afternoon at Fay's would be his last—if not during, then on the dark road right after. His way of thinking, stretched far out, had snapped back. He could no longer afford it.

Afterward he bumped up the mountain, taking curves one-handed, in some way pleased by how little his headlights revealed. Sitting back as deep as he could in his truck, he never pushed the stick forward to turn on his brights. Four miles from home a buck appeared like a long-hidden memory, completely clear, its consequences real. A streak of white ran the nose, separating near-perfect circles of chestnut brown. The eyes themselves did not seem alarmed, just inquisitive, as though the leaping animal, its head turned to see him, were about to remark: *Of all places, I didn't expect to run into you here.*

He couldn't understand how quickly the blood took the paths of the shattered glass—it seemed immediate, all of it had bloomed before him as the body slipped down the hood. Turning on his brights now, he watched the red following every fissure. Its back was turned to him, keeping a secret.

He spent ten minutes with the carcass, bereft, surprised by it. He wanted it to twitch its golden ears. On the shoulder of the road he stroked the places where the fur was not clotted. In the end he could not abandon it: he hated the idea of the body among the scrubs, uncovered. Rather than lifting it by the hoofs, he carried it by its back, honeymoon-style, into the bed of his truck, where he wrapped it in the shadow plaid blanket he'd kept there for Fay. Perhaps he would bury it. The thought was a comfort, but in the vision he had he could see himself doing it, could see his shoulder blades working as the shovel raised up. What did it mean if this was your fantasy of yourself, a view that didn't include your own face?

At their cabin all the lights were on, yellow flooding from the bedroom and kitchen and living room, because Elise liked that, the idea that every object in every room was visible to her, instantly reachable. The pearled pink toothbrush, the Japanese tea set, the driftwood shelves in the living room where Vincent kept his things up high.

Inside she acknowledged him by shifting her position on the couch, opening her body slightly from its fetal curl. He filled two tin buckets in the kitchen and carried them precisely, the horizon of his shoulders never drooping, the water in its containers barely thudding. He had brought a headlamp but in the end worked without. The light from the house was enough to suspend the body, and he could feel that it was already lighter, had already lost significant blood.

When he returned, to the noise of the television set she had fought bitterly to acquire—*Wouldn't some actual quiet do you good,* he had said, so many times she mocked it—he switched it off without looking in her direction, fetched a chair from the tiny kitchen. He did not want to speak to her from the couch, where they would feel each other shifting but stare at the same wall. To her advantage was the fact that he had not been home in the early evenings the past two months. He had stayed late on the base, working on a paper about the lift and drag of delta-shaped wings. Her imagination of the time he spent with Fay was much greater than the reality, and he couldn't prove she'd been gone.

He asked what she had been doing with herself the last week, the question thin and light and in conflict with the way he phrased it, sitting upright with his fingers tented.

She was conflicted by his interest in her, swallowing a smile, sitting up and then reclining back. Finally she spoke evenly, a departure from the typical poles of her falsetto laugh and her sharp, dark pronunciations.

"Thises and thats. I started a bird feeder from the old toaster box."

"Paint it?"

"I didn't quite get to that."

"Drive out to buy some?"

"No."

"Drive anywhere?"

As with the television, she had filibustered for a car that made no sense there, a Bel Air in a silky pink, and she almost only ever drove it to get it washed. She was as elegant and flawless a driver as she was a dancer, approaching four-way intersections with her eyes light and chin up, taking left turns with such ease not so much as a stray penny slid across the dash. It was one of many traits that had almost won his devotion.

"No," she said, not without cheer. Nowhere on her face was the bar where his girlfriend worked, the hundreds of dollars she had littered there. They were cruel in the same way, he and Elise, pointed. *When I walk in the door and make this gesture,* he had told her once, digging an index into his temple, *it means I need quiet to think.*

There were no more questions to be asked, there was no more probing to be done, without mentioning Fay, which he would not then or ever. It was only ever going to be a look that passed between them, a source of power that allowed her certain freedoms in behavior.

His elbow on his knee, his chin in his hand, he nodded, and then he stood and brought the chair back to where it lived. In their room, the covers and sheets he had tugged at and smoothed that morning had been slept in again. The bed looked like an envelope ripped open. Lying in his undershirt and briefs, he turned out his bedside lamp. He chose a memory of her and he followed it, Fay reaching for oranges in a grove they had driven to some months back, her mouth twisting as she punctured the fruit with her teeth. Her gestures clunky, her complexion gone patchy with joy—hands on his abdomen, he fell asleep.

He woke to Elise reaching for him, slipping two fingers beneath the elastic band of his underwear. It had been six months or seven. After he came his mind floated awhile, passing over the ends of sentences he'd heard that day, some childhood bike crash whose lead-up he always remembered, then settled on the buck outside, that thought unrelenting. He slipped on his long johns and was out the door, pausing in the living room to grab the things he needed, moving two inches every few seconds so as not to wake his wife. On the porch outside, where the temperature had dropped, he thought, nine and a half degrees, he slipped on his boots and laced them, pulled them tighter than they needed to be.

Strung up on a pine, lit variously by his moving headlamp, the animal reminded him little of what it had been, the expression it had made midjump. He could hear Ernie instructing him as he moved his knife in precise, centric lines above the hooves. His thumb between the skin and fat, his index finger fur-side, he began to pull and it came away easily, working with him to become separate from the body.

HE HAD GUTTED IT WITHIN the hour, and it bled out through the morning, through his next day of work. Of course he considered she would have to watch that through the window. They ate it for the duration of their time in California—he insisted on it.

13.

The image of Elise waiting for her, in the depth of two P.M. blue, was less frightening than threatening, less the sound of the crash than the broken window through which anything could come. Walking toward Elise, she believed that if someone were to push a hand up the other woman's neck and into the blue-black of that hair, she would feel it in hers. Vincent's wife dangled her feet in the pool.

The shirt she wore was his, Fay knew, and hated, yellow gabardine onto the tag of which Elise had sewn his initials—*VK,* letters Fay had thought about and drawn on the backs of receipts and sometimes her hands, the narrow angles that went so well together. She had taken it off him before. Elise wore his denim well, too, a button fly, a cord of rope cinched around it. She was taller than Fay had noticed during those nights at the bar, the rounds of her shoulders as big and perfect as Christmas oranges.

Fay settled on a canvas chaise near her, fingering the pilled military green canvas where it met the metal curve on the frame. She found herself looking for a pair of shoes, then understanding that there were none, that Elise had driven there barefoot. In forty-five minutes the first customer would show. She could hear Lloyd where he moved somewhere behind the shed, investigating a plant with his mouth. There was the sound of the planes. After sitting still a minute she slipped off her sandals, a weft of red and orange leather coming loose at the heels and toes.

"You have beautiful feet," Elise said, using a hand while she looked for the word, two fingers tracing a line that moved up and out.

"The metatarsal?" Fay said.

"The metatarsal. Did you think I wouldn't find out, or didn't care?"

"They're not beautiful. They look bubonic."

It was all she could say. She sat up straighter, a chin hooked on her shoulder as she surveyed the line of the backrest, the seat she did not deserve. Standing up, she waited for a question she could answer.

"You'll be amazed by how quickly it happens to you," Elise said, "that you're on just the other side of real beauty."

"I thought it was his job to think about. I thought worrying about another person's marriage was useless."

"Your face, your body. Elbows go first."

"If not me, someone else, I thought."

"This you were wrong about. Not to my knowing, at least, or no one who mattered. Immediately, with him, him with you, there was a change. It used to be he was so quiet I'd think he'd left, and then the whistling. You came into his life and then I always knew where he was in the house. 'Zip-a-Dee-Doo-Dah.' 'Way Down South in Dixie.'"

"But you're so beautiful. Everybody looks at you."

"Everybody looks at anything with lots of moving parts. A separate comb for the eyebrow, a different cream for mornings."

"The truth is I almost never thought of you," Fay said. "He never told me your name."

Fay had not known she would say it. The tear that ran down his wife's face, the low muddle of vowels that came from her mouth, seemed to surprise Elise, a choice her body had made without her. Elise ran the heel of her hand along her lash line and took her feet from the water, crossing them in front of her so that her heels touched her thighs. Hands on her knees, she looked like a very young girl, someone whose greatest ambition was to master the spelling of her own name.

"I guess he didn't choose you for your manners."

"I'm sorry." Fay sat again, her hand on the lip of the pool not far from his wife's.

"Are you? Do you have any sense of the long tradition you're acting in here, the very old story?"

Elise had pulled a pack of cigarettes from her front pocket and was gesturing with one, seeming glad for the power an accessory granted her. Surveying Fay's hand, she ashed less than an inch from it.

"I'm not sure what you mean," Fay said. "If you'll allow me this, I'll say nothing about his being married appealed to me."

"I won't. Allow you that."

That the mockery in her voice was tender, somehow, made it worse, Fay thought. The clouds beyond the inn's U of buildings had formed a kind of wall, a view of the sky that seemed to separate this part of the world from the rest. She was tied to this woman, she understood now, had been since the moment Vincent placed a finger on her ear. To love a man who belonged to someone else was, inevitably, to love who he had become in service to who they made together, the jokes and compromises, the turns in language. There would be terms he used for both of them, Fay thought now, *rosebud, babe,* certain observations or anecdotes he tested out on each. Had he told Elise about the badge he had designed for himself as a child, the symbol he had drawn everywhere, taken from the dollar—an eye in a pyramid. Elise cupped some water in her hand and let it down the back of her neck. Had he slept with them both on the same day, had his violence or passion with one meant his kindness or quiet with another.

"It's possible when I was your age I would have seen it the same way, although I wouldn't have been stupid enough to act on it. Of course I wasn't running around the Mojave Desert in just my overalls. You probably believe that this is limited to you, to the two of you, to whatever—"

Fay gestured toward her cigarettes and Elise nodded.

"Bond. To whatever strange, sad thing you see in how you are together. It has no say on what your relationships will be like later in your life, you think, it has no effect on the men who know about the affair you two have had, their wives if they've told them. You think this is a mistake of place and time and unhappy for the three people it directly touches, if you're nice enough to include me. You probably imagine, sure, some trouble in the meanwhile, dust that will settle or blow away."

The conversation was splitting Fay in half, creating one part of her that wanted to argue about the ideas set down, another that felt hot under accusation and told her to run.

"I wouldn't say that exactly, but—"

"You wouldn't say anything exactly. You're what, nineteen? Twenty? The whole point of you is that nothing is exact. That's the appeal of you to others and even the appeal of you to yourself. Let me finish."

Fay looked around her to the things she knew well, begging them to return her to the time before this. The trough where Lloyd's name was painted, the curtains of the rooms that moved erratically like the lips of people sleeping. She saw something then that she couldn't understand, that Charlie's window was open, close enough to hear, and she believed she saw the light shift when her sister moved through it. It was the first time, in their life together, that her sister had not come to her rescue.

"I want you to hear this clearly. Every time a younger woman takes up with an older man, there is a little bit of power taken from some woman somewhere else, and I don't mean just the person he's lying to. Because it sends a message to the man that his options extend in a way his wife's do not. That message, then, is printed on him for other men to see. Those men go home a little different, that night or another. Maybe they try less at small things, how-are-yous, a cold that comes on in the middle of the night it's their job to get up for. The little additive concessions of marriage. They think, What am I giving my whole self over for just yet. If I wanted to, if I saw it, there's still some window I could scramble through. Maybe it's only open a crack in their minds, but this lets in a breeze."

"I'm not going to see him again," Fay said, blinking, not yet convinced, with the remote hope this would keep Elise from talking longer. She remembered the feeling of being caught stealing, age six, the town grocery, four malted balls taken from the five-sided glass jar with a low opening in front, two along either row of molars, her mother putting out a hand and barking in the spring light of the open door. This was her feeling now, that nothing could fix what she had done, what her body had insisted on taking.

"And the side of the women. For your sake we'll just leave aside matters of money, here, though that's forgetting a great big part of the fire. Can you imagine what this does to birthdays, to mirrors? We start to believe we are lucky just to be returned to. Every year is another mile made on a deflating tire."

Her voice kept catching on itself, snagging on peaks, certain words in that moment painful to pronounce. *Birthdays. Mirrors.* Elise took his shirt from where she'd tucked it and wiped at her face, speaking for a moment through the fabric, shrouded.

"And when it comes to others, other marriages, the women we know and confess to, the news is not good either. The ones whose husbands leave we examine for signs of failure, did she stop taking care of herself, we say, and dark old parts of us see it maybe as contagious. Single women become a misfortune we avoid like any other. We say hello in the grocery store, but we don't look into their carts."

Fay was trying to focus on her next few hours, imagining the hot towels under her hands and the napkins to be restocked, and then she was weeping a little also, the specific pain of having humiliated yourself, having chosen that. On her body still were marks he had left, ribbons where she was sore that changed how she moved. Why had she needed no convincing? Lies to herself about her independence aside, she saw how she had wanted to become Elise. Then, now. She did not want to be the forbidden thing. She wanted to be the trusted clock on the sunny wall.

"Maybe we're having a few too many tears," Elise said, "over someone who once canceled his birthday party because he found out a rare owl was roosting just a five-hour drive away."

"The other day he drew the waitress a flowchart about what he wanted to eat," Fay said. "If not mashed potatoes, then string beans, but only string beans if no greens with roast chicken."

"She throw that away in your sight, or . . . ?"

"Waited until the kitchen, sadly. He said, *Does that make sense?* And she said, *No, and not dollars neither.*"

"Did you give her the Nobel for her perfect work there?"

They laughed and fell quiet again, separating at the places where they touched, knees, the backs of arms.

"Nice to know what a nasty thing you are," Elise said. "I was thinking ingénue, I was thinking pink Play-Doh brain."

"Will you tell him about this?"

"I was actually thinking I'd take a photo of the two us, frame it in the kitchen and wait."

"Why not take a few, consider a collage?"

"Macaroni frame."

When the first car pulled up, Fay did not move. Whoever it was could wait. In the last she saw of Elise, her head leaning out the driver's-side door into the dust, wrist bent right over the wheel, it was possible to imagine some other reason for their knowing each other, that she was not leaving but picking Fay up for a last-minute trip. They would pull money straight from their pockets, they would turn at a sign that said VACANCY.

"Forget him," she sang. The blue of the day had rolled over, was stretching into something thinner, the clouds now like what was left on a plate.

"Forgotten," Fay said.

14.

There was something about her, the men's faces said, that had become a little off-putting. Gone was the woman who sensed an empty glass behind her, gone the three-part pivots to empty an ashtray and grab the seltzer gun in one go. The quips, the authoritarian bellow when somebody got antsy and started rocking the cigarette machine. The books she had returned to reading any chance she got, dog-eared and underlined in forest green—they were gone, their tenancy of her time vacated and replaced by a cheer they all could feel was suspect.

It was a subtle change, visible to them only because they'd grown so fond of the way she slammed doors and drawers shut with a raised back foot. That equine gesture had not been the first or last that had earned her the commendation *a horse worth betting on*. Now she took indirect trips between deserted tables and the bar, carrying glasses only a few at a time, and she was inordinately touched by the most minor human expressions, smiling too long at a pair of pilots with their arms around each other's necks. When business was slow she could be seen with both hands dangling far across the bar, her head pillowed by her forearm.

Her etiquette became exaggerated, rich in apologies, some unnecessary and some when she had forgotten a drink or a meal, another change that became dependable. Charlie, who had retained a more active interest in her business since the episode with Elise, watched Fay with a dark curiosity, sometimes intervening, listening for the drinks she took and reminding her which she had missed, slinging an arm around her hip or slipping a saliva'd finger in her ear when she seemed lost to the room.

They had started closing together again, as they had when Fay had first arrived—still recognizably the girl their parents had groomed, still shocked by the decision she had made to come, in many ways her first.

At the end of a long week together, the corners swept, the nozzles of the cola machine sunk in pint glasses of hot water and lemon, they hung their feet in the pool, their skin made a fluorescent pale green by the underwater light Charlie had saved for and installed herself. They had emptied the pool to do so, and after brought Lloyd and a pack of beers down the steps. The horse had hated it, paced around them making viscous snorts and tipping his head at the world above.

"Fay."

"Charlie."

"What is it I always told you?"

Fay rotated her submerged ankle in polite curiosity.

"Happiness is good health and a bad memory. Farts are art. Don't trust that fuckin' expiration date. Always a few more days left."

Her imitation was perfect, the characteristic pointer finger flung toward God.

Charlie caught the laugh in her throat and dismissed it. Grabbing her sister's hair, she squeezed too hard.

"I belong to you, is what I meant."

"Ah. That. And the inverse, of course."

"Which, Fay, is and will be true. But I'm a little worried here.

I have this nagging little committee in my head that says maybe I failed you. Maybe this was not the place for you to come, the incessant committee says, or maybe it was, but now it's not the place for you to stay."

Fay sewed up her face into something smaller, her lips diminishing, her eyebrows pushing to meet.

"Where would I go?"

"Committee is divided on that. Votes and recalls, all day long. Gavel on the podium. But I'm wondering if back to the parents, maybe just for the time that you're—"

"The time that I'm what?"

"Oh fuck it, Fay," Charlie said, the alcoholic impatience showing itself. "Do I have to mime it for you? How long has it been since you bled?"

It had been impossible that she was pregnant, far too expensive a thought, so she had not examined it. She could have been naked in front of her sister, the way she went about feeling herself then, detecting the places where she was softer, acknowledging for the first time the inflammation of her breasts.

"Jesus Christ—was a carpenter," Fay said. Vestiges of her early life always arrived in her mouth when the present was hard to speak.

She snorted and began to cry simultaneously, a sonic contradiction that amplified as it bounced over the water. Charlie ran her oil-smudged hands over the chest pockets of her overalls, searching for her pack, and in that moment Fay slipped into the pool. The cream of her shift bloomed around her, fat and wide when she floated, slick and straight when she kicked her legs back. She swam hard for ten minutes, surfacing just to tap the curb at either end, and when she finally crawled heaving onto the concrete she looked like something the ocean has rejected and spat back onto sand, each stringy part of her pulled a different way.

Fay turned her cheek and opened one eye in Charlie's direction.

"I have a friend in LA who could," Charlie said.

"No," Fay said, singsong. "I made him. I should bring him here."

Everything about it, the certainty of keeping it, her unfounded conviction about the gender, silenced Charlie, who could do nothing but slap a hand to the wet pavement in performative solidarity.

Charlie fetched a towel for Fay and some scotch for herself. She moved the rough cotton over her sister's fine hair without love, not adjusting the pressure when Fay whimpered. They separated soon after to their rooms. Two hours later, Charlie appeared in her window, all her broad muscles locked, having found no way into sleep, and looked toward her sister's. The room was totally dark, totally still. It was as though the demolition of her life had come as no surprise.

Fay was unconscious ten hours, hardly changing positions, not even when, in the early morning, Charlie pulled away at high speed, the radio on, the gravel fleeing the tires' rotations, killing the silence of the place.

15.

In the weeks of testing in Texas, following interchangeable men in scrubs down reflective hallways, Vincent did not often think of Fay. The examinations came as a relief, for there were very few decisions to be made, only instructions to be followed. Missing was his compulsion to map out an area as soon as he entered it, determine north and south, imagine the crossings of roads or the meetings of hallways. He needed only to do as he was asked, albeit the asks were tremendous.

On a robin's-egg-blue vinyl stool he sat while a spectacled, wordless man squeezed syringeful after syringeful of ice-cold water into his left ear. There were no guidelines given, no questions asked as the liquid found the canal, just the shock and the understanding that it would keep coming. At no point was he confused about his obligation. It was to do nothing, to remain still as a houseplant, to not shift on the paltry surface area of the stool, to not look around the room at the cabinets or the clock or the door. To not wipe at the excess running down your face, down the neckline of the clothes they dressed you in, to not flinch when it reached your torso. When the experiment was over, when the door opened and another man appeared, and Vincent stood. "Thank you," he said to the blank man in the blank room—of all things, he said thank you.

How could he have thought of her, when. This time he followed the man up a set of stairs, and he placed each foot at a ninety-degree angle with the next step—the oldest part of him believed that was lucky, important. He had tried to say goodbye but her sister had been waiting outside instead.

Sleeping, she said.

Can I wait.

She's very tired.

Within the next room was a chamber almost as big, all glass with a backless wooden bench he could barely make out for all the steam. He knew without being told that he was going in alone, and again he thanked the man who opened the door to his next discomfort. Thank you, sir. They had included a thermometer, a cartoonish one the size of a baseball bat, had welded it to the wall he faced. He did not think of Fay there, because he knew it would raise his heartbeats per minute, and they would take note of that as a sign of frailty, and besides, he could not afford the one-degree rise in internal temperature her image would incite. One hundred forty-five degrees Fahrenheit. The sweat, he felt, was not something his body had produced for the occasion but a feature of his physiology, something he'd lived with always. The only picture he admitted to his mind was that of a walk he'd taken along the canyon of the Rio Grande. It comforted him, the thought of those curving walls of stone, the river, not so wide, that divided ways of life completely. The water like some kind of decision being made, over and over for miles, steady and green between the cliffs of peach stone. When the door opened—how much later he didn't know—it was not relief he felt, just an awareness of conclusion, a town he was driving away from, a belonging he had decided to give away.

She could be sleeping for months, Charlie had said.

They greeted him with a towel and led him to a long line of shower stalls, where he brought his arms over his head and curled his toes and watched the cold water run down the slant of the tile into the drain. A fresh set of clothes, identical to those he had saturated with sweat. Shortly after another man, this one older, his clipboard thicker with paper. The man made a gesture, a pointer that went back, and Vincent followed him out.

The next three feet of hallway terminated in double doors, which opened onto a wider stretch of linoleum. Through glass on either side he could see people working, carrying stacks of paper or typing alone, but he did not turn to observe them. At the entrance to the next room the man cleared his throat to speak, a thick wrist already on the knob. "Come out," he said, "in two hours."

When the latch took, the sound short and minor, the room was without light. Vincent heel-toed to what he believed was the center and he lowered himself, slow inch by slow inch, into a squat, from there into what Ernie had called Indian-style. His hands on his knees, he began to sing, his sight unavailable but his grandmother's Scottish tremor there with him. All choruses and verses included, he knew, ate five minutes, for she had insisted on singing it precisely at midnight on the nights they were awake and together, and he had dreaded it, her gaudy tremolo, and learned to diminish this by knowing when it would be over.

You'll take the high road and I'll take the low road
And I'll be in Scotland afore you
But me and my true love will never meet again
On the bonnie bonnie banks of Loch Lomond

Twenty-four fives. He did not think of the concept of two hours, of what that could fill, a matinee in Technicolor or the drive from Edwards to Los Angeles he'd sometimes taken with Fay. A meal at Canter's, why not, just her perfect teeth around a soup spoon an occasion. He tapped the floor at each conclusion, briefly, to remind himself of the advancing count. Aware he had taken fifteen seconds to get settled, he left the last chorus unsung, and when he felt for the door it was exactly where he thought it would be.

The light was surgical, examining him from every direction, and he heard the click of a stopwatch. He saw the scientist in the chair, the positions of his brow and jaw in clinical gravitas, saw him break part. The grin was wide and toothy, directed at the timepiece, gone in a blink.

She could be asleep the rest of her life, the sister had said.

Two hours, he learned later, and two seconds.

16.

Getting in touch with her parents had not proved as easy as either she or Charlie suspected, and the change in them, their sudden remoteness in the world, was something she almost admired her first weeks in their new home.

Their phone number, the same for thirty years, had been disconnected, and the letter she sent, forwarded to the Petaluma address, took weeks to reach them. Ashamed of their daughters, tired of the country club gossip, Fay's mother and father had purchased a rambling farmhouse in the northern part of the state. They had driven the nine hours along the coast, silent on a twisting road.

FAY HAD READ THE REPLY aloud to Charlie on the porch, their feet propped and a little crowded on the same milk crate, passing a bottle of beer back and forth.

Dear Fay,

We have moved away and are now just north of San Francisco. A bus leaves twice a day from the city to Petaluma. Enclosed are a

map and a schedule. Send us a telegram when you are sure of your
arrival. If at all possible, please dress for the trip.

C & J

The sisters had cackled at it, clutching at each other's elbows.

"If *at all possible,* please don't arrive in the nude."

"If clothing *is* worn, please remove all rodents that may be clinging to your attire or dependent on you for food."

"If at all possible, stow away inside a tasteful trunk. Using your forehead like a battering ram, heave your way onto the platform without breathing audibly or alarming any of your fellow passengers. Make it appear the trunk has been delicately placed there by a respectable steward of the railroad."

She had still been under the impression that the trip would prove merely an interruption of the life she'd been living, a belief whose bottom fell out the first time they took her to dinner. Her mother knocked on her door before with the dress Fay was to wear, something with an empire waist that would hide the fact of her bump.

A week before she left, disturbed by the Santa Ana winds, Lloyd had gone missing, four days in which all of Charlie's syllables elided and she drank only one jam jar of water. "What in shitfire you think goes into beer!" she yelled when Fay asked. When he returned, striding into the bar with a pejorative sigh, Charlie spent fifteen minutes with her head pressed to his. Fay's going-away party, two nights later, had been informal, unnamed, a secret between the sisters that the men didn't suspect. That night Fay was quick on her feet again, taking orders from across the room by gesture and wink, a pointer raised for a martini up, two fingers pinched on her nostrils to indicate dirty. Her sister was on the guitar, playing Hank Williams—*Her personality made me want her.* That she and Charlie both mounted Lloyd, Fay's chin tucked onto Charlie's collarbone, and disappeared for twenty minutes, seemed a return to business as usual. The men smoking by the pool had seen them way out, their bodies one slumped shape, a two-headed thing that could not carry itself.

KINDNESSES IN HER PARENTS' HOME were indirect, a stray sweater folded neatly where it was left, a fire lit in anticipation of another's return. Fay, the growing hump in her stomach set low and unyielding, helped with the patch of edibles her mother had planted in a hurry to remake her life. She watered the rows of arugula and corn and spoke idly to the chickens as she gathered their eggs, marbled brown and coral pink. Her father drove her to doctor's appointments, more careful with left turns than she remembered, and when she came home there was lunch waiting, covered by a butler's tray. Alone, she ate the tomatoes peeled and cut back to resemble flowers, the ham and apple muffins. The house sat high on a hill and the bay windows were poorly insulated, a breach of the outside world on the domestic that her parents would never have accepted before. As Fay sat at the table situated between them she could feel the winds she imagined were headed for the town, a place she watched every day but had rarely visited. Something had changed about her mind. When it came to a problem it couldn't solve, it would point, somewhat lazily, to dying. Or you could kill yourself, it thought for her, your mother's Seconal, your father's Smith & Wesson. She was disturbed but learned to think around this, a rude guest at dinner whose comments you ignored.

As she became bigger she was less content to remain on the property, and she felt keenly that this anxiety belonged to her child, that he wanted to see and know and had soaked up all there was in that silent home, on that golden hill. Her father caught her hiking the three miles to the small downtown—a hardware store with a taxidermied brown bear in the window, a movie theater with a marquee that wrapped around the corner, a mostly stagnant estuary—

and insisted on driving her. He pulled into a parking space and opened his newspaper, told her to take as long as she needed, but what she needed was for no one to know where she was, so she only skulked a few blocks up to the grocery, where she bought nothing, then returned to the car.

17.

It was Charlie who gave the baby his name. The drugs had disguised Fay, hidden her under thick blankets of light and sound. The appearance of her son, finally, after thirty-six hours, had not made words more available. Just the fragility of his head, how easily it could break, cowed her, checked her impulse to touch him. How could she name him, narrow his life that way? "You do it," she said to Charlie, who had appeared, cigar already lit, halfway through. In a letter a month before, Fay had offered a rough due date but not an invitation. Rather than bringing them in with the rest of their letters and bills, their parents had left the envelopes from Charlie, two a week for almost half a year, in the mailbox for Fay to find on her own. If she left one half-read on the kitchen table it appeared soon after under her door.

"How did you know to be here?" Fay asked, time wobbling between the walls of the aquamarine hospital room. Thoughts seemed to be arriving in the wrong place, a taste in her mouth or a weight in her hand. How to confirm that her sister was indeed near her, her son still not arrived. It was the smell she finally trusted, the singular odor of Charlie, pomade and tobacco and pine-scented mop solution.

"Been calling around different hospitals in the area for about two weeks," Charlie said, rolling the baseball cap she held in her hands. "Pretending to be the father. Some of those nurses got pretty fond of me by the end. It's sort of a shame they'd be disappointed to see the body attached to those vocal cords. Particularly Lindy. I sang to Lindy while she looked up records and whatnot. Lindy sounded like a hot mug of water."

"It's 'cool glass of water,' supposed to be." Fay was trying to get her hands to spread, trying to prop herself up. "'Tall drink of water.'"

"Have you ever had hot water? With lemon and honey? When you really needed it?"

Fay was laughing and crying, the two feelings coming to her at the same time like warring radios. There was the sound of nurses speaking in the hall, there was the pinch of her legs as Charlie settled herself at the foot of the narrow bed.

"Lloyd sends his regrets. Couldn't make it. Thought this might be the weekend he'd finally lick his own asshole."

"What do you think I'm doing in this hospital"—Fay was imagining her tongue pushing the words out as she said them—"but attempting to do exactly that. Safer with medical supervision." She made a monocle of her thumb and index, the other fingers framing her cheek, then smiled as if surprised at her new talent. The high was cresting, holding her open.

Charlie nodded. "A very good prank on the folks. No progeny, but—"

The cigar she replaced with a Lucky, which dangled about three-quarters across her bottom lip, an indication she was happy and settled. Recognizing this raised Fay's body temperature, and then with a wave of the drug she disappeared into a worry. What did it mean that it had not truly bothered her to be without this, old signs of old love? Five months she had been with her parents. If she had sometimes felt starved of conversation, missed the path an overheard argument cut, in the main she had not been unhappy, had filled her pockets with fallen buckeyes and felt glad not to answer any questions. Was it wrong to believe you went on as yourself even in the absence of the people who helped you become it? She thought of Vincent rarely, how he might have reacted even less. She was glad to be without whatever comfort he might have offered in the hour he had to spare, and anyway she could not be sure. There had been the man in Los Angeles, there had been the look on his face above her, more determined than Vincent's, less compromised. It would be easier to raise the son of a man she had not known than the son of a man she had failed to. In the hospital her mind snapped to certainty about it, that it was his, Raymond's. Her limp hand in her sister's stringy, sun-speckled one, she followed the relief of this to sleep.

WHEN HE CAME FAY WAS surprised by his weight, the fact of it when divided from her body. She kissed him vaguely, near his left ear, and he coughed. Charlie waited with her hands clasped behind her back, her chin tucked, and when Fay handed him up and Charlie spoke she was equally hard to place, the salt gone from her voice.

"What'll you call him," she said. "If I press my thumb here"— she pointed at the chin—"will he have a cleft or what. What will his name be?"

Fay was aware now of the doctor and the nurses, how they were waiting to take him to some station of sanitization or to offer some remedy. What was wrong with him? Claudette and James stood in the background, polished and withdrawn as people waiting to see a priest. She could not remember anymore which names she had considered. All names sounded like people she already knew, people who had failed to fill the spectacular title of her son.

"I can't, I don't think."

"Wright," Charlie said.

"Like the flying brothers?"

"Yes."

"Yes."

"Wright!"

"Wright."

Hearing his name where Charlie held him on her chest, Wright curled a hand in resignation. It seemed he was gesturing back toward Fay, toward back where he'd come from, as if to say he had not been told, had not been ready.

18.

HOUSTON, TEXAS, 1961–1963

Elise was happier here, tucked away in the row of identical houses painted in a range of mauves, the driveways all glinting in the early mornings with the cars the dealerships had leased for nothing to the men like Vincent. They lived in as close proximity as they worked, in a cul-de-sac without a sidewalk, and their bodies, subjected to the same diet and regimen, were nearly facsimiles. The push of Texas heat was constant, the power of the air conditioners soul chilling, and life here sometimes felt only about managing the two extremes, pulling on a sweater indoors and dragging a handkerchief across your sopping neck while out. Elise had bought and bought with the determination of someone under deadline, a pitcher with hand-painted stripes of primary colors and eight matching glasses, as though some inspection were approaching, Danish teak sconces that resembled horns, as though someone were coming to make an assessment and say this was or was not a home and a life. The bills were large, and he sorted them on the long walnut dining table with foldout leaves, the few hours he was home, paid them but barely on his government salary. Her parents, calling from their Garden District mansion in New Orleans, would not believe how little money he made. She took out a line of credit at the department store. Nine of the astronauts in his class had bought in this development, but they were kept so long at work that they rarely saw their houses, hardly dug their toes into the deep carpet or marveled at the spring of the toaster, and it was their wives who napped and ate and twisted the telephone cords here, building a community that existed below or inside the men's daily lives.

He saw the most of his wife in a crowd, every spare hour now consumed by a dinner party she or some other woman on the block threw. They were rigid and high-pitched, multicourse affairs for which Elise did her hair, the dishes topped by increasingly elaborate garnishes, lilies made of sliced tomatoes and egg yolks and endives, bow ties of lemon wedges and pimiento strips. At these events the men hardly spoke or adjusted their chairs. They had risen at four to run five miles and eat three eggs, to not blink during the talk led by the German rocket scientist who sliced nonstop at the air with his hands, to ride parabolic arcs over Houston just for the thirty seconds of weightlessness at the height of them. In transit from one obligation to another Vincent heard the other men pretending they were less exhausted than they were, leaning on reliable jokes. Dark jabs at the German, *Arbeit macht frei*. Speaking like a man running a carnival ride and waving an invisible cane. *Step right up into the vomit comet!* They had learned quickly to pat a man on his back if he hurled and tell him *Happens to the best of us* but also to keep track of how many times the others had retched versus how many times you had, and worry if the latter was approaching the former, and do everything possible to keep your flight suit pristine and avoid that admission of weakness. Swallowing vomit became a perfected skill. This is what they were thinking of at these dinners, not the pink and cream Jell-O layered and chilled at a diagonal to make bold stripes. They were immune to the small defiances of their children, barely recognized by the family Labradors and basset hounds. There was at least half a chance any story recounted had happened to somebody other than the teller.

Friendship was not what he felt for them, but he was not unhappy to see them at his dinner table or sit at theirs. He could understand why they sat the way they did, Dean Kernan and Wally Lacey, shoulder blades nailed to the backs of their chairs, why they ate as they did, Jesse Gordon and Dick Lovett, seconds and thirds in preparation for the marathon of tomorrow. To see them was to know how he was seen, which circumvented love or hate. Sam Bisson was the exception.

A veteran in a field were there were no veterans, Sam had been the only one to make it from the Mercury program to Gemini in anticipation of Apollo, and he spoke rarely and impeccably. Vincent had once and only once heard him misspeak, mistake the number of minutes into a lunar rendezvous that the lunar module would pass behind the moon—one figure of thousands they were meant to memorize, easily forgotten, easily forgiven—and it had grieved him so that he apologized like a person who has arrived hours late. Early in their training, he and Bisson developed a reputation among the others—*Hey, it's the Dour Dyad*—and it surprised no one when they chose houses next to each other, built a fence with doors between their backyards and front yards. Catching each other gardening in the mornings, Elise and Sam's wife, Marlene, clasped hands across the wood peaks. Sam grilled for the four of them and his two children. Spread out in reclined patio chairs, protected by citronella candlelight, they sighed or laughed into the alien blue of the pool. Vincent and Bisson traded notes, ideas they had about the mechanization of the simulators.

The months in Texas hurtled on, spliced by day flights down to Cape Canaveral or weekends in Johnsville, where they rode the centrifugal wheel, trying to surpass the record of sixteen g's, the backs of their cheeks pinned by their ears. Though there was no time for a hobby, for the first time in his life he could imagine one: the goggles he might wear while woodworking, the easel he would place in the sun.

When the new astronaut class was selected, when he saw Rusty strolling into the room in a line with the rest of the proud faces, when Rusty acknowledged him with a wink that lasted too long, he felt cheated, then foolish. Why had he thought some guarantee had been made, some injunction that sealed off his old lives from his new one—why did he believe he should be the only one to remember Fay, that horse? During the commute home came a dark possibility, a thought he felt trapped in the car with him. It was that he had always relied on his success to separate him from the time and people he'd manipulated to reach it.

Rusty and the wife he'd acquired during his graduate program in Los Angeles, Janet, were hosting soon and often after their arrival, themed evenings to which they always invited the *Life* photographers. Tiki torches and coconuts, cowboy hats and plastic feather headbands, their toddler twins running through slapping fat palms to open O-mouths as they yodeled. Vincent hated these parties but they were required—that his image there be captured.

"Heard something funny about an old friend of ours," Rusty said to him one night, catching him in line in the bathroom. "One Fay Fern. Something that might particularly interest one Vincent Kahn."

There was a flush, the sound of a faucet, a whistle as the water ran. Vincent nodded.

"Hard to trust what you hear, isn't it? I imagine I'll read about that once it shows up in the paper," he said, excusing himself into the door that had opened.

19.

Letters from Charlie, unopened, asked what her plans were, when she might be leaving, why she hadn't responded, whether it was money she needed, whether it was a car. She kept them in a neat stack on her bureau under the childhood ribbons Claudette had saved and repositioned here on the mirror, reminders as she fell asleep about who they believed her to be. The spelling bee where she had cried hidden in the red velvet wings, the tennis tournament she had won in the middle of a heat wave. I have a child, was the first thing she thought when she woke up, whether she could hear him or not, a slow fear that poured her out of bed. She kept waiting for the news to change.

He held blocks in primary colors, mystified by them, possessive. A banana was a gavel, he commanded the room with his judgment. Who she was didn't matter, she thought, what she had believed or fought against—the life she had chosen in reaction to her parents' had ultimately folded her right back into theirs. Claudette spoke to her and to Wright in almost the same voice, asked almost the same questions. What would you like to do today? What would you like to eat?

It was welcome to them, how she was diminished. At the dinner table her paralysis presented as excellent manners, no, yes, either is fine with me, thank you. If she wept over the roast beef, or while sitting out the afternoon on the wraparound porch, they presented her with the baby. A year passed like a matinee she pretended not to have mostly slept through, accepting what had changed and working out the events behind it. He took his first steps in the green-gold grass with the view of the town hung in fog behind him.

She watched television with her father, game shows, the news, an activity that rewarded her muteness, her lack of anything to say. *Truth or Consequences,* flat riddles posed by a jaunty host to faces as indistinguishable as loaves of white bread. *Why was the wife concerned that her husband was a light drinker? Because he'd drink until it was light.* Her father laughed at them, slippered feet crossed at the ankles, the same delay as the studio audience. There were commercials that mystified her, the joy of them. *Why do girls in love always look so beautiful,* the television asked. A woman in plastic twirled to unheard music. *It's because they always walk in the rain. Noxzema.*

Her allowance each week was twenty dollars. His first words were a sentence, "No please." On the last day of July they watched the footage of the partial eclipse, men streaming out of tall buildings in San Francisco holding cereal boxes to their faces. In the fall a black boy enrolled for classes at a college in the South and her father changed the channel on the riots, cars turned over on a lawn before the Doric columns of the lyceum. After a silent dinner, meat loaf shot through with a ribbon of orange cheese, she returned to the couch and changed it back. Her son remained in the dining room, sitting high on a booster and refusing to eat. When James heard what Fay was watching he did not enter, although from the frame of the door he made his dismissal clear, a hand waved in diagonal across his face as if at a bad smell. There was a shot of the governor's car rolling onto campus, white faces warped in joy at its arrival, and it took her a moment to understand he was there in protest of the student, an Air Force veteran, the grandson of a slave.

This event her parents did not discuss, life on land with people, but when the country had prepared for its first orbit they behaved as if in anticipation of a celebrity at their dinner table. Claudette baked in advance, shortbread cookies that looked like rockets.

Her parents stood by her door in the morning, tapping together without rhythm, her son in Claudette's arms pawing at it, too. They had brought her coffee and she blinked, gathering a robe around her gauzy nightgown as she stood in the door frame. The coverage was already on in the living room, and the sound of it unsettled her, as did the benign smiles of her mother and father, people who had seemed incapable of delight for as long as she had been aware. Cronkite's voice had never comforted her, that low bleat sounding like someone reporting from the bottom of a pit. A freckled man from Ohio, his face calm and clean, rode an elevator up the tower and boarded the capsule shaped like a badminton birdie. He was to ring the planet, hurtle around it waving bravely. On the enormous Atlas rocket, thirty stories tall and pale as milk, he waited as his audience did for the boom. When it came it disfigured the whole image, filled the frame with smoke, and then the camera struggled to keep up, losing it and finding it, losing it and finding it, the point of the rocket darting in and out until it was a nebulous white shape in a sphere of gray. The image was like a disease seen through a microscope, a vivid, frantic mutation, and all of it, the great furnace of the takeoff and the low human babble and the wind's dilating of the reporter's talk, sounded to her like an evil distraction . . . *Has passed through the area of maximum dynamic pressures,* the television said. Fay's parents clapped politely, stunned, unaware of the look on her face. It was the first day their country encircled the earth, and the first day she hated her country.

20.

Something had changed, they knew. She was always leaving her shoes somewhere, then the slippers they offered as corrective. It was a kind of self-neglect that enraged them: barefoot by the refrigerator at midnight, barefoot as she carried him up the stairs, a sideways angle that made him laugh, singing the songs her sister had. As though a solution were just a matter of the right slip-on loafers, Claudette suggested a day in the city, see the Easter displays at the department stores. Wright stayed behind with James, something Claudette suggested, girls' day out, with a wink her daughter did not acknowledge.

In San Francisco Fay could not be moved to touch the dresses, hold up the bracelets. Her mother, tired of looking behind to find Fay seated again, reading on a mirrored stool, handed her the car keys. "Why don't you listen to the radio. I'll meet you in the garage in two hours," she said. Dressed as her mother had instructed her, in a just-purchased celery chiffon dress with a high collar and empire waist, she took the first bus she saw.

Against the concave orange plastic seats she was aware how she appeared, how people might imagine her. A young bride glowing between two parts of her life, money in her purse, a collection of Pyrex in her cabinet, some man who knew her childhood nickname with her photo on his desk. There was no way to correct these assumptions, the looks from denim-clad people her own age that went right past her. She committed herself instead to the window, rode the whole way curled around to look out it. On the street from which the bus got its name, Fulton, she pushed the door open. She thought she could see a stretch of green several blocks down, a place where the city opened, and she walked with a hand on her abdomen, her few things in a white leather coin purse swinging at her as she went.

The Victorians she walked under were trimmed like cakes, pinks and blues and violets competing for attention, some with balconies full of plants and others with hand-dyed curtains, and when they let onto the green horizon line of the Panhandle, a long and narrow park you could see across but not around, she was taken by a muted panic, thinking she could not remember the last hour she had spent that was free to her direction of it. She was not in possession of her life, she knew. Suicide crossed her mind like a breeze, nothing that could be helped.

It was the stands of eucalyptus, their smell, and the streets across the park that led in dramatic angles upward, that urged her onto the lawn, where she lay down in a triangle of sun and waited for a thought that was calm enough she could follow it.

Gathered in a loose circle—the girls in linen jumpers and blouses that tied at the neck, the boys with glasses pushed midway up their foreheads, the collars unbuttoned—were a group of students, no older than Fay. She sat five feet away, pretending at contentment. Their scratched leather book bags weighed down foreign newspapers, encircling their talk, one continuous, mutual, angry sentence, elaborating, diverting, returning.

"Special forces, they say—"

"Advisers, they're calling them, they're calling people who are terrorizing a country the size of—"

"A country smaller than California—"

"Smaller than California, this nation, and operating pretty much the same since the fifteenth century, and what kind of advice are they giving? Have you ever extracted any wisdom from a chemical that—"

"—kills forests, eviscerates crops that have only served as the primary source of food for hundreds upon hundreds of years, not to mention what kind of—"

"—effect that's going to have on, oh, people, little kids, babies not born yet, old men trying to live out the rest of their time, and Kennedy meanwhile—"

"—has got a good show we can watch, a dazzling program about celestial exploration that will affirm our country's inherent valor! He's our nation's hope, our nation's cleft-chinned blue-eyed hope, he's got a—"

"—beautiful wife so he must be virtuous above all else, for only the good end up with the beautiful."

There came a collective sighing, reshuffling of papers, and they sat back on their hands or forearms, seeming certain, to Fay, in a way she wanted to be. It was this that moved her, that admitted the boldness required to stand and approach them, looking like she did, a frilly confection, a person who did not belong to herself.

"Excuse me."

As they looked her over their disdain was a unified front, even their collarbones thrown forward in a way that indicated disapproval.

The boy who had talked the loudest sat up, twisting a dandelion between his thumb and forefinger in quick, angry rotations.

"Mrs.—"

"Actually not a missus at all." She prepared for the next moment like a swimmer, surveying a distance and committing her breath to mastering it.

"Costume courtesy of a deeply embarrassed maternal figure, a disguise for the mother of a bastard. Fay." She flashed her left hand, bare of matrimony, waggled it. In the air was the suggestion of the ocean, in the mild temperature the threat it would drop.

They opened around her admission, relaxing their jawlines, tugging their socks up. One canted a hand over his eyes to see her better.

"Given my current incarceration, I'm wondering whether I could borrow one of your newspapers there. I could send it back by—"

"Take it," someone said.

"Subscribe to it."

"Get that special jelly and mimeograph it and—"

"Give it to someone else."

The boy with the tortoiseshell glasses who had called her Mrs. unfolded and refolded the paper, aligning the sections, running a firm index finger down the seams where the crease had loosened.

She waved goodbye, the thing she had asked for held between her ribs and bicep, crossed to the roads she'd admired before, the houses set at forty-five-degree angles, and took Central up to Haight, the strain in her thighs a discomfort that nudged her more awake. Another park waited for her, and it was there she unfolded it, on a plane of grass that followed a sharp incline. The wind that moved the pages almost animated the images, girls bent over rubble, corpses lined up with their shorts around their ankles, men with the waterline at their hips as they crossed the mangrove swamp with a gnarled child on a gurney. Once she saw them they were a part of her, the mosquito netting of the makeshift hospital dropping into the depth of the water, the limp penises of dead men exposed for their families to see.

SAYING HER NAME LATER, CRIPPLED at the elbow by shopping bags where she stood in the driveway, her mother rapped on the passenger-side window. Fay stayed as silent as she'd been on the ride home, an artifact behind glass, what happened around her immaterial.

21.

They strolled her parents' patches of tomatoes and sunflowers, Fay and Wright, they discussed the path of a worm. Her love for him arrived late and enormous. The more she practiced she found it was possible: to live one life in your mind, furious and predatory, and another out in the open, quiet and untouched by foresight. On the margins of her devotion was paranoia, a worry that the pamphlets and underground newspapers she read, the hate they scavenged in her, would taint her, so she tried to read only when he was asleep, to speak to him only in the light sounds her mouth had invented the day he was born. It was a voice that knew nothing of children fleeing their homes, ducking under the slant of their thatched roofs on fire, or of the American teenagers who had carved notches into the backs of corpses, placed the removed eyeballs there.

She was sickened by the masculine bark of her country, the sports someone who looked like her could never play, and in some lower register she was delighted by the warmth of her son's scalp under her hands. She could not imagine a place for herself in the decades to come, and in the long, cool evenings she launched Wright in the air—*again* was the word he loved—while her parents clapped. If she would never be a wife who waited for a husband in a

warm kitchen, she would always be a mother who delighted in the
opening of her son's life. Fay had never made so many promises to
herself, never bargained at length with her worst intentions. Shortly
after his third birthday, there was an afternoon picnic with his favorite hen, a moody queen of green-gray chevron, when he declared
his life's aspirations. She had to tell him he would not grow up to
be a chicken nor marry one. As he sobbed, his earnestness total, she
cackled and held him, and though she could crawl inside the complete joy of that minute, she knew she could not stay much longer.

She found the ad in one of her parents' papers, a humanitarian
aid group with outposts along the Amazon, and within two weeks
had obtained and returned the application, a few details forged or
omitted. Somehow she believed that his presence would disqualify
her so she ticked the box that said *independent housing preferred (not
recommended)* and decided she would disclose the fact of her mother-
hood once they had met her, seen the seriousness of her face. From
a chest in the attic she retrieved her old Spanish textbooks, their
margins littered with additional vocabulary from the phone calls
she'd had with Charlie—a language their parents wouldn't learn
and so the one they'd always communicated in—*motherfucker, pubic
hair, volcano, criminal, gonorrhea, devotion.*

When the letter arrived she read it barefoot outside, two fingers
pinched on the raised flag of the mailbox. He was inside with her
mother, trying to make a straight blue line on yellow paper.

The next day she told a small lie in order to borrow the car—
she wanted to attend a group for young mothers a few towns
away—and they were in San Francisco in forty-five minutes flat,
Wright made silent by the hills disappearing into the wash of fog.
"We're going to get our passports," Fay said, her nose at his when
she pulled him from the car seat. "Password," he said. "Pass-port,"
she corrected. The word was a gentle indictment of their life in this
country, the first promise about their future she made blind.

22.

Fay became the disgrace of the program almost as quickly as she had become its star, her foolishness considered as large as her sacrifice had been.

Her high school Spanish was fluent in under two months, a magnet snapping into place. There were tiny towns that had been named after American companies, oil or chocolate, some officially and some still bearing another name that was never used. In stilted three-room homes on their outskirts she arrived in the evenings with bags of books and taught men deep in their forties to read. Daytimes she spent with children, writing out groups of words in chalk, having a natural feeling for teaching, knowing that only by presenting the knots of vocabulary that existed in their minds would she offer a way into English. She disregarded the American textbooks, hokey lists of hobbies and places that meant little to these children whose mothers were Shuar or Macabea, *scuba diving, soda fountain.* Instead she asked them to describe their lives and gave them the words they used most often, tools their fathers used to hunt, features of rivers. Her hair fallen into her face during sharp turns of enthusiasm, she listened for any unfamiliar phrases they used, exuberant or desultory, and learned them. There was a certain bird, a hoatzin, with a fantastical appearance skewing hideous; the distinctive smell was its defense against predators. It spent its life on bare branches that hung low and close to water, never hunted but very alone. Stinky turkey, they called it. When she could sense their attention growing porous she would pivot in the moody light and say, *What am I to you, a stinky turkey?* It always got a laugh. Her son was with her everywhere, a giggle that presaged a crash. He was like a celebrity, his presence burnishing the mundane. She avoided the stalls at the open-air markets that sold three- or four-foot-long coffins and then she began passing them on purpose, trying to identify what the feeling would urge her to do.

Repatching her clothes until they were more that than the original, refusing to seek treatment after stepping on a nail, she was loved but ridiculed—by the people she helped, by the people who had trained her to help them. Her students, visiting her home, were confused to find domestic conditions equal to or worse than their own, and she ignored the question on their faces. What did it mean about a person if she could afford a new dress, a floor that was not dirt, but refused it, and did that make her more trustworthy or less? Claudette and James came to visit exactly once, and she put them on strict quarantine at their hotel room, where she brought what she had cooked over a fire at home and would not touch the room service they ordered, rotisserie chicken and flan. That their president had died was like the color of their eyes, something anyone could see, and that she would not say his name they took for a sign of her grief.

What difference was this making in the long run, she began to ask her supervisors, a husband-and-wife team who tugged at visible crucifixes, Ted and Ellen. This changed the lives of a few individuals, but how did it address systemic poverty? She wrote letters, to people in the States, the man who had given her that newspaper in San Francisco, others like him, members of Students for a Democratic Society and then the Young Socialists of America. In March, on a bridge suspended by hundreds of bicycle tires, she removed a camera from the neck of an American tourist, a bald man who'd been framing a group of indigenous children, and pitched it in the river. In April Ellen and Ted called her in on the rumor she'd been discussing birth control with a girl of thirteen, and the gestures of Fay's hands were too large and too quick, a palm slapped too many times on the desk, two fingers tapped to the temple to indicate where their brains should have been. Consider this a warning, they said, to which she said she would consider it little, if at all. In April Ellen asked that she distribute a certain shipment of diapers. A donation, Ellen said.

The shipment had arrived without standard paperwork, Ellen said, and Fay would need to unpack a box and get a count. Her pocketknife wedged in her teeth, Ellen whistling nearby, Fay pushed some papers from the table, vocabulary sheets, color-by-number printouts of hooded figures around a manger. She knew the song Ellen was whistling, "Jesus Loves the Little Children," and believed Ellen had chosen it with her in mind. Pulling out an individual diaper and unfolding it she was alarmed to see the words printed there, a slogan, a command. She had bought this brand before, blank.

Red-or-yell-ow-black-or-white-they-are-prec-ious-to-his-sight. Because Ellen wouldn't sing it, it was up to Fay to supply the lyrics in her mind.

Choose——the diapers said. A logo sat dark under the text, ink to be animated by the small body that would stretch the surface. She put her hands where the legs would go, wrenching the fabric to its limit, trying to distort the advertisement.

All-the-chil-dren-of-the-world.

Everything A-OK, Ellen said, somewhere very far from her, a question Fay responded to with a gesture as anodyne, a ring made of thumb and pointer and the three fingers behind splayed and rigid. Stacking them in threes, she carried the twenty-one boxes to the company truck and drove them eighty minutes to a dump, Wright singing out the window and pointing at clouds that spoke to him with a carrot. There she emptied each, making sure the contents mingled, the diapers stiff and white settling against the frames of cars and halves of sinks. She never returned to be fired, never inquired after the last paycheck.

Life would have to happen more deeply inside her, she decided. She had the job at the hotel in under a week, the room that came with it where she floated flowers in wooden bowls of water and taught her son about numbers, about animals and weather. At the school where she enrolled Wright, he was in love with a moon-faced boy who sang with his shirt pulled over his mouth, and in the room where they lived she believed he was happy, writing this boy notes though he could not really write, making drawings of his face that she taped for him by the mirror. *How are you,* someone said, and she said she was perfect, because her son was in love. He could read very early, he wanted a camera of his own. For his fifth birthday they took the interminable bus to Quito, rising from the rain forest to the cordillera. He walked up the aisle, asking other passengers how old they were.

Her Luckies she gave up, because they were packed by people too young for not enough money, and replaced with papers and sacks of loamy tobacco. She went from writing two letters a week to ten, and became cold to her sister when she called, intoxicated, to do her impersonations of American actors or report in depth on the contents of Lloyd's vomit. "What is it you actually care about," Fay said. "Call me when you're sober," she said, surprised at herself but also not inclined to take any of it back. There was a pause and she heard Charlie's teeth around a bottle cap and the drop of a quarter into the jukebox. "Call me when you shit out whatever rotten thing it is you ate," Charlie said.

There was very little Fay needed, she thought. Her life was becoming a line.

BOOK TWO

1966–1972

Consider the genuine glories of the movement. The varied ways in which it retains the allegiance of its members. The subtlety and flexibility of its teachings. The loftiness of its ideals. Finally, what all this amounts to is the creation of a certain type: the member. Far from conspiring to overturn society, as many people suppose, the movement operates mostly upon itself, not upon the world. And for what end? To knit together ever more tightly those who belong.

—Susan Sontag, "Old Complaints Revisited"

1.

The day he met the man with the missing left finger, Wright had spent the morning building a town, murmuring to it about what it was. At the long picnic table of the dining loggia, sitting on his knees on the bench that ran the length of it, he arranged his blocks in great walls that he tore down with a violent push of a plastic truck. There was an earthquake, he decided, a bad one. The detritus lay on the sandstone floor, a curiosity to the birds who wandered in. He was furious and merciful, famous to the tiny people he had created of stones and matches—their beds were moss, their dreams his invention. It had rained until noon, the pressure unrelenting. The wide leaves of the mangroves still dripped water just beyond the open eastern wall, the wooden ledge he would lean over in test of his courage.

At the inn where Fay cleaned and cooked in exchange for a suite, the owner, Lucinda, kept the news of the labor strikes on the radio. Fay and her son were something of a joke to the people who watched them go by, a unit whose lostness was so woven into them they could not see it. Her Spanish was effective but not without its eccentric flourishes, for she had studied certain tenses and subsets of vocabulary largely on her own, and she was respected but vaguely pitied there, someone whose real feeling was always disguised by a word only partially chosen.

His mother and Randy appeared above him, casting shadow on the roads he had poured of sand, Fay's eyelids hooded and her mouth a little open. Her skin was pink and damp and there was a smell to it, a slurry of salt and sweat. "Sweetheart," she said, her wiry arm looped around the stranger's abdomen. "This is my friend Randy. He runs a reading program at the prison."

The man did not treat Wright as other adults did, chucking him under the chin, offering him fruit. His name didn't suit him, the jauntiness of it, the singsong conclusion. This was not a man, his posture communicated, who stopped to greet just anyone, who felt any pressure except the kind he generated on his own. His real name was the sound he made leaving a room, quickly. His real name was the doors he would not close.

Randy only nodded at him, a gesture Wright had seen men offer others in a line of urinals, and shifted slightly in the jeans that sat high on his hips, noticeably worn around the five-button fly. On the lapel of his jacket, thin corduroy in pale blue, were many pins, mysterious symbols and exclamation marks. THEY ALSO DIE WHO STAND AND WATCH, one said. His eyes were very pale, his blond beard shot with gray. He resembled Paul Newman until he showed his bad teeth.

"Far out," he said, pointing at what Wright had made. "Can I?"

He didn't wait for an answer, just pushed the plastic ambulance down the thoroughfare. Then they were gone, laughing through the misty courtyard, disappearing into the room where, despite there being two beds, Wright and his mother had always slept together. Their quilt the color of sage, their lamp draped with her lilac scarf.

Soon Lucinda came to get him. Would he like to go up to the roof with her and see the birds, the crested oropendolas who made sounds like bowling balls plunking into deep water. He wanted to make her happy so he took her hand, he climbed the ladder, he watched the small bodies light in the deep green of the leaves. But he could hear it still, his mother and that man alone together. She was laughing in bright bursts, and then it became so quiet he thought she had fallen asleep.

"For god's sake," Lucinda said, when the noises came. "Is that necessary? Is he building a house with it?" She put her hands over his ears.

Soon, his mother had often said, *you'll be teaching me, my love.* Lucinda's hands on his skin, the birds beyond them coupling and recoupling, in some way Wright knew that something had fallen away. It was a surprise in the way of a burglary, a mauling of native order, the arrangements we are not aware of having made until they are disrupted.

RANDY HAD BEEN A SOLDIER, Wright soon learned, in a war America was still fighting. Transmissions from his native country were foreign to him, the footage of marches, the dubbed commercials for liquor, and he was curious about this war, his body eager to hear the stories and reenact them—make guns of his hands, the sounds of explosions with his fat, wet lips.

The stories didn't come. Wright's disappointment at this, once he'd digested it, turned to dread, because when Randy did speak about it, unprompted, his voice changed. It spiked. He lifted the needle from the turntable, he abandoned meals, he calcified in the one chair in their hotel room and would not talk or move at all.

Did he want to go, he asked his mother. He volunteered, yes, she said. But he hadn't been given all the information. He was very poor, he had few options. It seemed to Wright she had given him several answers, testing out the effectiveness of each.

2.

Randy did not relax into life around the inn, the long breakfasts of instant coffee and juices of every color, Lucinda's gassy baby learning to walk on the humus of the courtyard. He looked all day like someone waiting on a platform, someone who had no time for even the small, pleasant distractions. Reaching to stroke him, four-inch reddish tufts coming from her armpits, Fay seemed to grow calmer the more agitated Randy became. "You're right," she was fond of saying, a firm hand on his shoulder. He never spoke of the finger he had shot off in order to be discharged, and only in brave daydreams did Wright ask him. He always smoked without his hands, the lit thing bit down and finished in a minute.

Randy was not ashamed to ask for money and Fay was happy to give it, glad to reach into her fringed suede purse to thumb off bills with a licked finger. When she was not making beds or cooking stew or switching out locks that the afternoon rains had slowly ruined, she had begun teaching yoga. She had taught herself, advertised by flyer, spent a week of early mornings with her machete clearing a space down the path behind the inn. It was not far from the waterfall. She learned to raise her voice.

Before and after these classes Randy could be heard taking advantage of the new audience, quoting statistics about the death of Vietnamese children, naming the exponential increases in U.S. nuclear armament. Wright attended each, a devoted figure in the front row. His mother's body, bent this way and that, was a testament to her way of being in the world, more than others, Wright thought, bound to it differently. Few people came, four or five women who were loyal, subjugated by bugs despite the citronella candles Fay placed around the perimeter. Randy often abandoned his straw mat halfway through the practice, stalking off from the topiary of upside-down bodies, the left feet high above the hips, to smoke between the enormous roots of an ancient tree. Fay never said anything about it. She smiled from the cloud of her linen caftan, protected by something no one could see.

The language of it sometimes scared him, imperatives from which return seemed unlikely. *Pull your face up to touch the sky,* she would say. *Breathe into your elbows. Feel how much of your body is water.* Her voice became a parody of itself, throatier, punctuated more frequently by exhaled notes of contentment. After she had said her last om she fielded questions about positions, asked them to demonstrate then adjusted them, placing two firm hands on their lower back or tugging their heads up to elongate their necks. That his mother was as available to others as she was to him, as magnetic and imperious, had only just become clear. In his worst moments he fantasized, cold and jealous in the way of someone who needs to be touched, of cutting her hair in the middle of the night, moving the blades at a glacial speed in the total dark.

If Randy loved to hear himself talk, Fay loved to hear herself listen. She took pride in the forty-degree tilt of her head, the murmur of agreement when it mattered most. There were few instances in which she could not tolerate being the silent receiver, few outrageous reactions she could not meet with some placid, clement response. Though Wright resented this about her, how much she shared herself with every person she met, it made the occasions when she snapped or bristled all the more frightening. He was always aware of the other part of her, ready to whip her braid forward and curl her upper lip. When Randy was the target the room became another place, the talismans of their lives taking on other meanings.

THERE WERE MOMENTS HIS MOTHER was located so far within herself she could not be reached, and in hours like this Wright touched her, rubbing her back or braiding her hair. One such afternoon in March, Fay held her body in a twist on the bed, her right knee crossing her body above the left, a limp hand draped across the meeting of thigh and calf. Randy was out, one of his walks, through the pink and green gazebo in the town square and over the river. Wright lay behind her, whispering at himself, trying to make the strands even. He wanted the fine hands of an adult— the fingers that could tie the necessary knot, reach into the wallet and pay for things in shop windows.

As he concentrated, his exhales came a little clotted from his mouth. He was the child who never breathed quite easily, a lesser health that gave him an adult quality, for he could complain about symptoms, identify patterns in their uptick. His sniff and rattle distracted her and she turned, kneaded at his sinuses with the pads of her thumbs. Soon she was hunched over him, her hair slipping out of the inept braid and falling around him. She was the most in his possession like this, diagnosing an ailment, her torso contorted to better see him like some tree that grows in the direction of sun. Fay rose and was back in a minute, spreading the Vicks VapoRub over his neck, squinting to see where the application was thinner.

"On the count of three I want you to breathe in through your nose and imagine you're somewhere with a beautiful view, maybe high up a mountain. One, two, three." Randy stalked in as she spoke, carrying bread and flowers and his Polaroid.

"There's my sweet family." He used this phrase often, as though it were a slogan, and he had a side like this, a part that wanted to photograph them. He had shown Wright how to use a level, drilled him on multiplication tables as they walked. "There's my sweet family," he said again, nuzzling the door frame a little, his thin denim sleeves rolled up and the pearled snap buttons halfway undone. Wright loved him at these times, his enthusiasm for the makeshift slingshot, how he inserted their names into American songs. He had crooned a perfect Brian Wilson as he sang his revised "Surfer Girl," Fay's palo santo his microphone, *Do you love me, do you Wright and Fay, Wright and Fay, my little Wright and Fay?* Today he was buoyant, managing the door with an exaggeratedly light wrist until the air of the room closed around him.

"Where did your walk take you, love?" Fay sat cross-legged now and patted the space next to them on the bed. Randy's nostrils began to flare as he examined the place she gestured to, as though there were some threat there, a roach or a scorpion, that he would have to artfully remove.

"That does makes me think of those bodies," he said, each word a little louder than the one that had come before, the middle of a conversation he had begun without them. "Those who were lit up. Those who bought the farm."

Randy let out a moan then that used all parts of him, the shoulders thrown back making it louder, the tensed calves making it deeper. Fay leaned to the side, blocking Wright's view, and threaded an arm around back to hold on to his foot. From behind her Wright brought a hand to her belly, pressed his head against the place where the crepe of her halter top met her skin.

"We're going to have to get it out of here," Randy said, and soon he was in the bathroom, rifling through the shallow shelves of the mirrored cabinet, opening the few sticky drawers. She chased him in with her mouth set. There was the clatter of jars, the swishing of the shower curtain and the clicks of the rings. She was speaking his name, the meaning different with each iteration, a prayer, a threat,

a command. "Where is it?" Then the stick and release of his sneakers stopped, the faucet came on, and he was standing over the bed
again, lunging at Wright with a twisted washcloth.

They were before Wright on the foot of the bed in an instant,
and she had Randy's hands behind him, her torso atop his and her
knees spread on his back. She spoke into his ear, her lips contract-
ing and releasing so quickly that her teeth appeared like flashbulbs.
Wright could hear only every other.

"Ever

Fucking

Touch

Not his

War

Will be

Out

Not

Ever

Understand?"

They were silent a minute, five, Randy's breathing grinding
down from its panting, and finally she freed his hands. Wright
had hidden his head in the crumple of sheets so that only a slice of
vision remained, but turned when Randy lay his face near him. It
was totally changed, open to other people as it had been closed, wet.
"I'm sorry, pal," he said. "I'm so sorry."

At the door Fay gestured with a scoop of her shoulder for Randy
to go. He stopped at the long bureau, surveying the things there,
the Mamas and the Papas record with its lush colors, the end of an
incense stick that wilted over the long wooden holder. Then he was
gone again, leaving behind the sweet smell of his sweat.

"I forgot something I shouldn't have forgotten," Fay said. "You
did nothing wrong."

She sat on the end of the bed, speaking to him in the mirror,
her hair made wild by the struggle with Randy.

"The war Randy fought in was, still is, evil. That's really the only word for it. Teenagers killing boys your age, being urged to kill. Told that was their purpose, denied privileges if they did not, socks, meals. It was an experience so frightening that it latched on to the rest of their lives, to their futures, too—have you ever had a memory come at you for a reason that didn't seem really clear?"

"I think so. Songs."

"Right. Exactly. A sound is one way we associate, and so are other ways of sensing. Smell. Is another."

She had her right palm half in her mouth. He imagined she was keeping her organs in, imagined them pouring over her pink bottom lip. For the next quiet minute he prayed they wouldn't, knew they would. It would be his job to clean them. It would be, somehow, his fault.

"That Vicks VapoRub that we put on you tonight, it means something different to Randy. It doesn't mean medicine. In the war they put it under their noses to keep from smelling other things, so that scent immediately brings him away from us, to a time when he was very scared."

Wright did not ask what things. He heard Randy say it again: *Those bodies. Those who were lit up.* The fear of the evening had exhausted him and he brought his knees to his chest, falling into a thin, taut sleep.

HIS VISION SANDY, HE WOKE a few hours later, alarmed by the lack of other sounds in the room. When he pulled the linen curtain he saw them on the ground, his mother's caftan around her hips, Randy's ass lean and puckered. Their bodies moving in concert reminded him of trains, motion made of other motion, the undying violence of wheels.

3.

The day they got word of Bisson's assignment, an orbit—not a landing—was the last time they were photographed together, their foreheads kissing by the tank of a grill in Sam's backyard. Nowhere in the set, published in full color in *Life,* was Bisson's dense mood, the misery. The ongoing contract was a third of their income, essential considering the life insurance for which they couldn't qualify, and it went to contingency funds for their families. As the program raced ahead, the distance between how their lives felt and how they photographed grew rapidly, until the only time they put on shorts or read was when stage-managed to do so. That their lives outside of work had become performances sent them deeper into who they were when inside it, a place without possessions or memories.

The first orbit of the moon was not nothing, Vincent said to Bisson when they were alone, after the announcement was made, strolling down the gray linoleum hallway where every step sounded off a report of echoes and their reflections swam gleaming near their feet. Bisson dipped his chin half an inch, the smallest agreement he could give, and passed a hand down the back of his neck, the buzz cut his wife had given him on their lawn the night before while his son and the Kahns watched. He had not spoken since the meeting.

The news came from Anderson, who had been one of the first to make the parabolic flight that qualified as space travel, and who had, shortly after, left a routine physical with the news he would not fly again. He had stayed on as head of crew operations, choosing the men who would go on each mission that he could not. A heart murmur, Vincent thought, was a term that aptly described the mood Anderson gave off, someone whose wishes were so accustomed to being swallowed that they became a defining quality of their own, a slightly sad forbearance he afforded everyone but himself. The gold tie clip that Kennedy had given him was ubiquitous, the only part of him that asked for attention. He was the first person any man called when he was feeling sore or childish. Tall and too pale, Anderson solved the problems of others because his were intractable, hidden away in the dark of his body.

Bisson had been named the commander of the trip that would circle the moon but not land on it because he was the best of them, a painful fact everyone in the room understood but would not mention. Being the best sometimes meant to be trusted with the worst, or at least the uncertain introductions. Of the thirty-six men, Bisson had wanted the landing the longest, had watched its inky beginnings sharpen into a striking line.

Anderson made the announcement first thing in the morning, no rap of the knuckles or campy whistle. They had discussed the wearable coolant in the suit, the issues with the latest command module hatch. Bisson's nose fell three degrees, but—because Anderson loved what they all did so permanently that it seemed to have become a line on his face, and because he had taken countless calls from upset wives and turned them placid, and because he had fought with superiors just to get the astronauts naps or Cokes or a day off—Bisson thanked him, the disappointment changing even the way his mouth moved around his teeth. He stood up and offered his hand like he would a hero a slip of paper on which to sign an autograph. "It is and will be an honor, sir," he had said.

They had commuted together that morning in Vincent's Nova and they approached it together where it glowed blue-gold in the last of the afternoon. Knowing what the next-best thing to being alone would be—Sam loved to drive, enjoyed the minute theater of traffic, believed a cloverleaf on-ramp was the country's great invention—Vincent slowed his pace, called out Sammo, and pitched the keys overhand. Bisson lit up involuntarily, receiving the crenulated jangle of metal in his hand, and then he gave the hood a little knock and stepped into the driver's seat. The radio never went on. They had been separated.

Vincent had no more than stepped out of his stiff leather shoes and removed his socks, run a finger between his toes to remove the lint that had accrued there, when it went off, the red phone NASA had installed in his living room. On news of the assignment, *Life* wanted to come over and photograph Bisson. What if they all got together, perhaps some grilling and swimming? He was not allowed any answer but yes.

Elise he found in the bedroom, where she was perched on the window seat painting her toenails, her posture serene and the lacquer's smell pervasive. He did not even need to explain, only to say, "Barbecue, thirty minutes." In chignons and playful sailor's trousers, she had become a master at last-minute appearances— those brittle years in the mountains were gone; he had watched her shed them. There was nothing about their time in California either needed to remember, and this was a promise between them, a more potent vow than any other. Evenings she read to him and he clutched her hand.

Beside him in their walk-in, her hair a shellacked topiary, she pushed at the clacking row of wooden hangers. "This one," she said, pulling a shell-pink button-up, "with the tan slacks, the cotton, not the linen." She set his coffee on the vanity without a word. They were ready in five minutes, passing through the gate that connected their yard to the Bissons'.

The first to greet them was Eli, eight, who daily papered Bisson's windshield with drawings of guns and cougars. Today he paced the ring of adults in a New York Yankees cap, a Secret Detective glow-in-the-dark watch he had sent away for. A blue jay feather dangled from a leather string around his neck. He was bedecked like this always, in pieces that might make the difference in getting his name spoken aloud. Occasionally his voice broke through, piercing the conversation that happened a foot above him.

"Dad? Should we scuba-dive the pool?"

Soon they were splayed, Vincent and Elise and Marlene, in pastel lounge chairs by the chlorinated blue, the smoke from the grill hanging between them. Bisson wouldn't move from his place by the barbecue, and the photographer was unhappy, pivoting aggressively because of it, every angle of attack, every adjustment of focus. He was a short man with a gap in his teeth that sometimes whistled, toes that pointed toward each other, and they hated him with delighted sport, mimicking his attempts at artistic direction the moment he left. *I'd love one,* Sam would say to Vincent, hand on his chin, *where you're looking constipated in the hammock. Don't act constipated—be constipated.*

"I'd love to get one where the men are talking while the wives look on," he was saying now, "a little concerned, a little proud, maybe from the poolside, you know what I mean?" Leaning across the balsa-wood console that connected their chaises, Elise and Marlene began to whisper, their trust in each other real. No one had commented on Bisson's silence. It was as if his life could go on without his participation in it.

The photographer had just pinched his pants up at the thighs and squatted, just begun to adjust his focus and to murmur directives at the women—"A little more somber," "A little more scared," "Marlene, are you frightened," "Elise, are you relieved it's not him"—when Eli's backlit silhouette appeared twenty feet above them. On the roof his bike looked like something else, sleeker, the blue paint steely in the shadows cast by the peaks of the dormer windows. "Ittttt'ssss Eli," he bellowed, undressed save a helmet and the snug Speedo he wore to swim practice and a throw blanket he'd tied like a cape. Marlene was up on her wrists in a second, scrambling to stand, straining her voice and yelling for Bisson, who was watching this unfold as though it were something televised. Vincent, next to him, slipped an arm around his neck.

Eli's jaw was set as he pedaled off, his eyes fixed on the deepest part of the pool, and the clicks of the camera were all to be heard for the hardening moment that preceded the splash, which went on a minute and soaked an eight-foot radius. It took too long for the kid to resurface, a viscous revolution of time in which the broken water refused to return to glassiness.

The blue of the sky at six was frail, and this was something that happened in Texas, a feeling the land was more important.

"The moon," Vincent was saying in Sam's ear. "Who needs it?"

"Oceans and witches," Bisson said, his first words in ten hours.

They were applauding like devoted fans as Eli rose up coughing, his hand with its woven summer camp bracelets preceding him. Marlene and Elise scowled at this, the danger their husbands could see as diversion.

Oceans and witches became a joke they'd say to each other in passing, code for anything they could not control and so would not offer another thought, the unhappiness of their wives, any future beyond the immediate, all that went on outside the program. The last photo taken of them was barely that, just their heads pressed together, just their posture the same, extras in an image of a shouting boy driving blind through pale dusk.

4.

MORONA-SANTIAGO PROVINCE, 1967

They woke Wright before sunlight one day to ask. Did he want to go to Quito? The bus left in an hour. Their minds were made up, his mother's hair wet, her fingers pushing earrings through her earlobes as she spoke. She was happiest this way, about to leave, the kind of person with teeth marks on her passport, dark sunglasses that remarked to passersby she was on her way. Why now, he wanted to know. Would they spend the night. Finally he agreed, curiosity just outweighing his silver fear.

On the bus he had hoped to sleep but the blinking driver kept the radio on as they rose from the rain forest into the height of the cordillera, taking curves that sent leather purses and soda cans into the aisle. Fay and Randy sat ahead of him, whispering as though they were building something complicated in the dark. Finally he dipped into a nap, dreams as jerky and protean as the ride.

Walking on the cobblestones spaced wide and uneven, his thinking bleary and stunted by the sight of buildings so much larger than any he saw in his daily life, Wright followed his mother and Randy into the crowd of people without asking any questions. He assumed a festival, the birthday of someone famous, and soon they were immersed in it, a commotion without a center. Babies twirled at the top of the crowd, on shoulders, on the tops of their parents' heads, the masses having bled from the sidewalk into the street. People weren't moving anymore, but sound was, a knot of screaming that approached in flashes.

As the motorcade of astronauts approached, packing the mob tighter, Wright began to understand what they had not told him. His mother and Randy were part of a unit that was within the mass but apart from it. They were not, like the other people, bringing their mouths to their hands or pointing for the benefit of their children or wiping away tears. These would be the first men to orbit the moon, Bisson and Bailey and Slate, but Randy and Fay had not come to cheer. Their shoulders forward, their eyes cut straight through the hum of bodies to the men in the cars.

The astronauts wore white linen guayaberas and leis, and they waved in precise twists of the hand and torso, a paean to a kind of manhood he knew nothing about. He wanted to climb into their laps or inside their bodies, be the organs animating them or the pulse beating.

The group his mother belonged to, fifteen or so, began to separate and hand out the signs they had carried here, plant their feet in a way that signified an offensive. Some were professors, still wearing their teaching clothes, sweating dark ovals in the armpits of their white shirts, others students, bedraggled, their hair uncut, their postures uneven from the heavy book bags that hung from shoulders. Their expressions were like pools in deep shade, offering only the occasional reflection of the world around them. His mother and Randy and one other veteran—a man who wore an upside-down flag, and whose left sleeve was pinned up to where his arm would have started—were the only Americans. NO MORE BREAD AND CIRCUSES, said a sign. WE ARE NOT DISTRACTED BY YOUR SPECTACLE and HOW MANY CHILDREN WILL DIE ON THIS PLANET WHILE YOU COLONIZE ANOTHER?

"The crimes of America are not forgiven," his mother chanted. "The crimes of America are not forgiven!"

Though the chain of cars tried to pick up speed, the crowd made acceleration impossible. The three men in the convertible, their abbreviated haircuts identical, their shoulders dusted with rice, stopped using their hands to wave, bringing them to their faces instead, ducking, kissing their knees. Bodyguards climbed from one car to the next, insects in tailored suits. Over the mass of people, through the air so thin it was named the cloud forest, flew spoiled tomatoes and week-old fish heads, the dead eyes engorged and fixed on the sky.

5.

1967

Rather than being the place where his life collected itself, Randy's sleep was like another life. He muttered, words that were recognizable and acronyms that weren't. His hand shot out across the night table between the two beds, clearing lamps and Fay's bangles and the rocks Wright had polished. He sat up and slapped his feet on the floor and gave low, brief grunts, affirmative answers to unheard commands, and then he crawled across the bed he shared with Fay, the points of his knees everywhere, the spread of his palms making the mattress spasm.

Wright woke at all of it, and he spent his days sick with lack of rest, always feeling a step behind his wants. The great plans he had for them aside, his Lincoln Logs stayed loose in his palm. He subjected everyone to the pain of his last adult tooth coming in, howling and pointing at his mouth, surprised they could not feel it.

He was the first to read the telegram, which appeared under the door one afternoon with the shadow of the person that pushed it in. He had not answered the knock. Though the euphemism typed there was beyond him, the message was clear from the context. Standing in his bare feet he took the dried flowers from the vase that Fay kept on the bureau and he emptied them out, breaking off the stems, placing them at a diagonal bias around the square of bad news. She returned soon after, her back pushing the door open and her arms full with rolled straw mats, the smell of her sweat moving with her.

Near the Fisher-Price record player he'd long grown out of, his paper planes and Randy's stack of letters, ribbons in blues and greens that Fay kept to tie her braids, the thing kept its secret. He pointed. She gave an odd laugh, the kind made mostly of fear, and she picked it up with care not to displace the flowers.

Eyes closed, Fay twisted her body to the left and then the right, and then she crossed to the bathroom, where he could hear the anemic shower go on, the echoing thump of her footsteps as she shifted. She emerged in a towel knotted at her breasts, her hair so full with water that fat beads ran from it at every point, and fell face-forward onto the bed, her covering detached around her, her right knee bent and her left arm shot up as she let go her first sob. He didn't know what to do, so he read it again, and then he lay down on the bed opposite her, thinking that she deserved to be watched.

> *CHARLIE PASSED*
> *PER WILL*
> *PROPERTY TO BE SOLD TO EDWDS*
> *PROFIT YRS*
> *NO FUNERAL*
> *CONDOLENCES*
> *PLEASE ADVISE RE: HORSE*

SHE PASSED TWO WEEKS PROPPED up by pillows, receiving guests that way, things spread out around the shape of her body under the sheets, a postcard of Abbott and Costello squabbling, pale purple flowers, plates of chicken and rice, crucifixes of wood and Lucite and braided leather. Lucinda was there at least once a day, telling her again that her work would be there for her when she was ready. Rising only to use the bathroom, to place the occasional phone call in the front office, Fay nodded at everything said to her, would you like the curtains open or closed, what did you dream of. Her sleep was so fitful, so foul with sweat, that Wright and Randy shared the opposite bed.

He wondered when it would be over, but when it was, when she got up and spent all day conditioning the back of her head, when she mopped their tile floor with that flat and myopic look, he wished for that time back, the afternoons when what she had lost had made her soft and useless, and had not yet begun to change her.

She assured Wright, when he asked daily, that they would get back to the books they read together, things she assigned outside of his regular schoolwork. He was spending more time alone than he ever had, the money his mother gave him fat in his pocket, slipping in and out of the nearby restaurants that all served plantains and roasted chicken over rice. One day he returned from school to find Fay and Randy sitting in front of their room, propped up by the nubbled wall, tears slipping untouched down their faces, laughing a little every few minutes. It was Charlie's horse, they said, it was Lloyd. Fay had arranged for a caretaker until something more permanent could be settled, but Lloyd had chewed through his reins and shit in the drained pool and escaped. A pilot flying over had seen him running like hell, across a landing site and the winding highway, and then he couldn't see him anymore.

6.

Her own horse, everybody said later, into their cups, into their palms.

Charlie got into an argument with the schoolteacher she loved, her girlfriend of five years and a secret to everyone, in her room early in the morning—the wrong time for a fight, she thought. Shouldn't the ass crack of morning be the time for the complaints of the body? That was the first thing she said to Angeline, who was unhappy and devoted and had asked about some plans for the holiday. Her sister had been gone from the country almost five years that had felt like a cavity, a mostly occluded pain that might reveal itself barbed and whistling for reasons you didn't totally understand.

The question was, What are we going to do for Christmas? The assumption it built upon had not been discussed, or Charlie could not remember discussing it.

The horse was a drinker, too. She made him that way. Could grip the bottle nose delicately enough not to break it, then tip it back, one beer in one go.

What had she and Fay done for Christmas, for example, her girlfriend said. Charlie waved in a general outward direction, a gesture that probably looked like fuck-it-to-hell. In fact there was a shed she meant, beyond the pool, a crosshatched door painted white, then blue, inside it a cardboard box reinforced at the corners. Popcorn strings dipped in glitter, the tabs of all sodas consumed in the fall of 1958 worked together with copper wire to make the topper of a Christmas tree, an experiment that had ended badly. *Honey,* Charlie had said, *which race car had a hair ball.*

A beautiful creature, hard to say which color. She taught it to dance to "Mack the Knife." "Hey, Good Lookin'."

But the gesture was all she could make. Angeline set her jaw and began putting things in piles and systems, the beer cans into the trash, the change that came from Charlie's pockets at the end of the night into denominations.

Are you under the impression you treat me well, her girlfriend said.

It was a miracle that horse had learned to be around it at all, the sonic booms all damn day. A matter of time, someone said, maybe.

She could not answer. At that Angeline shook her head and disappeared into the bathroom to fill the water for the percolator. Charlie's voice went up, lost its core. You probably don't even need electricity for that, hothead. Plug the thing into yourself.

To keep herself from speaking any further she walked out, boots unlaced, naked under her red union suit. The sunrise was a civil war in pinks and she tore through it to where he was sleeping. Almost never had she ridden him this early, because she woke with headaches most mornings and needed to keep the world as still as possible, a thing she could see but that she would not touch. As they set out he was distracted, surprised by tiny flowers he had seen every day of his life. She'd forgotten her patience, lost it in the bedroom where it was clear for the hundredth time she was not the woman for the job. Thoughts of love were not enough—she could not thread them through to the other side where they were felt. She had one hand on the saddle and another hanging, an open pint of Beam tugged onto her middle finger.

Could have been some new test, a noise he hadn't heard before. That he was half-asleep. Or could have been nothing, the mystery an animal has kept his whole life and then needs to get rid of.

When he first picked up speed she was grateful. She thanked him. It was her turn to be surprised by the things she found familiar, a last look at the inn that had begun, fifteen years before, as an ink drawing circumscribed by the moisture ring on a cocktail napkin. Inside the velocity of his gallop, the things she could see became thinner, reduced to their most startling element. If you flattened its colors the desert was not beige but purple. Miles from the inn and crossing the highway, the car that nearly got them was only a sound.

Irony is they made it across. Guy driving almost crashed, seeing them.

She had stopped kicking, stopped saying his name. Whatever they were doing, wherever he was taking her, happened where speaking left off. She had belonged to him, always she had belonged to him, and it was a beautiful favor he had done in allowing the world to think the opposite. When he succeeded in throwing her she let go with a chosen freedom, knowing a locked body broke more easily.

Irony is, his loyalty. If he hadn't come back after he threw her, who knows.

As he doubled back, a shadow galloping toward her, she put a hand over her face, a final vanity, irrelevant as any. He had come back to find her before the glister of ten miles had really left him, and could not know precisely where he was going, where his feet would land when he leapt the line of chaparral—it obscured the flat place where he'd lost her.

7.

It was the color of the lemon that had struck Vincent, a yellow so unlike anything else in the room, the industrial slates and grays, his lilac-jawed colleagues. Sitting atop the Block 1 command module simulator, the lemon had a shape so flawless he might have charted its curve, nature's haughty perfection. Then he got the message. Bisson had put the fruit there to say what they all knew.

The press had lighted briefly on a rash of departures, engineers who had walked at the unreasonable timelines, the tests that did not account for certain variables. But the stories Americans wanted were of those born needing less sleep than the rest of us, of the many colors of a rocket launch at dawn. They did not want to hear of young, educated men shaking their head at the repeated mention of the assassinated president's words—*before this decade is out*—of their voices pitching up and wheedling as they insisted on more time. They did not want to know about this crew of astronauts, preparing for the simulation launch of Apollo 1, gesturing to each other, protesting as diplomatically as possible. They had spoken against it sternly, against the Velcro on the walls, against the nylon netting that the oafish technicians thought so handy, above all against the hatch that required a screwdriver, but these aspects of the module had remained. Under the lemon balanced on its peak, Vincent had briefly seen the triangular shape of the command module as menacing, the point that would narrow overhead a message of diminishing returns, but he let the thought go as soon as his mind would let him. He told himself fear was always a part of respect.

Vincent was at the White House when it happened, having witnessed the signing of a treaty. Space would not be militarized. The stiff afternoon bled into a series of cocktails, handshakes, group photographs. Tan shoes on teal carpet, wallpaper of pale gold stripes. In the minutes Bisson and Slate and Bailey had suffered, Vincent had been speaking to the First Lady about cayenne pepper as squirrel repellent.

When he returned to his hotel suite at dusk, the carmine wink of a message punctuated the room, the cuff links he had decided against on the dresser, his engraved shoehorn by the door. He had not turned on the bedside lamp, and he got the news in the dark. He could imagine what had gone wrong immediately. He saw the lemon, saw Sam placing it there with his thumb and forefinger and a smirk. He saw all the exposed wiring in the command module, resembling the blueprints of cities where it lined the floor, uncovered for the sake of decreasing weight at any cost, and the technicians marching in and out all day; he saw the bolts on the hatch, felt the ten twists of a screwdriver required to free them. He heard that pissing sound of the oxygen tanks.

What he found himself asking, in those odd negotiations made in the shock, was that Sam die in flight, or at least fly in death. Perhaps it was not too late to send him up, perhaps the body could be strapped in and—no. The world brought him back from the thought.

He answered another call from the center when it came in, nodded through the talk. "Thank you, sir, for the information," he said, although the voice said nothing new, although the information was evil. There was nothing to be solved today, nothing to be decided, but he knew they would make calls all night. Then there was a knock, room service, and the distance even to the door, where a pinprick of light came in through the peephole, seemed insurmountable, something his legs would not do. What sort of misunderstanding had there been, who had believed he might want fries or some damp club sandwich. He dreaded any obligation now, even food. But because he had never in his life let a knock go unanswered, he got up anyway. "Thank you," he said again, to a face he did not see.

It had been an oversight, the ice cream, something planned days before that the center had forgotten to cancel when the launchpad caught fire. They had wanted to celebrate the signing of the treaty, the anticipation of the landing that it seemed would finally be theirs. They had dyed it a marbled silver, the perfect globular scoop, had imitated craters with fine dimples in the surface. At a jaunty eighty-five-degree angle was a paper flag on a toothpick, the stars hand painted. He set it on the nightstand, near the phone that filled him with hate, and when he woke five hours later it had melted down the shallow bowl, over the blond cherrywood, and into the drawer with the Bible.

8.

He flew in early the day after the fire, DC to Florida, in a plane lent him to fly alone, something he insisted on, and fought to be placed on the review board. At first Anderson shook his head, put one hand on his elbow and the other on his pockmarked face.

"Uh-uh. No. Nope. Kahn, I can't believe you, really I cannot, it is beyond— Do you understand that I do not want to cause you any more pain?"

"I see what you're saying, Anderson, and I respect it. Might I be placed on the incident review board?"

"I see. You're going to just keep asking it, just like that. You are like my fucking son. 'Might I have fifty cents for a soda? Might I have fifty cents for a soda?'"

They were alone in the room together, a rarity, and Vincent knew it would not last long, that soon someone would stride in and tap a clipboard and make a demand, ask for a signature or a second opinion. Anderson was standing, the chalk expanse before him a mess of equations and names and roman-numeraled lists, eager to go, eager for Vincent to let up.

"Might I be placed on the review board."

His face hidden and his back bent and his palms flat now on

the table, Anderson was quiet a long time. He was not wearing the tie clip Kennedy had given him.

"You really want that, Kahn? You want to see the up-close photos of the body? You want to see how he was sitting as he died?"

Vincent stayed where he sat. At his back were diagrams of a collapsing lunar vehicle, a rough topographical sketch of the Sea of Tranquility, but he never turned to see them.

"I don't want that," he said. "The word here is *need*."

He held Anderson's eyes with a focus that, in his life up until now, he had almost only ever used in the consideration of something inanimate, a machine that needed his guidance, the half-inch pieces of a model that could fit together if he concentrated enough. As Vincent knew he would be, Anderson was the first to let go. He whirled around, his hands bound behind his back, and said it like a curse: "Eight o'clock tomorrow." A shadow appeared in the door's glass window but vanished soon after.

IT WAS THE FIRST THING he thought of once he was awake, of the accordioned arm of the space suit still bent, of the recording he had listened to over and over. *How are we going to get to the moon if we can't talk between two or three buildings . . . fire in the cockpit, there's a bad fire!* It had been Bisson's job to remain at the controls, and he had, fossilized on the command couch, his spine still long and his shoulders set back.

It was a liability and an embarrassment, grief, something akin to bringing a small child into adult places, waiting to meet its next need, muffle the shrieks and cries, follow it where it crawled. He would find himself hamstrung with it, his hands going numb on the steering wheel on the interstate, and an hour later he'd be shot through with anger, swatting at houseflies as though they were toxic. He forced himself to recite facts, his grandmother's full name, the Boy Scouts' pledge, his flight school's phone number, his parents' address, his wife's birthday. Sylvia Inge Kahn, *to help other people at all times, to keep myself physically strong, mentally awake, and morally straight,* Oakplain 0748, 322 E Street, May 8, 1932, things about his life that had always been true. The only relief came in the meetings, where at least the thing that harassed him was visible, where it was the committee's job to say why it had happened, to promise it would never happen again.

HE TOOK NOTES ON EVERY minute, pausing only to take a pencil sharpener from a corduroy case, asking any piece of information he didn't like to be repeated. "Say that again." He spoke the phrase so often it became a joke to others in the halls afterward, a steely fool's reaction to a thing one couldn't change.

Lightning split your car in thirds, sir. Your wife gave birth, but it's half horse.

Say that again.

In his graph paper notebook were drawings of the command module, the scale exact, red pencil highlighting the Velcro netting under the command couch. Next to it he drew up a list of its synthetic composition. The wires that ran from the equipment bay to the oxygen panel he rendered in pale blue. "Can anyone tell me," he asked, of the room of five other men, "how many times precisely the techs walked in and out and over these during the tests that day?" There was a silence, a shaking of jowls. "Why not?" He wrote the phrase neatly in capitals: *167 POUNDS PER SQUARE INCH (PSI) ABSOLUTE ONE HUNDRED PERCENT OXYGEN.*

When, after two months, they drafted their letter to Congress, *pursuant to your directive,* when each scrawled his signature across the front page, *each member concurring in each of the findings,* when Anderson opened the room's door outward with a half bow and they were all free to go, *no single ignition force of the fire was conclusively identified,* Vincent was the last to push in his chair, to straighten its back against the round vinyl table.

"Wait there a second, Kahn." Since the fire, Anderson had often arrived with his shirt misbuttoned, the look on his face of someone who has slept too long. "I wasn't half as close to him and I still feel guilty every time I have a hamburger or see a good commercial."

"Yes."

"So I'm telling you this because I am imagining you may need or appreciate it now, although the official announcement will be at the end of the week. I'm scheduling you for Mission G, all right?"

"Mission G."

"That's right. With Rusty and Eugene."

Vincent ran his palm from his forehead to his chin and then he nodded and then he coughed.

"The landing."

"The landing."

He coughed.

"The first."

"No shit."

Everything about the rest of the day was different, everything giving off a kind of charge, the smell of a sharpened Ticonderoga a taste in his mouth, the splinters in his ice cubes something he watched carefully. Pajamas a miracle, sleep an award!

9.

CAPE KENNEDY, FLORIDA, 1969

It was in the aquatic green light of the simulator that their old lives returned to them, slipping right on like something tailored.

Only that once had they spoken the word, her name, the sound like one your body made, though it had been clear, when Anderson had asked—*Hey, weren't you two at Edwards at the same time?*—that their nods yes had been a thought of her, Rusty of some act she'd denied him, Vincent of some closing conversation she had never granted. That he should share his trip to the moon with Rusty, Vincent thought, was a good play on the part of fate, vicious but not without its humor.

Through the two triangular windows of the lunar module simulator, a televised image of the moon grew clearer in detail. He stood with his hand light and alert on the toggle that controlled the speed and cant of their descent, his glutes taut, his knees bent imperceptibly inside his full suit.

The lunar module—they called it the lem—would fly face-down, their bodies parallel to the lunar surface, 3,800 miles an hour, as Vincent observed the craters and boulders and gentle concavities. When he saw it, when he identified the place that was smooth and clean and would gracefully receive them, he would right the contraption, with its three spindly legs, and begin to float moonward. He spent every red light and hot shower and commercial break considering it, reviewed the procedure while lathering his face with shaving cream, during staccato sex with his faraway wife.

The second man on the moon was not the honorific Rusty had imagined. It was clear in every gesture that he wanted his hands on the controls, not his voice feeding information to the people on earth. It was especially vivid today, the way Rusty bit off the numbers, altitude one hundred eighteen, inclination thirty-three point five, the way he kept his eyes on the button that read LUNAR CONTACT, which would light up blue if all went as planned. When Vincent felt the thruster stick, saw the image of the moon begin to warp and tremble like something in a county fair fun house, he simultaneously knew what was expected of him and that he would not do it.

"Kahn, hit abort," Rusty said, and then he began hissing it. "Hit abort, hit abort, hit abort." But Vincent wanted the chance to try, to see what could be done, to watch all the warning lights go on. Because in the communications between moon and earth there would be a delay of one and a third of a second, and because he knew they had replicated that in this simulation, he stole that time to strategize, to consider what had prompted the angry whirl and what would unmake it. When the image of the landing site froze, the Sea of Tranquility before them, when they were meant to imagine the lem had crashed and they would die on the moon, Rusty put his mouth to his right hand, the plane between his thumb and his index finger's first knuckle, and he bit. Vincent leaned back and closed his eyes and thought of his first contact with space, the X-15 over Edwards, the bend of the horizon against a black as he had never seen: total, and certain, and very briefly his.

THE CREW QUARTERS WHERE THEY spent their days before the launch were spare, practical, built, like everything else NASA had, by experts in a hurry. A dining nook fit four, though there would only ever be three on an Apollo crew, and the vinyl booths were padded but anemically, one of many reminders that comfort was not the objective. Cabinets ran above it on either side, stocked with canned goods approved by the on-site physician, and to the right was a refrigerator filled with steak and with eggs and carbonated drinks donated by companies seeking an astronaut's endorsement. On the opposite wall of the main room sat a couch, hospital-gown green with teak legs, which was as tasteful and uninviting as all else in that room.

Eugene, who'd insisted on Jeanie from the beginning, tried to save dinner. He had been the obvious choice for the position—to orbit the moon while Vincent and Rusty stepped onto its surface, to wait like no one else had ever waited. Affable, inquisitive, he painted marshy landscapes in his free time, showed up with dabs of browns and greens on his hands, brought their wives pale roses clipped from his own garden. Jokes and stories he kept like they were cherished gemstones or heirlooms, things he knew well and pulled out when the time was right.

Tonight, over the plates of chicken baked in mushroom soup that had been waiting for them in the oven, over the sounds of the forks moving as quickly as possible, Jeanie tried. They hadn't spoken since the simulator except to say *bathroom's all yours, phone for you, press briefing on the table there.*

"So there's this drunk who approaches a police officer, and he's wobbling, weaving. Says officer, some fucker has stolen my goddamn car. Officer says, where'djou see it last? The drunk brings up his hand, where he's been holding something real tight. It was right on the end of this key, the drunk says. Officer says listen, buddy, why don't you go home, get some rest, sober up. Your car's still missing in the morning, you come into the station and file a report."

Jeanie paused, trying to bring the table to him, his palms spread and clean, trying to bring them toward each other, his face lit up by the glow of his cheeks. There was no sound in the room save the tines on the ceramic.

"Listen, the officer says, while you're at it, pal, for goodness' sake zip up your pants. Your business is as exposed as a weather vane. And the drunk goes, oh shit—"

Jeanie paused, a fork held aloft now, a scepter.

"They got my girl, too."

Rusty performed a loud laugh, bringing up a bottle of beer and tilting it in Jeanie's direction. Vincent scooted out of the booth, a triangle of napkin on his mouth as he stood. He left them without a nod, washed his face without looking in the mirror.

"Must be nice," he heard Rusty say, "to be the only person who's ever known anything."

He waited until his skin was dry to answer, the towel refolded.

"I guess you'll never know for sure." He heard Jeanie laugh, then stop himself. The bottle opener again.

He fell asleep thinking of the simulator, his hands curled as they had been on the controls.

In the week before the mission, he dreamt of next to nothing, a room that was nearly blue, a voice he could almost hear.

10.

There was nothing different about the day, the four o'clock alarm, the steak-and-egg breakfast, the twenty push-ups he did with one arm behind his back, except that by the middle of it he would be leaving his planet's orbit. At five fifty-nine in the morning he took his last breaths of raw air. At six the mechanisms of the helmet met his neck ring and the temperature became precisely seventy degrees. On the shag-carpet floor of the van that took them to the launch site, from six twenty to six thirty-four, he never moved the oversized yellow galoshes meant to keep his lunar boots pristine. With the occasional bump he felt the shift of all the apparatuses connected to him, the accordion rubber around his knees, the silicone-compound slip-resistant tips of his gloves, the liquid cooling garment that fit around his crotch and core. All of them reacted a quarter of a second behind his actual body, a well-trained chorus that agreed.

As the elevator took him up, the gentle trundle along the Saturn, passing the second and third stages of the rocket, three hundred and twenty feet, he could see the million people that had covered Cape Kennedy, transforming its color and shape. The orange groves dotted by folding chairs in pink and blue, the minor waterways by yachts named after wives and mothers, the beaches by figures in bikinis and Speedos that spiked volleyballs and lit grills and dug umbrellas deeper in the sand. Somewhere on the Banana River was the enormous cruiser where Elise squinted upward or didn't, her elbows cupped by other wives, her white wine refilled by men from the Mission Support Office in Texas.

Slicing the light were shadows of helicopters, which carried the late and famous over the islands and beaches. A descendant of Napoléon, Johnny Carson, the man who had invented Styrofoam, an actress whose purple eyes people said were a genetic exception. The months of simulation had trained him not to miss sound, but for half a second he wanted it back, to reverse through all steps toward the full and imperfect world.

In his ear the voices said the same things they had for months on end, and as he listened he felt at the things in his pocket, a package of mint Life Savers and a plasticized photo and a two-inch lilac sock. Now he crossed the red iron bridge that led to the command module, now he had his gloves on the handrail above the hatch. Now he was swinging in, the curve of his spine and the tension in his abdomen the same as they had been in the five hundred attempts that had preceded this one. It was a lovely, clever miracle, how well it actually worked, that if all gestures and accessories were familiar and repeated so too were your thoughts.

He sat in the commander's seat, the abort handle an inch from where his left hand sat in his lap, Rusty next to him, Jeanie the farthest, their cheerful radioed confirmations of protocol in his headset. Four anonymous hands appeared in the periphery, white gloved and agile, and they pushed the hatch closed.

—*How is the booster doing,* Rusty asked.

—*It's perfect.*

The bridge that had brought them in swung away.

—*Access arm detached.*

They had five minutes left, he did not need to be told. There was total comfort in knowing, in every half second of his life ascribed to a rigid itinerary, every organ in his body monitored by someone in that vast hall of machines. It felt like coming back to his childhood room, the things he had sent away for, the piggy bank whose contents he knew exactly.

—*Spacecraft.*

Together they brought their shoulders back, the three of them, and they spoke from the same want at the same moment.

—*Go.* The struggle of the rocket against its clamps registered in his toes and chin.

—*Liftoff.*

Beneath them went the first stage of the rocket, seven and a half million pounds of thrust, wresting them from the rocky beaches where lost things washed up and the houses where televisions never went off. It was impossible to hear, unavoidable to sweat, unthinkable to think.

In thirty seconds it was done. The silence and the stillness came in politely, gingerly, pointing things out to him. Through the window was an unadulterated blue, shy and even and kind.

—*Apollo 11, your trajectory and guidance are go.*

Then it was black, and then it was black, and then it was black.

IN THEIR FLIGHT SUITS, HELMETS off, they waited, mothered by the orbit of their planet, the lights on the wall of gray computers pulsing red and teal, the zero gravity a tempting and placid promise, a push that told him his body, all its abilities, were no longer necessary. "How is everybody feeling in this zero g," he said. "Headache, palpitations, nausea?" Jeanie spoke first, the boy in him coming through. "Everything fine, except that I feel like some shitty uncle is holding me upside down by my feet."

Rusty: "Nothing. I feel nothing unusual."

The first sunrise was a reinvention of color. The Hasselblad was nowhere to be found, and Jeanie floated through the cabin, pushing off the command couch, his tape recorder playing "The Girl from Ipanema," naming the stray objects over Astrud Gilberto's crooning.

"Anybody lose a felt-tip pen? A legal pad? Anybody missing a single Life Saver?" Vincent laughed, the first time he had since they had straddled the rocket, the sound of it incongruous with the thousands of mechanisms of the craft.

"You so much as lift that perfect candy-cum-mint toward your mouth, Jeanie, and you will never see your wife again. I only have twelve." Jeanie went on swearing to himself, adrift behind them.

"A big mother like that, a little embarrassed to have lost a— Rusty, you don't see the Hasselblad anywhere below you?"

Rusty stayed where he was, his eyes on the checklist in front of him.

"I've already looked for it." Then Jeanie was bright again, buoyant, snapping their photos like a honeymooner. "Hiding in the aft bulkhead!"

Vincent was glancing at his watch in every free moment between system checks—he wanted to acknowledge every minute, to check it against the flight plan, to inhabit the time fully. The Speedmaster gave him minutes as well as miles per hour, the tachometer a broad circle that encompassed three others, faces in miniature that would function as stopwatches when the time came to conduct their experiments. Jeanie was against his window now, fiddling with the excitement of an expert, adjusting the camera. Stretches of white, stretches of green.

"Trees and snow! I can see trees and snow."

The men from earth were in Vincent's ear again, spitting argot, entirely scrubbed of their Southern drawl or Midwestern lilt.

—*Roger,* Vincent said. —*Reading you loud and clear. Our insertion checklist is complete, and we have no abnormalities.*

He wanted to say the phrase to himself, *translunar injection,* to be alone and to feel amazed and to say it for nobody. He signaled to Rusty and Jeanie that it was time, and they removed their suits from where they had strapped them beneath the couch, placed the bowls of the helmets on, and felt with delicate twists, finding the places where they caught on the neck ring. They sat back in the white leather, the seats each slightly ruched by six metal buttons, and they began the preparations for the launch of the rocket's third stage.

Before him the wall of computers gossiped, some of them spitting out numbers on scrolls that began to twist as they grew longer, some of them bleating like an EKG. Somewhere beneath them was a perfect circle of planes, moving over the Pacific and capturing the exactitudes of their ship. He thought of them as he left earth's rotation, the men in those planes, the ocean on its own schedule, ignorant of their program. He had been eighteen when he saw it first, swum off the edge of the continent, felt the saline shove of a twelve-foot wave, and wondered—held down without air, in the little light admitted from above—whether this would have been the other world that ate at him, had he been raised along it instead of in Ohio, where the plains ran under the sky in polite deference, no hill or peak in sight, declining to compete.

The burn took six minutes, and then the moon took them into its pull.

—*The Saturn gave us a magnificent ride,* he said.

—*You're really on your way now,* said the men on earth. Again they removed their helmets. Jeanie patted Vincent's head and without asking handed him dried pears, peanut cubes, freeze-dried coffee. It took time to remember to chew. The dehydrated food went unattended in his mouth though his saliva gathered around it.

IT WAS A PLACE WITHOUT analogue, speed here unlike speed anywhere else. Nothing out the window became anything else, reminded them of their modern power. All they knew, by their remote native planet—increasingly smaller, progressively bluer—was that they were farther. The feeling in him was of waking from the purest liquid sleep, soft bodied and alone.

The buttons they pressed in the next ten minutes were each like the breach of a serpentine curve, the way narrowing as the endpoint drew closer. CAPTURE/PROBE. Exploding bolts lifted the shell from the lunar module, the quivering half-life of the release impact longer than anyone had predicted. EXTEND/RELEASE. —*Let's go,* Rusty said. RETRACT. DOCKING PROBE. A red golf pencil in Vincent's peripheral vision trembled where it floated. OPEN.

AS THEY DRIFTED DOWN THE tunnel away from him, Jeanie grinned to Rusty and Vincent a little too long, trying to impart something, a message that would become clear when it was needed. His instructions were to leave them, if the lunar module failed to fire. There would not be fuel enough to wait on their dwindling supply of oxygen. Vincent tried to offer him something in return, to say he understood, that he knew how those hours without radio on the other side of the moon would be, a time colonized by one grim thought, but his nod barely registered beneath all the protection that obscured it. Before leaving the cramped area where they had spent the last three days, they had flown through an eclipse, the sun slipped behind the moon, the moon lit up and examined by a light source that was hard, at first, to place.

What is that, Jeanie had said, and the word, which Vincent had never heard or read or spoken, came immediately to his mouth. *Earthshine.*

THE EAGLE SEPARATED FROM JEANIE; the first word they heard from him was *goddamn*. In their ears he took in a short breath, inadvisable because it would raise his heart rate. As he pitched the craft over, Vincent spoke to Jeanie like a father removed from his son by a body of water, coaching him in a jump from a rock.

—*We're beautiful here, Jeanie.*

—*You are? Looks to me like you're wrong side up, babe.*

—*One of us is.*

The relief came through in Jeanie's laughter, too big for the meager joke. Vincent and Rusty stood now, this ship even smaller than the last, their feet restrained by thick straps of Velcro, harnesses wired to the floor tugging at their hips. It was nothing like the flying he had worshipped for so long, but there was a part of being erect as you maneuvered that made a certain sense to him, all of you awake and unfurled and ready, and it was this, and the thick error handbook clipped above, and the magnified sound of each breath courting the last, and his pulse points drumming correct as a metronome, that made him sinfully happy, left him as quiet as he'd always wanted to be. All answers and questions were faint nags that he sent and received on another plane. An automatic part of him responded to orders and queries and another poured itself out the triangular window, where the moon hung in the black, a boon and a study of grays.

Twenty minutes passed, an hour. The descent engine ignited, and then they fell down the front side of the moon.

THEY FLEW OVER THE SURFACE, checking their alignment against the sun's center through the crosshairs, calculating angular rate by the landmarks they passed, over peaks and valleys named after other astronauts' wives. The time had come: they were closest in orbit to the moon.

—*Radar checks reflect a fifty-thousand-foot perilune.*

—*Roger,* said the voice on earth. —*Copy.* Then they waited, ninety-six seconds in which Mission Control was perusing their situation on every level, listing off temperatures and pressures, typing and scrolling and whispering, preparing an answer that had never been given before. Rusty did not look at him and he did not look at Rusty. Then Jeanie was with them again, his voice clipped and tender.

—*You are go for Powered Descent Initiation. Houston recommends your adjustment of yaw by ten degrees to the left.* Rusty's mouth moved forward around his teeth, adjusting for some solemn gesture or remark, a habit Vincent remembered from Edwards, and they began their thrumming way down, the 16 millimeter camera above them just activated, what would survive if they did not. Something too bright in Rusty switched on, and he began reciting numbers they could both very well see on the screens in front of them, numbers already available to the echoing room full of people on earth. Vincent understood this, how he was trying to stitch himself to the moment better, make all possible adhesions. —*PDI Pad one-oh-two, thirty-three, oh-four, thirty-six. Oh-nine fifty, minus oh-oh-oh-oh two point one. One eighty-two, two eighty-seven, oh-oh-oh, plus five six nine one nine.* Below them were the landmarks they had memorized, the Sea of Fertility, the Sea of Crises. It was a place without oceans, and they had named every bit of it after water.

Vincent moved his hand over the docking target, a red cross missing its bottom half, and he began to pitch the lem faceup. The earth was before them again, polite, accusatory, haughty with color. With every second they were a mile farther, and after only a few did the alarm begin to go off, its insistency suddenly the focus of everything, its attendant yellow light altering the cabin. It was a 1202, one of thousands, and he had to ask. —*We're a go on that alarm,* the earth said, leaving the details unknown. The 1202 had not abated when the 1201 went off, and the men on earth again would not feed him any explanation of the computer's objections, so he tried to think of the flashing as a kind of encouragement. —*Same on the 1201. A go.*

The shrill complaints inside were of little importance compared to what he saw out his window, which was not what he had prepared for. They were below two thousand feet and he did not see the place, wide and flat, an amenable valley of level dust, designated for their landing, though the computer urged them there anyway.

Instead he saw a crater, deeper than he could guess, its bottom a dark without texture. Around it was further bad news, boulders ragged and pockmarked and as wide as sedans. He communicated his decision to continue with a question. —*How's the fuel?* Rusty sacrificed his concentration on the navigational system to shoot him a look, and the shallow blue of his eyes was a message for Vincent, a color as flat and inflexible as any serious threat. —*Take it down,* Rusty said. The fuel light was on and Vincent knew very well what chance he was taking—anything more than what had been apportioned for descent would be taken from their departure—but he switched the system to manual and canted the craft back a little to brake how fast they fell and begged his eyes not to blink.

They had just passed the crater, he had just identified an area that seemed promising, when the sheet of dust, a disc of tan and rose and gray, reared up in protest, spread around them with the opacity of a sail. It moved with them, the dust, thicker as they flew lower. The fuel had dipped beyond the point it could be quantified. It was in this way that they landed, running on empty, surrounded by the surface particles kicked up in disruption, their destination a place that would be revealed to them only after they'd gotten there.

VINCENT AND RUSTY HAD REACHED another world but spent the next two hours inside, relaying data, describing the colors and curves through their window. He felt a dull pain inside that stretch of time, knowing that next came a prescribed four-hour period of rest. Vincent was the same person as he had been twenty-five years before—the boy chastised for hiking ahead of his troop to identify an owl, the boy who bought a Schwinn at five to live on his own schedule. He declined to answer his mother's cheerful questions about work; grieved the baby Elise had lost but kept that from her; loved Fay because she was a secret from the rest of his life, a person it seemed he had invented in that hot, shabby room.

His first task on the moon would be to practice leaving it. On his first step off the ladder, he was to jump and reach for the last rung, ensuring that the climb back into the lem would be possible and painless. Nothing was done without an elaborate meditation on how it would be undone. It was not lost on him that this professional inculcation had not mapped onto his life outside of it, that everything and everyone else he had treated like part of some child's diorama, essential pieces transposed and removed as he wished.

When their rehearsal for egress was done, the system checks completed, he radioed to earth and made the request that was loudest inside him. Sleep was impossible.

—*With your support, we advocate for extravehicular activity beginning about one hundred minutes from now, following the scheduled mealtime.*

They told him to stand by. Rusty, his eyes out the window, was quiet for the first time since they had left Jeanie. He had let the cage of circumstance settle. A minute poured in, five. *One Fay Fern,* Rusty had said, that afternoon in Houston, using just her name to deride her.

—*We thought about it. We support it. We're a go.*

First they were to eat. Before even the discussion of the meal Rusty retrieved his Personal Preference Kit, and Vincent pinched the bridge of his nose, knowing what was inside it, the wine and the wafer. It was only a vial but he resented it anyway, how it was costumed, how everyone in the Bible-sworn country would agree a man was right to take communion on such an occasion, how everyone in the office had denied what they knew of Rusty, that he'd once found his Porsche on a street he hadn't known existed, once taken a communications secretary to a topless bar in a remote part of Cocoa Beach and left while she was in the bathroom.

"I am the vine, you are the branches," Rusty was saying, the maudlin way he drew out the words reminiscent of a daytime television evangelist. "He who abides in me, and I in him, will bear much fruit."

From the front porch where she kept a bowl of candies for

neighborhood children, Vincent's mother had taken every occasion to speak to the press about her son's faith, which she called quiet and unfaltering. The media preferred that message to the one he'd given. When asked, when assaulted with a mic and a boom and a hot light that ate at his vision, when questioned to speak on the divinity of the mission, when fed leading queries like *Does your belief in God, Mr. Kahn, give you confidence in undertaking the unprecedented,* he had answered in evasive mazes. *My confidence in this mission comes from something ineffable, and also from the men in Houston, in Cape Kennedy, at the Jet Propulsion Laboratory in Southern California. It comes from the tests we have completed, over and over, from how we have walked underwater to approximate movement in the absence of atmospheric pressure, from our geologists' studies of rock formations similar to those we have seen on the moon.* Then a protest came, always a but, a mic shoved farther, a jawline and a bow tie dug closer his way. He would smile as he had at pastors and professors, then raise his hand and dip his chin.

"Feeling holy?" he said to Rusty then, off radio so earth couldn't hear.

It could not be unsaid. Maybe Rusty determined his punishment then and there, or maybe it was a decision made again and again, a cold drip of anger that kept his finger from the trigger of the Hasselblad when Vincent passed before him. Save where an arm or leg intruded on something else being captured, save his backside in the foreground of an image of the planted flag, there would be no photos of Vincent on the moon.

THEY SPENT NINETY MINUTES ASSEMBLING themselves, connecting hoses to valves, locating the monocular and the stopwatch, inflating the suits, activating the cooling units in their backpacks, depressurizing the cabin so that the latch would release. Running under all these systems was another, unknown to the voices on earth, one that told Vincent how to curve his back or swivel at the hips so that their bodies would not touch.

Finally they worked silently on the handle of the latch, Rusty pushing on one side of the fulcrum and Vincent pulling on the other. When it came they each laughed, little boys who have found the forbidden room unlocked.

—*The footpads of the lem are not depressed very far,* he told the people on earth, looking backward from the ladder. —*The surface is powder-fine.*

His right glove curled around the last rung and his left foot lifted, he let go.

The landing was gentle. As he looked out he knew that the place had granted him entry, would allow him his visit. He made his perfunctory leap up to the lowest rung of the ladder and then he uncurled his glove again. On a looping wire attached to Vincent's suit and stretched taut, Rusty passed him the Hasselblad, and he began on a panoramic series, ignoring the men in his headset. —*Did you copy about the contingency sample?* He could feel their asking, and he could feel Rusty waiting, —*Planning on that contingency sample, there, Vince?,* but he wanted a few more moments alone, time to document the solitude he had hunted all his life. Finally he drew the scoop-tong from his belt. It felt as though every part of his body was involved in the motion, concentrated on it, the slight bend of his torso, the squat in his calves, the grip of his feet. The bag attached to the tool he filled with powder, the different rocks he could see, scanning for any variant he might miss.

The moon was everything he had loved about the high desert, landscape where nothing was obscured, available to you as far as you wished to look, but cast in tones that better fit the experience, the grays that ran from sooty to metallic, the pits dark as cellars. Most astonishing was the sky, a black he had never seen before, dynamic and exuberant. With a grin he realized the only apt comparison. It was glossy like a baby girl's church shoes—like patent leather.

He had been given his ten minutes, and now it was time for Rusty to exit. He found himself more generous, coaxing him down, participating in the banter he knew Rusty wanted.

—*I'll practice partially closing the latch, but I won't practice locking it,* Rusty said. —*An inspired plan.*

Jeanie's voice cut in on cue.

—*You two babes scientists or what?*

THE FLAG, WHEN THEY UNFURLED it, seemed foreign to him, sad and irrelevant in the way of outdated technology. The pole they were meant to plant wouldn't, the surface being too fine and shallow, the subcrust obdurate, and he held up the stars and stripes while Rusty made insistent, varied jabs. That it finally caught at all was vaguely disappointing, a concession to them he wasn't sure they deserved. As they drew out the telescopic arm that ran the flag's length and would make the pattern fully visible, he remembered the meetings. *Why not let it fall down naturally,* Vincent had said, *why push for the appearance of wind on a place that is singularly without it?* In the end they had settled on this, an illusion that would tell the world this place was not so unlike ours.

With the flag mounted he felt his body straighten in anticipation, knowing he was free now to focus on the tasks assigned to him, the collection of rocks, igneous and magmatic, pale blue and shrimp pink, but then they were speaking at him again, earth was, saying something about the president.

—*President Nixon would like to speak with you.* That he could feel cornered on a place unpopulated and uncharted was a surprise to him, and he spent the next three minutes trying to forget that itch, to make out the staticky congratulations coming from the Oval Office. —*As you speak from the Sea of Tranquility,* the president said, *it reaffirms our commitment to peace on our home planet, to the unity of all people on the earth.* Vincent heard the political lie and he came up with an answer. As he did so he let his bladder release into the garment that cupped his groin, a distraction from the ministerial statement he did not wish to make. —*It is an unparalleled honor to represent not only the United States, but all the people who have looked up at the moon and wondered.*

In the next hour he took twenty-three scoops, never out of sight of the lunar module, his back to Rusty, who was planting the seismometers they would leave there. Vincent had thought he was resigned to the limits of the mission, content with the two and a half hours he had been given, but a message from earth, coded to protect the American public, told him his heart rate was up, that he should limit his activities. Something in him had revolted, desperate and insistent, and he began to run.

—*We recommend termination of extravehicular activities in just under ten minutes.* Pushing off from one foot and then the next, the crater coming closer to him, he ignored the questions from Mission Control, which were arriving with fewer niceties. As he approached the rim he could hear his breathing and he could see his home, rising above the slope of the lunar horizon, confident, complicated, marbled with colors he knew he would not experience again. He removed the tiny sock, the photo of Bisson at the wheel of his car— one tanned arm draped over the wheel and the other hand turning the radio knob, his eyes open to the route ahead—and he placed the things on the rim, tucked both under a boulder he could barely lift.

This was the real misfortune of the people on earth, he thought: they had made their lives somewhere they had never really seen.

11.

The stamps Randy bought a whole roll of, one hand holding Wright's and one reaching into a tight front pocket and pulling out Fay's money. The stationery he took from the inn, which Lucinda deducted from Fay's paycheck.

"I don't care," Wright heard Lucinda say to a visiting friend, Belen, a woman with indigenous green eyes and an elegant way of interrupting, "what he does, so long as she's happy with him. It is like the person who you visit who has a chair in a stupid fucking place—"

"You do not say how inconvenient. You just step around it." It was off hours and they were drinking *café con leche,* petting a brindle stray cat when it came around. He was hiding in one of the empty rooms, listening under the window for the piece he needed.

"She has forgotten how to wash her asshole alone. About the boy, of course, I worry. He is becoming a person and she just stands there."

They spoke about Randy's hygiene, his volume in all things, but did not ask to whom he was writing so often, biting the ends of pens until the plastic splintered. The talk moved to Velasco, his fifth term, all of them laced with coups, and they joked cruelly about the holes in his power, how he retired military generals like a kid revising the fantasy. "I don't like how that cat is staring," Belen said, pushing invisible glasses up her nose as she sniffed. "That cat is now retired."

Wright resolved to ask Fay about the letters, to get the answer using the voice he had cultivated to sound especially young, especially blithe. He had different ways of being with his mother now, exaggerating his sadness to incite her pity, mocking her spells of anger so she would thread him into the largeness of the feeling.

All afternoon the rain competed with the light. As it died he found her in the room, reading with a pen in her hand. *It is foolish,* she always told him, *to imagine knowledge will be loyal to you. You must be loyal to it.* He crawled into the bed next to her, his head at her feet, his legs over her torso, and pulled at each brown, callused toe, a sensation he knew she loved. He heard the book shut. They had always lived like this, each with total access to the other's body, still showered together. He could remember breastfeeding, asking for it.

"God," she said. "When you do that it feels like every part of my body is standing up to wave."

"How does a kidney wave?"

"I guess it just leans in one direction. If that sounds sad, just imagine some of the other parts. The intestine, basically just one five-foot-long squiggle, can't really do anything but sort of push and squash."

"Sad."

"Tragic. And yet: I know my intestine is waving at me right now. As you pull on that very toe, I know you have made it truly happy."

The only light in the room came from a string of Christmas bulbs tangled in a mason jar, some nod to American kitsch that Wright did not understand. When he was very young he had called this hour the shadow shine and sometimes Fay still whispered that to him, *The shadow shine, the shadow shine,* pointing to a dark shape moving across a wall. It was a phrase that had become synonymous with anything tender or flighty, a thin red dog they met that would not quite come near, a look that came onto Wright's face when a question thrilled him as much as it made him afraid. The meaning had mutated, become a nickname, referring sometimes to how he saw the world and sometimes to the world that was him.

"Mom?"

"Yes, my sweet."

"Who is Randy writing to all the time?"

"Friends, family."

"But before he said his friends all died. Before he said he didn't have a family—"

Wright wouldn't look at Fay but he could feel, beneath him on the mattress, that she was firming up her posture to deliver a statement. He had introduced the question too soon, knew the answer would be too short.

"He's writing to some people in the States, a group of men and women with similar ideas about how our country treats other countries and how it treats its own citizens."

"Has he met them?"

Slipped in the wooden seam of the mirror opposite them were photos he'd taken with the camera Randy was teaching him to use, and he stared at them now—Lucinda on a phone call with someone she believed to be an idiot, her eyes mostly their whites and her fingers spread taut on the counter before her. Fay's soapy heel on the lip of the tub, a book splayed and puckered on the bath mat.

"No," she said, "but he was connected to them through a friend who is also a veteran and who also opposes the war. There is a whole group of them, young men who were drafted to fight and are dealing with the consequences now. And there are others, people who didn't go to war but want to end it, people who want to end the way America polices other countries just for having different ideas."

She was speaking to him too slowly, as though describing a view that was blocked from his vantage, relating only vague impressions of shape and shade.

"But so they're writing every day? They're best, best friends? What are they talking about?"

"Mostly about change."

"Change how?" It was completely dark now and when she bucked her hips he would not let her rise toward the lamp. He thought of all the ways he could recognize his mother, by scent, by the shape of her ankle, gemlike, sharper than any other part of her. He believed this would be important someday, that there would be an occasion on which his understanding of her would be tested, and he was going to be ready, to prove that before anything else she belonged to him.

"Okay, okay. Change on the most fundamental level, how Americans think about other Americans, how they think about the rest of the world, whether they think about the rest of the world. How to get people to see past their front lawns. How to get people to think about how their lives unfold on the backs of others."

"How does Randy think he can change that?"

"Well, there are a number of ways, all of which involve getting people to think. There's education, there's demonstration, there's symbolic action."

"What's a symbolic action?"

"It's an act that summarizes something much bigger or longer, in a very public way, so that people who might not otherwise think of that something will begin to."

"An example being . . ."

He had learned the shortcuts through the airy way she had begun to speak, and he deployed them like the politician all his mother's secrets had made him. Certain turns were required in a conversation with her, from ignorant to mindful, from son to something else.

"Do you know you are the only nine-year-old who says 'an example being'?".

"An example being—"

"Okay, an example being—I've told you about teach-ins, where a group of people set up in a public space and lecture and distribute information through pamphlets and what have you."

"And that's a demonstration."

"Right. A symbolic action, an example of one, is called a die-in, which is when a lot of us get together and we wear costumes and makeup that bring to mind the Vietnamese people who have been killed in the war."

"Why do you say 'us,' Mom? We've never done that. You and me have never pretended to be dead." As he spoke he tried to cover fear with emphasis, but the boil of his body stepped in front of his speech, making his talk quicken.

"*Us* and *we* are pronouns that help to emphasize the global nature of all these problems. Saying 'they' is the same as saying 'not me, not my problem.'"

"I understand," he said, the phrase he had learned to use when he could not.

"We can talk about this as much as you want."

"How about as little," he said, a minor fury coming to his mouth now, remembering things he'd heard Lucinda say. "It's weird how your voice sounds like his voice. It's weird how you forgot to wash your own ass without him around."

She was silent, then conciliatory, treating him like a boy much younger. Her bribes he declined, a story, a bath floated with flowers. She could run to the kitchen and caramelize some chocolate. He wouldn't answer, only set up on his own bed with a basket of scrap paper and began practicing a new design of a plane, the Dragon, thirty steps he'd memorized. He could feel that his mother was watching him, her arms crossed, her tangled hair pushed all to one side, brown and red and blond, could hear how her breathing had quickened. She swung her feet over the side of her bed and strode to the bureau, the wide sleeves and skirt of her kimono creating a slight wind that moved his papers around.

"Goddamn, woman," Wright said, echoing a refrain of Randy's. "On your way to the hospital? I'm doing stuff here." She was placing a hunk of pot in a grinder, the snap of her wrists gone sharp with anger. He knew what was coming, the voice she would use.

"I feel sad and unloved when I'm spoken to with sarcasm. I would appreciate, in the future, if you expressed any frustration with sincerity."

It was called an I-message, a device for the discussion of feelings that she had decreed as rule in the room the three of them shared. *Okay, babe,* Randy had said, *4–0 on the cry message.* Wright had laughed until he saw his mother's face. It seemed that she had slipped into Randy's politics totally, his way of thinking, but with hers he could pick and choose. In the adult world where they argued, the male mind was a cathedral, cool and stony, and the female a colorful junk sale, surprising but inconsistent.

She leaned darkening on the dresser, her hair tied up in an ugly knot, the smoke filling between them until she began to cough and displaced it. He hated the smell of it, hated the way she looked as she inhaled, her eyes shut to everything, hated how after nothing could interest or upset her. He began to throw the planes at her, first in gentle arcs, then angry lines. It didn't take long for her to go, less than a minute, and she left the joint smoking in the ashtray. He brought it into the bathroom and pissed on it.

IN BETWEEN DREAMS THAT NIGHT were the sound of their voices, the flint of the lighter catching again, a Stones record she asked he turn off. "—action met by action. No more protests, no more slogans on paper. If our government continues to destroy, then we must destroy the government." Wright woke to the sun rising and his mother on the floor, her hand moving fast across a page, the inn's stationery spread around her like a corona, the thin papers catching all the light.

12.

What persisted about the tours, 237 countries, the palms and fingers of a thousand diplomats meeting his, the view out the window prairie or alpine or smog choked, was the game Rusty had about telling women's ages. Vincent could see it from across a ballroom or down a table all busy with crystal, the look on his face just before they submitted. "You know, I can tell certain things about a woman by her hands," he would say. "Would you like to see?" Probably they imagined appealing vagaries, a line down the middle that meant luck in property, the prominence of a vein that revealed a stubbornness in love, and anyway who would say no to this American, whose face that summer was ubiquitous as water or money.

"Of course," they'd say, and remove their hands from where they sat folded on the table, or gesture to the passing caterer and set down their empty champagne flute on a platter, their beaded clutch on an elbow-height table. They were politicians' wives, mostly, relegated to the side, the colors they wore chosen based on the colors their husbands did, and it must have been a welcome question, Rusty's, some trick that considered them as individuals, that would say *you personally are, you clearly have, you likely want.* They always agreed, wearing wedding rings and Bakelite bracelets, their cuticles pushed back to emphasize the purity of their lunulae, the pads of their palms treated with shea and paraffin and vitamin C.

He would look awhile, cupping the wrists and tracing the indexes, transferring their palms from one of his hands to the other while the color of their cheeks deepened in happy embarrassment, and then he would say a number. Sometimes it took a moment, sometimes they waited for a possible amendment, thirty-seven what, exactly. Possible grandchildren in your future? But if they looked at his face they knew immediately. It was a kid who had Saran-wrapped the toilet seat on April Fools', left plastic dog shit on the family kitchen floor. Thirty-four, thirty-three, forty-eight, fifty.

"The hands don't lie," Rusty would say, delighted, always the same line. Then there was the moment they had to giggle like the girls they weren't, hinge a hand at the wrist in mock admonishment. Smile like *how clever*, smile like *what fun*. Vincent saw more than one leave the room after, feigning illness or actually ill. A hand low on the stomach, a knuckle pressed to a temple.

It occurred to him often, the polarity of it, how what he had been hired to do required precisely the opposite skill set that these rooms did. He remembered the things Elise had told him, yardsticks for small talk. If it's Wednesday or later ask about the weekend coming up, if it's Monday or Tuesday ask how was your weekend. Before you make a statement think if it can be a question. The spouses didn't come on every trip—the others had children—and when he called her, which he tried to often, she would sometimes say, bothered, vicious, "Are you nodding? You know I can't hear it if you nod."

Elise had told a story that wasn't entirely true about an inability to conceive, and *Life* had latched on to it, captioned a lilac-washed image of her looking into the distance. She had become a celebrity in her own right, making guest appearances on call-in radio advice shows, saying *This is Elise Kahn* as though she were saying *I have loved you forever*. There were the ads—a rouge company had asked for her endorsement—in which she held a phone to her ear and a pointer finger under her elbow. *Shouldn't You Look Like You've Just Gotten Some Good News?* He knew she would leave him when the publicity died down. It was a feature on her face now, a part of how she ate and moved and slept. The worship was gone, how she had always said *Do you like this dress, Are you excited for tomorrow, Can I take your jacket, Have you had your vitamins.* "Sorry it's later than I thought," he said, one night, from the Netherlands. She said, "Not a problem." She said it too quickly.

"I have to tell you a story," he said. "A Jeanie."

That was the way they were referred to, by everyone who knew him. *I've a got a real Jeanie to tell you, a Jeanie that out-Jeanies them all.* He lived for others, learned how to tie balloon animals for his children's parties, kept birthdays in a daybook that was with him on the way to the moon, knew the piano, knew the guitar, had once stopped a scuffle in some Cocoa Beach bar by walking across it on his hands. Even Vincent loved a good Jeanie. Sam had introduced the term without explanation: none was necessary.

"You know this rule that your head is never supposed to be taller than the queen's?"

"Elise?"

"Which?"

"Which what?"

"Which queen?"

"Any queen."

"I don't know it, but I don't doubt it."

She was smoking and painting her nails, he could hear it and almost smell it. How many times had he asked her to keep the windows open, but she must have loved it, the chemical bite of smoke on plastic, and couldn't he have just avoided that room?

"So tonight we are leaving this ballroom where the ceremony's been, and of course Rusty's had too many, but Jeanie also. The sort of thing where you're served some mysterious liquor in little cups, and no one is telling you what it is or what's in it except that it's a local specialty. So Jeanie was doing his usual act but a little bubblier. I heard him threaten his acrobatics, which thankfully the handler caught and nipped in the bud. Poor Susan, God bless Susan."

He had his toes knit into the carpet of the room and was talking to fill the distance, the dread of coming back to that house that belonged to her now. He no longer knew where anything was at home, a Band-Aid, the hot-water bottle, some souvenir he'd held on to for reasons unclear. The only room she hadn't touched was his office, and it was cut off from all other rooms, untouched by the cleaning woman, riddled with ancient to-do lists and books he'd only ever begun.

"And the queen," she reminded him. Talking to Elise now was to be a walked dog, pulled back from distraction by a snap of her wrist.

"Right. Susan finally gave Jeanie and Rusty this look, *Enough is enough,* and we all said our goodbyes and headed toward the stairs up to our rooms, Jeanie in front because he's a little top-heavy, and then there at the foot returning from who knows where is the queen. She is incredibly old and incredibly tiny, and Susan's face takes a hard left into fear when she sees the queen is also ascending. It's clear this is to have been avoided at all costs, because to follow the etiquette is nearly impossible, while walking, given the disparity in height. But Jeanie, who apparently has not forgotten this stricture, and who is pretty loose from the liquor and lest we forget a college acrobat, just takes this as a challenge. I have never seen a body move this way, Elise. An animate noodle. His knees and hips were sort of skewed in a Z, and then his trunk hunched way over and his head knit forward to listen to her. He had to keep the posture from step to step or the top of his hair would rise above hers. Finally they get to the first landing, marble columns, brocade benches, you know, and she turns down the hall and we all wave until she's out of sight. Then he says it, very quietly, 'Kahn, my ankle, it's snapped like a twig.' I had to carry him the rest of the way and Susan's still in there with the ice, and the thing three times its size and Jeanie's going, 'Goddamn the queen! Goddamn the queen!'"

She refused to laugh. The silence was clean. A decade before it would have delighted Elise, the debutante in her, this story in particular, absurdity in the name of politesse. She was committed now to a kind of remoteness that was an imitation of his. Of all the things he had given her, his cruelty. The way he had treated her was reified here, finally, in the yes-and-no answers, the delay in her reaction not unlike that of the CAPCOM, far away on another planet.

The tours passed like this, the main events the personalities of other people, the tide underfoot her unhappiness on the phone. He knew, it beat at him, that on the other side of this was a life without a center, and so he tried to approach time slowly, as if to trick it—turning fruit in his hand before he ate it, singing out the song that came into his head in the string of rooms where he slept, for the first time in his life, without his watch on.

BACK IN THE COUNTRY AND deep in the fall, they had five more stops and even Susan was deteriorating, emerging one morning with cold cream dotted in mounds under her eyes. At a college where the masonry was tawny and spotted with moss, in an auditorium that smelled of old graham crackers, the three of them sat on metal folding chairs and took questions from the meadow of hands. The answers were as automatic as the sensor in his garage, the light that appeared when needed. Pauses built in, punch lines demographic tested. Between speaking he took sips of water, held it in his mouth. He made a game of hours like this, how deeply could he retreat, how involved could he become in his digressive train of thought. He remembered every bed he'd ever slept in, moving systematically back in time, pillows and sheets, quilts and windows. He alphabetized his records, Debussy, Dvořák.

He surfaced to a changed room, Rusty and Jeanie canted at their trunks, looking back into the wings for the person who would correct the mistake. $24 BILLION THAT DIDN'T GO TO WITHDRAWAL, a sign coming toward him said, held so squarely aloft it seemed to approach on a track. They wore masks, synthetic hair on rigid plastic, brown and haloed in orange, backlit in the flare of afternoon, the primate features exaggerated at the cheeks and teeth, and moved in formation, four rows of two. WELCOME, NIXON'S MONKEYS. As they began to charge, the auditorium lighting caught the teeth of their zippers and the metal of the pins on their jackets. THEY ALSO DIE WHO STAND AND WATCH. The security officers flowed from the sides, let wild into purpose.

It felt like something that happened without him, the water glass, what he did with it. A hand closed around his ankle, pale and freckled and with dirt under the nails. He had only tipped the thing from its place on his knee. It could have been an accident, he thought, as he watched the shocked fingers unlatch. A baton already out, he saw, ready to fall on the pale line of the neck.

Susan was ushering the three of them off almost immediately, her hands up like a traffic guard, as if she might easily separate the future of the men from the anger of the students.

IN THE MAKESHIFT GREENROOM OFF the auditorium, among racks of period costumes and props, papier-mâché boulders and a canoe leaned up against the wall, Rusty gestured with a Styrofoam cup. Leaving the stage had been an admission of guilt, Rusty thought; youth hysteria was a disease they shouldn't be tolerating. Jeanie, hands in the pockets of his suit, would not stop nodding, would not wait for the conclusion of a thought to agree with it. Rusty closed his hand around what was in it. When the Styrofoam split, the coffee came through the seal of his fingers. *"Fuckit,"* he hissed, shaking the scalding drops off his hand and onto the brown carpet.

There was no car scheduled yet so Vincent stayed, listening to them rage, quiet as he was famous for being, on god, on his family, on the death of his friend.

No respect, they were saying, since when did reaction replace discussion, the trigger-happiness of protesting now, the college students automatons. If his muteness before had been a fence around what mattered to him, the questions he wanted to speak with alone, today it was otherwise. When he faced those masks, when he saw those signs, he had felt utterly unequipped, somewhere very close to obsolete. He knew there was some conviction he was meant to articulate, but he could not imagine what his walk on that planet, unpeopled and soft with slate dust, had to do with the pain or yelling on this one. What his mind brought him, in that dusty back room, was the tinny sound of a stall warning in the first plane he ever flew.

"We're going to go back out," Rusty was saying, an index driven into the flat of his palm. "We've got to make a statement." Susan was looking at Vincent as though she might soon take his temperature, send him back to bed.

"Go ahead," he answered. "Free country." He crossed his legs at his ankles, his position clear.

"Is this not real to you," Rusty said. "Is there a fucking thing on fire that would matter to you?"

He didn't rush getting up, remembering his yellow cardigan, his package of mints on the vanity. There was a side exit down the hall, the door minor characters passed through after speaking one line, and he took it.

EVEN HE COULD SEE THAT the photo was unfortunate. The security guards reaching from either side toward the boy in the mask, a fist already at the collar, Vincent's wrist bent up high like someone keeping a treat from an unruly dog. The band of water not yet broken by the hidden face. WHO'S AFRAID OF A LITTLE MONKEY? read a headline.

Two weeks after this came a call at home, the red phone that had almost stopped ringing. Elise was watching tennis, bare feet tucked under, a thumbnail in her mouth. He heard the grunts of the players as the president's voice came through, saying something about POWs. Would he do a tour in support of them.

"I will have to consider this," he said, which meant he would not.

Elise read the piece, when it came in the paper, section C, and left it folded back on the table—Rusty's smile the same next to the young men in wheelchairs as it had been next to aging queens. Vincent did not read that article about the war, or any others.

13.

Wright woke up to his bags packed, even the stones he had collected cleared from the dresser, and traveled to the airport in pajamas in protest. Fay hadn't told him sooner, she said on the plane to San Francisco, because she wanted him to absorb all the things he loved about his life in a sincere way, unfiltered by worry about the future. He knew that was the smallest part of the answer, and spent the line in the airport thirsty because he was sobbing, sobbing because he was thirsty. The heft came, he was sure, from Randy, who had sent more mail in their last month there than he had in the last six, whose general agitated personality seemed to have sharpened, clarified. Their last night at the inn, unable to sleep, Wright had heard Randy in the courtyard, reading to Fay, a clipped chain of words that changed his voice and substituted the anger there for certainty. He had known they were words on a page because he had never heard Randy speak that way, without interruption or angry discursion, without a *fuck* or a sigh. *Make no mistake. The wealth of the United States of America is the blunt consequence of its imperialist relations with other quote-unquote less developed countries, of the labor and natural resources we have stolen or abused. The Pan Am jet you rode to visit your aunt, your angora cardigan with the pearled buttons, the television you worship, the bananas you pack in your children's lunches, the tires on your family sedan and the oil that makes it go—all of these things are not, have never been, will never be yours. They were made in and are the rightful property of the rest of the world, of Venezuela and Vietnam and the Philippines, of all the lives you the American public have conveniently forgotten.*

The illuminated icon of a seat belt had just gone off and Randy was walking the aisle, grabbing headrests with his right and left hands, breathing in an audible way. Before him the soda he had emptied and peanuts he'd devoured, Wright could hardly bear to look down the foot-wide stretch of carpet. Randy had stopped, had placed his left fingers on a seat a foot in front of him and kicked his right leg back and up. His right hand met his right ankle as he leaned farther forward, his eyes closed in what Wright knew was the Dancer. It was a position he had watched his mother take for long minutes in the middle of the jungle he already missed, calling out *nat-a-ra-ja-sa-na,* hinging at her hip, flying a flexed arm before her.

People had begun to notice, to look to and from Randy, to their seat partners and the people across the aisle. Fay, in the middle seat, read a book and ruffled Wright's hair and smiled benignly, unmoved. He had just pressed his hot forehead to the ovular window when he heard a flight attendant begin to speak, using another voice than she had when offering *Cola juice coffee tea liquor? Cola juice coffee tea liquor?*

"Sir, I'm going to ask you to return to your seat now."

"Why's that."

"What you're doing is unsafe for you and your fellow passengers."

"Why's that."

Wright could tell, by the tightness of Randy's speech, that he was still in the posture.

"Should there be any turbulence, you could injure yourself and others. I need you to return to your seat, sir."

"The sign's off. The announcement said 'feel free to stretch your legs.' What am I doing here but that, do you think? Is it possible that you're just a little uncomfortable with how I've chosen to express myself here? Is it possible that some honesty might do both of us a favor here, ma'am? Betty?"

For reasons he didn't understand, because he wanted to mainline shame, Wright tore himself from the window and sat up on his knees to watch. He could see that Randy had released the pose and was standing on both feet.

"If you don't return to your seat now, I'm going to have to report this to the pilot, sir, and he'll—"

"No need for that, Betty. It's a beautiful country we live in, the US of A, don't you think?"

When he returned to them he kissed Fay with force, a hand slipped under the far side of her neck, and then he brought the metal tooth on his lap into its buckle.

"Better tighten those seat belts, *folks,*" he said, loud enough that the three heads in front of them, white and blond and brown, turned.

IN THE BEGINNING THE COUNTRY—HIS country—was beautiful to him, and they saw so much of it, the purple sand on the beaches of Big Sur, the eaves of Victorians in Syracuse piled with snow. Somehow Randy and Fay had returned to America with so many friends, people who hugged them at the door and brought them into rooms where there were countless others, smiling and waving. They napped like puppies on floors where cushions had been placed like puzzle pieces, Wright pressed against his mother and pushed to sleep by the sounds of fifteen people breathing. Sometimes the houses were bigger, and the three of them had a door they could close, and others he was banished to play in yards that were barely that, anemic patches of grass bordered by warped chain-link fences. There was that word again, the one Randy had spoken like a rule so often at the end of their time at the inn, everywhere. *Shelter.*

A kid named Ocean explained it to Wright, what it was their parents were doing, what the maps spread on the floors indicated, what the shopping bags they were always bringing were full with if not food. He was ten and more freckled than not, his hair cardinal red and unbrushed down his back, his teeth all at war with each other. He stole his mother's Salems and kept them behind his translucent ear.

"My mother wouldn't bomb anything," Wright said. It was late November, somewhere in upstate New York, the sky a deep and undifferentiated gray, and all he had on was a wool cardigan Lucinda had knitted him, a loose weave that did nothing to protect him from the weather. They had been at this house a week, long enough to suggest they would probably be here another. If there were something on the ground he could have kicked he would have, but there was nothing of any weight, some colorless twigs, the linked plastic rings of a six-pack.

"Sure she would. What do you think she brought you to a whole other continent for? To see the White House?"

"In the summer we're going to—"

"Grand Canyon? Niagara Falls?"

Unaccustomed to being mocked, the only response he could fashion was silence. On the cuff of his long-sleeve shirt there was a patterning like lace where he had chewed it, and he put it in his mouth again, tasting the spit from yesterday trapped there.

Ocean kept his shoulders close to each other, his lips open only as much as was necessary to get the words out. The few other children were undecided about him, sometimes seeking his approval about things they made or found, lanyards or foreign coins, sometimes leaving whichever unheated room he had entered in his deteriorating blue parka, its bits of polyester filling escaping in tufts. All Wright wanted, on that miserable patch of dead grass and concrete, was some leaves. The world without any green felt acutely unsafe, a place where rest and privacy were impossible.

"What are they bombing," he said, his eyes on the maroon Saucony sneakers Fay had bought him during their layover in the Miami airport, his first brand-name shoes. He asked the question with a kind of insouciance he was just learning, a behavioral experiment of the many that made up his life now, pushing the syllables out of his mouth like they didn't mean anything. Profanity he tested when he thought he was out of earshot, while he was on the toilet. *Fuck you,* he would say, then *Fuck me*—something he'd heard his mother exclaim in bad traffic, her hand smeared down the gearshift.

"What are they bombing?"

"You name it, anyplace that belongs to the politicians and the pigs. Police stations. Courthouses." In Ocean's phrasing, in the guttural way that he said *pigs,* there was the voice of his mother. Annabelle made soap of ash and butter, and she wore a braid that she often held curled around her fist as she spoke from a door frame, and the stories about her were like a perfume she wore, invasive once you were close enough. She had a law degree from Columbia and had once performed an abortion in the back of a moving van. His mother had mentioned these bits of her biography to him the first time they'd met, her voice low down in the thrill of it.

"Why." The question was too simple, that of a child much younger, and Wright was finding it harder to keep up the posture of someone who didn't care, given the wind coming in the loose weave of the sweater, the pit bull barking on the other side of the leaning fence. His English had an accent that got in the way of him, and the late afternoon in autumn in the Northeast looked to him completely incorrect, like the world had been shaken of all that was good about it.

The other five children were moving closer to the conversation, and seeing this Ocean pulled a match from his parka, dragged it across the bottom of his shoe, put a Salem in his mouth, and started to smoke it. Today he held it between his middle and ring fingers, an affect he was trying on.

"There are about as many reasons as there are people in New York City, which is eight million, which I know because I was born there. Why because the government doesn't care about other cultures and it makes our teenage boys go off and die and it's poisoning Vietnam's natural resources." Ocean was playing at conviction, Wright could sense that, and he could feel that he was going to push back, as he did against his mother, work him until he ran out of rehearsed answers. The way he was angry had started to become the way he was.

"But why bomb if bombing is what they're doing? Isn't that like saying it's all right, to, to—" He looked for the word. "To ruin?"

"No, idiot. It's saying what you're doing is not going unwatched! It's saying that destroying others will lead to others destroying you! It's saying—"

"That we're not any smarter. That we couldn't come up with anything better." He felt his shoulder blades spreading as he said so, his body opening to the argument. His breath reached all the way back. Then his head hit the ground. Before the pain settled he was almost happy for the warmth it provided, every cell inside rushing to alert him to what had just happened, embracing him in that way. He knew Ocean was hissing over him, Wright's wrist in his hand, and then he felt it, the real heat making its way inside him, the Salem deep in the pad of his palm.

Later, as they sat in a room upstairs on the only square foot that was not stacked with mimeographed papers, his mother treated and bandaged his hand. Fay told him how sorry she was, that the burn would become a scar, that Ocean was a smart kid but not blessed with any patience, that eventually it would fade, but Wright would fixate on it for months after, the wound his opinion had gotten him. He would check it like a clock.

14.

The other people with children had peeled off, vanished like the soft part of a body during some season of trauma, revealing only the mangy thing beneath. He and Ocean were the only ones who remained, and Wright kept as far from him as possible, pretending sleep in situations where it was inconceivable. Their positions on their mothers, their feelings about the movement that kept them in places like this, two-by-fours nailed over the windows, cockroaches so fearless and reliable you could name them, could not have been more different. Ocean had the look of someone waiting to be let in, a person underdressed and anxious at the door. He begged to attend the meetings.

All day Wright read, whatever he could, mildewed brochures on woodworking he found in the basements of the empty houses where they slept, paperback mysteries he stole from the drugstores where the adults bought saltines and batteries, Trollope and Austen he took from the shelves of libraries. He was ten. The more he populated his thinking with other text, he believed, the less he was vulnerable to the ideas of Shelter. He would hear one of those phrases they repeated so often, *Destroy to rebuild,* and mentally counter it with something he'd read, the more innocuous and benign the better, *Joinery first requires common sense and reliable tools,* picturing the phrase word by word in his mind until the angry spoken thing was gone.

In the privacy of his sleeping bag he fashioned a kind of helmet to keep out sound. Around his thickest socks he wrapped duct tape, pilfered from the collective supply closet, warping and massaging them until they resembled cups. They fit around his earlobes, connected by bands of tape, doubled for strength, which crossed his crown and circled his forehead. Over this went a knit cap, powder blue and bearing the monogram of a parochial school in Ohio. The absurdity of it, the bulkiness, made him look as removed as he felt. He owned few things and guarded them with all his energy, a pamphlet on the state parks of California he had long since memorized, a three-inch bureau that belonged to a dollhouse he'd never seen.

It was a certain type of meeting—louder than the rest and identifiable by peaks and lulls in which the members of Shelter slingshotted insults and reeled from those dealt them—that he had fashioned the contraption to avoid. They had named these sessions, called them Group Criticism. He had seen one first in Syracuse, from a landing on the stairs, his head pushed through the space left by a missing baluster. In the room below they had pushed everything to the borders, forming a crater of gapped wood flooring rimmed by books and folding chairs and piles of papers. Fay had stepped forward from the circle their bodies made, dressed as she had begun to in a thin suede jacket that obscured the beauty of her shoulders.

"Society cunt," they said, "little queenie, are you gagging from that silver spoon."

"Would you have gotten here without your daddy's money in your pocket."

"Without Randy's cock in your mouth."

"Think because you're a grade-A fuck you'll be exempt."

"Think this is a rough game your parents will hear about."

"Think because you're a mother you deserve some other treatment."

Watching it, the greatest wonder to him was how she took it, nodding sometimes, her biggest movement to bite off a crescent of pinky nail, her face like someone in the audience of a film, turned to something bigger than her, ready to feel what she had paid to. Finally she was absorbed back into the circle, and into the middle high-stepped Randy, his T-shirt worn to a kind of perforation, his sunglasses shadowing his face though there was not a lamp on in the squat.

"Here he is."

"Such a hero for shooting off his finger."

"What'd you shoot before that, how many kids."

"Were you a good soldier. Rape some women for the hell of it."

"Already burned their houses anyway."

"Even if you didn't you watched."

"Does being here make up for your time as a cog in the imperialist mechanism."

"Such a revolutionary. Such a freethinker."

"Never mind at the end of the day you want some woman to worship you. How's it feel to be fucking a woman smarter than you."

"How long until she says no more."

"Two months."

"A month."

"How do you even get it up."

Randy received it with his head tucked and his hands in the back pockets of his jeans, noiseless, but the way the wings of his hair moved betrayed him, how they twitched irregularly with the violent intake of his nostrils.

It was a way of systematically deconstructing the ego, his mother said, when she came to Wright later, a shape around his body sometime after midnight that woke him. Freeing it of its comfortable lies, so that the individual could recede and the revolutionary could step forward. He had not asked, had not even acknowledged the presence of her on the mattress except to scoot to its edge, and he hated the rehearsed way she had begun to speak, the built-in gravity of a perfected phrase. There were strings of days when he slept alone and others when her breath in his hair was like weather, and he didn't know why, though he suspected it had something to do with Randy, how their relationship had changed.

A fight had raged for a week in the boarded-up house, which was heated only by the detritus burned in a cracked granite fireplace. Wright watched the splintered legs of end tables disappear into ash, cheap sneakers curl like dead leaves. The argument had begun with his mother and Randy and spread outward, sides drawn along gender lines and then dissolving in shame once that was apparent.

Randy was the vocal advocate, the one who found a way of working the phrase into most conversations, *Demolish monogamy*. He and Oz—who had once posed for a photograph in which he and Annabelle fit, kissing, inside the same oversized Shetland sweater— spoke of the constraints romantic love imposed on the mind. The individual, Randy said, cannot devote himself to a movement when he is devoted first to another individual. Monogamy is a trap in our thinking. Fay had stood on the sidelines of the half circle that formed around him, nodding with a knuckle in her mouth, and afterward devised an errand.

Wright accompanied her, both of them in sunglasses and bala-clavas as they drove through Newburgh, a city of beautiful, ruined houses where no one wanted to live. The things hanging from the rearview mirror, feathers Annabelle had laced there at a happier time, swung when the gearshift lurched, blocking and revealing his view of Fay's crying.

Later that week, when she began sleeping with Oz, who was narrow shouldered in wire-rimmed glasses, someone for whom the appropriate quotation was always available to be spoken quietly, a graduate of a school he referred to only by the area in Massachusetts, Randy punched a hole in a wall. The issue seemed to be that she had chosen a single alternative, rather than the diversity of the five other men in the house. "That's not freeing you ideologically," he hissed at her, to which she said a stony total of nothing. *MASCULINITY IS POISON,* someone wrote in tidy ballpoint capitals next to the buckled crater of plaster his fist had left.

Oz, over a cauldron of bulgur and little else, suggested to Randy that he watch the two of them together sometime.

"I'd rather watch you fuck yourself," Randy said.

"Enlightenment called for you," Annabelle chimed in. *"Long* distance." It became a line they repeated often, all of them but one.

WRIGHT PASSED HIS DAYS IN his mind, with the textbooks Fay had pilfered somehow, all of them bearing the name of the previous owner, Brock Stevenson, a figure he imagined with great jealousy, a boy on a bicycle with braces on his teeth. As often as she could she looked over his work, and the way she squinted one eye when recalling some formula, the way she reached for analogies to better explain, were some of the last moments when she was familiar to him. She taught him the Pythagorean theorem and how to steal, only from corporations, only necessities. In a K-Mart parking lot she kissed him when she felt the bags of rice tucked into his waistband. *A value system is living and dynamic,* she had said, *changed by forces working against it. Any linguist will tell you that the only perfect language is one never spoken,* she said.

They behaved as though the smallest of pleasures were anathema, a distraction from the mission at hand, watching each other for any sign of joy and snapping when they found it. Someone's hot sauce was poured out and left empty, a patterned scarf thrown on the fire, a joint flushed down the toilet. The first week of February, with a line about how they must take advantage of whichever resources were available, Annabelle skinned and roasted a stray cat.

15.

Standing outside the closed noise of a classroom, imagining what might be kept in the row of lockers he faced, Wright was thinking still how easy it had been, the concrete walkway that cut through the snowy lawn, the oaken double doors unlocked.

There would be books inside, of course, but also lunches, sandwiches cut at the diagonal. Trumpets in cases, shoes just for track, cameras, maybe, keys. Imagining this, possessions in the dark, accessible only by secret combination, gave him a longing that was almost sexual.

When the door opened to reveal her, tall and black in pleated slacks that revealed the point of her ankles, pink polyester kissing sensible heels, he apologized. She was placing a sheet of paper in a folder attached to the outside of the door, on it the word ATTENDANCE stenciled in red, and when she saw him she kicked her foot out to keep the door open.

"New here?"

Wright brushed the hair on his head to the right, full of a strange feeling, something that could have been power, the idea that there was nothing about him she could know if he did not tell her. The thought ran around his mind and sharpened to a phrase: *nothing about me, nothing about me.*

"This the class you're looking for? Mrs. Henderson, English? Ninth grade?"

He could not lie, he thought, if he did not answer. She smiled without her teeth and opened the door wider, bowing in a dramatic way to let him in. It was almost too warm. The desks, blond wood and slightly tilted, looked like they were listening. He loved how they were a contained system, each married to an attached plastic chair, and the odd wish he had was to sleep under a row of them, crawl in between the margins of sneakered feet. He was shorter than the tallest student by a foot, but not entirely an exception in the study of bodies. Puberty was nearly a sound among them, a song some of them knew and would not sing to the others.

It was something he had never experienced before, the whole room turning to him. It put him in mind of being bathed. She asked him his name, and it was as if the lie were supplied by not his brain but his body, so automatically did it come.

"Brock"—he swallowed—"Stevenson."

"Your name is Rock," someone howled, a boy who was sitting up on his haunches on the chair, leaning forward on the desk like a sphinx. He was thin and tall, the bones of his wrists exposed by a sweater too short, and Wright wanted to kiss him, the novelty of another boy, another incomplete body. "Rock, Rock, dumb ol' Rock." He said these words again, drumming them out on the skull of the girl in front of him, who had an Afro crowned at the hairline with one pink bow. Mrs. Henderson cleared her throat and snapped her fingers twice, to which half the room snapped back once. She did it again, the hand raised while she faced the chalkboard, and this time all of them snapped back. The sound was as moving and surreal to him as the rest of the space—watercolor self-portraits hanging from clothespins on a string that crossed the windows, the blotted faces backlit by drifts of snow, three shelves

of books and a stuffed chair in which to read them, a sign that said
BRING ONE HOME THIS WEEKEND!

"Brock Stevenson," she said as she finished writing. "Is that the
correct spelling? Or is it a p-h?"

The beauty of the perfect cursive made him want to admit everything right there. *Not my real name, don't belong here, haven't been
to school in almost two years.* Again he did not respond.

"Tell us what you know about yourself, Brock Stevenson."

The face he must have made was of real torture, he thought,
because she laughed, her mouth open so wide he saw a silver filling.
She was tilting her head now, a palm curled on her cheek.

"I ask everybody new," she said. "It's just a way of attaching
your life to ours. You can tell us anything you want, anything that
comes to mind. Some people start with where they're from, or what
it is they want to do or be."

He believed for a second that he might answer with something
witty and avoidant, *America's first talking horse, a fly on the wall,* but
it didn't come. Instead he cleared his throat and said only, "Here."

The boy who had called him Rock, still sitting on his feet in his
chair, could not come up with the correct rejoinder, and it appeared
to make him uneasy. Wright's final sincerity was an odd weapon, or
the total lack of one, a message that any cruelty would fall on him
without resistance. Tipping her head the other way, Mrs. Henderson indicated a seat at the front. He could feel her examining what
was missing, a backpack, some identifying document, a pen even,
some proof this had been the plan at all. From her desk she removed
a notebook, wrapped in plastic, a new sharpened pencil from a jar,
and she set them on his desk without a word. He did not thank her,
and he hated himself, and the scarf around his neck, too, pink and
synthetic, woven through with metallic thread, obviously meant for
a woman. Inside of his sneakers were plastic bags to keep the snow
out, and he believed everyone would hear them, so as he walked he
hummed a piece of a song, a choice that did nothing to cauterize

his strangeness. "He think it's the fuckin' Grammys or?" said the sphinx. *"The winner is Rock."*

It took a minute, after this, another two rounds of snapping, for the class to quiet again. The howling at who he was aside, he spent the next two hours refashioned by happiness, his scalp prickling with what she taught them, the grace and freedom of thoughts that weren't his.

WHEN SHE SPOKE, MRS. HENDERSON, WHEN she put an idea forward, it was like watching someone decorate a room very carefully, hanging things where their colors made sense, shifting the position of a chair in relation to a window. Her confidence and flexibility created his. He was breathing more. They were discussing a novel he had read and it felt like a miracle, the only indication in recent memory that he was a good person doing the right thing. His hand was up the whole time, the fingers all spread an inch apart, little force fields between them.

"Why do you think," Mrs. Henderson said, "the writer keeps the protagonist's name a secret until the end of the book? Why is he only called the boy?"

"Because he believes he does not deserve one," Wright said. "In keeping it from us, the writer helps us to feel the anxiety he does, of being without a role or purpose. Revealing it only after he has suffered tells us how suffering has its merit, and can make identity feel earned as opposed to given."

Though his hand had been up, she had not called on him, and he believed this was why his answer reduced her to silence. She had her hand over her mouth as if to keep from expelling a belch, and he apologized, twice. There were construction-paper silhouettes of the city's buildings running the wall to her right, there was the sound of a water fountain going off in the hallway outside.

"Never apologize for your intelligence," Mrs. Henderson said, something about the skin around her temples activated, looking at

him only after she'd spoken. After another silent moment, a girl in the back made three kissing noises, and then the classroom erupted, the plastic seats squeaking against the metal they were welded to and the sour smell of bodies in the winter deepening somehow. By the time she had the room organized under her again, everybody snapping back after four tries, the bell rang. "Have a good lunch," she called. "Don't eat an apple for a doctor, eat it for yourself."

She didn't have to ask him to stay after. He knew.

The room, emptied, did an eerie impression of itself, the props strange without the actors. He'd closed the notebook but opened it again.

"I forgot to ask for your pass," she said, moving a wet cloth over the chalkboard, then leaning against the clean green. Her fingers curled around the slate lip of it, the nails trim and short and unpolished. *PASS,* he wrote, in capitals in his notebook, and then he circled it. She made eye contact but then looked, he thought, at the scarf, the haircut he'd given himself in a third of a mirror. He wondered if she could smell more than his bad breath—the essential badness of his teeth, the crumbling of which he often dreamt in clinical detail.

"I forgot to get a pass."

Wright told himself this was not technically untrue, that it had not occurred to him to try and this was a kind of forgetting, but he knew the question was coming he could not avoid, and he steeled himself against this, curled every toe.

"Do you know where the office is? You'll need one to come back here tomorrow. That's something I have to sign off on."

"I thought I might not need a pass if I came prepared." Even chewing the skin around his thumb as he was, he could barely get through the weak attempt. He considered the seams of the carpet as he said this, the white of the baseboard paint.

Another conversation ran through the spoken one, coded to an extent that lay beyond him, and his attempts to divert it felt sloppy.

"Being prepared is a wonderful thing. I wish that were all we asked of anybody. Where were you before this?"

"I was in another country," he said. The truth rendered him more of a captive, the fact he hadn't elaborated a question passing now over her face.

"How old are you, Brock?"

"Enough to know better," he said, a joke that didn't land. Her jaw gained some definition, a slight firming as she tried to imagine his angle.

"You're welcome to take that notebook," she said, pulling on a hooded parka. "I'm going to bring you to the office now."

"I can go tomorrow on my own," he said.

"I insist."

They walked with her hand light on his lower back, he stopping twice to tie his shoes and tuck the plastic bag back into the rib of his sock, she speaking the names of people she passed in the hall, first and last, like they were punch lines, students and other teachers. "Edna Roberts! Frank Dibbern!" When they passed a shuffling white-haired man wearing a tie embroidered with balloons, she whistled like a catcaller and he blushed.

"I think I forgot something in the room," he said to her, standing in front of the door on which a word was painted in decaying gold leaf. O F C E. "My pencil."

I forgot all my clothing, he might as well have been saying, *the only photos of a life that's gone now.* She pulled a Ticonderoga from her pocket and pressed it in his hand and fit her fingers around the knob.

"I look forward to seeing you tomorrow," she said, a lie for his benefit.

"I won't be late this time."

She nodded and squeezed his shoulder, and then she was a shadow behind the frosted glass, and then she was a good person he had only imagined.

"I'm supposed to call my mother," he said to a face behind a high counter. Under its fiberboard he pushed at a wasteland of dried gum with his thumbnail. In his periphery an Aqua Netted bob, helped by red fingernails and clacking bangles, did its nosy thinking.

"Hon, are you new here? Do you look like somebody? He looks like somebody. Doesn't he, Nance?"

A phone passed over the chipped surface and he dialed without thinking, the first response of which he'd been sure. Wherever they went, his mother grilled him on this until he spoke without stutter: the number of the pay phone closest in the network of them Shelter maintained across the country. In the receiver he heard it being dialed and imagined the stall, the corner of a vacant lot where a gas station had poisoned the ground. He had watched them step into it, his mother or Annabelle or Oz, as though it were an expensive and powerful car, pinching the doors closed with two fingers, looking around at what was possible inside it with great admiration. They had chosen it for the surrounding desolation. Only once had they found someone else in the booth, an older woman wearing clothing from every season. Wright had watched Oz and Fay standing on either side of the grated glass, tapping out a rhythm with the heavy rings each wore on their fingers, looking away with slapstick mischief when the woman looked toward them, then groping and kissing for her benefit.

Randy answered on the first ring, speaking in code Wright could understand, something they all said to each other.

"That you, Ralph?"

"I need you to pick me up," he said, and muttered the address of the school. Annabelle's teal van rattled around the corner ten minutes after he'd stepped outside, and Randy spoke only once on the drive back, not even a full sentence. At an intersection he pulled back on the fur-covered gearshift, sucked in a third of a cigarette in one inhale, and said, pointing at Wright but keeping his eyes ahead on the traffic, "All of our lives in danger." Randy made a gesture with his hand, one that meant, *All of it, gone*—a fist puffed on to bare the fingers flat, a dandelion blown away.

In the office the secretary had gasped, in the middle of the phone call, and Wright believed she knew: who his mother was, the sort of things she said with her eyes emptied out of feeling. But he had been wrong.

"I've got it," the secretary had said, and giggled, high and bright. "You know you look just like Vincent Kahn? It's the first man on the moon, Nancy, right here in our office, and he's calling home sick."

16.

A brittle two months later, Fay and Wright lay in the bed of an ash-blue truck, covered by potato sacks filled halfway with lentils, making a journey from Philadelphia to New York unseen. "You can't just reinvent my life completely without telling me how it's been changed," he told his mother. Wright's body in the sleeping bag fit exactly between the steel ridges of the truck. His birthday cake that year had been a Twinkie Oz held out in his palm, smashed from hiding it there.

"You could start with why are we in this truck, covered up like criminals, instead of a regular car with seat belts and an AM/FM dial." He had been in the country twenty months, never allowed to actually live in it. They hit a bump and his mother's involuntary moan, the light peal of fear, worked at his anger, softened it temporarily.

"We're in this truck because my name is attached to an activity that the government considers wrong."

"Which activity would that be?"

"Along with other members of Shelter, I engineered an explosion in the Philadelphia courthouse. We put in a call beforehand, we always do, to evacuate the building."

She was speaking from a script, the words arriving without any adjustment for their circumstance, and he wanted to unsettle her somehow, pull her hair, douse her in water. All the answers to his questions he knew already, but he wanted to make her say them.

"And why is your name—"

"Afterward we issued a communiqué explaining our actions, which went out to newspapers, and I signed my name at the bottom."

He craned his head up toward the unzipped mouth. He saw a slice of a billboard, the word *YOU* in black against white, and a toothpick of sky, and a crow passing over. In his teeth he felt each car and truck that overtook theirs.

"I love you. Please say something."

His arms were slipped down inside the torso of his too-big thrift store sweater, his ass was flush again with the truck bed. Between them was a change neither could articulate, that love could go unwanted, could become someone's defense against her worse self. It could run over the object without mending anything.

"Kansas," Wright said. "Bird feeder, truck stop, fork."

He fell asleep soon after, his fury with her turned a strange sedative, his feeling about the noise and the road and the vibration of the truck newly appreciative. It was something violent he could climb into, something that would take him in.

WRIGHT WOKE IN NEW YORK, his anger burned off, the world around him still again, his body attuned to the climatic facts of April: air that turned over into a chill every few moments, a morning sun that was invasive but not warm, the leafless trees planted in rows. Hands above them worked methodically, removing the things that had hidden Fay and Wright, and then four knuckles rapped the top of the cab and they knew to hop out, to follow the fingers flapping against the palm that meant *This way* and *Now*. In half a crooked block they were up the stoop of a brownstone, the steps with thick margins of cigarette butts. An exhausted wood foyer, a row of brass mailboxes, an apartment that was much like the others. The furniture was scant, a few school chairs scratched with initials, a pink velvet couch missing a leg and propped up by three bricks. Leading the way like lily pads through the unheated space were a series of worn bath mats, warped and ovular and square, puce and mauve and gray.

"Is this Fay," Annabelle's voice said, an arm gesturing from the kitchen with a wooden spoon held high in her hand. He stood at the periphery, surveying the room for any place he might comfortably sit, while Annabelle embraced Fay, lifting her off her feet and twirling her, praising her, making her kneel, knighting her with the unclean spoon. Soon the people sprawled around the room had risen, a redheaded woman in a shapeless dress, a man with perfectly round glasses and his hair in a top bun, and they hugged her, too, telling her their names, congratulating her. "So rare," he heard, "such confidence." They touched her hair and turned her face. "Court stenographer! We thought for sure we were fucked after Oz got chased out by that security guard. How'd you get in without a badge? Tell me you wore a little plaid two-piece, brought in a portable typewriter." He watched his mother's pride, realizing it was foreign to him, that he had never seen her filled this way. "I brought in a typewriter case," he heard her say, the light in her voice bringing out their laughter. "That's where you put it? A genius, a genius." Annabelle stepped in and hugged her again.

With the lightheadedness of someone very hungry, Wright made his way around them toward the toilet, the closest door he could close. He sat as long as he could, comparing the cracks in the room's plaster to the constellations he had taught himself, until someone knocked.

Back in the main room he saw that Randy, who had arrived in New York a day before them, was perched on an ottoman, his eyes mostly closed and his hand rubbing at the back of his head. Occasionally he glanced at Fay, who was still surrounded, and bit down on the insides of his cheeks, moved his splayed hands down his thighs and up again.

"Everything's all set," Annabelle was saying. "Randy and Fay and Oz and I will go around knocking on all doors. Everybody in this building is gone by eight thirty and until six. Leroy and Nadine, seven to seven. The Kiehlmans are on Long Island till Tuesday. Mr. Porter has nothing but work. We'll have it built by five absolute latest, in the building by eight."

It was the first time Shelter would target the living, a ball for returning military officers and their wives, and it was a debate he had heard Randy win over the course of months. Small remarks late at night, articles about increased armament taped to a dining table. Wright thought of the dresses, inverted flowers he'd only seen on snatches of television, how the tulle and silk would lift in the explosion. He took a pack of cigarettes from a nylon duffel collapsed by the door and he stepped outside, invisible and eleven. He hated the feeling in his throat when he smoked, and he felt he deserved it.

THE GIRL APPEARED FROM BETWEEN two cars, her nails badly painted and her hair ironed to a stiff point. She was somewhere between fourteen and sixteen, and he had never seen a pink bra through a poncho or a freckle on a bare hip. She asked for a cigarette and then a lighter and then for him to tell her if he recognized a bit of a song she had in her head and couldn't place. There was a protest in Washington Square and she wanted to know if he would go with her. She didn't ask to hold his hand. He was wondering about the street they were on, looking back at where they had turned from, trying to connect the roads in his head, but she told him it was the only part of the city, Greenwich Village, that wasn't on a grid. Wasn't that a trip? Also, she said, she was Brianna, and she knew right away she wanted to make it with him. It was an expression he was not familiar with but the meaning was vivid, because no one had ever held his hand like that, like she was trying to feel underneath the skin, to animate the bones there according to her wishes.

When they came up on the park he tried to locate it on the vague map he was drawing in his head, filling out the streets on the four sides. The crowd of people was livid and thick, broken only by the fountain and landscaping. To calm himself he looked through the triumphal arch that crowned it all. Garlands, eagles.

Brianna moved through the battery of people and kissed the ones she knew, a boy who almost cleared seven feet and wore necklaces down to his waist, a girl with feathers and dandelions sewn through her braids. She had not brought signs like the others, double-sided with messages. She did not shout, as the others did. Her long arm his leash, he made unheard apologies, tried to bend around the shapes of other people that seemed fixed. It was like they had been born there, the protesters, fossilized against the jostling of the police or the threat of bad weather. On their signs were photos of boys that were dead, boys that could have kissed them or thrown them baseballs, dripping numbers in red and blue that advertised the death tolls of the Vietnamese and Cambodians.

As they emerged from the crowd he found the world outside five degrees cooler, raked by wind. Brianna was shivering, the poncho and the holey jeans an attempt to expose herself that was working too well. Her skin was an amphibious blue, her posture and walk too open for the pace of the city around her. She had a friend's place where they could go, she was saying, where there would probably be a room for them, making these statements in a perfect imitation of innocence. He did not want to follow her, but because he could not articulate why, he still thought there would be a way to trick himself into the opposite feeling.

The apartment they soon entered was a close imitation of the one he had left, the people fifteen years younger but the accidental feeling of the place the same. He nearly didn't notice the two bent figures, so low were they to the ground, the beads of their spines evident even through their light sweaters, and he could not place the scent of whatever their Sterno on the floor was warming. He was still not accustomed to certain American smells, foods that listed polysyllabic ingredients, cheese that came in cans. Neither turned to greet them, just rotated their shoulders farther into the task. Brianna didn't acknowledge this, just gave him the smile of a person deep in a private, satisfying routine.

Directly past the boy and the girl was an unlit hallway, swaths of wallpaper falling down from the ceiling. The way they hung made him long for the jungle, the passageways of vines and webs and bromeliads. He had to remind himself that he would not return to his mother, would not give her that satisfaction, that he was here with this girl to do something that would separate him from Fay in a sense that he both could not imagine and knew would be permanent. "I have a good feeling about door number three," Brianna said, a laugh in her throat. She felt a pride, he could tell, in the run-down places she frequented, in how unfazed she was by any dark room. When she turned the knob she giggled and closed the door again, but not so quickly that he couldn't see the sallow bodies moving there, the man with his eyes closed and the woman on her hands and knees.

He was five feet and three inches when he walked into the next room, where Brianna pulled out a matchbook and four tea candles she had jammed into her shallow macrame purse. There was nothing on the floor but an empty Coke can and a newspaper laid to cover a spill and a cot, which was mottled brown and white and yellow. "I bet I can find us a sheet," she said, and he waited in a squat with his eyes closed, a position his mother prescribed for calm, feeling the grit of the floor through the thinning soles of his sneakers. He wished she hadn't lit the candles. He didn't need to see this place, didn't want to remember it.

She returned with an uninviting bundle, an old attempt at white or beige, and she spread it over the cushion. Somewhere in the place there was music, warped, at first only the refrain coming to him. *What I really want to know is—* She lay there while she took off her Lee denim, her floral bra. There was no underwear to be removed and he was still squatting and he thought her pubic hair looked too stiff and she was waiting for him, calling him baby—"Come here, baby, I've thought of you all day." He was helpless against the command and he crawled next to her, his back to her face, shivering. She moved her hands over the down jacket he was still wearing and unzipped it, she undid each of the five buttons on his jeans, she slipped a hand across his abdomen and then she stopped. *Has he taken any time to show you what you need to live?* Wright was not responding correctly, tightening instead of loosening, and he could feel her calculating, calling other cases to mind.

"I don't think," he said.

"You know what I'm going to do," Brianna whispered. "I'm just going to put my hand there. I'm just going to put my hand there until you want it to be there." As her fingers cupped him, firm but unmoving, the smell of the room, resin and malt liquor, began to leave him. He started to feel that part of him stutter, then fall back, then move closer to her hand. It wanted to fill her fingers, to force the grip apart. She said there you go, and then she turned him onto his back. He could hear the wick of the candle crackling as she licked her hand and brought it between her legs. As she slid onto him he tried to think, begged himself to think, to come up with a reason why a part of his body would agree to something he did not want. She was hideous on top of him, all her bad teeth revealed, the peach hair that covered most of her thin ribcage frightening, her face contorting like she was trying to get rid of a stain. That their bodies were connected made him feel he should not observe her in this way, that finding her ugly made him uglier, so he closed his eyes. She moved for a while longer like that, rubbing forward in a kind of violence, the sounds she made no different from those of anger, his body in hers a problem she was going to eliminate, and then he lost feeling in his left calf and his right. His eyes had only been open a second when it all went hot, then numb, then black.

HE LEFT WHILE BRIANNA WAS using the bathroom, leaping over someone who had fallen asleep near the entryway, running on the balls of his feet. He was on the street in under thirty seconds, then taking every turn he could, stopping only to retie his shoes, his urgency foreign in this area where people seemed only to sit on benches and smoke. "What's the rush, little man," someone yelled, to the laughter of an audience Wright couldn't see, "trying to get your balls to drop?"

He'd been panting ten minutes when moody starts of rain began beading the back of his neck, and he knew she couldn't be chasing him, that she'd taken the part of him she wanted, so he climbed up a stoop and stood under the awning, mostly convinced he did not belong on this planet, considering ways he might die. It was of great comfort, imagining this, the subway car oncoming or the river meeting him as he fell at great speed, all thoughts he'd ever had erased, and soon his heart rate had returned to normal. He began to enjoy the rain, how it forced all these people into cafés and bars and revealed the city to him. His legs outstretched, he bent his toes in their murky nylon toward him, newly resolved. Fay could do whatever she wanted, but he would enjoy these cities where she had dragged him, their canopied boulevards, the light coming off their buildings. He wasn't going to hide in those rooms.

He was patting his hair back in place, counting the change in his pockets, when he noticed the van he recognized as Annabelle's rolling very slowly toward him. The engine was still running, the sound like some animal huffing deeper in its search, when Randy and a man he didn't know emerged, taking the steps two at a time.

17.

Randy was in the passenger seat and he never looked back at Wright or Fay, only occasionally at the man driving the car, who never, in the next three hours of traffic and country, fiddled with a radio knob or cracked a window or said a word. The evidence of Annabelle was everywhere, the turquoise dream catcher hanging from the rearview and the crate of typewriter ribbons and the tip of the gun that he saw sliding from under the front seat, but Annabelle was not living. Neither was Oz. That was the only information given him when he entered the car, where his mother's hair, tied up in a bun, fell over her forehead at sudden stops. "Don't forget to tell him about the neighbor," Randy said. "A fucking teacher, for chrissakes, Fay, a black man, how does that look?"

"We made a mistake" was all she would say, a hand light on Wright's knee but her eyes affixed to the traffic.

"Are you going to do it, or should I," Randy said, once they'd cleared city lines.

"I promise we're doing this for your own safety," his mother said as she slipped the blindfold over him. The only sounds for the rest of the drive were the voices of tollbooth operators, fifty-five cents, the shifting of gears, the drift of food wrappers and stray pennies migrating under the three rows of seats.

Even at dusk he could see that the A-frame cabin where they arrived was unsuited to their circumstance, serene to the point of parody, a place where a tree bloomed pink needles out front and a three-legged cat roamed the grounds with its simple mewling wish. Someone, of the many who received the Shelter newsletters that Annabelle and Fay typed in capital letters, who had cheered at the destruction of courthouse lobbies and Pentagon bathrooms, had taken pity on them.

Knowing he wouldn't get an answer, he didn't ask where they were. He didn't know the name of the man who'd been driving, but when they were all out of the car Wright watched him stretch, his right heel up on the bumper of the VW and his long fingers around his toes. Fay and Randy stood just behind him, quiet like they never were, their eyes seeing no farther than the foot in front of them. His mother cradled a brown paper lunch sack and he could see some gingham and cotton protruding from it, his favorite blue T-shirt, incongruous as a wound. The driver continued to sigh, bringing his arms above him in a V, twisting at his waist, rotating his ankles, jogging in place, unaware or unconcerned that they all had nothing to do but watch him. He stopped and turned and they followed him up the cement walk, which was littered with the rosy debris of the tree, and then on the porch they waited as he felt along the inner sides of the eaves, grunting at the reach. When the key took and the door heaved inward, they heard the flick of a switch and the tinks of filaments, and then they followed him into the spill of light.

HE WOKE UP AS HE had fallen asleep, his mother's body enclosing him from multiple angles, her ankles crossed around his and her left arm running from his hipbone to his shoulder. She had begun to cry, the night before, when he had stiffened at her touch. He was looser now, the morning coming through a cracked window, and comforted by her smell, the tea tree oil and rosewater, until he reminded himself he shouldn't be. He extricated his arms and legs and stood barefoot, surveying the cabin. The room held two identical beds, the frames old and high and metal, and on the wall between them hung a shadowy watercolor of a tree grown through a window. Randy was asleep in the other, his lips an inch from the wall, his low-heeled boots still on.

It had been weeks since he'd been alone in any quiet, and he was relieved, as he entered the main room, by the sight of the driver still sleeping, his arm dangling from a pale blue love seat. In a small kitchen in the rear of the place, he pushed aside the white linen curtains that fell over some inlaid shelving, picking up and turning pickled lemons and beets, mason jars of sugar and flour and corn-meal. There was muesli labeled in neat capitals, and a white-and-red-checked cloth over a tiny table he set it on. Milk in a hip-high fridge, the glass jug unlabeled, a thick layer of cream on the surface. A passing car honked and screamed around a curve, and he heard everyone in the cabin begin to groan and shift.

Soon his mother was near him, her hair down again, with a prosthetic cheer and a hand on his neck. "Alan tells me there's some beautiful hiking just up the road," she said. "A series of waterfalls, and it's ten degrees hotter today than yesterday. Doesn't that seem lucky?"

He would not speak but he nodded. It was months too early to swim, a few lives removed from one that was lucky. They were out the door in ten minutes, the driver left behind looking over a map, Randy trailing a few feet behind, aphasic and chain-smoking. They ducked around a bend in a rusted link fence and then they were on the loamy trail, the insistent sound of the current a kind of permission for the fact they would not talk.

When they came to the first, some of the rocks black and slick and some disguised in verdant moss, the cascade of mountain water dropping into a clear pool, he felt joy but wanted to redact it. Her face open with hope, she watched him, and he stared her down until her mouth closed and her head bowed. They kept walking, the three of them, each separated from the next by about eight feet, enough that they could not see each other around a bend and the sound of their footsteps was eaten by the violence of the water. There was less moisture in the air by the minute. Wright removed the sweatshirt he'd been wearing for forty-eight hours and tied it around his waist. They passed two more waterfalls, each falling from a greater height, each pool deeper and wider.

At the fourth pool, all narrows and shadows, he stopped. On either side, just above the surface of the water, slick plates of rock shot out, leaving only a foot-wide corridor. At the widest point, near where the flow from above terminated, was a granite shelf—and he saw he could begin sitting there and let the force of the current shoot him free. Some of the trees were still without leaves.

"You shouldn't let him fucking do that," he heard Randy say. "That current is nasty. Probably forty-five degrees."

When Fay caught up his shirt was already off, hung on the branch of a tree, his fifty-cent thrift store jeans next to it. As Wright felt his way along the rock wall, right foot over left, he heard her voice, a chirped admonition that she began but gave up on, and then he was near where the water would push him, and then he was shoved off, charging down the path the world gave him, breaking surface and seeing only when it allowed him to, the shock of the cold a very real threat that kept him from breathing.

At its slimmest the way through was only twice as wide as he was and he went planklike in fear. The water deposited him twenty feet downriver, and he heaved himself onto the flat and warm stone, gasping and coughing. He had wanted her to watch the violence of it but she was already gone. That he could hear Fay and Randy shouting—he would not let it matter, he thought, because he did not love these people. His attention, from now on, his study, would lie elsewhere. The shape of his life, when he could finally control it, would not include them.

"You just couldn't let me," he heard Fay say. "Had to—"

Randy's voice came in low and tight, every word bitten off with the least possible effort.

"—on your own trip, little girl. Not my ego that peacocked and killed our comrades."

Wright pecked his way back up along the rocks, thinking up a future for himself, a split-level house and a piece of chalk he gestured with before a room of students, and when he reached his mother she was squatting with her head between her knees, wobbling as she keened. At the sound of his approach she looked up, her features remade into a face he didn't recognize, starved, toothy, patched with red.

"Is it my fault they died," she said, her eyes rooting around in his as though solace were something that could be stolen.

She must understand I was not there, he thought, and then, seeing the way her hands crossed to hold her own shoulders, he knew that she would have asked anybody, any animal. In that minute she did not have a son.

Maybe he heard Randy hustling down the path already, maybe Wright knew he'd be listening for the cars on the country road, putting together a story, arranging his hips at forty-five degrees and this thumb at ninety. Later Wright believed he had. His mother never heard from him again, that man who had spent that first night in Ecuador with her and each after that, returning only once to the room where he'd been living with his few cheap things.

18.

He thought he had become used to the meals one could gather in the aisles of gas stations, but the next two months played out on another frequency, each day distinct from the one before, presenting another set of challenges. In the first week they had a borrowed car, a loan from a member of Shelter who was still communicating with her, and Wright watched Fay's hands, always at ten and two, the speedometer at exactly the legal limit. When they managed to get to one of the houses where Fay once would have been welcomed, it was silent, barbed, the people drifting through the rooms shaking their heads and sighing, kitchen to living to bath, bath to living to kitchen, as though on the track of some children's railroad set. There were no books open, no maps spread. There was never the smell of food.

Soon they were hitchhiking, Fay lying as much as necessary. They were on their way to a commune, New Mexico, The Last Resort, or they were traveling to an aunt with pancreatic cancer, her remaining days in the double digits, and their Greyhound had broken down. Wright couldn't see how they presented, he and his mother, but they must have given off some smell of misfortune, because people seemed quick to pity them, to stop asking the questions with the sad answers.

Then it became clear, at a motel where a clerk with no front teeth asked why Wright wasn't in school and why she looked familiar, that something had changed, closing the world to them. A photo of her, scavenged from an article about Charlie and the bar, had appeared in the papers that morning, alongside a photo of Randy in uniform and the two deceased members of Shelter and the black schoolteacher their bomb had killed, a man who had died because he stayed home with the flu. The network of pay phones went largely unanswered, and the statement, sent to fifty-six newspapers, was of a different tone. Randy's name appeared beneath it.

We of Shelter are devastated by the loss of an innocent life and of our comrades. We are forced to reconsider our violent ideology, which we developed with the belief that we could enact change. We thought that by mirroring, on a small level, the way this country has treated others, by meeting shock and terror with shock and terror, we might as a nation begin to rethink our identity and become a more compassionate force in the global community. We were wrong, and now we are quiet, and we will remain that way for the foreseeable future.

She read it in sunglasses at a concrete table at a rest stop. They were between rides, having terminated the last early, a man who had asked if she was saved in a way that felt like a threat. She took out a pen and an envelope. He saw her parents' names printed in capitals, the addressor listed as Bess Rainy, but he refused to ask her why she was writing to them after so many years without a call. Her secrets held no interest anymore, and the thought of his grandparents, how she'd removed them from her life, made him silent. He would run toward the things he knew she'd rejected—a room kept neatly in your honor, photos that described you becoming yourself.

FAY NEVER SPOKE OF RANDY and Wright never asked, though there was a certain face she made that Wright sensed was a thought of him, her lips parted and eyebrows reaching for each other. The conversation she made was benign, remote, never impeached by the events of the last six months. I wonder what type of tree that is, she would say. Do you think the people who designed cars meant to suggest a human face with the headlights, the grill, or was it a function of the subconscious? Do you like the red that house is painted, or does it remind you of a stoplight? He knew they were running out of Charlie's money, knew that Randy had run off with half of what Fay had saved, because they were camping more and more, sometimes in state parks where Wright surveyed the other families, the Coleman coolers and rigid bedtimes, sometimes on farmland off the highway, places they ended up when they were tired of holding out their thumbs. Where are we going, he would ask her, not because he believed there was an answer but to communicate his total disdain. After a man with a shotgun had unzipped their tent and spit on its fly and given them one minute to go, somewhere in Pennsylvania, Wright offered to turn her in.

"I could do it for you," he said.

They were following a two-lane country road, barely lifting their feet to make the next steps.

"Here she is, Officer, the white woman who rejected her general luck and wealth to become an amateur bomb builder and inadvertently kill a teacher. She didn't mean to, she just wanted to impress the creepy radical she was fucking, I'm not sure which one."

They didn't speak for the two miles into the next town. The only event was a truck passing, its expulsion of air examining their dime-store T-shirts stiff with sweat. When she pulled her fifth cigarette from the box he asked her for one, feeling with some satisfaction that he could hate her for either response—if she agreed for the heresy of not treating him like a child, if she denied him for the hypocrisy of casting him as an adult. He was only a step or two behind her, close enough that he could press the tip of his sneaker down the back of her heel, which he did. After a minute she lit another one on hers and passed it back. In a café where the water-damaged wallpaper was a faded sixties pattern of interlocking flowers, in a town with three stoplights and a bar called Father's, she went through the classifieds with a pen and circled the cars for sale nearby. It was an apology, he understood that, an ill-advised risk she would undertake in the name of his peace. If the person on the other end of the ad did not look at her too long, they would have four doors they could lock. She left him in the booth with instructions not to leave and was back in two hours, keys in her fist.

Her seat belt threaded too tight across her chest, the rasping sedan struggling when she steered it onto the highway, she turned off the radio he had turned on.

"None of this was as I expected it," she said. "You have to forgive me."

He straightened his spine and sucked his cigarette and looked into the moon.

"There is nothing I *have* to do," he said. "You taught me that."

THERE WAS A BEAUTIFUL LIE of a month in which she found a job, a home aide to a blind woman in West Virginia, and they resumed some version of their life in a rotting carriage house transfigured by kudzu. On a porch that looked at an anemic stream, Fay set full pots of coffee on a milk crate and he pointed out birds from his dog-eared guide. She spoke to him glancingly about quantum mechanics, the difference between serpentine and alluvial soil. Before long a visiting cousin showed up and looked too long at Fay. She told Wright, at ten that night in the bed they shared, they'd be leaving at sunrise.

"You're one of those atoms," he said, refusing to get up the next morning, speaking to her from under the sheets. "Exactly. You don't exist except for when other people look at you, and that's why we're in this position." She spent an hour kneeling there, trying to touch his hands, his face, whispering.

The cousin in question saw her carrying him kicking through the pink light, and the blind woman heard what he yelled, an adult profanity. "Who is that," she said, groping to turn on a lamp, an old reflex. In the evenings he had rubbed the pads of her feet as she listened to the TV, described to her the faces of the soap opera actors.

Cunt, he had screamed. She could not believe it was the same boy.

SITTING IN THE FRONT SEAT of the car a month later, reading the newspaper she had sent Wright into the gas station to buy, Fay learned about a bomb in the bathroom of the New York State Department of Corrections, an admonishment to a system that had killed three rioting prisoners. As she scanned the article again, as if looking for her own name, she pulled at the yellow foam coming free from the ceiling. The second explosion came not long after, the Capitol.

They had reorganized, the communiqués appearing in the newspaper populated with the phrases she had so often spoken. Far from telling her she had been blamed, they would not tell her anything. From the silent car he watched her dial in the roadside phone booths, boxes of light that appeared like projections onto the dark margins of gravel, standing with one foot flat on the opposite thigh. Her face opened when someone picked up one of the numbers she'd memorized, but it was always another forgotten person, waiting for word from an old life, asking her please to get off the line. Then, one day, an answer, a message—he could tell by the way her hair fell around the phone and her shoulders crawled forward. She pulled a pen from behind her ear and wrote on her hand.

19.

1972

Her mouth open as she worked the tweezers in the motel bathroom mirror, her son in the next room sleeping ragged through a sinus infection, she removed her eyelashes one by one. It had been a year, more. She wanted to hang it on her vanity, the explosion, and was telling herself the story of that. On the counter was a twist-tied bag of sea salt she had bought for him to gargle with, in the garbage can the four Band-Aids she'd excised from her feet, pea green and puce, detritus of a lost battle. There were the blisters, then the fungal infection she had developed in her toenails, something she tried to hide from him. Some were half an inch thick and crumbled like old pastry.

A feeling of cleanliness now lasted a minute, less. Even the drip of water down her back seemed to know something about her, what she'd done, who was dead. Of all people, a schoolteacher with the flu. It was possible not only her physical health had been compromised, she admitted. Her hand had brushed away cockroaches from places they were not. The old thoughts of suicide had returned, a little changed, fantasies that more resembled memories in how long they went—it was as if she could remember killing herself, but also the placidity of the world after, how her leaving had bettered it.

She removed them one by one, the only light the pale three P.M. gray that came in through the window. The idea was to transfer the fear of people looking at her onto them, make them afraid of staring too long. In the foyer of the last diner she'd been brave enough to enter, the poster of her face was a nightmare that swelled in tinny horror when she saw it also included him, his passport photo, age nine and a half. He had looked for most of his life like someone just stolen from sleep.

Freed from her eyelids, they fell to the wan pink of the plastic and curled there. A lifetime ago or two, on the high wooden benches of Union Station, her mother holds a palm out to her, the little black comma upon it, and asks her to wish.

With her top right lid done, she blinked once to clear away any she'd missed and began on the bottom.

Her thin feet flat on the cold floor, she stands in the center of the circle of Randy and Oz and Annabelle and the others. *Do you think because you're beautiful you will be an exception?*

Her son had not spoken to her in seventy-two hours, and the last word he'd said was *no*. The question she'd posed him was *How can I make this time more tolerable for you?* She had not talked with her sister in almost seven years, a fact that did not feel separate from the fact that Charlie had been dead for five. If she were brave enough, she thought, if she were limitless in feeling, some communication would be possible anyway. Their last conversation had ended in a kind of threat—*Call me when you're sober*—and Charlie never did, maybe never was. The second movement of grief was less violent, a feeling of stupidity that barked occasionally at the fence it couldn't cross. In the year since the explosion, she had carried Charlie's letters everywhere and reread them in empty bathtubs, marking up lines and paragraphs as though to make the message new. Her sister waves from her horse, she underhands a can across the pool.

One whole eye lashless, she felt the child's pride in taking a punishment without upset. Here are her parents, a look exchanged across folded hands, shocked by how little it bothers her to be sent to her room. Being alone had never frightened her enough: she had never outright believed what the world would have her, that she was measured by who she was to other people. That was vanity, too, she thought, her eyes weeping at the pain now—her belief that she was an invention of herself alone.

She had said, to the reedy male voice on the phone, that she would have to think about it, although she knew she had no better option. She was interested in what they could want from her in the way she might be in a shop window, a fantasy constructed in her absence, adjustments in tone and color already made. The Shelter member who'd relayed the details had offered few, then hung up—a name that was unfamiliar, an organization she hadn't heard of because it had not, until very recently, existed. She had waited four days to call, or two, what constituted a day now transformed by the parentheses of sleep that had become irregular.

No, Wright had said, an answer less to what she had asked and more to his whole life, his feeling about it. *Going to disappear,* he had whispered in his sleep one night, a threat that frightened her so much she had turned on all the lights and the television.

Her eyes done, she began on her brows. It was not for other people—that was a lie. She could recognize them more quickly now, the parts of her thinking that were designed to appease.

It was not for other people. It was for herself, it was to be kept from mirrors. It was to remind her how ugly she was. She remembered his wife speaking the word, by the pool of the inn. Elise turns to her, smoke pouring from her mouth. *Can you imagine what this does to mirrors?*

She had not known she was going to call until the moment appeared, ripe, easier than the alternative of stepping back outside into the winter. A pay phone inside a heated garage, just visible through the door behind the gas station cash register, the mechanic, in a T-shirt improbably white, who, when she asked, spread a burnished hand and welcomed her back.

Inside the booth the plastic was milky, on the blond wood bench a slight recession, the place where people had gripped it while they called home to report on the cost of the damages. She believed the receiver would ignite when she spoke her name. The men who'd come for her were inevitable, and she imagined them all day, Navy uniforms moving toward her in formation.

"This is Fay," she said. It had been four months or six since she'd spoken it.

"We're so glad to hear from you," the voice said. Already the conversation was familiar, the confidence of the synecdoche, the young man speaking slowly for many. Their long acronym he explained to her with a green zeal that put her in mind of her age— she was thirty-three, older than she had ever imagined becoming. Her fantasy of herself had concluded.

They wanted to populate the last Apollo launch, he said, with images of the people who had suffered under the American hegemony. Vietnamese children, women who wasted their lives as men's secretaries, the assassinated members of the Black Panthers, the students slain at Kent State.

"We are against racism and repression," he said. "We are against misogyny and capitalism and war."

"How about plastics," she said.

"What?"

"Are you against those, too? Hundreds of years to degrade, some of them never. Might be room for one more letter in your title. Tack a *P* on there."

He did not laugh and she did not apologize. There was the phrase *smash the era that failed us,* there was her imagination of how he looked as he spoke, crossing an austere apartment, books the only clutter, his slim finger purple with the cord wrapped around it. There would be other people in unraveling sweaters, mouths open as if to indicate what he said to her came from their mouths, too. She did not mention how he and the young people who admired him were not the first to make this connection, between the war on this world and the spectacular fight for others. The black reverend who had marched with two hundred people and twenty mule-drawn carts to Vincent's launch, the signs about how the program money could be spent.

"We want you to be the face," he said, "to give the talk. We were inspired by your early work in Ecuador. It could only be you," he said. "What we need is an icon."

She did not point out the contradiction, the space between *only* and *an*.

There were three weeks until the launch. She asked for time. The mechanic, glancing at her occasionally when he emerged from inside a propped hood, mimed a flapping mouth with his hand and grinned, misunderstanding the look on her face for some domestic exasperation. In return she waved, high and tight, which she knew was not quite the right gesture. She had been too long removed from the codex of them, the small things people did with their bodies to signal respect for each other. The weather out there, the smell inside, the danger ahead.

That had been five days before, a number she was certain about. Time had tightened for her again, snapped into efficiency under what she was going to do. She had turned her curiosity toward an end and it was an incredible comfort, warm, forgiving of everything that had led to it.

The faucet running, she swiped a wet hand towel along the counter until it was clean. Back in the room, all she wanted was to crawl into the tight cheap bedding and sleep with her son, but she knew she needed to be awake when he saw what she'd done to herself, to explain it. The bigger piece of your promise as a mother was your ability to interpolate, rush before the oncoming menace and explain the ways its shadow was shorter than it seemed. Of course, she was the thing with the shadow now, the threat to be explained. Without the frame of lashes surrounding them, the slate of her eyes took on the quality of something abandoned to the elements, part the color of what they were but more the color of what they saw. Waiting, she left the television off, the curtains drawn, the water that fell from her body where it pooled.

He woke up twenty minutes after the sun went down, his eyes adjusting to the change in light at the same time they adjusted to the change to her face. Two hours had passed and she could barely explain what she'd done to herself, now, let alone Wright. In the first years of his life, her parents had often mentioned how strange it was—that he did not really resemble her.

"You're out of your mind," he said, passing a hand over his face in an adult way she had not taught him. From the dresser he took her rollies and a violet plastic lighter and stepped outside, a book under his arm, almost thirteen and a person without her. She said nothing when she passed him on the balcony, just handed him the hat he'd forgotten.

On the way to the pay phone she looked in the rooms she could, gnarled feet crossed daintily on the made beds, shirts thrown over lamps to make the light another color. She descended a set of freestanding steps, concrete fixed with glitter, like so much of the country both hideous and unremarkable.

"Yes," she said to the voice on the phone. Fay believed she could see his hand, how it brought the others in the room closer to the receiver. In the news that had not stopped reading, the polls were clear. The majority of Americans were for withdrawal, and of those who disapproved of the war, the great part disapproved of people like her. In the month between Philadelphia and New York they had received a letter from a priest imprisoned for burning draft cards, a man with a face so long and noble that his pacifist message seemed painted on it. He worried Shelter had become what it wanted to eradicate. *Shouldn't a revolution,* he had written, *differ vastly, in action and feeling, from the forces it hopes to dismantle?* Annabelle, in the days before she died, had mocked it, quoting it with her hands folded behind her back in the way of a clergyman.

In the year since the bomb, Fay had taken to speaking their names aloud, Oz, Annabelle, Charlie. *What did you say,* her son had whispered, any time he heard this, as bitter about her degeneration as he was afraid.

The metal cord snaking around her wrist, she watched a man by the vending machines push his forearm up inside it to a Snickers that was caught. What Fay planned to do she did not tell them, then or ever. She would be part of their message and distinct from it. The voice on the phone began to talk about the speech she would deliver, and she alluded to the safety of the line.

Under all thoughts, her son. In leaving hers, she would give him his life.

20.

For the first time in his life, Vincent Kahn kept irregular hours, sometimes remaining in bed until the light thickened into the shadow play of midmorning. The future yawned before him, bored with his misery, sick of his preoccupation with the zero-gravity simulations that had taken place underwater, the *Life* photos of Bisson grilling, the release of their collected piss into the black of space. *What's the most beautiful thing you saw?* A reporter to Jeanie. *Urine dump at sunset.* Laughter that locked everyone else out.

The time that lay ahead had no investment in him, and he had no interest in it. He paid the boy who delivered his newspapers to deliver his groceries, too, always the same, leave them 'round the side of the house, if they're out of something don't call to ask after a substitute, just use your judgment. Campbell's tomato soup, eggs, milk, hot dogs, Cream of Wheat. His body was no longer intrigued by the smell or heat of food, and it took him an hour, sometimes, to shovel in a meal, the dish growing cold on the table of puckered magazines and coupon circulars.

In the days after their launch there had been the quarantine, the scientists in hazmat suits taking samples of their skin and blood and hair and piss, two weeks of it, and then they were released into the circus of publicity, the violently confettied parades where he kept his mouth closed so as not to swallow any of it, the press conferences, the microphones coming for him from every angle, the handshakes with their soundtrack of a flashbulb's fizz. It was over in six months.

NASA had offered him a job in administration, a sort of waiting room for whatever the next conquest might be, and he lasted less than ninety days there. The funding was cut, the landings no longer televised, the last of the Apollo missions to be canceled, and he had no confidence that his appointment in a corner office would ever become anything else. He could not wait twenty years there for a pension, getting pains in his neck from bending over paperwork, his legs asleep under the desk, all for the salary of any middling government employee. There had been no party when he left, no card passed around. He had walked to his car, already packed with the few things he was taking, and driven straight to Ohio, leaving behind his home with a realtor, Elise in her new marriage.

She had left him in the fall of 1970, made the announcement in the morning and spent the afternoon stocking the fridge with heat-up meals in Tupperware. Two weeks' worth, she said, but Vincent stretched it to four.

He was a policeman, a widower with blond twins. People called him chief and he called them sport.

Vincent returned to his home state and took a house near his mother's. Two bedrooms, east-facing windows, a kitchenette. With his father dead she was thrilled with all the tasks Vincent's return afforded her, the *House Beautiful*s to be pored over and the casseroles to be delivered. She was the only one who rang his doorbell. He had accepted a job at the university an hour away and taught two classes a week, his body turned almost exclusively toward the chalkboard. At the beginning of the semester he made it clear that no questions about his past work would be acknowledged, and he instructed those who showed up to his office hours and asked anyway to drop the class. After a spring and a fall he had typed up a letter of resignation and slipped it, the eight-by-eleven envelope, in the department head's cubby, working it a little so that the edges of it were flush with the diagonal corners. *Good night and good luck,* he said to the three secretaries whose desks stretched from the front of the room to the back, but he didn't stay to watch their three chins tip up, to hear their chairs swivel as they began to whisper.

There were so many intricate nightmares that Vincent felt he deserved, but they never arrived. Instead he dreamed of the mission's minutiae, details that became, the moment they parachuted into the Pacific, men with the defining moment of their life now behind them, totally and forever irrelevant. He dreamed of the typed labels on the medical kit that hung like a calendar—DIARRHEA STIMULANT SLEEPING PAIN ASPIRIN ASPIRIN ASPIRIN. The object that was both scoop and tong, the solid bucket and the metal teeth poised over it, reminiscent of a whisk sawed in half; the notepad that snapped onto his knee with a leather strap, ensuring no aberration went undocumented; the Hasselblad cameras mounted on poles like birdhouses, the shutters activated by triggers they pulled with their thickly gloved fingers. There was a tiny bag of shark repellent. There was a tin box that promised to desalt the ocean, make it drinkable. There was the Omega Speedmaster, the miles moving up around the rim as the faces in miniature, thirty seconds, ten, encircled by the regular hands of hour and minute, ticked down.

He dreamed of all this but almost never of what happened in real air on earth, the relationships and the stopgap homes that he had tried to grow into sideways. Never of being a husband, the arguments across their oaken dining table, never of being a child, the small voices of his parents beckoning him back from the paper airplanes he flew through the wind tunnels he'd built—fans and cardboard boxes. His sleep wouldn't consider the flat of the country, the trolley cars trundling through cities, the rideable lawn mowers purchased on installment plan.

HE HAD ENTERED THE TIME, so long fought for, when he was truly alone. There were no parties, no silk bow ties that he could feel against his larynx when he spoke. It was not beyond him that his present solitude was made possible by the vestigial *Life* money, by every moment he had allowed a camera into his friendship or marriage. He spent the mornings reading, biographies and accounts by naturalists in parts of the world he'd seen only in parades, and the afternoons at his first aviation school, flying old routes in planes that shuddered at any change like some abused animal. He had loved them first and wanted to again, but he heard himself curse— like flying a secondhand vacuum. That he could have traveled so far from the boy he'd been, bicycling out there to pay for his lessons with his saved-up coins in a knotted handkerchief—the flights made him aware of every knot along his spine, every potential cavity and source of arthritis.

If her face came up on the news, still wanted, still missing, he changed the channel. He thought of her as an expression of his own unhappiness in California, an unwise purchase he'd been lucky enough to pay off. Even commercials were beautiful now, and there was one he liked particularly, a life insurance ad that followed a red rubber ball on its long bounce from a child's hands on a lawn to a father's lap by a fireplace. He had dreamt once of the man she'd killed, the schoolteacher, that he'd been with Vincent on the mission but refused to check the time.

21.

He woke thinking he heard birds nesting in the motel room. In his gray briefs he pushed aside the curtains, roughly starched on a warped plastic track, but there was nothing behind them—the same parking lot, a big rig painted with bubbles and the slogan IT'S THE REAL THING, a gas station with a scrolling marquee whose last numeral had stuck between six and seven. Behind flimsy pocket doors, the closet's hangers stayed secured to the rod by loops, the shelves above them still empty. A radio, he thought, a television in the next room, but when he stepped into the hall the sound faded.

It was coming from the bathroom. He placed the pads of his fingers on the door, which sat a full inch above the wan tile, and slipped in. The chirps were coming from inside the walls, he thought, perhaps behind the shower where the mold had been painted over. In the fan built in to the ceiling, through the radial swirls of plastic that would animate at the flip of a switch, he could see little bits of dried grass and plastic, hear the squabbles of adjustment. He tried to explain it to himself, how they were laid there, how the mother had left them. A hole in the roofing she had flown through, the gap soon patched so she couldn't return.

There was only one switch, light and fan. He looked down at his shoes, the duct tape wrapped around the balls of his feet to cover a hole. Sitting on the rim of the bathtub, he began to pull it free, the adhesive trailing behind the silver in protest, the shape of the ribbon becoming warped. When he was done he tore off smaller pieces with his teeth, tasting the bits of stiff dirt and concrete that had made their way in, and then he began to cover the plastic rectangle that held the little lever, isolating its position at thirty degrees, hardening it there, pressing his fingers along the edges of the tape with his full weight. How long would it buy them, keep the blades off? Three days, a week, depending on the guests to come, how indifferent they were to their surroundings, how clearly they wanted to see their nipples and beer guts and crow's-feet.

He stood with his hands on the pink vinyl counter, appraising himself in the mirror in the low six P.M. light. A child still, he thought, removing his shirt and watching the demure curve of his shoulders as though they might fill with musculature as he evaluated them, reflect what he had done with Brianna, what she had forced him to do. That she had fucked him had not allowed Wright to enter some new version of himself, only made it clear how far he was from the one he needed.

His hand on her jaw, he sat on his mother's bed. All he wanted was to tell her about the predicament of the birds, see her face turn at the injustice of it. She smiled in a way that felt alien, as though the teeth and lips had received inadequate instruction, and took his fingers. That she had removed her eyelashes was a fact he declined to acknowledge further, knowing there would be some symbol she saw in it and would ask him to consider.

When she'd returned that evening he had refused to look her way, locked his jaw and raised a straight arm, the remote a seamless addition at the tip of his fingers, to the television. *The Price Is Right* baffled him completely, the prerequisite knowledge of the things you had already bought to guess at the value of the things you might win. Money, in America, was a party you entered and could not leave. The longer you stayed, the more you imagined the happiness to be found on the other side of the room, if you could just work your away across.

"There's a protest I want to attend," she said now, speaking as slowly as she had when disciplining him as a toddler. "It has nothing to do with Shelter, though they reached me through them. You'll be glad to know that. The invitation came in some days ago but I wanted to sit with it awhile."

He waited, his bowels turning over, for the thing she was concealing to show itself in some euphemism, for the faltering in her careful phrasing. She had called Shelter *a collective focused on change,* Randy *a boy whose life was taken from him,* his missing finger dexterity sacrificed to condemn one. There was always, with her, some gauzy lingual veil fallen over the truth, some other conversation taking place on the inside of the words he could actually hear.

"It's a demonstration to take place at the launch of the last Apollo mission, organized by some brilliant college students who see the country's space program as a distraction from the systemic abuse and disenfranchisement of so many. They want to form that association in the public's mind."

"How," he said. He wanted the truth while she had no acolytes to defend it, no distractions to offer him, no other room to enter.

She was sitting up now, cross-legged, her hands spread across her knees. She spoke with the fidgety air of an expert, pushing some hair behind her ear, rotating a raised palm for emphasis, like someone explaining a procedure that had become a simple matter of muscle memory. Just a talk, she was saying, just a supplement to the images the group would provide, of the people forgotten by the American spectacle.

He was silent now, as distant from her as he could be, in the far corner of the room with his forehead resting in the wedge. Only faintly, under the sound of all the blood in his body pounding in his ears, could he hear the room.

"I'm not coming," he said.

"America has to see what it has done to its future," she said, weakly, for the first time he could remember not convinced by her own rhetoric.

"Who are you talking to? Who do you think is recording this right now, *its future*? We're two people in a very bad motel in Georgia, and I'm not its future. I'm just your son. That I'd gladly give up."

"I know that. I understand that, how I've failed you. I want to free you of this. I want you to become who you are. I've been in touch with your grandparents, and they say they'll take you. They live on a hill in California. I was pregnant with you there. We grew tomatoes together, you and I, we fed chickens. You'll recognize it."

"Recognize it. I'm sure that feels nice to believe."

"Come with me."

"No."

"You would do it knowing you had a new life ahead of you. A gas stove, a Labrador, oil landscapes on the walls. Clean laundry every Sunday. Starched. They are nothing like me, my parents. They would always be the same. Will you come?"

"What happened to how you felt about me? What happened to 'you'll be teaching me, my love'?"

"Do you want to live like this any longer? Coin-operated beds, a hospital if either of us needed it out of the question?"

He knew she was talking to herself now and he let her, his face only changing with the colors of the television he'd got up and turned on again. Verdigris. Cyan. Ancient, modern red.

"The moment it's over you'll be free to go. If I sent you now you'd be recognized on your way, if I sent you now it might keep me from this. Will you come?"

ON THE BUS TO FLORIDA he told her about the birds trapped in the fan's chamber, the bits of duct tape he had repurposed. Her eyes went glassy and her palms opened, and she looked as she had by the waterfalls, between then and now so many days where nothing was said, a winter that had left them both with a bronchitic cough.

"That's so kind," she said. "Your compassion is an indelible part of you."

"They'll die anyway. They'll starve."

Late the night before, after she begged him, squatting, *I need you to come,* stroking his head, *this way America might learn what it needs to,* leaning her spine against his when he turned again to the corner, *the very last time,* looping a forefinger around his big toe, *I can't make it there without you,* rubbing the lobe of his ear, he had assented.

Ahead of and behind them were people who looked like they had been passengers all their lives, waiting for the time they were told they could eat or sleep. A half hour into the ride the bus swerved to miss the gnarled metal debris of an accident. Fay gasped and put her hands to the ceiling, but Wright only looked down the aisle of thinning purple carpet, his sight on the windshield broad and high.

22.

The last letter Claudette and James got from their daughter advised that they keep their television off on a certain evening, and on this point, for perhaps the first time since Fay had been a ballerina in a crown of milk braids, they trusted her. Though she had not mentioned the radio they avoided this, too, even the sight of it. To the question of her son they had agreed, remembering how patient he had been with peas, with the dog who sniffed his fat diaper.

The night in question they ate outside, on the balcony that looked over their animals and their town, anticipating the other's request for wine or butter before it was spoken. James had given the housekeeper the evening off, thanking her for the meal she left in the oven. It was one of their chickens, a lemon from the tree that straddled the hill beyond their bedroom window, rosemary from the fat row of herbs where the cat slept afternoons.

They set the cast-iron skillet the bird had roasted in right on the table. Claudette sat with her hands on the slight shelf of her belly, her round bun moving a little as she tried to see to each edge of the property, as he carved away the breasts. The knot of hair, the red-blond she had given her daughters, had always been an indicator of her hurt or fear or love, as much as any expression she made, even anything she would say. When she was free it became freer, wobbling as she performed an anecdote or bent a look to some question, and when she was furious it was erect and visible, making sharp turns, the thing that was apparent because she would not show her face. It was high and tight, now, reddening the skin at her hairline, tilted to the landscape while she kept her chin tucked and ate. He never imagined what it felt like, to have that much hair, all the way down her back, to keep it locked up that way. If it hurt he didn't want to know.

The question of heeding the letter had not been discussed, but on the calendar by the pantry Claudette had circled the date in fine blue ink. There was the air of a wake to the way they ate. Neither sipped any from the crystal glasses of water before them, but once their plates were empty they drank without interruption, draining them like children who have come in from a long time outside. When he belched a little she almost smiled, although a correction passed over her face in half a second. In town that day he had bought her the cookies she liked, madeleines dipped in chocolate.

"None for me," she said when he appeared with the milk-glass platter on which he had arranged them in a fan, and he understood and felt ashamed. There was nothing to celebrate.

They had been prepared, the two of them, to accept some responsibility. Even the modest farmhouse they lived in now in Northern California, the transition from their life before in the south of the state—the lawns of their Spanish Colonial mansion spotted with imported trees, the parties they had gone to every year, the pink and green tamarisk whose feathery branches seemed suited to the ocean floor, the Whitneys' Valentine's gala with the sedated lion cubs rented for the evening—had been a concession to this, to the embarrassment of how far each of their daughters had gone from them. It was understood that, for the rest of their lives, there would be no company coming.

On the table she was folding her linen napkin in some elaborate way, to make it look like a bird or a flower, a talent she had been known for in the decades of dinner parties.

THEY FORGOT IT ALL OUTSIDE. In the night the carcass of the chicken in the skillet took on a coat of dew and the fog bloated the madeleines and upstairs their sleep was dreamless under the lights they left on. When he woke up to piss, he saw she was not even using a pillow, that she had her palms tucked under her thighs and one foot slid under the other. He had always known her to be unkempt in her sleep, Claudette, a leg hinged up at the hip in a crazy angle and a hand high above her, and had teased her about it, calling her the colonialist, saying, *Could you stay out of my country over here.* Tonight she was like an epiphyte, a thing clinging to its host, almost undetectable in the bed.

In the morning they each kept a leash to the other, never drifting from earshot. He was very aware of the radio that was usually on, local and national and weather, the detailed forecast that usually filled the rooms of the house. By the afternoon he was unable to concentrate on the most minor of tasks, some paperwork sent over by the accountant or the crossword puzzle folded back on his knee where he sat on the porch, and he called to her. "Trip into town," he said. Somehow he had adopted the belief that the news of their daughter, whatever it was, had their address, would reach them at home. The thought of a drive was a comfort. "A matinee," he said. "We'll drive by the theater and see." Implicit in this was that they could not check the listings in the paper.

They floated down the hill with the windows up and his foot never pressing the gas, Claudette in a dress he hadn't seen in thirty years, navy silk padded at the shoulders. She was a woman whose younger self had been eaten angrily by the older. He no longer knew her by her face or body but by how she used them, a way of crossing her feet when she didn't approve, tipping her forehead back to consider an alternative.

There was a soap she wanted and she asked if he would stop at the market first, and he waited in the car with his seat belt on, the metal of the buckle right in the line of sun and capturing so much heat he could feel it in his gut. She emerged ten minutes later, through the automatic doors installed that year, her purse open and the soap held like a ticket, and he understood from this and how she crossed the lot, her chin buttoned to her neck, hardly lifting her feet, that she knew. On the drive home, the marquee out the window forgotten, he kept telling himself that at the next stop sign, after the next crest of the hill, he would ask her what their daughter had done.

23.

As though she is just stepping into the store to grab a pack of smokes, something to unclog the drain, he waits in the car for his mother, vaguely surveyed in the rearview by the college student appointed to keep him—company, or from himself, or from her, whichever, the interpretation turning over as quickly as the Florida radio stations. Few mention the launch. There is Zeppelin, there is Bowie, there is the DJ witticism and the accompanying sound effect, zoom, kapow. All four doors are open.

She had spent most of the bus ride meditating, something he hated her for. Even the drool that gathered in the crook of her unmoving lips he hated, even the dairy-white moons of her fingernails on her upturned hands.

In the front seat Brad licks the crease of a rolling paper, his knees splayed so wide the soles of his Birkenstocks kiss, and pulls apart the sticky bits of green with his thumbnails. He passes this back without asking or looking at him and Wright accepts, taking in too much, the taste and smell like the sap of a fir tree. Gasping and coughing is a barbed pleasure, the idea his body might get rid of anything. Wouldn't it be good to eliminate an organ, any of them, survive on less, be made of less. There are Buddhist prayer beads hanging from the mirror, there is porn stuffed down the back of the seat, a white cock, a black one, a pink mouth too open.

When it hits any calm or pleasure falls shut, an old window on a pulley finally collapsing, locking him into somewhere too small to live for long.

In a cavity under the radio there is a collection of stray coins, filthier than he can bear to look at, coatings of gum and tobacco, shadowed faces of Indians. *Kill yourself,* he thinks, *stop living,* a quiet, peaceful thought. Brad is talking about direct democracy, or about Marx's idea of a human home, or about an ex-girlfriend he wishes would fall ill.

Wright looks for something familiar as he puts off accepting that he cannot stay here in this car. Where else can he go? The cigarette burn on his hand shines a little pink, years old now. His mother? His jeans gape around the knees, a disintegration he exacerbated during a year where all food was cold, all sleep was cut short. He had pulled at these holes in steel-sided stalls, on the sides of roads, during talks from his mother when his jaw was locked and he never said a word.

Brad's head tips back into some kind of dream, waking or otherwise it's unclear. Wright drifts from the car, a thing pulled by weather.

The parking lot at night is a metallic grid of the hundred ways he might go, the posts of light with their necks bent in a way that feels deferential. He goes toward the sound of people. There is a turnstile he walks through, an attendant waving him past, her face as distinct as a dirty puddle. Smells of cheese that is not all cheese, meat that is not all meat. The bleachers are perforated with empty spaces where he might sit and for a moment he forgets what he's doing, considers taking a load off, considers a souvenir baseball cap. A mom, a dad, a curfew, a bike. He has wanted places like this all his life, uniform rows of people, checking watches, agreeing that they are mostly the same, waiting on the same entertainment. For a moment he considers warning them, distracting them somehow. The rocket, past grass and stanchions and concrete, is the biggest thing he has ever seen. It's a question, or the clarity of its answer, that puts a laugh in his mouth. Has there ever been anything about which he had no doubt? The biggest.

He watches them hopping the barriers now, people he has never met but who are instantly familiar, the political buttons on lapels, the density of ungroomed hair, the looseness of sleeves. The signs come up like a time-lapse simulation of spring, bulbs breaking through soil. Blown-up photos heave up and down in alternating waves, a naked child running under a sky on fire, a sweatered figure standing over a body while a girl near him howls. There are call-and-response chants, there are mouths that seem never to have been closed. And, he knows, at the center of it, at the bottom of it, his mother.

They part to reveal her where she sits as he jogs toward the stanchions. He clears them in a T shape with the help of his left hand, the lightness of his body what makes the jump possible, the remnant narrowness of childhood. They have made a U around her, a frame from which she is meant to speak. The signs remain but go still. Coming from nowhere a voice mentions minutes, T minus two. The biggest thing he has ever seen prepares to become the biggest thing he can no longer see.

He is on the ground and moving there, avoiding ankles and knees as much as possible. The high has changed. Before he was only his thoughts, places and arguments, but now he is only his body, ankles and calves.

Her face, his mother's face, is quiet as the moon. Under his breath he speaks her full name, but there is no sign, in the curve of her bare feet on her thighs, the ragged weft of hair, that she imagines herself to be seen. She could be out in the orchards where she grew up, she could be alone in the dark.

He can smell it, the kerosene, sharp, precise. It gives her hair a unified or solid quality, incorrect and unreal as it curves around her face from the middle part, spreads pat as house paint over her heart and meets the bevel of her ankles. Annabelle had teased her: the only one not to cut her hair. Its color, its length, something people have always felt free to comment on, is it red, is it gold, does it change with the time of year, could you lasso a horse with that, hey princess could you escape the castle on your own.

Between chants a few voices acknowledge him.

"Hey, that's her kid—would somebody—what's he. What's *he*? What's *she*? That smell is—"

The knot of people seems like it's growing toward him, shoelace tips in duct tape, hairy shins dry and reptilian underneath, and then she opens her eyes. Not fully, just enough to see him, the bottom slice of the world, surface but not sky. A pocket of space tears open around her and he crawls through it.

There's an industrial strike-anywhere match between her middle and ring fingers, a sprout growing onto her open palm. He removes it without looking, eyes staying with hers. She almost smiles. When she replaces it, he pulls it again. Three times, four. What is it he thought he would say? The countdown of the rocket is at thirty seconds now, twenty-nine. He can feel the hum in his teeth.

She uses a phrase then that nobody else knows. She asks him to go. All their life it has gone this way, no commands, just questions. All their life, the illusion of choice. She uses a name for him nobody else ever will. He retreats backward, swallowing nothing wildly, the points of his knees higher than the crown of his head.

Nothing in his mother's life has ever happened slowly, and neither does this. She is skin then not, hair then not. The orange is oversaturated, a mean smear of one ugly color. It's not a consequence, an answer or reaction. It's a change of the channel, another story entirely in a sliver of a second. Ten, says the voice. Nine. He finds it easy to think, for a slow pour of a minute, This has nothing to do with me. This is something else.

24.

He woke with a dull awareness of it, the last Apollo launch, and had decided by breakfast he would not watch it, the broadcast they had conceded to make, sure to be pitiful. But the rattle of an afternoon flight left him nostalgic for the program, the beauty of the atmospheric burn, and at eight he turned on his Panasonic, thinking he would keep the sound off, lean back and wait for the rocket's color and smoke, the red becoming gray, the gray becoming the sky left behind. It was the only launch to take place at night and he could not help but see it as an admission of failure. Steel-blue standing lamps bent over the couch, their switches in reaching distance, but he remained where he lay, as darkened as what played out on-screen. He hit mute during a commercial break for Head & Shoulders, a man gripping a tuft of his hair like a twenty found on the street.

The press seemed unsure of where to find the patriotism of this moment, how to euphemize the fact that Congress had deemed all of it a frivolity. They were sorry, their postures seemed to say, their hands too loose on the microphones, their shoulders pushed forward, for the future they had asked the public to dream about. There would be no lunar colony, no vegetables grown in space, no shuttle that ran between the planets on loop, preparing the moon for its pacifist global future. As he watched their lips move around words chosen carefully, the rouge and shadow of their made-up faces attendant to their stoic presentation, he thought he could read some: *Watershed. John-F-Kennedy. The last.*

The crowd, he calculated, was a fifteenth what it had been when he had ridden in the van with Jeanie and Rusty. There was no one on the beaches, face painted and all-day drunk, no international cross-section of luminaries and royalty, no cacophony of French and Italian, Mandarin and Portuguese, Japanese and Czech. Slate-gray and spotted with empty spaces, the bleachers were lit like industrial holding pens for cattle. The cameras dithered in their path, zooming in on certain members of the crowd, their haircuts rangy and their clothing ill fitting, before cutting to the astronauts crossing into the elevator.

A time zone behind them, there was no way to tell Dean Kernan good luck as he crossed the detachable arm, no red phone in sight that would ring when something went wrong. You made this choice, he reminded himself, in that room that could have belonged to anyone, a place of few photographs or heirlooms, you locked yourself out of that life.

As the countdown began they rushed the fence that ran the perimeter of the launchpad, a group of lanky figures in denim and paisley and plaid, their hair flowing up and sideways from the force of the rocket, their signs warping in the blast. They planted their high-top sneakers and fringed moccasin booties and they held the poster boards by the corners. NO MORE BREAD AND CIRCUSES. DEATH TO AMERICAN DISTRACTION. YOUR MURDERED CHILDREN ARE NOT IMPRESSED. Photos pulsed between the text, the bodies of Vietnamese men piled in black silk, the body of a black man shot by the FBI as he slept.

From between them she appeared, protected by the fence of their bodies, her hair giving off light, the midcalf length of it as shocking to him as the saturated sight of her. Vincent bent forward, his front teeth on his pinky's cuticle. She was the girl he had known—that immaculate dancer's posture, that accusatory tip of the chin—and she was violently, potently, not. His body made a sound like gargling when he realized what was missing, eyelashes, eyebrows. There was nothing about her face that indicated it might break into surprise or fury, nothing in her eyes that would delight in anything around her. The station he was watching cut away to find the shot that would exclude her, and then he ground his thumb into the remote, two presses, four, until he could see Fay again.

Around her the bearded men and barefaced women held their signs and grimaced as the seconds wound down, nine, eight, and the force of the Saturn became greater. Vincent leaned forward and spread his hands on the glass tabletop. Seven. A child, maybe thirteen, appeared from behind the rooted legs of the protesters, his hands gathered in a fist at his stomach. Six. It appeared he was speaking, confirming some stricture with someone above, five, and then he kneeled where she sat, his face turned away from the cameras, only his shrunken turtleneck and blond-gold hair showing. Four. There was a kind of tug-of-war between them, a theft or an exchange it wasn't clear, and then he fell back on his hands, his knees raised high, his feet and palms working to get him away in a primeval crab walk that removed all feeling from Vincent's hands. She went up as the rocket did, as red and angry and determined to disappear.

Nothing in the room reflected what he'd seen, was changed by it, and because of or despite this he couldn't be in it anymore. He walked in his open robe to the car. There were sidewalks covered in crooked hopscotch squares, there were stoplights he flew past like the anterooms of dreams, minor scenes we disregard on our way to the promise of some real message.

He learned it two days later, his heart rate returned to normal. There were certain things he would be glad to remember, as glad as he had been while she lived. How she answered questions with questions, the bit of ink that was always on her face. A day he had parked a mile off and walked in, watched her for ten minutes she believed she was alone performing grand jetés over knots of manzanita, chin threaded to the sun, front toes piercing the future. That she had died almost didn't matter, he thought. The distance between them was the same.

BOOK THREE

1980–1988

The trouble with a secret life is that it is very frequently a secret from the person who lives it and not at all a secret for the people he encounters.

—James Baldwin, *Another Country*

Dear Mr. Kahn,

Is there a version of events in which you know who I am and think of me the way I do you? You're on my mind whenever I'm alone too long, and also during the point in a conversation when the other person begins to suspect there's something I've left out, a secret I've been greedy with that's kept me from some authentic way of being in the world. People seem to find me rude, outspoken about things that were better left unsaid—the obsolescence of religion or the overrated trifle that is the Beatles—but cold with the American small talk that is a comfort to them. It's true I never ask about people's families. There's a reason for that.

I've written all sorts of hedging introductions to this in the last few years, but maybe it's best now to just come out with it. I think that a long time ago you knew or loved my mother, Fay, who was the woman on the cover of Life with her long hair on fire at the last Apollo launch. I'm her son, in the corner of the picture, crawling backward out of frame. I'm Wright.

I wanted to say so right away because I know how much mail you must get. I would understand if you couldn't read it all, and I would also understand if you didn't love my mother. My own feelings for her don't look like that anymore. They look like those photos you sometimes see in the newspaper real estate sections. They're empty, these houses, price reduced, and you can tell how they were lived in,

*the dormer windows missing some shutters, the railings leaning away
from the porch, but you can't really see how they could be a home to
somebody else. Maybe that doesn't make sense to you. I haven't had
to explain myself much and I also haven't had much of an education,
three half-asleep years at the only third-rate college that would take
me and whatever my mother taught me before that. There were things
she left out completely but when something interested her she gave
herself over to it, which I guess a person could tell just by looking
at that picture. I know a lot about herbal remedies and human
anatomy, how to steal in bulk from K-Mart. My Spanish is still
okay. What I learned or knew best was her. I guess anyone could tell
that, too, by looking at my face on that cover.*

    *I'll get to it, Mr. Kahn, because you must be busy. Or maybe
you're not. What does a man do after he goes to the moon? A trip to
Hawaii must seem to you like a walk to the bathroom in the middle
of the night. When I'm the worst I ever am—which is a lot, and
I didn't die last spring only because the door in my shitty rental
happened to splinter and let me and the belt around my neck fall
down it—I believe I'm the loneliest man in America. Then I think
about you and with all due respect I wonder if you might be running
laps around me in that regard. In terms of isolation, tolerance of it,
your stamina is probably superhuman. I can't manage mine for much
longer, which is why the following.*

    *For a long time people were always recognizing me. I went to live
with my mother's parents, after what happened, in a small town in
Northern California, and I don't mean there, where I was given the
leprous status of an object of pity, and every churchgoer in a ten-mile
radius was sure to send me a birthday card. Any time we were in
another place, though, two towns over or three, some little old lady
or squinty trucker would say don't you look like somebody. (I was
thirteen, then fourteen, still very small. It was like my body wouldn't
accept my childhood was over because it hadn't been much of one.)
I was so shamed by this because I assumed they knew me from that*

photo, and I didn't want to be the boy in that photo. I wanted to have a Coke with my nice new normal grandparents. I wanted to whine about the heat or beg for jukebox quarters. After it happened I would have to go to the bathroom—don't you look like somebody— and stay there until Claudette and James came to get me. Even then sometimes I couldn't leave because I was afraid The Recognition would still be out there having his hamburger. I could tell you a lot about the restrooms of those restaurants, the pedals under the half- moon communal sinks that made the water go, the powdered soap always the same antacid pink. They would come, my grandparents, and tell me, honey there is no way, sweetheart, they just think you're cute, but I knew. Those people were just making sure. They just had to confirm it and then they would tell me that my soul was bad, just being the son of someone like that, that I deserved to be burned, too.

I understand now that no one would really remember the face of that kid, out of focus and barely in frame, because my mother was the exploding star of that photo, and because no one wants to think of these things in the same sentence, white boyhood and homegrown terrorism. It was for another reason. When my shoulders came in and I grew about seven inches in a summer is when these people could finally name what they had always known.

It's happened to me something like fifteen times now even though I've tried to avoid it, by not buying a ticket to the movies after all when I saw the cashier in the glass box start to look at me that way, by only going to stations where you can pump your own gas. I tend to avoid interactions in the afternoon, which seems to be the time people most want to speak their lazy, native thought. People say I look like you, Mr. Kahn.

It happened again yesterday, on a date with a woman who was kind enough to let me touch her, even though I hadn't showered in days and I got fired from my latest construction job for showing up late too many times. I tried moving the alarm clock down the hall, then to the kitchen, but my body would not be roused, could not face being a body again. I had taken her, Cheryl, to a bad Chinese restaurant where there was a dirty aquarium with no fish in it anymore and then to my place to watch TV, but nothing was on and she was annoyed by my milk crate coffee table and how bad my antenna was. She asked to see my room anyway, and when it was over in bed she was so happy, looking at me like she would have to draw me from memory, and I was so glad to have made her that way. I've been trying to figure it out all night, she said. You look exactly like Vincent Kahn. I asked her to leave after that and she couldn't understand why, shoved me playfully at first.

I'm sure I'm not the first person to have written you, claiming to be your son. It's a common delusion, isn't it? We want to attach ourselves to greatness. But the funny thing about me, maybe the first thing about me, is that I don't, Mr. Kahn. The fantasies I have are of houses in the forest, places without mirrors or telephones. I want to treat my thinking like nothing of consequence, stop hearing it like people do the traffic where they live. I want to see myself as secondary.

I can't claim to love where my mother's politics led her, but I'll tell you now I wasn't exactly raised a patriot, and it isn't exactly ideologically convenient, thinking what I do about who my father is. I spoke the idea aloud exactly once, to my grandparents, who looked at me as though I'd just seen my loyal dog shot and served for dinner. You've got to let that go right now, James said, and left the table. On a drive the next day, past cows and horses on the way to the ocean, he turned off the radio and asked me to listen carefully. My mother had not been well for some time, he said, probably from the time she was my age. There was no way of knowing what exactly had happened during those years at her sister's bar, he said, but her behavior had been reckless. When he asked if I understood what he meant, I said I did, and for a little while felt better believing that my father was not one man but somehow a stream of them. I was fourteen, and I imagined men pouring single file through some hokey swinging saloon doors, naked and determined, a parade of erections. If my father was no one, he was also in some way everyone, Southern and Midwestern, green eyed and brown, spindly and slowed down by his paunch, moved by a belief in God and changed in the absence of it. The first time someone likened my face to yours in the presence of my grandfather—it was a hardware store employee an hour north— James clapped a hand to the man's shoulder and laughed. The third time was a hostess at a restaurant, and we left without lunch.

The dates line up, when you were at the base near the inn that my aunt owned, where my mother worked when she left her parents. She almost never spoke about that time, as she almost never spoke about other things that shamed her, her parents' wealth or how when her sister died she hadn't called her in two years. Charlie's drinking had become such that people had stopped going to her bar, where sometimes the only creature behind the counter was her horse, Lloyd. He was an alcoholic, too. This I read in a posthumous profile, of which there were quite a few. My grandparents always expected to raise unforgettable daughters, but the ways Charlie and Fay became remembered eventually drove them inside. By the time I lived with them they had already taken up certain habits of the irretrievably unhappy, bickering viciously about things like directions and expiration dates, telling stories that had transpired decades before as though they'd occurred over the previous busy weekend. Everything they need now, food, laundry—never the news—is delivered.

I'm not writing for money or love, or to say there's a person I should have been that I'm not, now. I'm just writing to ask about my mother, if you knew her. Did you know Fay? I don't know anybody who does.

Yours,

Wright

P.S. For a year now I've been living in Texas, only about an hour from Houston. It's easy to find out where your house was, that cul-de-sac with the other astronauts—I think there's even a tour. But I wanted to guess. I drove down it at night and thought very carefully about which you might have chosen, knowing what I do about you from the profiles I've read. Of course I didn't have much luck. The same curve to the driveways, the same green of the plantings. Living like that, I would worry I'd disappear, Mr. Kahn. Can you explain it to me, the American idea that luxury is a house indistinguishable from the one next door? I've had dreams where I show up in the town where you live now in Ohio and I take a job at the drugstore downtown and wait for the time you'll come in, thinking it's inevitable—your head will hurt, or your clothes will be dirty, and you will have run out of the thing to fix it. Any day now, I think, he'll come in with a question I can answer.

November 16, 1980

Dear Mr. Kahn,

I think I called your mother last night, which I want to apologize
for right away. I was shocked to find her listed, under her maiden
name of course. She was very nice about everything, despite the hour,
I guess just after one A.M. there, and said she'd give you my message.
We spoke about a dog you had, as a child, which I'd read about. Poor
Shadow. There did seem to be some confusion—when she said goodbye
she didn't hang up but started sort of calling out to someone else. Then
she stayed on the line a long time. Is your father still alive?

I've waited a month to hear from you and again I know the
amount of mail must be staggering and I think about it, the piles of
paper, the cursive and capitals, and I wonder who manages that—
you? Where is it kept. Surely not at home. Maybe behind the lines
and clerks in some recessed room at the local post office. It's calmed
me to think these questions, at night in bed, a mattress on the floor
that I've covered with a quilt my grandmother made me. We are not
exactly speaking, Claudette and James and me.

It was too late, when it came down to it. I was foreign in every
sense. I ate things with my fingers that you were not supposed to eat
with your fingers, I bathed only when they reminded me to, I walked
barefoot around their property and through their house. They'd catch
me at midnight in the snack cupboard, wince at the dirty pads of my
feet, the calluses.

When Nixon came on I belched and left the room, which upset them and which even I couldn't understand—my leaving I mean, my disapproval of him, given how much I wanted to be apathetic and mild-mannered and not made of my mother in any visible way. I was already inculcated, already wary of American authority and the jowly speeches. When he resigned I came in and clapped, and my grandparents looked at me as they did the vagrants that occasionally made their way through our town, having managed the fare for the bus that came from San Francisco.

There was tenderness, too, Claudette teaching me how to use a steak knife, the power hon is in your forefinger on it, and remember it's guided by the fork you thread it through, James buying me my first tie and laying it across my bed, that fine white tissue and long navy box waiting for me when I got home from school.

I was behind in those classrooms in ways easily quantified and ahead in a manner those bespectacled women sensed but did not trust. There was an IQ test, an embarrassment James insisted on and paid for and whose results he put on the fridge, but I could not easily long-divide, it being a week in school I'd missed on account of some three-day hike my mother thought we should take, and when I saw that symbol, that line reaching left and slanting down and peaking back up, I felt fear as far as I could, lost feeling in toes and calves. I could not name the presidents, though they tried in off-hours, after school, to teach me the ditty of a mnemonic everyone else had learned. Wash-ing-ton Addd-ams, Jeff-er-son Mad-is-on, Mon-roe Ad-ams, Jaaack-son. I sang it back to them, standing, my hand on my heart as instructed, the chalk dust tunneling farther into my body, my eyes on theirs as insisted. But I could hear something wrong in the way I sang, tinny or hesitant or duplicitous. The Spanish priests and the missions they had founded up the coastline I could not recite, and when I raised my hand and asked in all sincerity whether the Miwok and Wappo and Tipai had said absolutely, we'll make bricks of cow shit and water, we'll hand over our cypress and juniper, we'll *take your God, I went straight to the principal's office, a pinched forefinger and thumb on my shirt's collar.*

I wanted to be their boy and their pride, poor Claudette and James, who had done maybe nothing wrong except to live by the rules given them, and I posed for the photos, face straight ahead, right fingers planted on opposite knee, their hands on my shoulders hot with love or embarrassment. James signed me up for baseball tryouts, bought and oiled a mitt, tried to show me, on the hill where my mother had been pregnant and known she would leave, how to swing a bat. Knees bent. Knuckles aligned. Feet and shoulders exactly twinned. He knew when he picked me up by the dugouts, didn't ask, nodded at me in some shorthand of comfort and asked did I want the radio on or off. I said on for his sake, because I knew his disappointment was big and probably symbolic. Five buttons, each another station, James punching through them with his middle finger, more age spots on his hands every day, rock stations he had put on for my benefit or enculturation, Jim Croce's "Time in a Bottle" topping the charts that year and humiliating him in a way I'll never forget—there never seems to be enough time to do the things you want to do once you find them—James pulling over and grumbling something about the back wheel but pacing the car with his hands on his face. Was he thinking of my mother, was he blaming himself for what had happened on the inside of her, was he just unprepared for how I'd arrive, not the son he'd never had but a person already formed, the deficit already carved out. He got back in and put on the one station he'd left for him, classical, and we drove back in silence.

Did she talk to you about them? I imagine no, or a little, or that if she did it was to express how their every habit and ritual was repellent to her, had always been. Of this I'm not sure. They lived in the south of the state then, not far from where you two met. There are still a few photos, ones Claudette hid under a loose board like this was all some English mystery novel. My mother waves from the orange tree she has climbed, her dandelion hair and white dress

blown around by the Santa Ana winds, her tiny fingers in a salute
or a sun shield. Claudette, wearing forties shoulder pads and silk,
holds Fay up to place the tinsel-haloed angel on top of the tree. All
childhoods look happy in photos, you might say—nobody grabs for
their Instamax when his kid has made another kid bleed in a game
that seemed innocent until it wasn't—but there are others, from
when she looks more physically like the person maybe you knew,
but also their daughter, someone who grew up on the inside of their
protection. There was a moment, however brief, when she was both.
Fourteen or so, a desk where she had placed her writing implements
in a container meant for it, wooden and perforated, so they stood up
straight as a forest. Textbooks and novels spread around her, open,
earmarked, underlined. A shy, proud glance over her shoulder. A
spelling bee ribbon she holds up for her father to see.

I admit I think about it, you and her, what sort of conversations
you had or if it was not, forgive me for saying, a largely verbal
relationship. I have known she was beautiful since I've known
anything. She must have been interested in your mind, is what
I say to myself. She must have sensed you were headed for the
extraordinary. I know how quiet you are in interviews, only the few,
best words, and I wonder if she brought you past that, made you
curse, which was always one of her powers. She would extract from
me opinions I didn't know I had. Her way with people, drawing
them out, was like those magician's scarves, silky and effortless and a
little bit evil.

It's late now, which I know without checking. 2:50 would be my
guess, by how the moon looks, the western edge obscured. I have to be
at work by seven, a roofing job with a guy who talks to me sometimes
about beating up his girlfriend. Tina. Brent has some regrets
about this but not enough to stop. Does she really think sequins are
appropriate for dinner on a Tuesday he says. Does she not know they
fuck with the light around her and ask for attention? I smiled at
this and neither of us knew why. Brent's company aside, I like it up

there, the higher the better, straddling the peak and laying down the shingles that will keep the water out. Sleep deprivation can be a kind of drug, a different type of consciousness, and I like how it makes all my senses more alive to the work, more moved by the view.

I want to tell you about what happened to my mother, at the end, but first I have to tell you about how she happened to me. My hope is that if I can explain it, how she vanished, then I won't need to disappear myself. Isn't it true we only follow or imitate what we don't entirely understand?

You don't need to worry that I'm telling anyone about this—if I tried they wouldn't believe me. Good night, Mr. Kahn. I hope you're the kind of person who sleeps well, proud of who you've always been.

Yours,

Wright

December 2, 1980

Dear Mr. Kahn,

   *Have you ever hit anyone? My mother would be heartbroken to
know that I'm capable of violence, she the detonator of bombs. She
would have said what she did was a kind of communication, and
that the brawl I started today at work was a way of eliminating the
possibility of any. I can't help wondering if it had been a roofing gig,
like I was doing last time I wrote, I could have resisted that part of
myself. Having only limited surface area to walk and think on, being
very intimate with the sun, slows down any reaction.*
   *Me and two other guys, both veterans, were redoing a woman's
kitchen. She is what you would call a classic Texan lady of the
house. How her enormous outdated beehive survives uncharred is
beyond me. The required amount of Aqua Net and the omnipresent
Virginia Slim, the nail polish wand that comes out at the slightest
provocation—these seem like a deadly combination, though I am
someone who fixates on a fire hazard, so.*
   *She had read that an open plan was in vogue and wanted us
to make two rooms a seamless one. Also she wanted an island and
loved the sound of the word and repeated it often. So I can just lean
over the island and talk to my guests while I'm fixin', etc. Fixin',
in Texas, is not a transitive verb. Among the things my mother did
teach me was grammar, a love for language, believing, apparently,
that an adult way of speaking would make me stick out less, not*

more. Did you like Texas when you were here? I somehow can't imagine it suited you but then you were probably as insulated from the outsized culture of it as anyone can be. I hope you'll forgive my presumptions. I ended up in Texas I don't know why, partially on account of your having lived here, partially on account of the movie Giant. *It was James Dean's last, something I watched on television in Ecuador, an idea of this country that predated my experience of it. Have you seen it? It spans thirty Technicolor years, and the actors all play themselves as they get older, all get the same violet-gray hair color at the same time, which comforted me deeply, the idea of parity and fairness in our dying. When I dropped out of the college Claudette and James paid for, I ended up on a bus to Houston, and I've spent the last two years floating around the state.*

We had anyway already knocked out the wall between the two rooms and hauled out the pink linoleum countertops and the attached wooden cabinets and most of their upheaval's detritus. Olivia was a constant presence, picking things up we'd just set down and trying to hand them to us. It didn't help anything, nor did my claustrophobia or allergies, both of which I acquired sometime in my teens and neither of which is a good excuse for what I did to Brent. I told myself in the hour after that if I had been near an open window, or if breathing hadn't felt like something that required concentration, I wouldn't have done it. Like my mother, I always have an accusatory finger on the environment. I don't like that, but I see it.

Brent wears his fatigue jacket to the job even though it's Texas in the summer and he has to remove it immediately to get to work. Shane is another story, always twenty minutes early, won't put together a full sentence unless it's absolutely necessary. He presents as a nonentity except that you turn around and he has sanded and planed an eight-by-ten piece of pine and sawed out the shape of a sink. Over the course of two weeks Brent has attempted to engage Shane with no real luck except the initial acknowledgment that yes, he had served. Brent's version of hello is cocking a head at someone

*and asking—You serve? He did this to me and when I said no he
squinted and said, Too young, as in what a shame.*

*Brent has cadged and leaned on Shane without getting any real
information, and I knew this was making him angrier and angrier.
Combat medic is my guess, he said, between surges of the electric drill.
Green Beret? You will kill me if you say Green Beret. By day five
or so he stopped guessing. You're a deserter, he said, and stared at
Shane whenever he could, even while caulking or hammering. Shane,
who has the kind of exceptional focus that sometimes comes to the very
frightened, used this as encouragement to work even more efficiently,
thinking, I could tell, toward the wad of money at the end of the gig
and the grunt from our supervisor in the smoky trailer office. The
only thing Shane did that made him a less than perfect employee was
to always leave five minutes before our scheduled lunch break, going to
hide somewhere that I never found out.*

*Fifteen feet from us, Olivia put on a Patsy Cline record and raised
her chiffon neck scarf around her mouth, unhappy and immaculate
on her plastic-covered sofa. She was insane, as was Brent, as was
Shane in a different way entirely. Though he had managed to
avoid it almost altogether, by going through me or interrupting his
work to fetch the tool he needed rather than asking Brent to pass it,
something came up Shane hadn't anticipated. The polyurethane had
to be applied almost immediately after the wax, and he had forgotten
to retrieve it from the truck. I was in the nearby bathroom pissing
when I heard his voice, the sound of which I'd almost forgotten or
never registered in the first place. It was deeper than you'd think, the
kind of voice that even in whisper reverberates. Brent, he said, I'm
going to need that polyurethane that's in the bed of the Ford awfully
quick. Is there any way please you could grab it for me? I could tell
by the ceasing of the drill that Brent had stopped his work on the
cabinets. You can't say two words to me all week and now you want
my fucking help? This is a Christian house! I heard Olivia yell. She
was oblivious to what was about to unfold, already into her second*

afternoon G & T. I just need it quickly, Shane said. Then we can talk. I promise.

That was the last thing I heard. I came back and Shane's brush was wobbling in his grip, dripping wax onto the surface he had made perfect, and he'd brought it up onto his shoulder to kind of embrace himself. His eyes didn't know where to go. I don't know how, but I felt certain that the fear he had then was the same as what I had felt hiding in those bathrooms as a thirteen-year-old, crouching on a toilet seat and wishing the earth would relieve me of my existence. It's our mistake, I wanted someone to say, not yours. You were right. You were not meant to be here, not like this, and we're taking care of it immediately. It sounds ridiculous, but the only way to put it is this: I believed Shane and I were the same color.

Brent advanced to whisper something in his ear and took a hunk of Shane's hair in his fist. He twisted Shane's hand with the dripping brush in it, all the way back until it lost its grip, and that is what got me started. I don't imagine you've assaulted anyone in your life, Mr. Kahn, and I'd like to believe that I'd be that person too had my life unrolled differently, had I always been worried about by someone else. I wear this turquoise ring of my mother's on my pinky, sharper than it looks, and the bleeding on his face was significant. A minute in Olivia threw her drink on me, which did nothing to put out the situation. I didn't have to pick up the spare piece of wood. He was already on the ground. Okay, he was saying. Okay, okay, okay.

Shane left with me and we walked, crossing the street to the promise of shade every few minutes. I didn't desert, he said. I told him I knew and that I wouldn't care if he had. I just can't talk about it, he said. I think about it enough. We were both leaving that month's pay behind and there were altars in almost every yard, crosses adorned with fake flowers and planted in multicolored pebbles.

I've been hiding out in my apartment a week, waking up to the messages Brent's been leaving when he calls early in the morning. Moving seems very likely, though the thought of surrendering to

*whatever punishment has some appeal, too. I like the idea of having a
face people in line don't want to look at. Before I go anywhere, I have
to visit Shane, whose mother called to let me know. He'd been living
with her since the first hospitalization. She thanked me for standing
up for him, and said even if she didn't condone violence she knew I
had probably protected Shane from some. There was one nightmare
in particular that he had described to her, something someone in his
company had done to a corpse. They had seated him in a chair by his
home and formed his fingers into a peace sign, so he would look that
way when his family arrived home. His head was basically gone.
Linda apologized for being so gruesome, but she wanted me to know
what had kept her son from sleeping. He is not crazy, she said, he
just can't get a good night's sleep, and what can you do without that?
I agreed. There is very little you can do.*

*Her name is Linda and she thought it might be nice to go together
for his birthday, his thirty-third, although she warned me that
the Thorazine might keep Shane from visitation hours altogether.
Do you know any boys like this, Mr. Kahn? I imagine not. Have
you thought about how strange it is that while you were treading
completely virgin ground this was going on below you, sometimes just
by the light of the planet you walked on?*

*The apartment won't be hard to pack. It's embarrassing, the way I
live. Cans of nuts the only thing in the kitchen, a bed on the ground
I've never once made.*

Yours,
Wright

1.

1981

Wright left Texas late in the afternoon and a garbled message for his
landlord on the office machine, apologizing for leaving so much behind and saying of course he understood about the deposit. Money
was something he could not care about, like a person to whom you
are introduced and can think of nothing to ask. The feeling was
mutual. He did not know what things cost and could not be bothered to compare the prices of similar goods, and he bought next to
nothing save an occasional manic spree after a paycheck—he would
emerge from a department store with a fishing rod and an unsea-
sonal sweater, a discounted blender and a white leatherette address
book. He was twenty and objectively beautiful, the mangy native
state of his body refined and filled by his jobs in construction. There
was someone people thought he looked like. He was frightened by
conversation and spent any looking somewhere else, a habit that
gave him the air of cockiness.

In the middle console of his truck he put two packs of cigarettes
he'd emptied into a bowl. He smoked a pack a day, Marlboro 27s,
and it felt like the punishment he believed he deserved. To wake up
and cough was a perverse pleasure. The man he'd assaulted at work
had finally made good on his threats to return the favor, show-

ing up at a bar where Wright programmed hours on the jukebox and played paper games of Hangman with the bartender Frank. *A quaint drinking village with a fishing problem,* said a sign above the bar. All pool sticks were attached by a generous length of wire to the wall, a measure that kept them from being taken out front and snapped in the service of an argument. Frank knew where Wright lived and had driven him there, three times Wright could remember, more that he couldn't.

"Hey, soldier," Wright had said when Brent sat down next to him, a poor opener that escalated things quickly. He was the one to suggest the parking lot. Brent was bored by how little he resisted, making up for what the fight lacked in an antagonist with whatever props were around, a fistful of gravel he rubbed into the side of Wright's face, a jagged piece of bumper left behind that he used like a bat on Wright's lower back. "Am I wrong or are you the type of faggot who likes this," Brent asked. He was genuinely surprised. On his belly Wright flashed a peace sign and threw a kiss over his shoulder. Frank appeared with his .22 on his shoulders, a hand slung over each end.

"I hear there's some good television on at your house," Wright heard him say. "I hear cable's a notifying miracle."

It had been no heartbreak to leave that apartment, which he'd decorated only with the occasional fortune cookie scroll Scotch-taped to the card table he ate on. The few visitors had been disappointed women. Imitation pearl earrings or turquoise belts way up the waist, pageboy bobs or hair that fell warm down the back, breasts high and mean or low and brown, all of them left confused about why they hadn't been enough. At first when the moment came and he couldn't, he apologized and excused himself to the bathroom, but lately he just fell to the side and welcomed them to sleep there or not. If he saw them later in the drugstore or supermarket he never greeted them by name.

The clouds as he left the state had a truant feel, thin and distracted. On the radio was the inaugural address, coming to him in two-bit phrases as he looked for a station playing something else. The president had been an actor, a B-rated cowboy who spoke out of the side of his mouth. Wright imagined him like this still, splayed on a horse in the movie posters he'd passed in the downtowns of places they never stayed long. *The watching world,* the new president said. *Economic ills, mortgaging our future, patriotism quiet but deep, the giants on whose future we stand.* After minutes of searching for something else, he turned the knob to off.

It was the weather, he told himself, that he wanted. Northern California had moods like his, the fog in the morning skulking guiltily around the hills until noon, a correlative to the half-dead feeling he had the first few hours he was awake. He respected the sun's expression there, mercurial and withholding, and how the light breezes turned over into something pushy and corrosive in under a minute. There was a shame in returning, and also he knew that the influx of information any new place required would pass right over him now. He'd spent the majority of his days off the last year in bed, wishing for a meal to appear as though that were something he could not orchestrate himself, newly frightened of things that had happened a decade before. The suicide attempt he refused to think about, how even for that he had not planned well. He put the belt in the plastic garbage liner, after, and wore his pants loose and low. The letters to the astronaut were similarly avoided, a part of his emotional life he starved out unless he'd been drinking, when he wrote and wrote and walked cockeyed to the mailbox six blocks away. He must have known if he left them until the morning they'd never get sent. On the way to California he ate sunflower seeds and sang to himself, Phil Spector's love songs, catchy and wicked. *He hit me and I knew he loved me!*

January 21, 1981

Dear Mr. Kahn,

    As I was getting ready to leave, looking through the things I own, I kept thinking—it's strange what persists, more arbitrary than I'd prefer. I have an old driver's license of Randy's that he gave me, I don't know why, some early token of love. I have a photo of Claudette I took with a camera they gave me, her sleeping face revealed in the leftmost third of the photo through a cracked door I made out of focus. A Bible my mother stole from somewhere and rolled joints from, a magazine I'm on the cover of, not the one I've mentioned.

    I don't imagine you'll know this, because it took even the press a few years to put it together, but that was not my first time, at the launch I mean, on the cover of Life. *I guess this is something you and I share, that we are some of the few individuals to make it twice. Of course I realize that worshipping coincidence is the province of the insane. No one knows I write to you, have I told you that?*

    Maybe you remember the photo. I'd argue the composition is the most striking thing about it, although my mother would say it's my face, the determination there. There's a row of National Guardsmen, diminishing in size into the distance, and facing them a row of people in their twenties and thirties. Where the two lines meet is a tree, fat and dark and with a canopy that hangs just a foot from the ground, one that was everywhere in San Francisco and which most people confuse with a pine. Actually, it's a Pacific yew, which you can tell by the little red berries it litters everywhere. I know my trees. My mother always said the way we show our affection for life is in our ability to name it. I would say she's right about that, although I can't say my botanical interests were so loftily motivated. If you are a boy without a door that closes, you quickly find and love any place that might hide you. The Pacific yew, fate bless it, gave me that.

In the first line of people, the sameness is shocking, and I don't just mean the starched epaulets and built-in belts that cut just under their ribs and the rounded helmets strapped on at the same one-hundred-and-twenty-degree angle. I mean the faces and the postures and the way they hold their guns, which I have to say seems gentle, the elbow a little loose to accommodate the length of the rifle as it crosses the torso. There can't be some military dictum on how to arrange your face, but in this photo the twenty sets of lips are identical, all performing something of an underbite, all looking like they're keeping something secret behind that lip, a match or a penny. Ditto the forehead, creaseless, and the stare, a kind that has always made me nervous, one that remains firmly on the line of horizon. They're all white, of course, all of them with their feet spread just wider than their frames and one cocked back, none of them obviously deviating from a general mold of five ten and a hundred and sixty.

The other line is another story totally, faces and postures as different as they come. One bearded man, a head taller than everybody—whom I remember as having some trail mix in his pocket that he kept offering the Guardsmen in a peculiar kind of taunt, saying, Time for a snack, boys?—is in the middle of a leap, has both fingers pointed and a knee raised almost high enough to clear a nipple. The woman behind him, masked in sunglasses and a cut-off pullover sweatshirt, is rooted in her feet and hips but with her torso flown forward and her curled tongue a millimeter away from licking one in the row of barrels. Shin'ya, a friend of my mother's who once took me to Japantown and bought me wooden sandals so beautiful I could never wear them, is there in that line, too. Her inquiring look coming up through her lashes, her hair falling down a dress I would remember even if it weren't for that photo—empire waisted and powder blue and always dirty around the floor-length hem. She was the one who helped me gather the flowers, that morning. My mother didn't attend any protests by then, thought of them as a waste.

I'm the boy, first in the line opposite the guard, with the chrysanthemums—they were white and purple—placing the stems in the guns. It surfaces every few years, the cover of some anthology. There are some secrets to the image, some undersides that would belie the message it sent of an American child demonstrating on behalf of other children, or maybe just a boy focused on keeping thirty of a million guns from going off.

I was angry with my mother when I woke up that day, for reasons I can't remember now, although I could provide you with a litany of possibilities and past offenses. The time she gave my cot to a fucked-up vet whose fetid piss I never got out, the money I'd set aside over months for the revised edition of Birds Over America *that she took from my duct-taped wallet and spent on brown rice and vegetables for fifteen people I'd never seen before. Shin'ya knew this and had invited me for a walk and to this protest in a way that felt adult, not like she was obviating a mother-son conflict as a favor to both of us but like she took real interest in me as an individual. I wasn't the twelve-year-old son of a woman whose politics she admired but a boy who could tell her what he'd learned, and while we walked in Golden Gate Park, she listening to me talk about the native and nonnative plants, I thought we might look like lovers. I was so emboldened by this that when we ran into a friend of hers, a man who said how long has it been six months and kissed her on the mouth, I accepted the mushrooms he offered shortly thereafter with a temerity that was unlike me. I was a kid who had once, when we had first arrived in the country, slept in a wolf costume mask for a week, comforted by the idea that in my sleep I would not be recognized. We ate them with some walnut bread Shin'ya pulled from her loose-knit white yarn purse—an object I would fixate on when I peaked—and a bar of chocolate the man, who introduced himself as Larry, a.k.a. Soft Serve, a.k.a. Cuttlefish, kept in his front pocket for occasions such as these.*

It's certain you wouldn't touch them, so I guess I'll tell you how drugs like those bring about a kind of splitting, unrivaled in my sober life—a division of the world into what we can afford and what we cannot, what we wish to understand and refuse to consider. Colors deepened around me, yes, and I saw into the root systems of trees and how far down the stems of the lily pads in those turbid ponds reached, but more so I became aware of my ability to instantly accept or reject. I loved Shin'ya, her mouth that was parted in surprise or disgust more often than not, the cut of her dress, empire waist as I said, which made her movement seem invisible, not related to a body. Also the copses of eucalyptus and a toddler running across a sandy path with a ball held way aloft in his hand, also the Victorian greenhouse that housed the Conservatory of Flowers, because the oxidizing copper detail made sense to me, the depth and microscopic dynamism of it. Then there were the things I hated, occurring to me as enemies the moment I saw them: The stone archways that cut through hills, five degrees cooler and host to a library of urine smells. Larry, who asked me how I was doing, little man, how I was feeling, once a minute. I remember that I couldn't look at my sweatshirt, something I'd worn almost every day for weeks—San Francisco is so much colder than it looks in photos—because the stains there, usually imperceptible, the coffee I'd started to drink and the plain chicken broth I sometimes had for lunch and the beer somebody'd spilled on me halfway through his argument with Annabelle, were suddenly vivid. Overlapping, layered by age and intensity, sallow and mottled and distended, they were a loud billboard of the things that frightened me about my life, how dirty it was, how much it was changed each day by how many different people. You'll notice I'm bare armed in that photo, though everyone else has the benefit of some suede or flannel, and there's a reason for that. I had abandoned that sweatshirt an hour before, making a sound of such relief that it delighted Shin'ya, and she followed me giggling as we ran from it. It was after that I picked the flowers, apologizing loudly to each stalk I picked.

That we made it to that protest at all is a shock to me. When we first lined up I could not look at those men in uniforms. I believed that my thinking and seeing had been altered permanently, that I would always be the prey of arches and clocks, bearded men and mirrors.

I don't remember the photographer being there at all. What I remember is seeing the row of barrels, all at the same level, and they were marked very clearly to me as being on the wrong side of the binary that the whole world had become, a string of horrible mouths that were starving but refused to eat. I should say that at this moment my fear was at its zenith. Each of my ribs felt distinct, not part of a system, ready to collapse at any second. My underwear, which had rockets on the elastic hem, some bizarre bid to any remaining childhood my mother had chosen for me, was ruined with piss. It occurred to me then that there was something I needed to be doing, and I loped up to the first gun and removed a stalk from the ragged bouquet in my hand and slipped it in, making sure the petals were flush with the rim, and then I made my way down the line. When I ran out of flowers, a wrist with bells around it appeared with more.

The image itself is so comforting that for a long time I wanted to believe what it said, that here was a boy making himself clear about the country he wanted, a child turning a weapon into something else. But if I look closely at it, the deliberate way my hair was arranged to block the periphery I was too afraid to see, the hipbones that shouldn't have been exposed in that forty-degree weather, I know what was captured there was a plea, simple and private, to slide down that time in a way I could bear. I've never told anyone this, *because I like the illusion better and I wouldn't want to take it from the people who might have been moved by it.*

A part of me can't believe I'm on my way back, and another knows it was inevitable. Have you ever spent any time in Northern California? It's almost always too cold to swim, but people still arrange their lives around the ocean. That you'll never read these letters has become a comfort to me. I can thank you for that, at least. I hope you're sleeping well, dreaming easy.

Yours,

Wright

2.

Wright's life in San Francisco revealed itself in a matter of forty-eight hours, coming to him like he'd called it by its name. He saw a boy in a crisp white shirt and apron and wanted to be him, so he forged a food service résumé, naming nonexistent restaurants and responsibilities with a certain pleasure, Debbi's Late Nite, oversight of the midnight rush, Alliman's Bistro, knowledge of a diverse wine list. He removed the wrinkles from his clothes by hanging them in the shower of the gym that had offered a free trial membership.

The second restaurant he wandered into offered him a position. It was a wine bar with a small menu where people ate on a slanted, triangular patio, the servers always placing wadded linen napkins under the tables to keep glasses of coastal pinot gris from sliding off them. The manager, Judy, was first a cigarette and then the body that needed it, and she spent ten seconds on the piece of paper bearing his name but a minute on his jawline and deltoids.

"Fucking Anthony with the legs just quit," she said. "Could you come back for the dinner rush? We have an opener but need a backup."

"Tonight?"

"No, babe, in the year 2020. Wear some silver leggings. I'll be the head in a jar, okay?" She immobilized her neck and deadened her eyes and began to speak in a kind of mechanized chirp. "This body was no temple."

Judy, the other waiter explained as the sun went down on Market, was a mostly lovable figurehead, there primarily to fill the duty of tasting the wines. He was sleek and compact, Braden, originally from Ohio, which he revealed in a whisper, and he did a practiced impression of her at the bar, the wobble of her fingers with the Camel Light, *Is it corked, I dunno,* lips smacking, *I have a feeling it must be corked but I need another sip to know for sure.* They were standing in the hall between the kitchen and the dining room, rolling silverware into napkins, the knives' blades slipped between the tines of forks and then swaddled in an elaborate fold Wright could not get the hang of.

"Congratulations on the nomination," he said. Wright took a breath and a quick survey of Braden's face and another set of steaming silverware from the plastic bucket.

"What?"

"Your résumé. It's up for the Nobel Prize in literature. A rich, devastating fiction, they're calling it."

"You'll laugh, you'll cry."

"Mostly the latter."

He was in Wright's ear the whole night, issuing an instruction, averting catastrophe, handing him the tapenade or soup spoon he'd forgotten, calling Wright honey in a way that humiliated him. Later he remembered only this, the voice coming to his rescue under the strings of lights that laced the wild-vined terrace, how natural Braden looked, making his body small and light to land an entrée at a far table, then dense and thick to demand some missing order in the narrow window that led to the kitchen.

Sitting at the bar afterward, in the shadow of the chairs piled on tables, Wright kissed him. In the long second before, when he was leaning in and taking Braden's face in his hands, he told himself he would have kissed anyone who had shown him a kindness.

Braden put a hand on each shoulder and pushed him away, humming a terse note like a machine malfunctioning.

"Nothankyou," he said. "I don't kiss boys who are pretending to be straight."

Wright stood and untied the apron from around his waist, removing the Bic and the steno pad, and he rolled it on the bar and then made a gesture to indicate his departure.

"Did you just salute me?"

He laughed, though his lungs felt wet and nothing was funny, certainly not the way he was living his life, following any impulse and then balking when it would not embrace him. Braden patted the stool.

"Planning on living in your car, babe?" he said.

Braden pointed at his clavicle, circling his index finger in a tight clockwise rotation.

"Oh god." The little laminate ID necklace from the gym hung on its fluorescent green lanyard, showing through at his top buttons. "It was there all night? You knew just from that?"

"Not quite. That and your Ford, which I saw you sleeping in on my way in this morning. I don't know, it broke my heart. I couldn't say anything. I had a feeling you'd walk off midshift anyway, especially after you almost spilled scalding consommé on that fairly charismatic baby."

He laid his head on the bar and Braden gave it a paternal ruffle. After they finished a bottle Judy had opened but forgotten, he offered Wright the room, walking distance if you could stand the hills, there was a reason men in San Francisco had such beautiful asses, rent he could make easily from a few weekend rushes, enough sunlight that it changed the feeling of the room, charged it. Like the presence of someone you loved sleeping in it, Wright thought, when he walked in, pulling loose cash for the deposit from his pocket right then.

3.

Braden's personality was like a feature of the apartment—crown molding, bay windows, his hungover voice coming down the hall in the morning. "I feel like a goddamned aborted murder." His cheerful march down the hallway, his singing in the afternoon and his culinary catastrophes, little bits of green onion that ended up flung far from the stove, remnants of yolk and demerara sugar that crusted in bowls in the sink. Around a mattress on the floor in his bedroom he had arranged a choir of antique ladders, peeling and leaning, and at the top of one a rubber plant he referred to as My Wife Doris. "Gotta get home to Doris," he would say. "Gotta get home to the wife."

Wright furnished his bedroom as though it were his vocation, adding or altering something every day. He bought a lacquered wooden tray, Japanese, that he kept on his dresser, and on it every night, next to the moisturizer he had begun using and a vial of cassia oil he dabbed at his throat, he put his cheap rubber watch and the turquoise ring of Fay's. Although it meant welcoming whatever draft or chill came in, he put his bed in the U made by the bay window, at its top the abandoned maple headboard of what had been a sleigh frame, and spread over its length a quilt he had splurged on, navy and maroon checked with cream.

At the ends of the nights in the bars where they gave away their money, laying it damp and crippled by the gin and tonics, they sat for photo booth pictures, Braden always the star, Wright waiting after in the sulfuric smell for the strip to fall down behind the band of metal. He hung the highlights in his room with wooden laundry pins on fishing wire. In the undisputed favorite, Braden poured a beer onto an unknowing Wright's head, filling the next frame with Wright's cursing mouth and sopping hair and leaving Braden, in the last, alone and delighted, hands to his cheeks.

That everything was new about his life, all of it the invention of a golden flash of time, did not feel strange or false because this was true of almost everyone he knew, boys whose families went exclusively unmentioned. They were, those buttoned-up people in pretty side-gabled houses, those Maries and Dons, those owners of station wagons and Kodak projectors, essentially only places his friends had once lived.

He spent the first three months there waiting for the moment he would be asked, sometimes leaving the table at the bar or the low-slung couch if the matter of hometowns came up, until he realized that in saying nothing he was communicating a great deal. Braden was the only one who knew about Fay, and he asked very few questions, something that made Wright grateful at first and resentful later—why was it only living parents who were the subject of the conversational offhand, did your mother cook growing up, were you raised religious.

Whatever anyone else assumed, a renouncement at Thanksgiving or the locks on the family house changed, was not, he felt, so different from reality, at least in visible consequence. It made him feel like one of many among them, those whose only life was the one that could be confirmed by others. The suede and denim layered against the fog, the gossip at breakfast, all the men he kissed, nearsighted or clean-shaven, deep brown or pale and blond, supplicant or adversarial, long and warm and alive.

October 3, 1983

Dear Mr. Kahn,

I know I said I wouldn't call your mother again, and I'm sorry. It happens sometimes when I drink, that I pick up the phone, and it might not even be a sad thing—I just want to hear as many voices as possible, before I go to bed, as many places. I'll call the late-night desk at the newspaper and ask what I might find in the morning edition, I'll call the mechanic with a made-up problem and ask for an estimate. I think POPCORN might be the most beautiful phone number there is—the sound of that woman telling me the exact moment one minute becomes another makes me feel like a part of the world's order. In any case, about your mom, she hung up the first time and didn't answer the next. She didn't seem to remember the conversations we'd had about you, the things she'd told me.

It's strange to be back in California, so close to my grandparents, without their knowing. I never returned the last letter they sent, just cashed the check. Although I keep telling myself I'll drive over the bridge the next time I have two days off, then I think—why? Why put any of us through that, the complicated lie of it? If there's anything I love about this country, it's the acceptability of calling shared blood an accident. I never knew my aunt, just how she suffered, at the hands of her family, because of who she wanted to fuck, and there's no part of that I'm interested in—the neutral

*pronouns and mysterious descriptors I might use, when talking to
my grandparents, to hide the fact that I like men. Is it possible it's a
kindness, not telling them?*

*There was a joke among the members of Shelter, that if you
wanted to join your dad needed to own homes in two climates. Randy
was an exception to this, and my mother was fundamentally not. It
occurs to me that a convincing performance of destitution, the trash
fires and meals of stray cats, was possible for her and Annabelle,
whose grandfather patented superglue, only because they had come so
far from the other end. What's funny is that who my mother became,
ashamed of her parents' wealth, turned Claudette and James further
into the isolation their money had afforded them. They moved from
Orange County, where at least there had been visits to the orchards,
civic committees and whatnot, to a house on a hill in a town where
they knew no one. By the time I got there, they had stopped taking
new photos.*

*The summer of the meat shortage and the oil crisis and the
Watergate hearings was my first with my grandparents, and I was
addicted to the television like some boys are to porn. Unrepentant
Nixon voters with bumper stickers to boot, my grandparents started
watching the hearings in support of my curiosity, perhaps thinking
that it was in avoiding political conversations with my mother they
had lost her. In the beginning Claudette, who usually relied on the
housekeeper Miranda to boil water, made popcorn.*

*At first it seemed like a mistake to me that the green of that long
table in the caucus room was the same color as the felt you'd find in a
pool hall. I remember saying so, what is this, the national billiards
tournament, an attempt at humor with my new family. Sam Ervin's
drawl was the soundtrack of those months, something that I left on
in my bedroom on the portable color set they'd surprised me with, and
maybe you remember how you could hear it change. In the beginning
the slowness of his speech was in the service of jokes, just a country
lawyer he said so often in the beginning, but then the protracted way*

he talked became about something else. He stopped mentioning North Carolina, a saying they had there. He started speaking only about that room, their reasons for being in it.

I was amazed by how living that room seemed, how there was always a cigar smoldering in an ashtray, or a wife of one of the witnesses adjusting her earrings where they kissed her fat chignon, or a photographer ducking to tie his shoe before he set up a shot. There was food and water and even, in the way people dressed—formality ratcheted down for the sake of the heat—weather: the top aides to the president with their summer buzz cuts and no suit jacket to speak of. I was twelve, about to be thirteen, and the hearings made me happy, even giddy, I guess because they made the country seem less like an oath and more like a conversation, one that could go dark or light or turn around and surprise you. On either side of me, Claudette and James looked forward to the clarification that would put the unfounded rumors to rest, and in the beginning they watched with the patient faces of people watching a child solve a simple equation, hiding what they knew well to allow him his moment of understanding. They were bored as they waited out the spectacle.

There was the map of the complex that the detective touched with a pointer. There was the phone with its organs exposed, McCord demonstrating, with his fingers light on the wires, how to implant a bug.

By the end of the first month, the solution had not come, and we stopped watching together. James would shut off my television if he passed by my room and I wasn't in it, and the minute I returned I would snap it back on. The faces of the witnesses had fallen into two camps by then, roughly along age lines, under and over forty, people who believed their life might change and those who refused to. There were the younger men, responding to the senator's questions in complete answers, aware of the left they had taken a while back and pleading with it, looking damp in a way that seemed permanent. They had been, just months before, men who had walked up their lives like a staircase, an easy and inevitable ascent, but now they were locked out. When they reached for their water it sometimes made me want to cry, because you could see it was the most relief they'd gotten from their rotten selves, the privacy of the moment formed by the glass and their tongue.

These were the witnesses I had a harder time watching, but I think it was the older men that got to James. I could hear from my bedroom the involuntary noises he made, sounds that were low and digestive. The facts that had gathered were rendering them and their way of thinking obsolete, and they wouldn't see it. What did the president know, and when did he know it? That Baker's question was so simple, and that their rejoinders were so acrobatic, so semantically complicated, was all anyone really needed to understand—if they hadn't already—that there would be no recovery. But they were close enough to dying, the attorney general and the chief of staff, their noses red and ruined enough, that they would not budge, contrition a way of living they had no interest in. They already seemed like things in a museum, taxidermied to teach a lesson about foolishness.

Even after James had lost hope, which I knew by the fact he had stopped watching entirely and had started visiting the kitchen in the middle of the night, hoping hunger had been what woke him up and not plain old loss and fury, I held out some on his behalf, or the parts of the child that persisted in me did. This was a dull counterfeeling to the awe I had for that room and the men in it, who had taken apart corruption just by speaking sensibly and at length. Still, for his sake, a part of me wanted some astonishing, improbable reversal, a joint revelation from the members of the Committee to Re-elect the President that would return my grandfather to the safety of his own thinking. How moved he had been, in the months after the re-inauguration, in the landslide against McGovern, a happy tear in his eye more than once over the morning paper in the cornflower-blue kitchen where the windows were never open. He had behaved like someone who, after *being long deprived of people who knew him, walked into a room full of them. "The silent majority" was a phrase he took from the president's mouth and kept with him, something he would say with an index raised, the three words representative of a long argument about the resistance that had ravaged the country for a decade and the sensible citizenry who'd had enough. But the neutrality of Cambodia, I would say, for instance, and he would shrug and lift a finger and say, The silent majority, and smile in the way that is the same as a closed door. I forgave him or tried, understanding his choice had been made less because of any speeches or headlines than because my mother had kept him from sleeping. He needed to believe the revolution that had taken his daughter was a corroborated evil, thought of that way by most reasonable men. The other answer was untenable, an understanding that would have undone him in the few years he had left.*

James stopped watching around the time that the eighteen minutes of tape showed up missing and the president's secretary tried and failed to shoulder the blame. That photo on the cover of Newsweek *was a punch line for all of it, her body contorted to reenact an impossible accident, a foot on a pedal beneath her desk and a hand on a red button on the receiver three feet away and her middle-aged torso trapped in a dress that could barely accommodate the gymnastic twist. Her face feigning normalcy above the strain was as perfect a symbol for the government as we'd see.*

The view from my grandparents' house was pleasant enough, made everything look far enough away, that it seemed maybe Claudette and James could ride it out in their fortress, sitting out on the porch where red rufous hummingbirds took those J-shaped plunges that seem like averted suicides. Stopping to look at the framed photos of their old life, they argued over the details—years and meals, guests and holidays. But even syndicated television, that reliable time travel, was no longer a comfort, given that on any day reruns might be interrupted with footage of the hearings. What had changed about

*the country was hidden everywhere, a joke shop trick ready to pounce
from the can.*

*They had tried to keep it from me, but I knew, from the women
picketing the grocery store and the gas station lines that sometimes
snaked around the block they had driven down just to avoid them,
that we were not living like other Americans. Claudette had Miranda
purchase flanks of pork that cost as much as she would earn in four
days, and once a week James sent her, in the beloved Mercedes he'd
previously barred anyone else from driving, to fill up the tank. I hated
seeing her in that car, perched on a stack of unread newspapers to see
over the dash. I recognized the fear in the way she sat. It was how I'd
behaved my first months in that house, frightened by all the things,
century-old chaises you weren't supposed to sit in, abstract sculpture of
glass and wire, each of them worth more money than I could imagine
holding in my hand. Why are you always marching around like a
soldier, Claudette had asked, her first tease, and I didn't say that I
had decided moving through the rooms in straight lines, taking only
clean, ninety-degree turns, was the way to keep from touching or
breaking any of it. They called me Little Old Tank and I laughed
with them, bewildered, some animal cornered and honking.*

*There was a week where Miranda couldn't get the gas. Her son
was sick and she needed to leave early and Claudette had said, Don't
worry about it. It can wait. There was an ease she'd adopted that
ran in opposition to how formally she dressed and how carefully she
cut the things on her plate. It was not some new-sprung generosity, I
know now, but a strain of defeat. She would not be running out to
meet the world and its plans anymore. It could make its way to her
or it could not.*

*She didn't know about the day James had in store for me, a
swim in the Russian River an hour north and some barbecue after,
part of an ongoing program to make me an All-American Kid that
embarrassed both of us, each pretending to enjoy it for the other's sake.
It was a war of attrition that had often reduced me to a wobbling*

center of panic and James to an old man in a parking lot, waiting for me to come out of whatever bathroom I'd locked myself into. He was going to teach me to dive that summer, an act that would have seemed absurd in the jungle tributaries where I had grown up, which had a way of arranging your body any way they wanted to. The goal was not to enter them separate and gleaming, in perfect human form, but to feel what was happening inside the water and mimic it as best you could. I was dreading all of it, the drive, the ugly pineapple-print swim trunks, the restaurant where he would make a point of calling me son in front of the waitress. What'll it be, son.

He saw the level on the tank as we coasted down the hill and became, in his seat, an inch taller, the only indication of his clipped annoyance. We'll be making a little stop, he said, as we passed through the light that came lacy through the patch of buckeyes. I could look longer at his face when he was driving, when he would not tell me staring was impolite, and as I studied him, I thought of Randy. Of all the differences, it was the ways they inhabited their anger I noticed the most. Randy had been transformed by it, a sketch of himself rendered in broken lines, reduced only to a furious shape, but James just lowered his voice and narrowed his eyes, limiting the visual intake of the environment that had wronged him, calling whichever malfeasance close to listen carefully.

The line for gas was twenty cars long, more. On the back of a hay-colored convertible, a young mother sat up, twirling her baby in the sun. From a dented sedan that was mostly bumper stickers, boys not much older than me rolled down windows to bleed smoke from their mouths. A couple in their early twenties had laid out a picnic in the bed of a pickup and were waving around red licorice like wands, touching it to each other's ears and collarbones. There was the war between three different radio stations, and the crescendo of an argument between two unseen men named Mel and Finn, fucking Cheetos in the mattress again one was yelling, and from somewhere behind us a child singing the alphabet incorrectly.

We waited there close to an hour, James not cutting the engine like everyone else did, turning it on every ten minutes to pull slightly up, but instead acting as if he were in the middle of an urban intersection at rush hour. What are you checking the side mirrors for, I finally said, a turtle that might pass you, testing out a sense of humor I wanted to adopt, but the weak joke died the second it hit the clotted air, and his foot stayed on the brake, ready to spring off.

In our town there were some enterprising individuals who capitalized on the gas line, guys with coolers on their shoulders saying ice cream, saying cold beer cold water, cold beer cold water. I could feel James conducting heat when they passed, not budging his jaw an inch when they knocked on the window that he had rolled up the moment they appeared at the front of the line. Don't look at them, he said to me. At the juncture when what he needed to believe was that the political moment was an exception—the diplomatic hiccup responsible for the oil embargo, the wobbly craven face the president made in all photos now—the capped-teeth men with their drumsticks and Budweisers and economy creamsicles, profiting from the waiting that defined that summer, suggested a normalization that he couldn't abide.

The car in front of us, a Volvo 240 in baked orange, was the only other in the interminable line that seemed apart from the microeconomy formed by the string of cars, also with its windows up, also emitting no sound. I could see what was happening in it perfectly, the heads and torsos framed through the back like a television. The woman in the driver's seat, whose fine black hair fell nearly to the gearshift, was wearing a red scoop-back leotard and bracelets of bells and wicker. She was intermittently kissing a man in the passenger seat, who would disappear one hand in the hair at her neck and slip the other down toward the pedals. In between bouts of writhing they didn't speak or touch or fiddle with the radio, just settled against the blond-wood beaded seat covers.

We were third in line when the guy with the cooler came around

*again, a veteran, I thought, because of the way he had of looking
at the people he took money from, too long and as if he were owed
much more. He tapped the window of the couple, who had returned
to a taffy of hair and color and fingers. When they didn't react, he
started for us.*

*A strange side effect of anxiety, Mr. Kahn, is a kind of
clairvoyance. What I mean is that when so much of your mind is
devoted, at all times, to the worst-case scenarios, when you become
a factory of troubling permutations, once in a while you will get it
right: if not the exact unfurling of events, the inciting incident or
pitch of a complaint or unhappy end result. A thousand monkeys at
a typewriter, et cetera. So that day I saw the rough heft of everything
that happened a second before it did, the vet knocking on the window
just as a station wagon left a pump and the kissing couple who
didn't pull up to take it, James seeing this and honking again and
narrowing his eyes as the knocking came quicker. This time the guy
with the cooler had looked in long enough to identify me as part of
his prime demographic, a young teen not yet welcomed to his vices
and still settling for sugar, and perhaps felt if he stayed long enough
I'd do his job for him, insist to James that he cough up the dollar.
By the third rap my grandfather's finger was already on the handle,
and he pulled it and swung the door open with his face fixed ahead,
probably already imagining the argument that of course he wouldn't
have looked to his left before doing so, because he would never imagine
a person standing right next to it, illegally, in what was technically
the middle of traffic. He lived his whole life like this, inside a series
of logic proofs that were sturdy and formidable so long as you didn't
admit desire or iniquity.*

*The guy jumped back, hit hard. Popsicles in blank plastic sleeves
and sweating Budweisers in their Fourth of July packaging dove for
the oil-saturated pavement. The couple through the window were bent
away from any outside noise: she had a knee up on the middle console
to twist into the passenger seat, and he was sitting way back to receive*

her, seat reclined, his knees in cutoffs spread as far as they would go. More horns were honking now, a sign that my grandfather took to mean he was right.

James moved around the vet with a lightness in his step I hadn't seen, some old version of himself. The man was bellowing about the loss of inventory, about what right do you have, looking like a horse in the way his teeth seemed to multiply as he got angrier. When James got to the driver's-side window he removed a handkerchief from his back pocket and wrapped it around his knuckles, and then he knocked. The spectacle of this was not lost on the line behind us, hungry for entertainment, and a horn sounded out—shave and a haircut, two bits. I saw her arm fly backward from the knot their bodies had made, the middle finger rise up, and then, without entirely understanding what I was seeing, another hand, my grandfather's, flying in through the door he'd opened, taking that profane gesture and literally crushing it. I didn't watch his face, the way his eyes moved as he did this, just how the way he had grabbed her reached other parts of her body, the vertebrae in her back scared very straight. When his hand took her hair, I turned the radio on and put my head between my knees. She's fine, he said, when the police came, look at her, believing as he always had that everything about a person could be known in a glance. He said the same thing to me, more than once. Look in the mirror. You're fine.

Wealth being a kind of wicked fame in small towns, my grandfather's name was known to at least one person in that line of cars. In the weeks after, teenage waitresses would seat but ignore him, the post office line would move around him to cashiers who claimed to be unsuited to the task his mailing errand required. Neither the headline that showed up in the local section, nor the letters to the editor it encouraged, were kind. Like the news of the White House, he refused to read it, and by the end of the summer they had canceled all their subscriptions. The rest of my time there I bought newspapers in

*town and shoved them down the back of my pants. Near the base of
my spine there was always an ashy halo of print, a word or two my
sweat had sucked off the page.*

*When I left their house at seventeen the mounting relief was a
secret they couldn't keep. They bought my train ticket to school in
August by April, all possible dormitory supplies by June. I caught
James whistling in my empty room. What a pleasure it must be to
enter that agreement with yourself, when you get to a certain age, to
say no more adjustments will be necessary. That two people could look
so eagerly toward the end of their lives was an astonishment to me
then.*

*If I write you these letters and you never read them, am I better
off or worse? In the offices of guidance counselors and therapists, the
emphasis was always on my past. If I could come to terms with it,
I could be on my way forward. But why is it my job to understand
what happened to me? Shouldn't that be the work of the people
responsible for bringing me here? You and my mother were more
similar than either of you would probably care to admit, each given
over to your program or movement, leaving very little of who you were
for anybody else. Tell me about yourself, said the college psychologist
I was forced to go to, on account of truancy, three purple weeks that
turned over in my twin-sized bed.*

*There was something I read about you, in a gossip magazine I stole
from the grocery store checkout, how when Elise divorced you it took
your mother visiting and seeing your wife's things gone for her to even
find out. This they painted as the nobility of your heartbreak, but I
know it was something else. You believe it's possible to live entirely
inside yourself, Mr. Kahn. I know because you gave that to me.*

*I was born in 1960, I finally said. What could I answer? What
chance, in the shadow of two people so contorted around their very
clear purpose, did I ever have of observing myself?*

I enclosed a photo I took the other day, of a homeless man asleep at the back of a bus. I loved the color of his dress, the blue sequins on the orange plastic. Doesn't he look happy? I hope you're sleeping well, Mr. Kahn, proud of who you've always been.

Yours,

Wright

4.

That Wright saw Randy one last time, gaunt and bearded, later seemed like something he should have worried about, a mean joke about the smallness of San Francisco, but in his life here he had given up plenty of his old self, denim that didn't fit right, a habit of apologizing at the slightest discomfort of his own. The thoughts of himself suspended by a noose from an oak tree, twisting over some golden farmland, were all but gone, the imagined weight of a gun pushed back down his right molars, the fantasy of thirty pills dissolving in whole milk and strawberries in a blender. Suicide had been like some billboard he had to drive by every day, he thought, a highly effective advertisement that adorned the horizon on his way to getting anywhere, and somehow, with luck whose longevity he prayed for, he had found a way around it. He had not forgotten how it was to live with that imperative in his mind, a two-word command he had heard from everywhere, and he kept the memory of it as a warning, to remember what kind of town he was living in and what waited on the other side.

The day was forty-two degrees and flirting with rain, and he had taken Braden's lunch shift as a means of making amends. At a bar two nights before, a place famous for the fact that no two chairs were alike, he had picked up a boy Braden had been eyeing for weeks, a painter who lived on a houseboat in Sausalito and was always faking concern about making the last ferry.

It had begun to feel to Wright like a thrilling game, how to make himself seen. It was automatic now, a certain glance, a jaw pointed in the opposite direction of the gaze, a way of standing, his hands woven behind his head, as though he were at rest even then. He understood that making this his talent had its issues, but it was the first time in his life he wanted to be visible, for people to ask, when he leaned over the shifting light of the jukebox or kissed an arriving acquaintance, who is that? Braden found the painter in the kitchen the next morning, while Wright slept off six well-gin gimlets, and after mopped the whole apartment, the aggressive smell of the citrus wax he used a telltale sign of his anger. "It's like you need every single person to love you," he said, when they finally talked about it, "no matter how you feel about them. It's the same old show, watching you after your third drink."

On the way home from the restaurant Wright was immune to the street, the florist who lined his windows with unusual cuttings in jars of water, the fire escapes where boys in women's furs sat smoking. At the corner store where he stopped for cigarettes and to scan the newspapers, a place he generally spent ten forgotten minutes, he heard Randy's voice. It was unmistakable, a sound that sent up the last decade in smoke.

Next up in the five-person line, shorter than Wright remembered, Randy was thin and ragged as some plant that has grown in a place where it is not supposed to, counting out some change with a rigid pointer finger. He was slipping coins along the top line of his palm, pinky to index. Wright put his paper back and pushed on his sunglasses and made his way toward the door with his eyes on his watch, an absurd impulse he was only half-aware of, as though Randy, if he spotted him, would assume he was late for an appointment and decide not to bother.

The hand on his shoulder came a half a block down. He saw the fingers over the line of his jaw, sallow and attenuated. He dug his scapula forward to remove them, spun around to better see the threat.

"Whoa, man," Randy said, his arms spread to embrace him. "I thought that was you."

Wright couldn't speak, only wait for what came next. He hung on that piece of time waiting for it to drop. Randy began to talk, as he always had, as though he were answering an audience, a single-file line of burning questions about his remarkable life. The flap pockets of his oilskin jacket were overstuffed and revealed their contents, a trade paperback, a misshapen bar of soap. His showy rhetoric identified him immediately, but there was a postural aspect that had changed, a shifting of his weight, a hedging air.

"In town for some big meetings. Not anything I can talk about, yet, but this administration is in for a real shock, let me say, if they think . . ."

The incomplete sentence he punctuated with a hitched-up wiry eyebrow, a smack of either palm to his jaw to crack his neck. He had been underground, Wright calculated, for eleven years. "Where you living, chief," Randy was asking him, as casual as someone very young to whom an address was a fleeting accessory. Everything about him, this man his mother had loved, ran in opposition to time, called it some old-fashioned joke Randy was above entertaining. This was the chief domain of the unstable, Wright thought, that they saw all minutes and years as having equal importance, not as the pieces of an elaborate construction, foundations and entry-ways, but some deep bowl of marbles, any of which could shift to become the most visible and relevant. Standing there Wright had a pneumonic feeling. He was sure he could have told Randy that Fay and Annabelle were around the corner editing the latest missive to the press, and Randy would have felt a great relief, followed him without blinking. "Where you living," Randy had asked, a jocular punch on Wright's elbow. He heard himself naming the intersection as he had hundreds of times, lightly, *Church and Duboce,* to cabdrivers, *right off the park,* to men he wanted to fuck. He had believed himself married to his new life, to the project of his future, but he saw now that at the smallest wave from the past he might consider dismantling it.

"Right on," Randy said. "Well, yeah, I can definitely stop by and fill you in. And speaking of that, could you loan me a little something?"

Why he agreed he didn't know. It was a memory that appeared like a taste in his mouth, Randy hunched over him deep in the jungle, covering the tight little-boy fist with his hand and pushing up his shirt to suck out the stinger of a wasp. Randy on his guitar in that hotel room where their three lives had been braided together, no sentence started by one of them left unannotated by another, Paul Simon, *mama don't take my Kodachrome away,* a palimpsest of interjections and half-remembered dreams and offers of dried fruit or clean laundry, a world of talking Wright had helped to make, and that had made him. From his front pocket he took his billfold and removed everything in it. He watched Randy walk away with it, the bills tight in his filthy hand. "I'll call you," he said, though Wright had not offered his number. At a certain point Randy stopped, and Wright thought he might turn, give off the kind of smile that had once bent a room to him, brief, enormous, but he was only looking at a damp cardboard box someone had put on the curb, picking up tapes and warped tennis shoes, trying to find something he could use.

5.

It happened in a moment, a look that lighted on Braden's face. He understood what Wright had never told him, the belief that was too foolish to say aloud. They had cooked breakfast for some friends, Tony—who was called Fucking Tony because he was forever making some fool-hearted mistake, taking home some transient who stole his entire wardrobe, accepting a catering gig that paid a third in coupons, what has Fucking Tony done now—and Jean, who was tall and French and had a way of making anything sound like an aphorism he had coined there on the spot. *The bagel it is better because of the part that is missing, no?* It was a line they howled and repeated.

They sat on two chaises, arranged to make an L around a coffee table, hunched over their plates. On the window was a spray of eucalyptus, lolling across the floor in the breeze from the bay windows were three nearly deflated blue balloons, vestiges of a birthday party the week before. *God bless your mother,* it still said in lipstick on the bathroom mirror. The television was on, the channel changed every so often by someone who forgot to pay attention anyway. When they had mopped up the last bits of hollandaise they sat back into their hangovers, sorting through the narratives of the night before, deciding what needed to be explained or forgotten. The three of them had gone out, a night at a friend's, poppers on the roof, but Wright had stayed home. He was trying to be curious about who he was when alone, among only the things he owned and had arranged himself. There was always a moment, a few hours into solitude, when he panicked at the simplest of decisions, to bathe or make a cup of tea, when he balked at the responsibility of a whole body. He had been in the city three years now and no longer felt that it could absorb him, that just by being inside of it something in him was being polished.

It was December 1984 and the conversations all seemed to be rolling the same way, a slant to the floor of how they were living that was becoming more pronounced. Who did you know who had died? How had he looked at that party in Diamond Heights, and was it only six months ago, and did you remember how he had corralled a group of them—yes, twenty of us walked there, that rope swing that flew out into the view. It was the year people started saying, low voices into cupped hands, *I almost slept with him, we had a date that I canceled because of a cold.* The men who were sick or gone were always talked about in terms of proximity, as one might mention a movie star, and it was true that their deaths had made them famous and abstracted, the whole of their lives reduced to whichever salient, adaptable anecdote. Anthony the ballerina who had once bottomed en pointe, Forest from Florida who wanted to die with his watch on.

On the television identical twin girls, fourteen and Aryan, leaned out right and left from a tandem bicycle and blew green bubbles of gum. A white woman in shoulder pads lowered her sunglasses at a white man in khakis. There was no one like them in the commercials for small cellophane candies, antidotes to migraine, juice so fresh it jumped from the glass and clothing so clean it glowed. There was pride in this, that their lives were unmappable, irreducible, existing under the known American fabric, but also fear, like some nightmare in which the mirrors when you pass by them are empty.

"He was always at the gym," Braden was saying. "He did hand-stands as a party trick."

"That's right. He liked to walk on his hands. I saw him do it down the middle of Dolores."

"Twenty-eight."

As was his role with them, Tony came in with a discursion, always looking, as he placed the opening remark, like he had just been woken from some sleep in the sun.

"The other day?"

"Yes, Tony." Braden had a cigarette in his mouth and was roll-ing pennies from the jar they kept by the door. He could only stand Tony's talk if he was accomplishing something else.

"Downtown. I saw this guy on the street?"

"Shocking. Foot traffic, in this city?"

"And as he was coming closer I couldn't remember his name or where I knew him from, and I felt so guilty. Cute, but very shad-owy, I mean some real unnecessary sunglasses, a bad Bogart trench. I figured oh, a very intoxicated conquest, because definitely I had a memory of him with his shirt off! So I decided not to be a puss about it and make eye contact. But our young friend clearly did not like it, because the more I looked at him and waved the more he looked the other way, and then I started getting angry! We've all been rejected. It is never a day at the fair, but still."

"It is to us like temperature," Jean said. "We only can face it."

"Thank you, Jean, profound, yes," Braden said. "And?"

"So as I'm about to pass him I straighten up and I say, real vi-cious, 'I'm sorry I fucked you and never called, okay?' He looked like he was going to flag down an ambulance right there. I was very pleased with myself and decided to walk all the way home, and about ten minutes in I realized where I knew him from. It was Tom Hanks."

The minute they spent laughing stretched and tightened and Tony got up and bowed, tipping an invisible hat. Wright had his face in the crook of the couch and could feel that the elastic waist on his pajamas had slipped around. He kicked his slip-on Vans in delight. In the silence after there was the flint of his lighter and a car passing below playing Donna Summer and the light turning over into afternoon.

"Hello!" Jean said, in a way he did they had ceased correcting, the way one might say, hey, you forgot your wallet, hey, you can't do that here. He insisted that the two were interchangeable, *hey* and *hello,* and anyway it mitigated his confrontational streak, because he was the type of person always accusing someone else of having spilled his drink. Instead of the charbroiled melancholy that was his nature, he gave off a kind of confused gregariousness, a near-constant state of greeting. "Hello!" he had said when a seagull shat on him at China Beach. "Fucking hello!" he repeated, disturbing a passing family, who could not imagine why this man in a leather jacket, with runny avian excrement coming perfectly down his side part, would be choosing this moment to make their acquaintance.

Jean had snapped his fingers and was pointing at Wright, his middle finger still curled under.

"Do you know who you look like?"

Wright shrugged and sucked on his cigarette, using it as an excuse not to speak. In his slippers his feet were pricked with sweat; in his mouth there was not even the memory of saliva.

"Vincent Kahn. It is crazy, it is exactly. No? All you need is the suit. We must fashion you one."

As he turned to Wright, Tony had his hands spread amenably on his thighs and his mouth a little open. Braden, who was tipping his head, then nodding with some conviction, locked eyes with Wright and stopped. The glance that passed between them was a whole late-night conversation, questions backed up to and answered indirectly, shock, exhausted laughter. Inside of it was the evening Braden had knocked on Wright's bedroom door and found him drunk at his desk, writing a letter, and he had barked *not now.*

Wright tucked his chin to his neck, briefly, as if to acknowledge to Tony this had been said before, but the confirmation was for Braden.

"I think there's nothing more boring," Braden said, "than insisting everything and everyone you've known has some counterpart or mirror. The referential is a weakness, I think. Abandon it."

His intellectual arrogance was familiar to them, what they hated about him and why they ran to him when they were frightened of themselves. Tony made an involuntary noise in his throat, as though Braden's idea itself were caught there. Rolling his eyes, Jean moved his hand quickly up and down a small invisible cock.

"What is the expression? Why are you being such a dirty blanket," Jean said. "It is Sunday and I am looking only to enjoy, lovely, relaxed, and you are face-fucking me with this philosophy."

"This wet blanket," Braden said, stacking their dishes on his arm and sashaying toward the sink, "cooked you a spectacular breakfast." Wright made his way down the hall with his hands on the western wall, someone caught on a shelf of rock, and he crawled into bed with his shoes on.

HE WOKE TO BRADEN AT the foot of his bed, sitting there dressed for the dinner shift, his hair still wet from the shower. The only light came from the streetlamps that had just turned on, the red paper lantern in the hall.

"What do you want to tell me," Braden said, "about that look on your face when Jean said what he did."

"Right now?"

He was buffeted still by sleep and tried to release it, sitting up and throwing the blankets off and passing a hand over his face.

"Right now."

"Which war manual did you lift this tactic from? 'Interrogate the prisoner on his most fearful secrets while he is mostly unconscious.'"

"Is it a secret?"

"'Ensure the prisoner cannot tell his waking state from his sleeping.' What do you mean is it a secret?"

"Is it a fact?"

"I told my grandfather once. A therapist in college."

"Only a fact can really be a secret, right? Otherwise it's just a sad thought you've been keeping to yourself. Something that isn't real can't really be confined."

"That's kind. I'm feeling very hopeful about this conversation already. The dates line up, Braden."

"Which dates. Tell me exactly which dates. This is not something she told you."

"The dates she worked at her sister's bar outside an Air Force base where he was a test pilot. In the Mojave Desert. Starting in 1957. No."

"What else. Is there a photo? Is there a letter?"

He knew how it would land before he said it, so he didn't. People say I look like him. *The referential is a weakness,* Braden had said earlier in the living room. He asked for his cigarettes on the dresser to buy himself time. He wanted to be his own creation, as Braden was, as was everyone they knew, and somehow he could not. Around the room were his shoddy attempts, the books about Greek architecture he had dog-eared, the photos of the two of them in the frames he had painted.

"Why are you doing this," he whispered instead.

Braden stood to turn on a light, the brass lamp with the swinging head that was clamped to Wright's desk. Stacked on the desk were the books he had recently read, a reminder of the information that was at his disposal now, and Braden picked one up and opened to a page in its middle.

"'The first conscientious objectors in United States history, the Shakers' pacifism can still be understood as revolutionary,'" he read aloud, and shut it. "I'm doing this because your believing this is keeping you from something."

"They believed god is male and female. What is it keeping me from? Tell me what it's keeping me from."

"That's the whole thing about prison, isn't it? You don't know what it's keeping you from. Anything could be happening outside of it, and you're lucky if you get a window."

"They knew exactly, about any object they built, where it would go in a room."

"I'm late to work," Braden said. "I'm sorry I can't go there with you. I would if it made any sense. I would if I thought it would help you."

The door shut and his heart rate tripled and he heard Braden gargling his mouthwash, humming "Happy Birthday" to time it. He looked around his room and thought about how nothing in it, except the ring on his finger, was something his mother had touched. If it had all turned out to be a mistake—if she had not died, if she had not left—she would not know where to find him, and if she did, she would not know what to ask.

6.

In the way we believe some door at home has been left unlocked, Wright felt he had the disease and knew which man had given it to him. Why the specific belief, he asked himself. It would be easier to keep it nameless and faceless, the thing ruining his body. It had taken him so long, twenty-five years, to love his body, to know what he wanted from it, what he wanted done to it, and now, he was sure, it was going, fleeing by night. There was no proof, not so much as a cold that wouldn't go away, but his certainty about it was the thing that woke him up every morning, what he argued with in bed every night.

The man in question had been Boy Scout beautiful, hair the color of a peanut butter cookie, silent until he became, on some issue—the superiority of a certain car, the history of the American railroad—implacably outspoken. They had fucked within an hour of meeting, upstairs at a dinner party, their places saved, leaving a few bites of pork left, on the salad plates a smattering of peach and pine nuts and gorgonzola. It was a guest room filled with the typical second-rate ephemera. Above the door a framed macaroni collage made by some child, in the corner a stack of *Architectural Digest*s, on the nightstand an ancient university anthology and inside of it some pressed flowers. There were six pillows on the bed, each in a different pillowcase, and in the thirty minutes they spent there he shoved his face in each of them. The man had been kinder than the circumstance demanded, kissed each of Wright's eyelids and thanked him. "For what," he said. It went unanswered.

When they emerged, damp and empty now of the dinner party impulse to follow any comment with a witty rejoinder, the room clapped. "I would ask if you'd like dessert," said one of the hosts, a mutual friend—a man who could name the year and designer of any piece of furniture you showed him, who was such a beloved uncle that nieces and nephews repeatedly ran away from their house to his—his hand aloft and fork pointed out, "but it seems you've already had some."

His name was Ben, and Wright saw him once more after that. He was a third-grade teacher and a hobbyist mechanic and a runner, the first one Wright had ever met, the first person who ever took Wright's cigarette from his hand and asked him to consider quitting. Wright took him up on the invitation, an address on the back of a library receipt, no phone number, a drunk omission or just a dare, visited him in the Berkeley hills, a thirty-minute walk from the train, surprised him where he lay under a Fiat from the fifties. "Wondering when you'd come," he had said, still under the car.

Wright sat on the hot curve of pavement, smelling the bake of eucalyptus and waiting for him to finish what he was doing. When Ben rolled out on the carpeted creeper, he took his time putting his wrenches away in an Army-green toolbox and then motioned toward the garage, where he washed his hands in a paint-splattered sink, then brought Wright through a door into the kitchen. He offered Wright some mineral water, then bent him over the tiled counter. On it was a wooden bowl of clementines, small and still bearing leaves, which Wright could, even a year later, see approaching and retreating as the two of them moved.

How did he know, how could he be certain? Hadn't there been

others, around the same time? Yes. The bathroom of a bar in the
city, a place where an aquarium gurgled behind the shelves of liquor,
a guy with a beard who had smelled uncannily of mold and held
his hand the whole time. Buena Vista Park, the underbrush taller
than his ankles, fog already in from the bay, a dog nearby barking.
A stoned afternoon in Sausalito, a houseboat made of driftwood, a
second time with the windows open onto the water, his name possibly Hugh or Kent, a moment where the pain or pleasure of it was
so large he could not see.

Then why Ben? For one thing, he had died. It had happened
in the same room, he learned, with the bowl of clementines. The
hospital bed and the oxygen tank and the life-monitoring apparatuses fit better there than in the dark back bedroom, where he'd
hung moody figurative charcoals of cities, another hobby he could
have made a profession. The nurse who came could clean him more
easily, there in the light and with the sink nearby. That he was
gone Wright knew because the host of the dinner party had said
so, matter-of-factly, continuing to walk and dodge panhandlers on
the street where they ran into each other, the way he said it an
odd semantic switchback, "Oh you know who died is Ben." It was
a necessary defense, to treat it like gossip. They could not stop at
every casualty or they would all be fixed in apoplectic place. Paper
sacks of groceries on their cocked hips, hair tucked into sheepskin
collars, they kept walking.

How could he be sure? It was something his mother had said.
He was loath to lend her any credence, and preferred to think of
her as an accident moving further into the past, but occasionally
she was as large as she'd ever been, scribbling her marginalia on the
years she'd left him to. There was a judgmental silence when he was
denying himself some vital feeling, and sometimes it came with the
image of her hands folded, features placid as a Renaissance cherub's.
This had been her way of denouncing an idea or event, by refusing
its projections onto her face. He had seen it anger people, Randy,

to the point of violence, ceramic trinkets launched across the room, tree branches snapped back, *Say something, say something.*

It was possible he had loved Ben, or at least that Ben had recognized him in some novel way, because he had felt an unfamiliar repulsion. He had turned down Ben's offer of a meal or a drive to a swim, his grandmother's chicken, a rope swing Ben said was downright Rockwellian. Even a shower he had declined, although he knew the water pressure would be perfect, the towels fluffed and folded as his never were. When Wright wrote down his phone number in the address book Ben handed him, a fine object embossed and clearly cared for, he changed the fifth digit. It was the first time a man had wanted to know his oldest memory, had tendered a theory on how he smelled. "Like a stick of cinnamon left its podunk town and got a fancy education," Ben said, then sank his teeth in Wright's shoulder.

The conversation was one of few in which she had used the phrase *your father,* the others being in reference to some genetic trait or strain in temperament she could not account for—the recurring ear infection that kept them up nights the year he was six, Wright's tendency to take apart machines and rebuild them. Other than this she would only say she had not known him well.

I can't say how, but it was like my body knew, the weeks after your father, that something had changed it fundamentally.

She had confessed this from in front of a mirror, loosened as she always was by her vanity.

The day after I took the horse on a long ride, which I almost never did, Lloyd, have I ever told you about Lloyd, because your aunt got nervous any time he was out of her sight for more than an hour. It was the first thing I wanted that morning, to squeeze my legs around him and knot my hands in his hair. He was a villain, this horse. A long story, but he shit on my lunch, once, when I left it on the porch to grab a beer from inside. Perfect aim, middle of the sandwich. As though his asshole were another eye.

He had sat on the toilet, as he did so often, watching his mother.

Her fingers along her jaw, her mouth pursing, then relaxing, her shoulders turning to catch the light as she tugged her shirt down or adjusted a high bun.

On my dismount he was switching a little and I rolled my bad ankle. This had happened a number of times, a side effect of a decade of ballet lessons, but this time I was weirdly disarmed by the pain of it. Charlie found me crying in my room and laughed, put my swollen foot on her lap and talked to it like I wasn't there. I felt the injury more keenly, is the point, felt betrayed by that tendon! Isn't that silly? But later, when I knew I was pregnant, it all made sense. I had felt I was responsible for more than myself, that my foot had belonged to or was responsible for more. Always pay attention to the theater of your body.

In the weeks following the afternoon with Ben, he had felt a quiet corporeal fear, something that altered his behavior in peculiar ways anyone would have noticed had he allowed anyone around. After a shower he stopped toweling himself off on a bath mat, in view of the mirror, instead drying and then dressing behind the curtain. He ate as though he might be caught and punished, barefoot by the fridge, at odd hours, without the proper utensils, forgoing seasoning or any modifying wish. The exercise regimen he'd taken pains to establish, the mat in the corner of his room under magazine photos of triathlons he'd sheepishly pinned there for inspiration, went from daily to never in under a week. He rolled it up and placed it on the highest shelf of his closet without asking himself why, obscuring it quickly with boxes of old books that he brought from back to front. Sweets began waving at him from everywhere. From the rear of a bodega freezer he pulled a coconut Popsicle, the lone survivor of the summer, and he ate it on the walk home in forty-degree weather, taking large sideways bites. In a Polish diner where he sometimes read the newspaper on nights he couldn't sleep, where the tables were always vaguely adhesive and the disappointed elderly waitresses were always out front smoking, he finished his borscht and blinked and made a beeline to the frosty display case and pointed at the largest slice of something called peanut butter pie. He ate it without stopping once for a drink of water. It was as though, in advance of disappearing, his body wanted to become as substantial as possible, to become more of a burden to the thing that would fight to erase it.

So this was how he knew, this was why he thought Ben, although it had been a year, and it was a suspicion he kept private, an illicit pet he fed only when alone. It made sense to him, that the first man who had made him want the things he had always been told he couldn't have, the house with the lights already on when he got there, the domestic squabbles over money and décor, the child who knew and loved his name—it made sense this would also be the man to take their possibility away.

How had Ben died? Perhaps their friends suspected what Wright believed by how intent he was on answering this question. What did he mean, they said, how had he died. He put the question to them cold, no warning or transition, as they walked uphill in clusters to the parties that had begun to feel like an elaborate performance, in the back rooms of bars between the end of one song and the beginning of the next. How had he died? Like all of them were dying, too quickly, like men three times their age. What did he mean.

If he was a fool to think there was something of how someone lived in how he died, so be it. But he wanted to know. He would not elaborate. He only repeated the question. How had he died, Ben? Finally, there was someone who could tell him, a man who taught in the same school district Ben had, a nebbishy person who often spoke with a palm across his face. Someone had given him Wright's phone number and they had arranged to meet at Tosca, where he had shown up early, his collar buttoned too high. Ben had loved it there, the booths as red and cheap as the wine, the waitress who lived in the back and managed the late nights in her gauze robe.

From the way he said Ben's name it was clear he had loved him, and also that the feeling had gone long unreturned. He had not been there at the exact moment, only Ben's sister had, but he had brought groceries often, stood by the blender a foot from where Ben lay and ground ingredients for the repulsive smoothies that might buy a few more hours. So how had he died?

"In the last two weeks," he said, "Ben developed this funny habit of rhyming."

"Rhyming?"

"Anything you said to him, he tried to match the last word. Sometimes he couldn't get the word, only a sound. It made him laugh. His jaw seemed to be the only part of his face that was left. I'm sorry. I don't know why I said that."

"Forget it. Why?"

"He was always so witty and I thought maybe this was to cover up for how sedated the morphine made him, or, this might be a reach, but to kind of extend the conversation and make it bigger. He knew there were so many things he wouldn't get to talk over, so this was his way of covering more ground, getting to say this or that one last time."

"And?"

"What, and? I don't know. I'm trying to give you what you're asking for. How did you know him? I never saw you around."

"Can you remember a specific rhyme?"

"Most of them were nonsense. Just words, just noises. Sometimes a phrase—I'd say, 'I'm just going to get a coffee,' and he'd go, 'Happy children are so bossy.'"

The conversation dried up, then, the disappointment bidirectional. There was always the strange metaphysical hope, in meeting someone who had also loved a person now totally gone, that the exchange of information would somehow remind the dead of their life, return them to it. Instead it was never enough, the salient story already half fallen away, existing only in the invisible ways it changed the person telling it. They didn't shake hands as they left, make any fake plans to reunite.

SOME MONTHS INTO HIS BELIEVING this, Braden, who always seemed to understand things about Wright before he had—pointing out the boy he'd go home with before Wright had even seen him, identifying an allergy to wool—sussed it out.

"Are you going to tell me what it is?" They were walking through the Panhandle, on their long way to the Steinhart Aquarium, a place Braden loved, the only one that kept him from talking.

"What what is."

"Why you've been walking around looking like a mugshot."

Wright laughed, he grabbed his hand.

He admitted what he believed in a roundabout way, mentioning only that Ben had died. Braden hailed a cab right there, insisted on it.

"What about the jellyfish," Wright said.

"They don't have any fucking bones. I think they can wait. I'll get one, too." Wright apologized the whole afternoon, for a traffic jam, for the emptiness of the watercooler. At the clinic Braden filled out the forms for him. There were no appointments. The test was new that year, and there were friends of theirs who would not take it. Why confirm your house was haunted if there was nothing to be done about a ghost, went the logic. Braden and Wright waited six hours, avoiding eye contact with the other men waiting, never touching the pamphlets spread on the table before them.

DEEP INTO THE EVENING THEY returned home and Braden began taking things down from the cupboard: olive oil, cocoa powder, cayenne. He baked a cake in a cast-iron skillet and they ate it with their hands, standing up in socks. No recipe, just some pioneer nonsense, he called it. Still, a little something to celebrate. But the results wouldn't be back for weeks, Wright said.

"We're celebrating the selflessness and sacrifice of me," Braden said, taking down the secondhand crystal he had polished. "We're going to have a bottle of wine about it."

Wright pawed at the bowl of batter and placed the last in his mouth.

"Know what I call you," Braden said. "My Li'l Burden."

"Good night, Li'l Burden," he called, later, from behind the French doors of his room, both their lights out.

"Fuck you, Braden," Wright said, the happiest he'd ever been.

Their tests came back negative at the end of the month and he bawled as he walked sideways down a steep hill, shoving into his mouth potato chips he'd bought blind, relieved to be relieved. For so long he had worried that what he actually wanted was to be eliminated, the choice made for him, no more sunny rooms with people in them.

7.

It took up most of a whole room, the mail, in uniform boxes taped and labeled by NASA, and everyone who knew him, few though they were, his mother and some childhood friends, was surprised that Vincent kept it. The letter regarding the forwarding had arrived in the summer of 1984 and he read it standing in the kitchen, barefoot, having just come in from tending to the tomato plant in the backyard. His feet were almost translucent in their age, the metatarsals beneath the skin more pronounced, like the original pencil showing through some painting . . . *no longer holding mail addressed to astronauts of your class,* the letter said . . . *budgetary limitations.* He lifted his left foot at forty-five degrees and stood on his right, then switched, an exercise he performed three times a day, morning, afternoon, evening . . . *happy to provide forwarding to your home address, or to another address you provide, in perpetuity.* Letters and packages from NASA had the same feeling as those from Elise, an ask from your old life that promised to be the last. Two years before she had sent a class ring he'd given her, the university's lyceum engraved in miniature, no note, and a year before that there was a package from NASA, his old Speedmaster, relinquished by the Smithsonian, which had kept them on display. The museum was returning them to the original astronauts for reasons unclear. By a month after the landing Omega had repurposed the special design and sold it en masse, the go-to gift for fathers and husbands who might measure the inertia of their armchairs. He had imagined some scene in public, a stranger's hairy wrist held up to point out a made-up bond, and put the watch away.

His life had become the small acts of discipline that had once punctuated it, the main events blotted out. He washed his car once a week, made his next appointment with the barber as he was paying for the last. His accounting was perfect, his laundry folded as if by ruler.

Why keep them if you won't read them, his mother's face said when she saw the stacks, but she had become, it seemed in the matter of one Sunday, too old to voice this or any other characteristic admonition. Her wheedling little questions were gone from their exchange. He visited and checked after her meals, now, rearranged the TV dinners in the freezer. Her hand and bath towels had begun appearing crumpled on her bathroom floor, and each time he came he folded and rehung them. Once she found him on the tile as he did this and tried to pass him the phone, the cord stretched to its limit.

"Somebody keeps calling and saying he's your son," she said, her voice as flat as the teal of her polyester pants. He waved this away, changed her number and made sure it was unlisted, and surprised her on her birthday with a cordless. She brought it to the grocery store and showed it to the checkout clerk.

In terms of the letters, it was a matter of practicality, he thought. What was the other option? Some PO box that he'd need to regularly empty of the letters? No. When the forwarding began NASA stopped boxing them, so he put them instead in the plastic bags from the supermarket that had accrued under his sink, and when those had run out and a new supply had yet to build up, he put the letters in loose and closed the door to the room. It was the one area of his life that defied organization, the place he would rather not look. The year before the landing, when the letters had begun swimming in, he had been told that they mostly contained suggestions, directives on what he should say when he set foot in that new place. He had never had any interest, not because he believed he knew explicitly better what should be said, but because he thought no one was more or less suited to know.

It had come to him on a run one day, as he pushed past the hoariness of sleep deprivation, a phrase that he heard as he came to a field of grazing cattle. It was almost as though they had supplied it, the bigness of their eyes. Anderson had asked about it often, wanting to run it by some committee. Vincent knew for months, what he would say, but told no one.

His mother lost her mind in the space of a summer that was arid and unyielding, even bemoaned by the little boys on bicycles, who could be seen on the side of the country roads taking breaks en route to the same destinations he'd sought out once, the creek bottom, the quarry, their radios sputtering from where they were tied with twine to the Ts of red and blue frames. There was no wind. She began calling him and posing questions that were like koans, rhetorically impervious but hiding some candor.

He was in the garage, the first time, sorting winter clothing, bagging some sweaters for donation, when the phone rang, and though he had decided to let it go it went on a long time, twenty rings, thirty. Finally he put down the turtleneck in his hand, navy, Scandinavian wool, a gift from Elise, and ascended the two steps inside.

It seemed there was no one on the other end, at first, but then she was there, his mother who had never asked him a question about the divorce, just opened the furniture catalogs she subscribed to and begun to leaf through them with a pen in hand. She had read out prices like possible names for babies. Blinds and sectionals, lawn chairs and ottomans.

"The clock is talking too much," she said.

"Do you mean," he said, "the bedroom alarm or the kitchen wall? That the minute hand is loud? Should we replace it?" She hung up. The next came two days later, five A.M. sharp, early even for him.

"No space for a tree in a house," she said.

He ran the three blocks there and found her in the living room with one piece of white bread in her hand, curled like a tube. No butter, no plate, no knife. She performed a girlish annoyance at the breach of privacy and he left on her insistence, but on the next visit there were eggs in forgotten bathwater, coupons stapled to a jacket. His mother had always treated him the same, had insisted, two days after the quarantine was lifted and she saw him for the first time back from the moon, that he comb his hair again before dinner. He wanted to afford her the same privilege, despite how far she had traveled—much farther, he thought, than he'd ever been. When she told him, the last afternoon in August, during the middle of the game show that was her favorite, that she was very late, that her ride would be in front of the movie theater any minute, he reassured her that her dress was perfect, there was no need to change, and then they got in the car. On a bench under the marquee, his hand on her neck when she let him, they waited two hours.

"Your son," she said, and he patted her hand.

She died without much awareness of it, bothered by any ceremony around her, swatting the pastor Vincent had invited when he tried to take her hand. The pastor, sitting with his scrubbed hands spread on his knees, called her by her name, Andrea, something that had thrilled her once, and made reference to her many years as a Sunday school volunteer. At the close of ten minutes, in the middle of one of his careful sentences, she tottered up and turned off the lights. They laughed, Vincent and his sister and the pastor, the way they might at a child who has said a taboo word without knowing it, but not for very long. The last thing his mother said aloud in this life was: "The ladies'." As in, *I need to use the ladies'*.

The matter of the letters was raised in her dying, because she left so much to be kept, much of it the story of who he was, the newspaper clippings and the locks of his baby hair. It had to go somewhere. His sister laughed meanly at the suggestion she take it all, her hands on her hips in their childhood kitchen where she had once, in private curiosity, chewed some dog food and then tried to put it back in the bowl. Sophie had been the first to idolize him, spelling her own name wrong months after she'd perfected his, and also the first to give up trying to know him. She had exploded during the Thanksgiving following his divorce, nearly a full year after, when she asked where Elise was and had to glean the answer from the ashamed look on their mother's face. *Please pass the rolls,* he had said, and she had, not before unscrewing the salt shaker and emptying it on the one golden lump remaining. Even this provocation he had not taken. He got up and announced he thought he'd take a walk, and she had said, as he pulled on a jacket, *You know, I used to call you a mystery, but even a mystery rewards you some for trying to understand it. My son got more out of his pet snake.*

Now, in the light of the open refrigerator, squatting in loosely laced running shoes and jeans that were too young for her fifty-six years, pulling out the crisper bin and passing a hot bleached cloth over it, she was less nasty, tied only loosely to the situation and its questions. She hadn't even looked up at the suggestion, which he had voiced without really thinking, that she take the boxes of clippings and grade school photos, the proof of his life their mother had saved. He had forgotten or never really known she was unlike the other women who had appeared in his life, pliant, just to grow around it.

"Why would I hold on to your childhood? What do you think I care about those scrapbooks? You're not famous to me."

He found her weeping, later, crouched over a box in the bedroom, a photo of herself in a hand-sewn costume of a plane, six years old, a bid for his attention that their mother had architected. As he turned to go she caught him leaving, and she threw him a look as though he were a chore too long postponed, some filth that had spread and changed.

It seemed preposterous to him that we should all be so beleaguered by our lives' arcana, have to decide about the college yearbook and the wedding reception album. How could we possibly determine their worth, he thought, and weren't we damned either way, cold and unsentimental if we let them go, hamstrung by nostalgia if we didn't. At the end of her month packing up the house he accepted her invitation to breakfast, a diner where they had gone as children, a place with high-backed booths and a wall of celebrity photographs that included nine of him. He could not understand why she became so furious when, after ten minutes of their sitting there in silence, he opened the newspaper. "Your things are boxed by the back door," she said as she got up. "Once you've got them, you can slip the keys in the mail slot for the Realtor. Thank you for breakfast." The bill had not been received or discussed. She was passing through the glass door and agitating the string of bells, she was making her way to her scratched-up car in the lot, she was adjusting her bangs in the mirror, she was pulling out, she was gone.

When he brought them home, the thirty-two boxes that she had carefully taped and angrily annotated, *Marriage-Edwards,* the only place for them was the spare room where the envelopes with strange handwriting already lived, and so he decided one evening, after days of stepping around them in the hall, with a hand on the back of his neck and a forkful of overcooked pasta in his mouth, that he had no choice but to take care of the letters.

He was of the age now that his admission to the movies was discounted, but he paid full price. On his bedside table were books in stacks, in his wallet no photos or ticket stubs, and he had begun knocking wood when he passed it, cabinets or tables, for luck in what he didn't know.

8.

YELLOW SPRINGS, OHIO, 1986

He is sixteen, this boy from Ohio, hired by the astronaut, and before this he walked dogs and threw papers and daydreamed of his
girlfriend, not even nude, just alone with him in a house, any house,
just pale and tall and his. For a few years now he has delivered the
groceries, always the same, leaving the bags by the screen door
where his checks are pinned once a month. He has never seen another car in the driveway.

When he took this job it was with some imagination of social
capital, of people in the hallways sidling up and wanting to know
what Vincent Kahn was like, and also of some mentorship the spe-
cifics of which he could not imagine—exquisite one-liners the astronaut would deliver in reaction to some reported crisis of the
boy's, advice so lean and infallible you would bend yourself around
it. Every week he hopes for some deviation indicated by a Post-it,
*I'm craving a Popsicle, surprise me, could you ride out to the bakery with
the marbled rye and buy the biggest loaf they have.* But there is only the
Cream of Wheat, the cans of soup, four tomato and two mushroom,
only the sensation of the screen door like all other screen doors,
wire that feels made of pressure-packed dust. He has begun, if he's
honest, to resent this job, the total and impersonal mundanity, how

it's eroded his ideas about this man and men like him. He grew up loving this town, riveted by the fistfights at the lasagna feed, well versed in the folklore of certain abandoned buildings—the house where the newlywed had sleepwalked off the third-story porch and died. He was proud to come from the place that had formed Vincent Kahn, but now he cannot help but feel that whatever remarkable civic element had assisted in making this man did not outweigh the smallness it must also have instilled. He will not, this boy, Sammy to his friends and in his own mind Sam, be living here a day more than is necessary. Every part of who he is will be by his own design.

He has secured admission to a university in a city where he has never been, Chicago, and knows at all times how many days of 1986 are left to live through before he will board the train there. Repeatedly, furiously, he has declined the offer of the family station wagon. He will arrive for the rest of his life alone.

On the day Vincent Kahn opens the door, he has sixty-three days, and he imagines all of them will be empty, an unendurable waiting room. Even his girlfriend has become a kind of redundancy, someone who loves a person he no longer wants to be, Sammy of the yelling cannonball and the joke bicycle with the clown horn. He knows this hurts her, that he can barely respond to her placid questions, would he like to go outside and see the moon, see the neighbor's Lab dyed lilac in a prank. Stephanie. In the spring he came in her mouth. It was an event long talked over and planned, but he wouldn't kiss her in the hour after, and also wouldn't apologize.

Sammy, soon to be Sam, is placing the bags on the two concrete steps of the side porch. For reasons unclear, to fuck with the astronaut in some small way, he is arranging them in an elaborate and nonsensical fashion, a V that straddles the three levels. Last week it was a circle. Maybe Vincent Kahn will fire him, which would at least require some departure from the script. This is certainly a note he could pin up in his dorm room, a dismissal from the first man on the moon. He is goose-stepping over them to leave, his Chuck Taylors laced in that special way that makes them look like isolated rungs, when he hears a sound he has not before.

Vincent Kahn does not speak. He waits for Sammy to acknowledge him. Later, alone in his bedroom, drinking a beer pilfered from the garage refrigerator, Sammy will note the power in this and decide to adopt it in his new life. Appear in a door, in a room, cast a shadow, wait.

Standing with a hand tented on the screen door to keep it open, the sleeves of a thin shirt rolled up, Vincent Kahn could almost be another middle-aged man in Sammy's way, someone telling him not to park or talk or smoke here, were it not for the eyes, their two different colors. He has read enough of his father's old *Life*s, has been indoctrinated with the myth, to know how much has been made of this, a rare condition that flagged him from the start. The words printed and broadcast are a part of how he sees Vincent Kahn, superimposed on the normalcy of the kitchen behind them, mustard yellow, *the eyes of two different colors that marked his destiny to belong to two worlds,* the outdated high-waisted denim belted around a visible gut, *the green of the earth that bore him and the gray of the moon he would conquer.*

The words are out of his mouth before he has thought them:

"Hey, coach!"

Not only does he call him coach, but as he does so his hips do this unexplainable buck, a pelvic thrust like an unwieldy toddler trying to shake the piss off. Why, why, why.

"Come in for an iced tea."

It is not a question. Inside he sits at the dine-in laminate counter on a stool that spins slightly, willing himself not to abuse this feature although to do so feels like a betrayal of the self. To spin on a stool, to shorten the name of anybody you know into something foolish and mocking, to leap up and brush your fingers on arched white entryways with your new height, to take a hill at full speed and black out the headlights as you crest it. He wants these things before anything else, food even, money.

"I thought you might take on another kind of work for me for the rest of the summer, Sammy."

"Sam," he says. It is the first time he has spoken it aloud.

"Sam. I had a dear friend named Sam."

There's a peculiar look on the astronaut's face as he says this, one that seems to possibly move from outside the body in. There's a silence. Sammy kills it with an ice cube he takes in his molars, a reflex the urbanity of which he has not considered. This snaps the astronaut back to the conversation and it crosses the boy's mind that perhaps he is reconsidering.

Vincent Kahn, from behind the cutout window that bridges living room and kitchen, threads his pointer finger through it and over the counter.

"See those boxes?"

A nod.

"Full of letters. Fifteen years and change. No idea what's in them. I can't bring myself to read them."

On the counter the boy knits his fingers together, trying to present as thoughtful and composed, but it reads he thinks as prayer, so he separates the hands and lets them fall open. It has the look of supplication now. Vincent Kahn seems to forget this is an exchange he has initiated. In his pocket is a handkerchief he removes and makes a point of and dots along his hairline, which Sammy is disappointed to see has crawled halfway back his head. He wants the man in the photos, waving from a motorcade, the worshipped center of ten thousand hands. He wants the snowy voice broadcast in every home, narrating morning on another world.

"Well?" Vincent Kahn says.

Sammy's tongue does not seem to belong to him. What has he missed, why is he here, where was the question? Sam makes eye contact now, longer than he has been able to before. The astronaut has the kind of discomfort, communicable, that transfers immediately to its witness. The boy sees now it is his task to prompt him, that the conversation has been abandoned, with its few belongings, at his door.

"The letters are from fans?"

"I assume. And the opposite. And some lunatics. Probably a good section of those in both categories."

Sam gropes for the man's intent, sort of pleading with it.

"You don't want to read them, but you don't want to throw them away?"

"This is correct."

"You want me to read them?"

"This is correct."

"And do what, exactly?"

"I had a thought."

He disappears for reasons unannounced and Sam opts not to move at all, not to survey the house he already understands as a disappointment. He doesn't want to note the lack of photos framed on the walls, the living room that seems devoid of life. No pets, no smells, no sounds.

Vincent Kahn returns with a document of some kind, creaseless as sky in a stiff envelope, and slips it across the counter. The incongruous ceremony of this, urgent and official in a situation that is anything but, is not lost on Sammy. For the first time in months he misses Stephanie, who threads her filthy Reeboks with glitter laces, whose face hides nothing. The feeling there, inside the two of them, is as far from this room with this man as possible—facile, riddled with punch lines and rolled-down windows. He wants Slurpees at the 7-Eleven, perfectly two-toned in a helix twist, cherry and Coke, pink panties, blue condoms, golden beer.

He wipes his hands on his jeans and takes the single piece of paper from the envelope. It is graph paper that has been run through a typewriter, the letters boxed perfectly by the squares.

"Just a start," Vincent Kahn says. "I would make more."

Profession, the text says. *Age.*

Current state.

Home state (if different).

Sane. (Y/N)

Unstable. (Y/N)

Summary of letter.

Most telling remark.

"Quarter a letter," says the astronaut. "Lunch included. Two hot dogs, one apple."

He has not once asked, but what can Sammy say? Can he say no? Two hot dogs, one apple, he will tell his friends, finding a real thrill in mocking this famous man.

Later that night he climbs the tree to Stephanie's room, new with feeling for her. She squeals when she hears this update, of all the boys, you.

She is on her period so he doesn't undo her pants but keeps a knee high and a little rough up between her legs. In between the feelings of her tongue in her mouth he looks out at her room, the transparent plastic phone she uses to call him, all colorful gears and mechanisms revealed. He leaves her earlier than he otherwise might, Stephanie with her hair a little oily and her shirt still off, to start in the morning.

Vincent Kahn has been up for hours when he arrives. It's he who has the appearance of someone showing up for a new job, not Sammy, whose breath in the morning is so strange that puffs of it feel textured, mossy with a liquid underside. Not Sammy whose sleep is so beautiful he thinks of returning to it all day.

To his credit, he is on time. "Coffee in the pot," says Vincent Kahn, but when he goes to it there is little and it is heatless. Eight A.M. and the coffee already cold. Vincent Kahn has reimagined the living room in service of the work ahead and he moves around it gesturing, Sammy following him the two steps toward the window or bending to something on the coffee table. There is a cup of sharpened pencils, weighed down at its bottom by a rock from the garden. A new box of paper clips, a stamp that says READ, a stamp with a scrolling date, a spiral-bound notebook that is already labeled. In view of the front lawn is a tawny armchair, overstuffed with an antimacassar, and Vincent Kahn gestures to this.

"I thought you could read there. Of course, anywhere is fine."

This Sammy does not believe for a second. If he understands anything about this man, if he knows anything already, it is that his ideas about how things should go are precious and flinty, inflexible.

"Any questions?"

Sammy knows he wants there to be questions so he scrapes at the edges of his mind, past the gold of a dream that is still the heft of it, to find one.

"Where's the bathroom?"

The first man on the moon slaps one hand to his jaw and points the other down the hall. "First door on the right."

THE DAYS PASS WITHOUT HIS acknowledgment, never discrete enough, one intruding on the next. The work is always the same, the markings on the graph paper, the way he bends to retrieve a letter from the box on the floor next to him. The silent phone, the darkened television, the few sounds of Vincent Kahn from the bedroom or garden. The voices from these letters are the only variable, snapping as though in opposition to each other, paeans and polemics, angry capitals and schoolmaster cursive.

Professor, he writes. *Barbershop owner. Secretary in a doctor's office, Kansas, Florida, Yes, Yes, No, Yes.* There are many hours when the work feels like a fool's errand, when he feels the frustration of a son toward his father, bored by some lecture on a tedious, obsolescing process. In many of the letters these people offer Vincent Kahn their thoughts on what he should say when he steps down from the command module, and in others they call him a blasphemer, treading on heavens not meant for him. The futility of this gives Sam a dull ache, just the decade-old dates at the top of the page enough to put a pearling of sweat on his body. Why now, why at all. He comes to believe it is possibly worse, what Vincent Kahn is doing, delegating someone else to sift through the praise and blame rather than just leaving it alone. Opening the letters to Sammy feels criminal, breaking the seal pressed there by very specific lips and hands. All his mother can speak about, when he comes home, is the weight he is losing, and it is true that there seems to be a secret body emerging from the one that has always held him. His hipbones are evil little jewels now. His teeth are more apparent in his face.

There is a fear when he opens a certain kind of envelope, one on which the lettering seems inconsistent. He comes to know it as a sign the author is possibly unhinged. Within a week on the job, he can identify a suffering or proselytizing person's *g* or *f* from two feet away. He stops making any plans with Stephanie, because he does not know how the letters will make him feel, and becomes instead the kind of person who only shows up late and without a call, whatever he's dealing with already partially mitigated by three to five Miller High Lifes. In his dark car alone he speaks the slogan aloud. The Champagne of Beers.

There is one letter that he reads and has to leave early. He pulls it thinking it will be an easy one, mistaking the lettering for a kid's, maybe because he thinks the name on the return address, Sweety, could not possibly belong to a person who has cleared eleven. It's a boy who is his age, or who was his age, or who maybe never got any older than his age. Sammy picks up the letter from the soldier and smells it, thinking somehow the essence of the country would have saturated it, a place that to him is just a word, a war too recent to have entered his history book, three syllables muttered by much older brothers and sometimes men outside bars but never by teachers or parents. Vietnam. There is no smell, anymore, though he checks.

Sweety tells Vincent Kahn his footsteps were the last television he watched before he enlisted. Once, on leave from training, he smuggled a brick to the public pool so he could sink with it to the bottom and stay there and pretend to walk on that surface. Also that someone in his company notched some holes in a corpse's back and shoved its eyes there, that he, Sweety, took a photo of this, he didn't know why, but when the print came back from the Army processing center in Saigon it had been censored with thick black lines, as if this were too gruesome a thing to be seen.

It is only eleven A.M. Sam leaves a note for Vincent Kahn next to the daily log he's meant to keep on the kitchen table, time in, time out, the number of letters processed, the year of the last he's read. Summer is unrecognizable as what it once was, dives from rocks and naps as close as possible to an open window. Now it is just this warm, awful room, all the time that surrounds it either the dread or consequence of what happens inside it. The only disruptions are small and tireless, moths that don't seem to fly but fall, the sounds of chained dogs barking. *I am feeling incredibly ill,* his note says. That night he masturbates to thoughts of dying, his own death, then others', why he doesn't know, perhaps to replace fear of it with something else. Hours later, the only noises in his parents' house the hum of appliances continuing, he is outside the bedroom where they sleep, sitting by their door, his face wet, his snot green.

August waxing, one day he shows up to find more letters have been read than remain. He is hurtling through the end of the seventies, cheating sometimes and just skimming, but anyway they have become more placid, the letter writers, as time has passed since the landing. They are enthusiasts who quote data, they are lonely people who would like to put a memory down on paper. Nobody believes, in 1979, that Vincent Kahn is a part of the vanguard they must persuade of something. He is to them like the light contained by an old photo. They are grateful to him. They hope he is well. Sam, in the chair where he has sat all summer, can feel the next part of his life sidling up to him and waiting. He drinks enormous glasses of water from forty-two-ounce promotional plastic cups Vincent Kahn has mysteriously kept, tokens of summer blockbusters and minor-league openers, and pulls from his pocket a drumstick with which he practices while he reads. Pink Floyd's "Fearless." *You pick the place and I'll choose the time.* He has it way up, past his shoulder and over the imagined high hat, when he opens the first letter, one of many from the same person.

As he reads he has a clear idea of how he'll be noting it, using that category Vincent Kahn created in a move of prescience, circling the Y by *Unstable*, but as he gets farther down the page he feels less certainty about that assessment. It feels too elaborate, on top of that too sad, to be a hoax. In a lie there's the hope for an outcome, there's a shortcoming being stretched around, but here there's only an admission, tired and without flourish.

He decides to put off its categorization and sticks it down the craw between the arm and the cushion, feeling some crumbs there and then some satisfaction at this human oversight, for Vincent Kahn's is a home without dust and stray coins. The next letter is a denier's, ragged with exclamation marks and worked over with underlines in another color of ink, and then another from the same writer, the accusation deepening in scope. Sam does a scan of the box at hand and the one that's next up, shuffling the dates as he pulls. There is sweat in the pocket between his palm and first knuckles, there is what he can only describe as an itch in his molars. Vincent Kahn is gone again, out flying one of the ancient planes for rent at the run-down airport at the edge of town. When he is home, when he does see Sammy, he doesn't ask about the work or anything else. He treats the kid like someone managing a laborious repair, an act that requires a specified field of knowledge and total silence.

There's a minute, less, in between the idea and the moment he follows it. He doesn't log out in the designated notebook. The letters, ten in total, he slips down the small of his back, and they fan out accordion-style as he rides his bike home. At every faded stop sign he checks with a hand. His bike felled on the front lawn, his backpack limp and unzipped in the foyer of their split-level, he makes his way to his room and he stays there. There is no sound of his life leaking under the door, the radio or the record player or the handheld gaming console.

In the morning, for the first time that summer, he shows up early, eighteen minutes to eight. He goes around back where the rosebushes and tomato vines are dripping, the galoshes Kahn wears to water them warm by the screen door. For the first time Sam uses his name, calls it out into the dustless house. The letters are zip-locked now: in his kitchen after midnight, he pressed the blue and red together to make the purple seal.

"Vincent."

He emerges from the hall still damp from a shower. There's something about the fragility of it, the volume of the hair killed by water and the mottled pink of the scalp revealed, that upsets Sam.

"Early," Vincent Kahn says, the surprise in his voice making it softer.

"There's something you need to see."

9.

Vincent let the teenager go after that, not saying why although of course he knew. *Something you should read,* he'd said, with an earnestness Vincent found endearing at first, Sammy with the holes in his jeans and a mouth always damp at the corners. The letters smelled like malt liquor and nag champa and had been refolded along slightly different lines. It was clear he'd taken them home and then who knows where—a party, some beer-blotted afternoon at the quarry. Just this was enough to fire him. *Later,* Sammy had said, letting the screen door bang.

He'd been amused. *Why's that, why should I,* an uncharacteristic joviality, hands spread by his ears. The idea that there were any shoulds in the life of this boy was appealing—Sammy who just let weather happen to him, never bothering with a raincoat in the summer storms, never turning on the fan.

Because there's somebody who's been trying to reach you a long time. Did you know Fay Fern?

Just hearing the name in his house was an incursion, an event that made him want to check the locks, back door, side door, front.

That'll be all I need from you this summer, he said finally, drawing what cash he had from his wallet, more than the boy was owed, fifty-seven dollars, and turning down the hall. *Good luck at university.*

HE PUT OFF READING THEM for forty-eight hours. He sent away the housekeeper from her usual appointment, something that baffled her from where she stood at the door. She could see stray items of clothing on the arms of chairs, she could smell the garbage he hadn't taken out and held up the feather duster like it was a possession of his he'd lost. He shook his head again.

Fay Fern. It was possible he had never spoken her name. She had been babe, rosebud, she had been darling, she had been a smell and a time of day and something he refused to title. He told himself a well-tooled lie about that, how something real between two people needed no classification or observance, maybe suffered under it. It was a way of treating her as he did, tugging down her overalls on some gravel shoulder and pulling her onto him in the driver's seat but not always stopping when he knew she was hungry.

Vincent scanned them in one sitting, early in the morning on the back porch, wearing the red drugstore reading glasses it had been a humiliation to buy, possibly a crisis. His eyesight had been remarkable, offering gifts in color and distance that were the envy of the other men in the program.

He spent an hour denying the possibility of it, a son, then two believing it totally, remembering something of how gentle she'd been the last time he saw her, unusually docile. She didn't pick at one thought of his, didn't make light of one annoyance.

By the next afternoon he had swung around again. Surely, her parents being who they were, they would have demanded some recompense. The Ferns had been famous even to him, a family whose parties you heard about once you were anybody. They had once flown two members of the San Francisco Ballet company down to perform directly on the long garden table that sat twenty, a surprise for guests after dessert. The story went that the plates had not been cleared, a small humiliation the dancers were meant to incorporate as a constraint. Claudette and James Fern would not have allowed their daughter, however far she had strayed, to raise a child alone. No.

Say they hadn't learned, he reasoned, believing, the more he remembered her, who she insisted she was despite where she had come from, that she would never have let that information reach them. Her sister would have had the number of three different doctors. Hadn't her first reliable punch line been the misfortune of conventional life? Once, in the aisle of a grocery store near Yosemite, an overnight trip they'd taken without a toothbrush between them, they'd been stuck on either side of a couple arguing viciously over types of bread, ignoring the bawling child in the seat of the grocery cart. She'd enacted an elaborate mime, stepping up some invisible steps and saluting the executioner, checking the imaginary noose around her neck with a vigorous thumbs-up. He had pelted her with grapes from their basket to get her to stop, had turned away to keep the family from seeing his laughter.

He decided the letters were inconsistent, sad and wild, entreating and then hateful, the handwriting gone jagged with accusations, the leaves of paper sometimes inflamed where the pen had pressed too hard.

They were not the thoughts of someone in mastery of them.

In terms of years it lined up.

A resemblance might be hard to argue with, he thought, or it could be chalked up to the reliable and boring hopes of most people. The last time he'd seen her she'd asked a strange favor, to drive her awhile to buy some dental floss. Her sister had taken the truck. There was something in her teeth she kept pushing at with her tongue. In the sand parking lot of the pharmacy she had stood with her back to him where he sat in the driver's seat, standing in a balance while she flossed, her peachy foot flat on her thigh. When she was done she waved the strand like a little lasso in the sun and let it drop with a mannered flick of the wrist, some private joke with herself. A small moment in the scope of things, meaningless, but hadn't she done everything that way, alone, her life an elaborate expression that admitted or needed little of the world around it? He couldn't say what had happened to her in the years before she'd built that bomb and killed that man, except that he was sure it was what she wanted. She had not lived her life, her life had lived her.

In the highness of afternoon he began to write, just out of reach of the sprinkler he'd turned on, a legal pad on his failing gray knee, starlings and warblers calling from the trees that shadowed him. *Dear Mr. Fern,* he wrote, aware the boy had only ever used his first name. He started the letter but didn't finish it, not that day or the next.

10.

Their apartment filled with poster board, thick markers and glitter glue and stencil templates. That Wright was unmoved by them, the things used in the service of shouting and marching—that he goose-stepped over them where they lay in the hall and pushed them aside to make room on the coffee table—became like a quality of the air, something both of them woke to and were relieved to forget once they left the house. In the beginning Braden had been tender about it, brotherly. *A group of us,* he would say, *are going door-to-door to get signatures, are meeting to write postcards to congressmen.* Wright would nod and say *Today isn't but,* would say *Definitely next time,* and after a few months Braden stopped asking. They never shared shifts anymore. At home and work they were circling each other, confronted with reminders but never voice or touch. Envelopes of tips with a name scrawled in capitals, a still-wet toothbrush left out on the sink, smudged water glasses baking in the kitchen sun. On the television Madonna danced backward through Venice, far from virginal, and a news anchor declared, one shoulder dug slightly forward, that under the current administration the NASA budget was projected to double.

Wright was out every night again, his hair long enough that

someone was always moved to pull at it. As he was standing in the shower one Tuesday a condom he could not remember losing appeared by the drain.

There was a morning when it turned. The boy Wright had brought home, too young and with eyes the color of cactus, was slipping out when Braden emerged from his room. From the kitchen Wright heard the greeting, flat and vicious. He was sitting in the bay window with a bowl of cereal, a foot hooked around the opposite ankle, when Braden appeared.

"Where'd you find him?"

"Oh, him? He was doing my taxes."

"Are you protecting yourself?"

Wright kept his mouth on the spoon so that he could shape his lips around it, register no reaction to Braden's voice. He said it again.

"Are you protecting yourself?"

"Yes, okay? Now can I enjoy my breakfast?"

"Sure. You can enjoy your breakfast, and you can enjoy your walk to work, and you can enjoy your favorite jeans, and later you can enjoy knowing your friends were dying and you did nothing about it. But I want to know why."

He made an exasperated gesture with his spoon, a vague lift, as if indicating some structural deficit that couldn't be helped, a crack in the wall that let in a draft. There was no way to begin talking about it, he thought, to begin explaining, because he suspected if he did he would never stop. It would have to be a part of anything he ever said. He did not believe that there was enough of him that he could add his voice to an angry cause and not give himself over to it, not become that sound. What he wanted was to transplant into Braden certain memories of his mother, wait for his friend to understand how she had taken on injustice after injustice until there was nothing else on her face, no bending for love or memory. He wanted to give Braden the smell of that brownstone in the Village, sweat and mold at war, in the days before the bomb went off and killed the sleeping neighbor, or the way his mother had moved the last few years, always with her chin clipped to a shoulder, always with the curtain of hair pushed too far into the lines of her eyes. How for the rest of her short life she lived as though entitled to pure silence, insulted and undone by the slightest sound. He remembered his mother, of whom there had been so much before Shelter absorbed her—well-tooled anecdotes and geometric neck scarves and a way of silencing a foolish comment with just a look—and what followed was that he, comparatively so little, so malleable and unformed, a person made only by the people around him, would vanish completely under any act of resistance. He couldn't go with Braden to the protest. There would be no way back to any normal life, grapefruit for breakfast or the click of a camera or the small, sharp possibility of love in any room he entered.

"You know, don't you, how many are dead at this point? Should I remind you?"

The spoon was still now where it lay across his limp hand; there was cereal in his mouth he couldn't bother to chew. He still smelled of and felt like the sex he'd had, a second time in the morning, his hair staticky and his skin flushed, and he believed this was something Braden could see, a crime as visible as an ill-conceived tattoo.

"Tell me," he said, the words coming from a numb mouth and sounding, he knew, teenage and insolent.

"Sixteen thousand one hundred two, two thousand sixty one in this country alone. But like, how were the baths, babe?"

"I wasn't at the baths. I don't need to go to the baths to find—"

"Oh yeah? What's his name? How about the one yesterday?"

"Peggy Sue, both of them."

The moment he could have apologized was gone, the light opening with the fog burning off, and then Braden turned to leave.

"Who your mother was doesn't give you a pass," he said, speaking in the direction of the hallway from the kitchen. "You don't get credit for what your parents thought. Some people are meeting downtown tonight to march on city hall. I'm walking over after my lunch shift. Eight."

"Okay," he said, the word sounding like an apology and a defense both. "I'll be there."

HE LOOKED OUT AT THE rest of the day from inside a haze, walking without a destination in mind, stopping at one point in a kitchen supply store for reasons unclear, skulking even there, darting out when a salesman asked him if there was something he'd like to see. Back at home he finally showered, something he always put off after sex. He liked smelling foreign, liked the idea that his body had become partially the province of someone else. Sex with men was the only place in his life free of interpretation, his mind relieved of its obsession to comment and criticize. Now it too was politicized, a comment on who he was and who he failed to be.

Naked in his room after, pushing his shoulder sockets far across his chest, rocking back on his tailbone to see the skin between his legs, he looked for the change that half of him believed he deserved, a small purple spot that would signal the proliferation of all other symptoms. It would be the beginning of a new season in his life, the last. Paper gowns, lines at the pharmacy. It wasn't there. He got into bed, his face in a rectangle of sun that was two degrees warmer, and told himself he would close his eyes for a brief, quiet moment, just until his skin was dry, just until he felt warm enough. He woke at 6:50 and at 7:10 and at 8:05, each time to the sound of a kneeling bus exhaling, each time telling himself that there was enough time, small and gentle lies that were obliterated when he finally woke. He waited for Braden to come home, the apology lachrymose in his mouth, an insistence on next time, a reference to a fatigue he couldn't shake. A certain way he would touch him, a hug from behind with one hand slipped up to cradle his friend's face. They had their cycles, he told himself, movements in which it was up to one of them to make declarations, to cook dinner unprompted or knock another time on the locked bedroom door. It was only a matter of focused generosity, and then they'd be back in their deep circuitry, a system of rapid-fire references no one else could parse, foreheads glued on a couch in the corner of some party, the annoyance and envy of anyone who tried to enter the conversation.

Wright spent three days waiting, leaving notes even when he stepped out for the smallest of errands, *I've missed you and I hope you'll let me make it up to you, What do you say to a bike ride to Baker Beach this weekend,* but they remained untouched where he'd left them, propped up by a vase of peonies or balanced on Braden's door-knob. He was sleeping somewhere else. When he did come home, it was difficult at first to name the difference, because much of how Braden behaved was the same, substituting lyrics of pop songs to denigrate their landlord, answering Wright's questions where he stood tweezing in the bathroom mirror with the poise and wit of a winning game show contestant.

It was not incremental—Wright didn't understand it, and then he did. It was his eyes: Braden wouldn't look at him.

On an evening hemmed in by rain, Braden was at the kitchen counter, dicing small dark mushrooms, a cookbook propped open by a wooden spoon along its length, the Supremes on the turntable. Wright sat smoking on a stool near the open back door that led to an exposed stairwell, a drafty clapboard pathway from which a neighbor's head might occasionally pop in. He could feel the weather that way, the small changes in intensity, and he knew it bothered Braden, the Midwesterner in him that believed a house should be what kept you from the disorder of the world.

"What's for dinner? Need me to do anything?"

"Chicken marsala. I need you to keep breathing."

It was his standard response, worn and familiar. They settled into a comfortable conversation, talk of Judy, calling her Mother, calling her Little Miss Middle Age. "How was she today," Wright had said.

"Besides the picture of health and beauty?"

"Yes, a given."

"Well, during a tasting before the rush she blew her ass like a trombone—"

"Like seventy-six of them—"

"Yes," Braden said, "she was absolutely leading the big parade. But so she blew her ass as she was pouring us this chenin blanc, it sounded like a two-hundred-year-old wedding dress being ripped in half by the angry hand of god, and then pretended to be frightened. 'Something fell, something big.' She made Shelly run down to the cellar and check."

The story brought a happy tear to Braden's eye and then, as he went to wipe it, he gasped like a moviegoer and started to swear. Wright rushed to his bent shape, spreading a hand on each shoulder, saying let me see, let me see you. The mushrooms in the saucepan continued to simmer, popping and hissing, and Diana Ross still came upset and proud from the speaker. Braden was screaming and whimpering and would not turn his face.

"It's the chili from the salad," he said, finally. "Right in my eye. Don't touch me, don't touch me, don't touch me." The insistence on this seemed outsized, as though it were his whole body exposed and injured.

"You need cream," Wright said. "An acid as an antidote." It was a piece of information coming to him from he didn't know where, a part of him that sounded like his mother, and then he was pulling some yogurt from the fridge and spreading it on a clean napkin he had worked into a kind of blindfold.

"I can't believe how badly it hurts," Braden said, in the dark of his bedroom, on top of the perfectly made bed where Wright spread the poultice over his face. "I know," Wright answered, believing Braden was speaking to him, but when he returned to the kitchen to finish dinner, he could hear him still repeating this to himself, murmuring like a kid who believes his thoughts don't exist unless they are spoken aloud. By the time the food was ready and Wright stood at the door frame with a plate, Braden was asleep, exhausted by the shock.

"How's the eye," he said, the next day, catching Braden in the hall when he came in drunk and late, taking his chin with two fingers to try to tilt it up. The looseness of his entry, the freedom of his body, was gone immediately. He locked his jaw and swiveled around toward his room, but Wright caught his shoulder, more violently than he wanted to, his advantage of height and weight suddenly clear. Little Bullet, people called Braden behind his back, or Naps, short for Napoléon.

"Look at me."

"No."

"Look at me."

Wright had his legs in a V now, either foot parallel to the base-boards, blocking Braden from the path to his room. A bottomless minute opened around them.

"Fine."

And then Braden did. Wright regretted the command immediately, for he understood that in refusing to look at him, Braden had, in some way, been protecting him. There was nothing in his look of who they were to each other, no depth or light to the glance. His face, regarding Wright's, was of someone in a busy crosswalk, staring ahead only for the sake of safety. In the twenty seconds that he stood there taking this in, Wright replayed every remark Braden had made that referenced this part of him. Talking about an ex whose name he had firmly vowed never to say again, about his bigoted mother whose birthday cards he marked, every year, *Return to Sender*. He had seemed so brave to Wright in these conversations, so in command of his life and what love or cruelty he allowed into it. It had never occurred to Wright he might pass to the other side of Braden's life.

"What is this? Why are you acting like I'm anybody else?"

"It's not even a feeling I want to have," Braden said, back to looking down now, picking something out from under his thumbnail, pushing his hair behind his ear. "I didn't even realize I was doing it, not looking at you, until the little habañero incident. Do you want me to apologize for something as crude as instinct?"

"I'm going to bed."

"Sleep well, sugar," Braden said, in the plastic chirp he used when taking complicated orders from entitled customers at the restaurant. Wright spent the whole night awake, one knee cocked way up by his hip and then the other, adjusting to the news that the life that had come so rapidly to him had run just as swiftly away. *We are,* Braden had said to the group of boys gathered in the living room, some months before, the wooden spatula in his hand a baton, *in a very real sense of the word, at risk for extinction.*

11.

He spent as much time as possible, in the weeks to come, away from the apartment, filling his leather shoulder bag with what would keep him away, books and bananas and dense ziplocked joints he wrapped in paper towels and placed in the inner compartment. He smoked on roof gardens downtown, places flanked by withering topiary and empty save the occasional forlorn banker, or in the bathroom at work, sitting on the closed toilet with both feet flat on the wall. He got high on the backs of buses as they strained uphill and watched whatever was left behind on the seats roll with the snaking curves, stray chips, forgotten ChapSticks, ambitious threads of urine. He woke in ten different bedrooms, twenty, places whose windows only faced another building, some with ladders to the roof, and took photos of each, though never the people they belonged to. Fishbowls, waterbeds, overflowing closets. The men attached to these rooms hardly mattered, although he kissed them goodbye, their necks pale as milk or sandy with freckles, although he thanked them, the men he had slapped and pushed and choked. He asked to be spanked, for a fist inside of him, for a belt around his neck. He tried every fantasy, every exit. When he did have to come home, when he miscalculated, watched his target float out the door with somebody else, he made sure to piss and brush his teeth at whichever bar, minimizing the possibility of a bathroom run-in. He left nothing of his in the common area besides a check for the rent. He could not imagine how long this might go on, but he also could not imagine very long at all. The time in front of him was flat then sheer, something he would fall from soon.

That the rest of their friends felt the same about him he believed because he had not heard otherwise. Held up during the marches that had become as ubiquitous as any other type of traffic, there was a popular sign, in pink glitter, in gold, in plain black capitals, spelled out one letter at a time on T-shirts worn by a line of people: SILENCE = DEATH. The change in the city was so total that the color and pageantry of it before seemed like a false memory. It was in the way that people behaved in restaurants and movie theaters, older women opening doorknobs with handkerchiefs, families moving rows because of their proximity to a cough. Where there had been gaggles of boys on the sidewalks, knit together by conversation and moving like pool balls inside a wooden triangle, there were now single men. They had canes and plastic bags from the pharmacy, they wore sweaters and sunglasses and sheath-y coats, anything to make the membrane between life and body thicker. Conversations were quieter now, birthdays celebrated like unlikely successes. Wasn't it enough, he asked, in his mind, to the sound and vision of Braden that never abated—a figure so real that he could almost get away without missing its corporeal counterpart—wasn't it enough that he felt sorrow about it? That he had ordered so many meals he couldn't finish. That he saw these men tapping down the street and wept.

No, Braden said in Wright's mind. *That will never be enough.* The adjudicating hand in the air, the soft palm turning over.

AND THEN THERE WAS A day when three hundred people called to him. They were black and green-eyed and slack-jawed and thin, blond and hoarse from shouting, linked to the people they loved at the elbow. He was sitting at a sidewalk café with a novel and his camera and a dwindling pack of cigarettes when the march came through, heard long before it was seen, the diversity of voices flattened into one protracted roar. As it got closer his shame became acidic. The whole mechanism was a spectacle to him, the way a chant would begin at the front of the crowd and move back and be replaced, in a lightning minute, with the next set of words. "Won't you join us!" they were yelling, the intonation spiking at *won't* and *join,* four claps in between to mirror the sound and insistence, and it was such a direct plea, so literal, nothing else required but standing up, that he did.

He was amazed by how easy it was, to see a moment and step inside it. Once he was within the river of them it was hard to believe he had been without. A man on his right gave him a squeeze as he stepped in and forgot about him just as quickly. When Wright tried to find him minutes later, the gap-toothed smile, he was gone. The individual was interchangeable here, a body moving the same way and a voice saying the same thing, strange, he thought, given that what they were yelling about was the right of the individual to continue his small, specific life. Boys on fire escapes blew kisses and then descended to become part of it. Ancient Italian men, their ceramic espresso cups aloft, their enormous watches drooping on their disappearing wrists, stared as though all five hundred of them were one defective or unauthorized thing, a car spewing violet smoke, a zoo animal loping down a sidewalk. They were moving north, taking hills without slowing. There was light on the water, boats coming in, and in the windows of houses families passing plates across tables.

He'd been among them fifteen minutes when he realized that the moment he was waiting for, when he would open his mouth and become one of the voices, was not coming. In knowing it he stepped out, as easily as that, over a curb and onto a one-way side street, and he took the lens cap from his camera.

THAT AFTERNOON, FOR THE FIRST time in weeks, he faced his home in the daylight. He took his shoes off at the door and stepped hesitantly through the rooms like a museumgoer, waiting for the beauty or the lesson to occur to him. Three lone sequins winked on the coffee table, pale green flotsam from some made-up occasion. On a windowsill sat a nickel and a bookmark and an open matchbook with a phone number written in it. The photos of who they had been to each other still appeared under magnets on the refrigerator, hidden partially by new layers of life, receipts and to-do lists and a Polaroid of Jean and Braden sitting on the shoulders of men Wright didn't recognize, holding up cardboard signs in capital letters. Left out on the counter was a watermelon, and he held it up and thumped it, something his mother had taught him, a revelation at the time—that you could listen to the insides of something. He opened cupboards and washed some silverware left in the sink and felt a loose knob on a drawer. He was fixing this, a tight twirl of finger and thumb, when Braden walked in.

"Thanks for doing that." His speech was still xeroxed somehow, the execution like that of a distracted actor.

"My pleasure."

He meant it. It was. Their life together, this apartment, had been the first occasion for Wright to stay with a problem, to understand and address it—a leak in the shower wall he caulked himself, a moth infestation they treated with sage and profanity. If you paid attention to the small, deepening dramas of the domestic, gave yourself to their remedy, you began to see yourself too as worthy of small attentions, as amenable to solutions.

He had learned to master problems around the house, perhaps knowing how ill equipped he was in others, those having to do with love, how it met respect. *You need every person to love you, regardless of how you feel about them. It's the same old show.*

"Anything else that needs fixing?"

Braden was quiet, playing it carefully. He was weighing how

much he needed help against the gratitude receiving it would entail.

"Well—"

"Just tell me what it is, bud."

Bud, kiddo, champ: this avuncular way of talking had been new to both of them, something they stepped into together from a lifetime of looking out only for themselves. It had been a performance at first, then a familiar joke, then a tender necessity. If your private life had begun too early, you needed, in this life, someone who spoke to you like a child.

"The wiring on the chandelier in my room."

In under a minute he was up a ladder, electrical tape around his wrist, the screwdriver down his front pocket. He was comfortable here, and he took his time. The view was the fire escape across the way, where two nudist lesbians kept forty plants that disguised them somewhat when they sat there, green on skin on green on skin, and the electric lines of the Muni, leaping when buses approached and sagging in their wake.

"Try it now," he said, and Braden moved to the switch, submissive, tame. "Try it again."

"Fixed! You did it. My handy dad."

As he descended he caught Braden's eye. It was quickly gone, his sight fallen back down on the floor, but Wright had seen an opening. Braden knew he'd cracked and was shifting a little in frustration, stuck on the far side of the room. When Wright grabbed for his right hand he spun around toward the window, threading Wright's elbow under his armpit, balletic even in this. For sun-bent seconds Wright loomed in the half embrace, taller, understanding what he was about to do and wondering why, knowing how little it would solve, and then with the other hand he wide-palmed the back of Braden's head and began to scratch it.

"You're fucking insane," Braden said, but he didn't move. Wright brought the hand on Braden's chest down so that it encircled his hips, and then he kissed him, once on the top notch of his spine. When their mouths joined it felt like an expert telling of a story, the time taken on all small and necessary parts. He crouched to meet each hipbone and bite at it once, something he knew Braden liked from confessions he had made as a friend. Wright was using private information in a way it had not been intended, leaping roles to steal back some intimacy that had been lost.

He knew that the important thing now was to not stop touching him, was for not a beat to register between the admission and the next handful of hair Wright took. What did he have that was not in thanks to Braden? The question was with him like another pulse point, a hammering behind his knees. He thought it like a mantra, *what do I have that you didn't give me,* as he reached around to loosen the belt and bring down the zipper. The afternoon stretched the shadows of everything in the room, the tendrils of the plants on ladders showing up as smoky ribbons across the wall where Wright had pinned each of Braden's hands. The bed in its range of navies looked deep and liquid, and they fell onto it without unplucking the hospital corners, a habit of Braden's conservative boyhood that had never left him.

"A condom," Braden said, "I think there's one still," and pointed to a drawer. He stayed the way Wright had arranged him, a knee drawn up by a hip and both wrists above his head.

It's as if you need everyone to love you. He moved his hand over the private things kept there, some movie stubs and a jar of Vaseline and a velvet jewelry box.

"Don't stop," Braden said, and for an hour they didn't.

12.

In the days after, the silence between them was different, less animus, more fatigue. Everything you could say to a person, everything you could do, they'd said and done it.

Something about how he'd been living had fallen away—the thrill of possessions had evaporated. Whether this was evidence of some maturation or regression he couldn't say. He wanted only whites now, only windows. He'd begun emptying his room of objects he had once loved, a copper diorama of the city found at a flea market, mixtapes made by boys whose names were gone. Through his third-story window he could see people stopping on the street where he'd put his things in boxes, pulling out raglan tees and badly framed watercolors. They asked the opinions of lovers and friends who squinted, imagining a life worse off or better.

On the television one night there was an old movie starring the president, and he found Braden on the couch in its rapture, a bong between his knees. *"Bedtime for Bonzo,"* Braden said, exhaling a fat train of smoke as he did, knowing Wright would be unfamiliar. He held the carb between his thumb and index like something valuable, a lucky stone. "Reagan is a professor who socializes a monkey."

He was handsome and clean in black and white, the president, speaking to a perplexed blonde, offering answers as though they were things he owned outright. In a bassinet between them a sedate chimpanzee blinked. Why was he doing this, she wanted to know, this simple girl from the country he had hired to help him, bland and pale and open to whichever wish of his. *It's fairly simple. A lot of people think they're born better than others. I'm trying to prove it's the way you're raised that counts. Even a monkey brought up in the right surroundings could learn the meaning of decency and honesty.*

Braden was asleep soon after, a hand high up his cheek, but Wright couldn't leave the room until it was over. He was trying to chart the distance between performances, the man on the screen now and the one who was asleep in Washington, the one who would not say *AIDS*. He saw only the ways they were the same, a firm gaze that seemed earnest and reassuring until you understood it as calcified and blinkered. When he finally stood and turned the television off, Braden woke up. It was as though, even asleep, he were made of and guarded by pop culture, and could not furnish himself with the permission to be alone.

Sometimes they kissed in the kitchen, in those weeks, afterthoughts by the refrigerator, tiny agreements. They said good night through the French doors that separated their bedrooms, they listened to each other sleep and wake up.

WRIGHT WAS POLISHING WINEGLASSES WHEN the letter came, or he was eating stale rolls of sourdough standing on one foot, or he was trying to keep Judy away from the new guy, whose name she was saying too often, every time he crossed the floor. It didn't matter, but for some reason it was this he thought of when the call came, from Braden, from home—where had he been when the note in its thirds appeared in their mailbox?

It had been a year since he had stopped writing, and he remembered the pages he'd sent with some embarrassment, hideous confessions so long unanswered he had come to believe they were as private as thoughts in the dark.

"Are you sure," he said.

"K-a-h-n," Braden spelled.

The lunch rush was blooming around him, wrists shaking out napkins, water glasses filling with light.

13.

The envelope was too thin. Wright turned the letter over without opening it, feeling it for some valence, and then he set it against a browning bunch of bananas on the kitchen counter, thinking he should eat something first, having skipped the meal after his shift. He had woken that day with an unusual happiness, a feeling like having a friend in town, someone whose joy would come in observing routines, the idiosyncrasies of a bad lock, the beautiful broken idioms of the man at the corner store. Everything—weather, the walk to work—had transpired alongside some witty commentary upon it, but the feeling was gone the moment the call came, erased. Stoplights were invisible on the walk home. Other people were cardboard cutouts.

He chose a record in no hurry, he diced an onion with his back turned to the envelope. When it had pearled in the skillet he turned off the flame and wiped down the counter and began to bark, stuffing the side of his palm in his mouth as he bent weeping over the sink. It had been the wrong thing to ever write, he thought, a vote against his easier future.

As he attacked the envelope the leftmost third ripped, and so reading it he had to hold the two pieces together. There was a bus passing he could hear and he wanted to be on it, there was clean air outside and he needed to be in it. Vincent Kahn's letter was brief, all capitals, all right angles.

DEAR MR. FERN,

HELLO.
THANK YOU FOR WRITING.
YOUR MOTHER WAS A VERY INTERESTING PERSON.
I DID NOT KNOW HER FOR LONG.
IF YOU ARE EVER IN OHIO WE CAN MEET FOR LUNCH.

—VK

HE TOLD BRADEN THE LIE first, thinking in doing so he was making it something else, a decision not contingent on a brief letter from a famous man. A drive to New York, he said, maybe a move, he wasn't sure. They were sitting in the living room passing a smoldering roach back and forth, holding it by a glittery bobby pin of unknown provenance. In the corner of the room their Christmas tree remained, strung with popcorn and cranberries they'd threaded on a little coke on a Tuesday, tucked into it some cardboard New Year's glasses that read *1986*.

"You're joking," Braden said. "You worked so hard for your life here."

"It's too small a city. If I wanted to know everybody's business, I'd move to the suburbs and read all the classifieds. I want to meet someone who doesn't know anything about who I am."

"Who are you?"

"Stop it."

"I mean it," he said. "What is it about who you are that's keeping you from staying here?"

"Don't you think taking this personally would be beneath you?

I'm not saying permanent, I'm saying I'd peek my head in, and besides I'd stop in Ohio on the way. California's not the only place. California's a lie we tell ourselves to feel better."

The smoke in the room made the conversation feel more casual than it was, an extension of any of the thousand they'd started but not finished, the time they'd travel to given the choice, half-recalled history lessons, an argument about the pretensions of Jacques Rivette or the sex appeal of Michael Keaton.

"Don't you think 'taking it personally' is a term invented by sociopaths to shame everyone else for having very normal feelings? When has my personhood not been affected by the world's action upon it? When did you become such an ice cube?"

"There's nothing I'm ashamed of that's keeping me from staying. But aren't you tired of walking into a room and having everybody know exactly how you became what you are? Don't you like the idea of getting to present yourself?"

"Traveling is a fool's paradise, et cetera." Braden waved some smoke from his face.

"I don't really think Emerson applies here. It's easy to feel superior about your identity when you're sitting in a caned chair alone on a pond. It's easy to say that changing the environment is a superficial fix, but also, no transcendentalist I'm aware of ever ironed out his sexuality for an audience over the course of years."

"He's going to let you down."

This Braden said quietly, a part of his exhale on the last possible drag.

"What?"

His feet crossed on the table, Braden wouldn't repeat it and he wouldn't say anything else.

"There's nothing I expect," Wright said. "So how could he?"

Braden shook his head and set the bobby pin on the rim of the ashtray. He was testing him with silence, a dare Wright always lost. His voice sounded like Randy's, and he thought his body felt as

Randy's must have, nothing about it liquid—all springs, all metal. He remembered Texas, he remembered gravel. The heat map of the body the day after a fight.

"No response at all? You'll just leave me with that hopeful message?"

Rubbing a hand on his locked jaw, Braden stood and left. In his bed that night through the French doors Wright heard him in the next room, a two-part cough that seemed to correct itself on the throatier downbeat. Wright heard him sleep but never got there himself, and at five he gave up and made coffee, took his book and the French press down to the filthy stoop. He watched a man pulling a shopping cart of possessions uphill, stopping twice to rearrange the system of tarp and bungee cords, each time losing a few inches to the slickness of fog on the sidewalk.

At six thirty he stood by the wall-mounted phone in the kitchen, the letter in his left hand, his mother's ring dull on the pinky of his right as he pecked out the numbers, thinking he could hear more of his body than you were supposed to, the breath but also the blood. The seventh digit, the ninth. There was something he was owed, or there was something he'd forgotten. When it rang he put the phone back on the cradle, then picked it up and pressed redial, glad to hear the sequence relayed evenly, the space between all parts the same.

"This is Vincent," the voice said, a greeting that stunned him in how it answered the first question he'd prepared.

"This is Wright."

"Beg pardon?"

"Wright."

"I'm sorry, what is? This is Vincent. To whom am I speaking?"

"This is Wright. Fern. This is Fay Fern's son, Wright."

The pause felt like the time spent trapped in a rotating door, the air that felt pressurized, the silence that held you hostage.

"Of course. What time is it where you are?"

"Excuse me?"

"What time zone?"

"California."

"Pacific Standard, you mean."

"Yes."

"Weather there okay?"

"What, it's—well, you can't see anything until the fog burns off, and that's about noon. It's forty now."

They were speaking about the temperature, he thought, and he ground the heel of his hand into a closed eye until he saw splintering reds. A second passed, three, time he didn't pass through but that hung from him. In a strange coincidence I'm going to be passing through Ohio, he understood he was saying, a lie that landed flat-footed. The call became a gas station atlas, routes that connected and didn't, are you writing this down he asked and Wright lied again. At the close of a phone call that was over in three minutes, Vincent Kahn spoke the name of an Irish pub franchise and a day and a time and then they repeated it to each other, the first thing on which they could agree.

In the days that were left he slipped a check for rent under a magnet on the fridge and rode his bicycle farther than he ever had, out to the seaside remains of the public baths that had burned in the sixties, and he walked the lines of the old foundations like a kid, hands out to either side. His last morning he spent seated at the foot of Braden's bed, already dressed and showered, reading the headlines aloud and the corresponding article if a thumbs-up appeared from under the comforter. It had been their ritual for years, the Morning News, they called it.

WINNIE MANDELA CRITICIZES REAGAN. REAGAN HOLDS FIRM ON TAXES. By nine the light had turned milky and he stood up.

"Go back to sleep," he said.

14.

He watched the Challenger explosion naked, the motel towel loose around his hips where he sat on the edge of the bed. Fourteen years since and just the sight of the bleachers, the way people held their cameras up, was enough to frighten him. At least it was the daytime, at least the colors of the Kennedy center were slightly different, given that. For thirty minutes he only got up to get an ashtray, only moved a finger to find the channel playing the footage again. He had twenty hours until he'd see Vincent Kahn, too few for anything to change about his life, to make it one he might explain easily across the table at a chain restaurant. At first the way the smoke branched looked fallopian, tunnels driven from a meaningful center.

In the American movie theaters where they spent their lives alone, they had been taught to love a blast, and so, at the sound of the explosion, seven people becoming sky, the audience in Florida had clapped.

Captions pointed out the silver-haired parents of a certain astronaut, a woman, a schoolteacher. The mother wore white wool and a white fur collar, the father's insignia of the mission sewn onto his jacket. In the moments after the boom, the grin he'd put on at the outset stayed—warping a little, the last to get the news—while the rest of his face collapsed. The smoke in the sky thinned and streamed down in feeble cords.

His hair fat at the tips with water, Wright watched the stands empty the way they must have the night of the launch, some of the Americans lingering in the chance the show would redeem itself, looking over their shoulders as they went. He pressed mute and saw he'd smoked five cigarettes and mentally cataloged his life. He owned three shirts and he had rotated two throughout the drive from California, leaving one for the day of, not considering the question of laundry once he arrived. He had kept it, navy and heavy flannel, separate from all else in his duffel, in a brown paper lunch sack with a little sachet of lavender, a habit of his mother's that had found its way back to him. She had worked to make their lives recognizable to them even once their days had deteriorated into strange cars and bacterial infections and potato chip dinners, she had believed in the permanence of scent. Cones of piñon she bought in bulk and burned wherever they went, the backs of dark vans, in houses where there was no heat. She had insisted, whenever possible, on fork and knife, on correct posture.

On another channel, the president. *We've never had a tragedy like this.*

He picked up the phone and punched in the number he knew.

"I knew you would fucking call," Braden said.

"Are you watching this and crying?"

"I'm on the damn floor. Jean is on his way. The dad."

"I know, the dad."

"Meet yours yet? Calling from a new life? Camping? Conversion therapy? Fun combination of the two?"

"Some motel. Amarillo, Texas. Listening to the president?"

"Yes, yes. And it's bad, but you know, I thought, maybe what we dying faggots really need to get Reagan to pay attention to us—"

"Is a spaceship. If we could just add some more explosions to the fatal epidemic."

"AIDS: where are the explosions? This whole time we thought they were bigots, but it turned out they were just bored. Nuance is not for everybody, you know."

"AIDS: coming soon in 3-D. Coming right to middle America, sooner than you'd think."

"We are going to throw beautiful parties in hell, girl, don't you think?"

"Extremes in temperature are equalizing," Wright said. "Nobody ever made an interesting mistake in full air-conditioning. Guest list?"

"Mussolini can't come but his team can design the gazebo."

"Fascist gazebo!"

"Obviously Marilyn, who I guess is there, if hell is real and follows the rules, so long as it was a suicide, which we agree it was."

Wright stretched the cord as far as it could go, almost to the dresser, and pulled out with one hand the pants he'd placed there two hours before. It was a habit he'd developed as a child, no matter how short the stay. He had used the soaps and the hand towels, read the laminate brochures propped up on the nightstand, even consulted the cheap Bible. The dyed blue carnations, set out at continental breakfasts, he'd turned into boutonnieres. Shower caps he collected in case of rain. He had wanted his suitcase to be heavier, he told her, when she found it full of parking lot gravel.

"Ansel Adams."

"Why is he in hell?"

"How egregious to think you could make a mountain more beautiful than it already is, how boring. Only a straight man."

"I miss you already, Braden."

"Vincent Kahn."

Wright was silent now, leaning against the foot of the bed with feet touching the bureau, feeling where the imitation wood would snap if he pressed hard enough.

"Why's that." The fun was gone from his voice, the laugh all absorbed by fear.

"For the cold bath he gave you, babe. I read that letter. How much do you think you deserve? Is the answer nothing? Is the answer whatever anyone else can afford, no matter what it costs you?"

"Okay, okay, Braden. What exactly is it you want me to do?"

"Are you listening carefully?"

"Yes."

"I want you to gather up your shit, your little lavender satchels and whatnots, and I want you to return your key and pay your bill. And then I want you to come home."

"I promise to call soon," he said, and hung up. His things on the dresser were small and useless, and he cleared them with one swipe of his hand.

15.

The sign on the freeway for the restaurant, an Irish pub, white curling text on a brown backdrop, showed up sooner than he thought it would, but there it was, O'Malley's, two miles, *Ye Olde Spot*.

Right off the highway, Vincent Kahn had said. *Most convenient for you.*

His temperature had ranged about wildly, near shiver to near fever. In his rearview Wright ran a comb through his hair, an act so unfamiliar to him that he thought he looked like a cartoon doing it, a dog trying to pass as human. He walked the parking lot of the strip mall with the sort of panic that is quick and bright, all silvery angles of movement. Carrying a plastic bag from the pharmacy, a woman leashed by four children emerged from a chain drugstore, looking like the kind of person who has never cried in her life. A teenage couple, sitting on the released tailgate of a truck, blew smoke in the direction of anyone who passed, the sleeves of their hooded sweatshirts warped from always being pulled over their hands. The smells coming from the restaurant were almost identical to the smells coming from others in the franchise, a town over, a state, and his plastic watch, a find from a quarter machine, something Braden had called Mr. Little Clock, told him he was two minutes early. When he passed through the automatic doors of the restaurant there was a sign that said WAIT TO BE SEATED and he walked right past.

Vincent Kahn was not in the restaurant and he waited ten minutes in a booth. Above the bar hung photos with the same sepia wear, a dirty child pushing another in a wheelbarrow, a one-room house at the edge of a cliff. In a frame in front of the cash register, a sallow piece of fabric was embroidered ERIN GO BRAGH. After the second time he asked the waitress to recite the specials but did not order she rolled her eyes and smeared a hand through the bangs she had sprayed so they arched up.

"I'm sorry, Kelly," he had said, reading her tag, but somehow speaking her name was a breach of contract, another loophole in American etiquette he would never understand.

On the table the evidence of Vincent's not coming mounted, four straws whose wrappers he'd removed, a children's color-by-number he'd completed quickly with the provided crayons in only greens and blues, the yellow-brown plastic pint glass empty of water.

"Policy," Kelly was saying, standing above him. "Federal, or whatever. Half hour with no order, and I have to ask. Waiting for someone, or what?"

It was his humiliation that spoke for him, wanting him to hear how stupid it sounded in the world of other people so that he could make the necessary correction, choose a life that made sense.

"I'm waiting for Vincent Kahn." His hands lying faceup on the table, he heard the radio fill the silence, a DJ saying the name of the song that had just played like it was the ultimate painful coincidence. *That's Bob Seger, with "Still the Same."*

"The space guy?" She was waving a hand over her turned shoulder, already on her way out of their interaction. "He goes to the other one."

"Where," he said, shadowing her across the carpet, three steps unfolding in the time he'd usually take one, and she said something he couldn't understand, named the same interstate he could hear now over the sound of the baseball game. "Four miles," she said, both hands running from the base of her scalp to the hairline, trying to give further volume to her flammable cloud of hair.

In the foyer where more framed photos covered the walls, he hoisted the brick of the phone book, attached by cord to the booth, and found the number he needed. The voice was as bored as Kelly had been with the mention of the name, Vincent Kahn.

"We don't take messages from fans," it said.

"Could you just tell me if—"

"Not at liberty to say."

"Could you just tell him I'm on my way?"

16.

There is no traffic, there is no obstacle. Wright hits eighty on the brief stretch of four-lane highway with his body singing, all gestures perfect, the blinker turned on with just a pinky, the foot lifting off the gas when he reaches the exit in an elegant wave to the future. The downgrade of speed is perfectly even. His chin when he changes lanes ticks over his shoulder like a dancer's.

At the restaurant where he comes once a week Vincent takes the last bite of what he always orders, corned beef and hash. The light is the same, smoky and bluish through the stained glass that ribbons the windows. There's no watch on his wrist, no clock he can see, but he knows that forty minutes have passed. That this is a skill other people don't have, to feel the hour slivering by the minute, has escaped his memory. He could be locked away in the dark for days and know exactly.

It's a bigger one, its own parking lot. Wright breezes through a foyer much the same, curving like a *C* to avoid a cluster of bodies who seem related, all smelling of dairy and sweat, all terminating around six feet in the same red hair. For five, they all say, when a hostess who is mostly the gum in her mouth asks how many. The photos above the bar are identical but arranged differently, the cash register with ornamental typewriter keys just like the other. He sees Vincent Kahn immediately, a person like any other person, a bald spot that looks as greasy in the light as the plate in front of him, empty but for a precisely folded napkin.

The person coming toward him has a look he's never liked, a glance that's wide but unfocused. There's a smell, too, new sweat on old, blue-green dime-store soap, tobacco's mean loiter on the body. He uses his hair in the same way she did, a curtain that gives him a dishonest advantage, an unmanaged part of himself that predicts many others. What was beautiful about her was never different from what was frightening.

Saying his name, pointing to himself as he comes down the carpeted aisle, Wright is aware of a vague impulse to raise both his hands, as though to communicate he is not armed. In pleated denim and a shirt so stiff it seems to hover outside his body, Vincent Kahn stands up and squints like someone trying to pretend he has not been asleep.

The boy's handshake is barely that, his eyes the same blue as hers, a color you couldn't trust for how it took on the surroundings. Before, writing that letter, taking that call, he believed there was something he might ask the boy about her. Now he sees the distance as precious and fought for, remembers that in knowing her his life had nearly lost its focus. Airplanes he let her fly, sleep he went without. His mouth tightens, his mind does.

Wright explains the matter of the mix-up as quickly as he can, the details all spliced with the word *sorry*. Vincent Kahn makes a small gesture with his wrist, the pillow of his palm turning out, as though screwing in a lightbulb.

"I already ate, but you should feel free," Vincent says.

As the boy orders, apple brown betty, CeeCee who always serves him writing this down in enormous, bubbly blue letters, the cap of the pen shot through as it always is with splinters, Vincent looks at his face. The bridge of the nose, the spacing of the teeth, the length of the philtrum. He believes it's important to consider them separately, apart from any instinct, apart from any feeling, all of which say *no*. The dessert is on the table in a minute, less, and now he considers the way the fingers hold the fork, the way the hand moves its fingers.

"Thirty-five hours from San Francisco, something like that?"
"I added some. I wanted New Mexico, I wanted to pass back through Texas. I used to live there."

Wright adds this as a kind of test, to see how closely Vincent Kahn read, to try to knit them together more. But the man across from him goes on to discuss roads, to name-check highways and landmarks. He mentions the surprising green of Arkansas; he cuts a hand vertically, from the height of his shoulder to the surface of the table, to indicate some directness of route. The letters seem to have as much influence, at the table between them, as another country, remote in time and weather, ruled by a different system. He tries anyway, his anxiety having reached its exhaustion, no longer compelled by the possibilities of rejection.

"I've never met anybody who knew her—before."
"Me neither, or at all. I didn't know her long."
"How long was it?"
"A year? Less? More."

It's the first lie he's told in a long time, Vincent, and he does it cutting one shoulder forward, his fingers spread on the plastic in front of him. He knows the answer exactly but thinks of anything else to keep it from his face. A bicycle he'd loved and crashed, brick red with blue fins, age six. The only woman he'd touched in the decade after Elise, friend from the golf course, lights out.

Wright digs his chin into the corduroy collar of his denim jacket, smelling the salt of the fog on it, feeling the difference of their lives as completely as he would water all around him. He had known they would be strange to each other, he had hoped they would make perfect sense. One more question, he tells himself, and if it goes unanswered it's no harm—he won't have any more than he did before. To imagine your mother before she was your mother, he thinks, at the same time he thinks everything else—to imagine your mother before she was your mother is to know the parts of yourself that were never a matter of your will or trying. It was awful to be made of anybody else, and it was all he wanted. The waitress, her denim hip nearly checking the table as she passes by with her platter of baked potatoes, looks back and forth between their faces, two times, four. A table past she stops and turns and opens her mouth to speak, but doesn't.

"Were you surprised? By what happened to her."

"*Surprised* is not the word I would use."

Looking at the boy's face, the features and how they work together, he feels the relief of it, something he had to see for himself.

"Your mother was a gifted person. She could find a reason to learn anything, all California tanagers in the space of an evening, takeoff and landing as fast as most pilots. Always a book. She never wanted to know less than anybody, never wanted it to be said she had not tried. The horse, what was it called—"

"Lloyd."

"She rode it standing up a mile on the bet of a nickel once, sprained her wrist. People thought the proud one was her sister, what was her—"

"Charlie."

"Yes. But she was just as much so and more patient, willing to give up more in the short term."

"She flew planes?"

"And she kept a good secret, apparently. That I knew. Yes, we flew some."

"What is the word you would use?"

"You look like her. Almost exactly."

It's less like hearing the words, *you look like her,* than eating them. He feels them in his body, parts of himself he'll never see. Wright understands now that Vincent Kahn won't speak the underside of it, the answer inside the observation, just name the similarities as he must observe them. The color of your hair, he is explaining, your feet a little bowed, too, sorry for my saying. A scent from the waitress, knockoff Calvin Klein that comes in a spray can, the heft of it right but the last note metallic, sheds her as she speaks. Dessert or I guess you already had some, anything else, just the check. Over the shoulders of the first man on the moon are paper shamrocks ascending and descending in their hang from the ceiling, and Wright focuses on these, the slight movement under the fans. Is it a lie, is it one Vincent Kahn was always going to tell or did it come to him in this booth. Why write. Why come.

"New York, is it? You're driving to."

The boy's disappointment looks like hers. Blows don't land on the face but disappear, almost immediately, into the body. He's striking, it's undeniable, absorbent of light in the way the most beautiful women are, and the waitress sees it too, and keeps looking over at them from where she's spraying down the curving glass case. Leaving his house he had told himself he was prepared for any outcome, a son who would make the rest of his life a long apology, baseball tickets by the ream, sleeping bags and fishing poles piled in the hall. Syndicated television, popcorn on the stove.

"Welcome to stay tonight, if you need."

Why does he want him to sleep there? To make the humiliation longer, starve it until it dies? It's a false offer, Wright decides, so he takes it, wanting, like his mother did, to push at the flimsiness of a façade. On their knuckles is the same patterning of hair, on their chins the impression of the same thumb.

"Love to. Follow you in my car."

The drive Vincent does without thinking, losing her son behind him at one point and only realizing when he honks. He throws a hand out the window to apologize. *But he can't drive my* Ford *five blocks to the drugstore,* his father's friend had said. A turn signal is a sound he's always hated, the clunky two-note stupidity of it. He waits empty minutes behind a station wagon with rear-facing seats. A boy with mucus trails the color of corn stares back, his fingers loose in his lap, his hair very clean.

Down Vincent's cul-de-sac the trees are young, the houses low, the budget sedans wood paneled. In the windows are naïve craft projects, Popsicle-stick wreaths and Scotch-taped finger paintings, on the lawns miniature stovetops and shopping carts in kid-friendly plastic. The greatest luxury of the middle-class childhood, Wright thinks, right here—life so dependably familiar that the notion of running errands, feeding and being fed, could be reenacted with an imaginative twist. There are no sidewalks, just driveways and curbs, and the fences, slight and cosmetic, suggest there's never really been a threat to any of this, never anyone who came and did not belong.

He has a can of hot dogs and cable with a number of channels and a good shower and he names these things aloud to no real response. To supply some sound he turns on the television. The president's voice is one he likes, an actor's training yes but a humble measure to it, only the necessary words. He's heard the address already, three times or four, the Challenger disaster, news stations playing it on loop. After Bisson had removed the lemon from the command module, his point made, he had tossed it to him, backward and underhand, winking over his shoulder. He knew Bisson had seen his life both ways, precious because it was expendable. Her son, listening with a hand cupped to his mouth, is making an expression he can't read. Some take comfort in seeing their faces in others, he thinks, they spend all their lives looking. It is a way of feeling the world has invited you here. But he was never this way—even as a boy, what he loved above all was the privacy of mornings, the theater of weather.

We've never had a tragedy like this, the president says, and Wright thinks of Braden, the way he keeps the number of the dead spring-loaded. There's almost nothing to look at in the room, brown shag carpeted and furnished in muted oranges and greens, but the one framed photo that sits on the stone mantel. A grimacing boy pedals a bicycle midair, hovering a few feet above a pool. A few days before he left San Francisco, Wright had watched him scrawl the latest in glitter on poster board, 16,116. *We mourn seven lives,* the president says. Jacket still on, fists in his pockets, he laughs, the undeniable punch line of the number. He imagines two thousand crews of seven, men who smiled at him on the street or undid his metal button fly with their teeth, exploding one after the other, the shuttles failing again and again to fly straight.

"Something funny?"

"I'm sorry. Probably just exhaustion." The room where Vincent Kahn leads him is as clean as it is empty. There is a mattress on a box spring, a nightstand with one drawer. He thanks him for the apple brown betty, he thanks him for the bed, he thanks him. With the door closed he examines the few things he can, the pale cotton curtains on pulley, a small, stiff towel on a mounted wooden ring in the connected half bath. The only question he could ask of the room is the drawer, and he resists it. In the living room the address continues, the president speculates on bravery. Because he knows the bed has been made with a precision he cannot replicate, he resolves to sleep atop and climbs on, shoeless. His right hand shoots out on its own, the fingers twist behind the wrist to pull the knob. Like somebody driving, his eyes stay straight ahead as he looks with his body. There's nothing, he thinks. In a second he turns over and switches hands, places the flat of the left on the pine and scoots it back. A weight there, something with different parts, metal, Velcro, glass. The first thing he does with the watch is turn it over and blow the dust from the face, a bubble of some depth and heaviness. TACHOMETER, the outside ring says, tiny white capitals over numerals that go to five hundred. Circumscribed by the twelve minute markers are three smaller circles, the use of which he can't guess, going to thirty, going to sixty, going to ten. The doubled band, Velcro, could reach around his wrist twice, and stitched on its inside is a label: plain, official. APOLLO/NASA. When he puts it in his pocket, cool and elegant among the crumbs and pennies there, he says I'm sorry to the alien room, less an apology for what he is doing than an admission of what he has done, the acknowledgment of what he won't take back. A post office or pawnshop, near here or should he drive awhile, he doesn't know. He will leave at five A.M., the rooms he passes through dark, the cul-de-sac at dawn taking on a glow piece by piece—the cheap plastic disc swing tied up in the tree becoming bluer, the saliva-worn tennis balls scattered by dogs appearing like Easter eggs under the bare hedges of rosebushes.

The judgment greets Wright as fact: there is nothing to be done about the way certain people come into the world, nothing to be done about the way the world comes easily to certain people.

Vincent had skimmed the letters for information, of which
there was little. The final months with her, she had sometimes
been cold and strange—*Your life is a promontory you carved yourself
and walked way out on,* she said—and he had waved it away, her
maudlin tendency. In two years, when the last letter comes, when
he finds it waiting in his mailbox after a last trip to Edwards, he
will read it carefully, more than once, not rising when the afternoon
goes to turn on a lamp. For now he sits, listening to the television.

We've grown used to wonders in this century, the president says. *It's
hard to dazzle us.*

October 17, 1988

Dear Mr. Kahn,

I don't talk to anyone about my mother. What I say is, she died.
I never want to catch a look on somebody's face as they talk to me
and imagine it's about her, like they're trying to identify the ways
in which who she was shows up in who I am. So I guess this was
practice, writing to you, for a someday when I'll pause between sips
of water and say, like people do, and I'm always so jealous of how
offhanded they can be, that reminds me of something my mother said.
My mother had a dress just like that.

Less like a person and more like an event, is how I think of her.
She was an accident I could not have avoided. Sometimes I ask if
this is also how she thought of herself. The days before the bomb
in the Village I saw it, however briefly. They were discussing the
number of officers to be in attendance, a guest list that Randy had
stolen somehow, and she said something like, a hundred and six, and
flapped her palm open and shut to say, gone. Then the look on her
face like a change in light, an old part of her almost coming through
to say, what?

What frightens me the most about who she was at the end, the
tendency I'm most afraid of having inherited, is how resigned she was
to all of it. She behaved as though every shocking fact, the bombings,
her face on the news, the most-wanted flyers in towns where we could

only stop long enough to eat, was part of the same inevitability—speaking, also, as though she and I were equal victims of the same circumstance, using the word "we" in ways that made me beat my pillow. We're both hungry, she would say, but it's our job now to focus on just making it to the next place. During a thunderstorm we watched from a motel in Georgia, I suggested to her she go find the roof of the highest building and wait to be struck. My temper had become a part of how we lived, something factored into how long or hard a trip might become. We didn't speak for four days.

They were farther apart toward the end, moments when she cried or begged and seemed to be looking for a way back into who she had been, and they passed like a sneeze. An hour later it would feel like a hallucination I'd had, her face returned to its rigid economy, creaseless and lightless.

If she hadn't met Randy, would she have found her way to Shelter? I want to think no, although I know this doesn't say great things about her constitution, Mr. Kahn, and I'd love to say great things about her constitution, particularly to you, whom I have reason to believe she loved, and who I have reason to believe humiliated her. I overheard her in a fight with Randy once, the first few months in the country, when she was saying, You're like every other man. You love the woman who worships you, and the ones you respect you fuck like they're trash. You love what you pity and destroy what you admire. I was stunned by this, the life before it must have referenced.

Was she against the war, yes. Was she angry. Was she wild. Was her life's lack of structure what allowed her to change it completely. Yes, yes, yes. But my mother, Mr. Kahn, was the kind of person who reassured spiders as she carried them outside. She wore a button that said "Children Are Just Smaller People," and wanted my opinion on everything, always, before I could even spell my name, and once let me paint what I know now was an incredibly valuable suitcase, a last gift from her father to her sister, with a very large and crooked portrait of a whale. She eschewed toy guns and once kicked Randy out of their bed for a night because he'd made me a slingshot. Is this the sort of person you imagine becoming a top twenty-five most-wanted domestic terrorist?

What happened in the brownstone in New York City was a distracted mistake. Whether it was my mother's distraction that killed that man upstairs, the fault of Annabelle or Randy or some combination I don't know, although I have my theories. My mother loved Randy, maybe in the same way she loved you, and by that I mean she loved the way he thought. I don't know if it was ever about how he made her feel. It was about how he made her see. What he didn't account for was how well she would see, better than he could, wider and farther and uninterrupted by rage. That she became the bigger star of Shelter was a deep shock to him, and even that she understood before he did, from where she was always standing beside him, a light hand on his elbow—how it would undo him. The image of a weaponized woman is a new one, I heard her say to him, during a sulky fit he had after Philadelphia brought her the fame it did, in the voice she had used to comfort me when another child had been cruel.

In the last months I knew her, in the motel rooms where she faded, my mother was a fount of American commercialism. Though she had spent years decrying the Television, talking about it in that vicious way—the Television has spoken, A true American consults first and last the Television—her position allowed her, finally, to understand its appeal. She mouthed the slogans in perfect mimicry. The electric pour seemed to be going both ways, from the television to her, from her to the television, the belief and its believer entwined ad infinitum, becoming interchangeable. If I had to choose the moment I lost her, Mr. Kahn, I couldn't. But if I had to choose the moment in which I knew she was lost, it was this, her mouth soulless around a jingle. MY BOLOGNA HAS A FIRST NAME, IT'S O-S-C-A-R. Easily, this.

Even as a child I could understand why it was her and not

Randy. He was incapable of hiding, from anybody, first of all himself. What woke him up in the morning was a litany of wrongdoings, those done by the country pressing on him as much as some cruel nickname that had followed him around his childhood playground. In the places where my mother could slip in undetected, hard to pin to a specific stratum, still adorned with certain formal gifts of her upbringing, Randy was obvious, all angles and ragged political patches. The war was on his face. She could put on a secondhand white overcoat, no buttons, all sash, and pass like a slightly unclean Lana Turner through the revolving doors of Brutalist high-rise municipal buildings. She could say beg pardon and ask for directions without anyone guessing what was ticking in her suitcase. Though she was the oldest of the women in Shelter, she looked the youngest, something if pressed she attributed to the inversions of yoga, and that she never wore underwear if she could help it.

One piece of Shelter's agenda, often left out in the TV movie reenactments, was the rejection of monogamy. They felt that in the work they were doing the romantic-sexual attachment was anathema, a sure route to a weakened purpose. Randy railed at her later for how free she became, slipping from one cot to the next in the early morning sometimes, but he was the first adopter, disappearing for days with Annabelle and then barely shrugging when asked about it, as if discussing matters beyond his control, road closures or outdated laws.

The Philadelphia bombing, of which my mother was arguably the star, incensed him, though he talked about it as a failing of ideology, and he was the one who pushed for a change in the model, who rallied for the practice of evacuating these buildings to end. It's not enough that they fear for their institutions, he said. They have to fear for their lives. He was the one who identified the officers' dance that was to be the target of the bomb that blew up the town house. Fifty military officers and their wives. Tuxes and tulle.

She was not only the one who planted it, in Philadelphia, curtsying her way in with a typewriter case, more than convincing as the part of the stenographer, but also the voice on the memorandum that so many radio stations played. It was coy but forthright, feminine but unfaltering. Someone likened it to Marilyn. Let it be known that America is now subject to the same obliteration it has brought elsewhere, she said. Thank you and good night. She had come into life with all advantages and she had scorned them, and that was a compelling argument for something being very wrong with the heart of the country, of course more so than Randy, whose missing finger was too personal an injury, too clear a sign of the ways his country had hurt him, not clear enough about what it had turned him into. To be truly famous here is to have lost or gained everything, reversed positions completely. The photo that had surfaced of her, beaming astride Charlie's horse, was in every paper.

The network of Shelter pay phones had almost completely regenerated by the time the AARRMW got ahold of her, and she believed, not entirely incorrectly, it had been changed to keep her from using it. Randy had his wish: he became the star. She went on trying those numbers months after they went silent, something like thirty she had committed to memory. I still hate to enter a Laundromat or arcade. The sound of the coins dropping sends me right to her fallen face.

The group that gave my mother her last stage had formed only shortly beforehand, and disbanded immediately after. The shock on their faces around her is part of what made the photo so famous—a mean, easy comment on how the radical left had eaten itself. She told them she would begin seated, or so went the account in the news. She said she needed to meditate before she gave any speeches, and I suppose that was not a lie. They were younger than I am now, but I have a hard time forgiving what they failed to see about her when she showed up. People in gas stations had seen it, at rest stops where she was afraid of the herds of children that bounded from station wagons.

Is your mom okay, said a woman on the bus I had watched stow three garbage bags of clothes in the undercarriage—leaving a bad relationship, she told me at a rest stop, keeping a hand over a very obvious bruise on her jaw. She must have seen how my mother insisted we switch seats four times, then fell so deeply asleep she tumbled, during a jerky lane change, into the aisle.

Would she have agreed to any protest that vaguely aligned with the way she'd been living before, to attach her face to a cause for the price of a bus ticket? It's possible. The car she'd bought, unregistered, had broken down. Our money was gone. She'd sold a belt buckle of her sister's, a figure on a horse with a lasso, the twist of rope spelling the words "WHAT FUN." But like all other decisions she was making then, she agreed to the trip to Florida having eaten only what came from motel room vending machines, never having slept more than an hour at once. Every person we saw, in those days, was someone who would make the call the second she turned a corner. Dogs were suspect, their sense of smell. Birds too cheerful. The sun too bright, the window too big, the sheets too stiff, the water too cold. There was no part of the world left for her, was the way she was acting. I know now that this was because she had turned her curiosity toward leaving it.

I'm telling you because I don't want you believing that what she did was some act of revenge toward you, that you were that big to her. Revenge is an act of pride, isn't it? And pride is an act of self. It requires a person to believe they have been deprived of something they deserved. My mother, Mr. Kahn, no longer had any sense of what she deserved. She didn't even have a sense of what she liked. On our last stop on the bus ride before we reached the cape, at the rest area where we were allowed ten minutes to stretch our legs in the aisles of a gas station, I watched her fill a cup of coffee with two packets of condensed creamer. She had always, with no exception and a fair amount of insistence, taken it black. When I pointed this out to her, she gave me a look of total guilt. I'm so sorry, she said, as if I'd be the one with the wrong taste in my mouth.

She had never loved the program, of course, and we took a bus to Quito to protest a parade for your friend Sam. She called Apollo Our Happiest Lie and said things like, Here's our country, dressed to the nines while its house burns down. All my childhood, she simmered about the coverage it received, talked about how it was the same, the money that lit the rocket and the money that killed the children. Two sides of the same coin. It makes sense that a country destroying life on one planet would need to lay claims on another.

When we got to the cape, my mother asked me something she hadn't in a long time, a question that for most of my life had given me a deep thrill: Would you like to take a walk? I never knew when it was coming, this question, and it usually followed a period during which some book or thought had kept her from me—she would have been quiet for hours, moving only to underline or scrawl in the margins. That she wanted my company after this had always seemed like the greatest compliment.

Passing the tents set up on the beach and the people tailgating in baseball caps, my mother looked at them with a kind of benevolence, like they were some hand-painted exhibit, quaint representations of simple, parochial lives. She was dressed more like she had when I was younger, in box-cut linen that diminished what was beautiful about her, and she asked me, as she always had when we started out, what I was thinking. I was sullen and I didn't want to say and for ten minutes I kicked a beer bottle along the sand in front of us, rolling my eyes like even that was a tedious burden forced upon me. I wasn't asking myself, Why isn't she afraid of getting caught? Why aren't her sunglasses on? She had her shoes, some drugstore espadrilles worn out the summer before, in her hand, and she started speaking in the automatic way people do when telling a story they know very well.

I don't know if you'll remember, she said. This was soon after we got here. Those couple weeks in Berkeley. Do you remember Karen and her baby Henry? He wasn't as curious as a baby should be, I always thought. And he cried at anything. She was asked to leave soon after this, because of him. Anyway, there was this afternoon. Henry'd been left on the back porch in a bassinet, someone saying what he hadn't gotten enough of was sunshine. The jelly for the mimeograph was on the oven, and I was stab-binding some poems written by the women of Shelter, and I didn't know where you were, but this was before things became so strict, and I wasn't worried. Then I heard the screen door open and saw you come through, carrying him. The remarkable thing was how you were holding him, textbook. All the women were mouthing at me: Has he ever held a baby? Has he?

I don't know how you knew. It took me four months to lift you naturally, because it's counterintuitive, holding a life that small— you have to start not with the heaviness in the torso, but the head, which can feel too downy, impossible to secure. You were inured somehow to the fragility of it. It's one of the first things I remember when I think, Who is my son? It makes me believe you will know what you need in life, and that those needs will always include the happiness of others.

I understand now, Mr. Kahn, that this was the version of me she wanted to remember as she went, a boy who was likely to survive without her, one who was possibly better off. For a long time I worried I had lit the match, because the way the photo was composed somehow makes that case, and because in a bacterial, bodily way I had hated her. Claudette and James, for all their fear of difficult conversation, always had the time to remind me of my innocence. She did that to herself, they would say. She did.

My mother had the presence of mind, at least, to keep me from the demonstration, or to try. She had arranged for someone to look after me in the parking lot, a short college student named Brad who was pissed to be kept from the action. We were sitting in his car with all *the doors open smoking a spliff and not talking. There were Buddhist prayer beads hanging from his rearview and in the seat pocket in front of me some porn magazine folded back and barely stuffed down. I could see most of the image, of a woman being fucked in two ways by two men, black and white, and the text said something about ebony and ivory. None of them were looking at each other. One of them had both her wrists. Her mouth was open too wide. The point seemed to be pain.*

Brad turned on the radio, eventually, and closed his eyes like somebody alone. The noise of it seemed like my cue to exit. With the doors already open, leaving was just a matter of swinging my feet onto the asphalt and going. I don't know how long until Brad realized I was gone, just that he didn't come after me. What you see in that photo, a boy holding a match as he crawls back, a woman sitting with her palms faceup on her knees, is true and it isn't. The peace on her face is less that than a total vacancy. Rather than cleaned out, abandoned. That match in my hand is one I took from her, ignoring the fact that a whole booklet remained, fighting, like the child I still was, with the small pieces as though they would change the whole. I know the papers speculated about the words that passed between us, what she whispered. Shadow shine, is what she said, which is how, when I was very small and living in another country, I referred to the ends of things, and how, finally, she referred to me.

She didn't believe in it, what you spent your life on, but I don't want you thinking that woman on fire had anything to do with you. That woman was empty of who she had been, someone invented a thousand times over in as many mirrors as she could find, and that was something her country allowed her to do.

We're just very young, my mother would say, scanning the headlines of the papers she bought religiously, shaking her head. I didn't understand then who she meant, that she could be talking about the nation as a whole. She had a tendency to see any system as living, a creature that might behave another way if only it could be enlightened to what waited for it. When she'd had too much to drink, my mother could be persuaded to perform the pliés and fouettés that had won ribbons in her childhood. She kept many of her gifts hidden, as women do, worried about what love their talent might keep them from. My mother hated her country, and she was a part of it.

Wright

17.

1988

Earlier in the bleached-out day a bird had gotten in, and the attempts to remove it were still visible hours later, a handprint on the window, the tented yellow caution sign where in the chase a pitcher of beer had spilled. A busboy had stood on the back booth's table and held up a broom, waving it like a carnival barker. Also a smell, the collective perspiration of the lunch crowd who had forgotten their fries to watch it play out, and the tiny bit of blood high on the wall of windows, noticeable only if you knew where to look. From the line at the counter of spinning seats and the two-tops that ran down the middle of the room, people had called out imperatives, close the shades, turn out the lights. The staff had nodded like this was helpful, but the diner was twenty-four hours, and the lights were on timers they had not been trained to change. The shades were mostly cosmetic, the floor-to-ceiling windows designed with tinted glass. Its shape was famous to every American, the peaked eaves that had once seemed futuristic, the color of its logo instantly recognizable, a yellow that only meant one thing. The chain's promise was a basic sameness, mild, uniform.

"—need is a sheet," someone had yelled, a voice that sounded like it hadn't been used in weeks. "Create a wall that di-rects it out of there."

So many had offered suggestions, loud with apparent feeling, but the bird had not survived. The table where it had finally fallen was seated now by a traveling family, a mother with wet wipes in her fanny pack, children in souvenir hats purchased at the theme park six hours away. Its body was wrapped in the promotional glossy about the seasonal waffles and deposited in the industrial trash out back. By the encampment of Dumpsters the line cooks smoked, holding their cigarettes like small, powerful tools, arguing about things that could not be proved.

There was a sign, identical to all others at locations across the country, that said PLEASE WAIT TO BE SEATED, but he had curved around it and settled at the counter. He was the sort of person other people noticed, particularly here where the only sound was the highway, particularly because he was hard to place. Nothing distinctive about him but the woman's ring on his finger, no ac-cent in the way he asked for a hamburger medium. Of course, there was his face, there was who he looked like. But it had been long enough that even that was slow to surface in the minds of people who stared at him. Was it a celebrity or just some man you had wanted to love you, some man who had gotten the job you deserved. The idea of a person on the moon felt like a curi-ous outlier, something that happened at the close of that furious decade like an isolated remark made at the end of a wild dream, and so instead of knowing, immediately, who it was he resembled, the people at the diner only behaved with a breath more deference, treating him as something familiar and beloved, nodding at him if he caught their look. Even the waitress, whose life turned on the appearance of a new face, who asked questions about marriage and money before the second cup was approved for refill, somehow felt it right to be quiet around him. Instead of asking what he took in his coffee, she brought out all possible answers, milk, nondairy creamer, nonsugar sweetener, more wooden stir sticks than could be needed.

The light was the biggest part of the room. It caught on the laminate dessert booklets, gave a forgiving glow to the baby's breath and carnations dyed antacid pink. Coming from the back was the sound of an argument, Alejandro who had tried to usher the bird through the doors and the cook who had mocked him out back for saying a prayer over its collapsed rib cage. There was the industrial fan from the kitchen and the crushed ice settling in enormous sodas and the highway, less like a series of sounds than a circle that hemmed all others in. Management encouraged staff to keep the television off. This would entice the customer to put his money in the jukebox, to make that meal his own by the songs that would recall it. People chose almost anything over silence. The waitress, who had woken up in the dense blue of four thirty A.M., crossed to the wall-mounted Sony above the bottles of liquor. She took down the remote attached to its side by Velcro and began to assault it, flipping channels for the reminder of options. In this life, the television said, or close to it, there was a terminally ill child, a toothy beauty in purple, who had made a miraculous recovery. There was a high-speed chase in a city that buried its dead aboveground, a woman who had fallen from a parking garage and survived, a millionaire who had lost it all, a lottery winner who had gained it. There was a cat who could sing, a house you could buy with a pool at the edge of the horizon. Her thumbnail on the rubber button moved with the instinct of hunger, orange polish put on yesterday and already chipped, three seconds better than six, each channel a wish made and granted in the same moment.

It was when he spoke that she really looked at him. "Could you turn it back," he had said. He had the sort of grainy complexion, freckle on tan, that made it hard to tell how clean he was. His fork he held in a way that was both very feminine and somewhat crude, like the practice was a new one, and he was being careful with it.

"Could you turn it back." He repeated this with a look on his face that was too big for the request. "The—the shuttle," he said. She snapped the fluorescent yellow gum in her mouth and she pressed the button in the other direction, three times, five.

. . . *niner,* the television said. *Soon to go subsonic,* the television said. *No changes to wind or weather.* Sixty-five miles from the landing site at Edwards Air Force Base. *Thermal protection heat shield. The first mission since the Challenger explosion two years ago, and a real feeling of pride in the audience. We've got celebrities in the stands, we've got Vincent Kahn.* On-screen a gray face, briefly, then the return to the blue.

Before its shape could be seen it was just an interruption in the sheet of sky, a manic deviation that needed to be corrected. Over and over, the camera lost it and found it again. Cutting through the blue, finally it revealed itself, a shape like an inverted Y, its chase plane beneath it then behind it, loyal as a child. Then it was a thing with wheels and decals on its side, and then it painted shadows on the dust. It prompted applause from hands unseen as it rolled through desert, whiteness of land so complete as to seem like water.

She was watching it, too, so she couldn't see his face when he spoke again, but later she remembered his last words. She always remembered walkouts. In her ten years waitressing she'd had something like twelve, and their faces were with her like old boyfriends, asking the same questions in her memory. Could she have seen it coming, their leaving? Was it a decision made in minutes or seconds? Was it anybody they would have let down, or just her? Was there anything she could have done? It upset her more deeply than she cared to admit. The feeling was not just being robbed but something under that, your time and voice and how you used your body, how you offered it to the comfort of someone you didn't know—that, also, made worthless.

In this case what was strange, what she told friends over all-syrup margaritas later, was that she'd watched him leave, turned around to see him pass through the first set of double doors and didn't think to look down at the bill he'd left untouched. He'd been so calm, stopping to use the restroom, knocking the wood of the hostess stand on the way out, that she hadn't suspected a thing. He had approached a truck in the lot and removed his keys from his undersized denim jacket and then—what? Thought better?

"He didn't get in the car," she told them, her hand cupped a little as if to catch the missing information. He looked left and right, then crossed the highway, walked into what she knew was a long patch of nothing, three miles of heat uncut by shade that led, eventually, to the border.

"Anything strange about him?" they asked. "Funny last remark?"

He looked like somebody, she said, who she didn't know. It would come to her. In her impression of him she was hushed, trying to communicate how he had spoken, like everything he said was something he had already, and didn't want to again.

"That's all I needed to see," he had said. "You can turn it off now."

18.

The story about him changed depending who you talked to, ten years later or fifteen, in the Mission or the Castro, whether the day had been bright on the hills or it had hardly bothered to reveal itself, stayed hidden by the gray weather.

He thought his father was the first man on the moon, a boy of twenty might say, in an oversized lamb's-wool coat that fell halfway to his bare knees, his face mostly its big green eyes under blue mascara. Such a sad delusion. Can you imagine thinking that while you were dying? Bradley, I think. Twenty-seven.

You're thinking of his friend, who got the what do you call it, the moon clock, the space watch.

What watch? What are you talking about, *the space watch*? How many have you had, Moon Clock?

In another version, sugary and miraculous, Vincent Kahn was the happy long-lost father. His son was someone most people claimed to remember and a good few, older, claimed to have a friend who had slept with him.

At a bad party in the Sunset, in a stucco building that had just gone up—a forty-minute bus ride and for what—somebody with an unfortunate scramble of teeth leaned out over the balcony, holding his cigarette between middle and ring finger. The depth of the park across the way could be felt, the people the city had forgotten sleeping on cardboard in the groves of juniper. The green had a smell, the damp had a color.

A real beauty, a real slut, who wasn't. He had a superhero jawline and this turquoise ring.

And did he ever say—

It wasn't a real talking-about-your-dad–type situation, but he had class. Left a note with a little drawing of a whale saying *A whale of a time,* which Andy kept, which I know because I cleaned out his apartment. What I heard was that he went there, where is it, Missouri, Ohio, where Vincent Kahn lived. And Vincent Kahn took him in, but it had to be very quiet, a national hero with a gay son, can you imagine?

You're telling me he's still there, living some secret life with his long-lost astronaut father? I mean, does this story make you feel good to tell? What are your thoughts on JFK? He's taken up papier-mâché with Marilyn in Bel-Air, right? Do you subscribe to the *National Enquirer* or prefer the thrill of buying it at the store?

Let him tell it, said a boy in a dewy drugstore lawn chair. Relax.

Believe what you want. Some people think he had it and died there, but I don't know. I like to think of them cooking breakfast, talking the headlines. And if it went the other way, don't you think it could be better? That at the end of your life you're entrusted to somebody who only gets to know you then? There'd be none of the comparisons, when he was healthy he was this, people crying just because of how your skin looked. Your identity would just be your transition. It would not be such an embarrassment, having to die.

There's a cheery little thought. Are there lightbulbs inside I could eat?

It doesn't not make me happy to think about.

Who was his mother, then? Who has the son of the first man on the moon and doesn't cash in on that?

You know, those guys could have whoever they wanted. I had an aunt who screwed a fighter pilot, they all started as that, the astronauts, test pilot, I can't remember which, and she said, she got too drunk at Thanksgiving, "That's a rough mistake I'd make *again*." His mother could have been anybody. It doesn't matter, for the story, who his mother was. History belongs to men, blah, blah, blah.

In another story, he shows up at Vincent Kahn's door unannounced, a twink in the wrong place, and Vincent Kahn calls the cops. The police arrest him somehow, on inadequate grounds, because Vincent Kahn is the biggest thing that has ever happened to this town and they're in his pocket. They humiliate him at the station, they make him cut off his hair with an old pair of office scissors. In almost every story, he has beautiful, famous hair. Kaleidoscopic, someone says. They sprinkle the cuttings over his county jail dinner and make him eat it, or they burn it like incense for the three days he's there. The smell makes him gag, but every time he gags they blow a high-pitched whistle, so he learns to swallow it. After this, the story doesn't know where to go, and it stops abruptly. Anecdotes like this, unbelievable cruelty in the hands of power, have become as dependable as syndicated television, and their entertainment value is the same, satisfying if you're looking for confirmation that the world is stacked in the same way it was a year or five before—in this case, against you, against people who look and talk and feel like you.

I don't need to hear this, says a man with a beard as neat as his sweater, pushing his cleared plate to the center of the table. Someone put on a record.

There's another version, told less often in the city, and it involves a small town in the redwoods. Guerneville. Before the men from San Francisco started buying up houses there, it was pronounced with a middle *e*. They decided better without—a stately two syllables sounded more like how the dank place felt—and the locals, over the course of two decades, must have slowly agreed.

Most often he's a little older, the person telling this version, than the person listening. Here it's a host and his visitor, a generation between, all told in the time it takes to drive from the main drag to the gray ocean. Snaking along the river, which drowns an early swimmer every March, letting up on the clutch of the Saab that's his pride, the driver takes the curves through the ancient trees, so dense that the rule, even at two in the afternoon, is headlights. The river takes its name from the Russians who settled it, who built wooden forts against the ocean and ran a pelt trade. Their rivals were the loggers, always American.

Anyway, says the host: the boy who believed Vincent Kahn was his father. For years he'd been writing to Vincent Kahn, something he was ashamed of, something even his best friend, who he lived with and knew everything, didn't know. He was a strange case, no family, very charismatic, maybe something a little off with his mental health. The sort of person who is at every party for months on end, then disappears for just as long.

Is it always so dark like this? What was his name?

Just for the next stretch, then everything opens up completely. The way the land changes here.

The host waves a hand, steering wheel to open window, to indicate his broad feeling for this part of the country. The boy reaches into the buttery leather of the backseat for another sweater.

A letter comes, one day, from Vincent Kahn himself, neither confirming nor denying. He packs up in a matter of days, telling some lie about how he was driving to New York anyway and a stop in Ohio was basically nothing. The friend was very active—he organized, maybe you heard of it, that die-in at one of the last bathhouses to stay open, that nightmare in SoMa, the exact number of men who'd died in the city, numbered in greasepaint on T-shirts flat in the street. Also a real cook. The kind of person who thinks, Oh, Tuesday: I'll just prepare duck for eight.

Around here the road rises, shaking off the old trees, and the river changes into something else, gaining salt and sand. Ahead is blond farmland, tawny cows at home in the serpentinite rocks that cradle it.

He has promised to call the friend, but nothing. It's not unlike him—some people are oysters, some people are clams. I'm not this way, I've never done anything alone in my life. Three people know not when I have a cold, but when I think I might.

Beautiful, the boy says. It's like it totally forgets what it just was.

Weeks go by, and then this package comes. Barely a letter, something like, I'll let you know when I'm on my way. Sell this if you need to. I'm sorry. Inside is this watch, enormous and decked out with all kinds of dials. On the strap, sewn to the strap, it says, whatever, NASA. An Omega Speedmaster.

They crest a high curve, a turn decorated with white feathery plants that grow waving in green reeds from between boulders.

The friend is furious, a real moralist, very unhappy to be in the possession of stolen property, but keeps this to himself. He does not sell it for rent, he finds some subletter. Their whole friendship has been an Italian wedding, shouting matches, big declarations, a fair amount of pleading. The watch goes in the drawer of his bedside table, a year goes by. A test comes back positive. His was the type, by the way, where he wasn't sick, wasn't sick, wasn't sick, then was *sick*. Anyway there are all the appointments and tests, no insurance of course, he's a waiter, he's twenty-six or twenty-seven. A month or two later he more or less loses his job, drops five plates he'd stacked on his arm for the second time, and to the two friends who come by it's obvious. Pneumonia, the hospital, let's go. They're rooting through his room to find his wallet, he's delirious in three sweaters, and in the nightstand they find the watch. He's babbling that it's from the friend, it's Vincent Kahn's, told me to sell it, and they're brushing him off, trying to get an overnight bag together, but somebody looks at that label and starts to think. He's French, something of a devil-may-care.

The windows are up against the wind now, and the driver barely slows to turn. If there wasn't enough light before, now there's all of it.

Long story short, while they're at the ER, he walks down to a pawnshop, the place on Mission and Duboce with the neon arrow, you've seen it.

He waits for the boy to nod in confirmation, which he finally does, fingers of both hands curled around the tan pull-down handle.

And he's fighting tooth and nail, because as it turns out, says the man at the pawnshop, this is a watch that was sold to the public. The French friend says what about the little tag sewn in that says Apollo 11, look how long the strap goes, obviously it's meant to go over a space suit. The French friend's English is bad, worse when he's angry, and the guy behind the counter, a beautiful Vietnamese man, still works there, anyway pulls out a magazine where he says he's seen the ad for this watch recently. He points out the similarities, and the friend points out the differences.

The boy's knees are up on the seat now, his left hand tensed on the dash. The color on his face looks daubed there by a preschooler. They come up behind a Toyota, a family of four in coordinated neon windbreakers, license plate Idaho, and overtake it with a long, mean honk that bleeds into the next mile.

Commemorative edition, he keeps saying. Commemorative edition.

The driver takes his hands off the wheel to ape the gesture of the man at the pawnshop, hands raised as if holding two platters by his ears. The boy's hand shoots to the wheel.

Commemorative edition! He acknowledges yes, the differences, the Velcro, the patch, but he asks the friend, and what can the friend really say, how can you verify? How can you prove it? No proof, no money. And this makes sense, of course. Fame like that, prestige, really we're talking about power, it can't just pass from one hand into the next. There's no trickle-down. It's nontransferable. It would only be truly worth something if Vincent Kahn sold it, and it would never be worth it to Vincent Kahn to sell it.

He got no money?

No, no, he got some. Be patient. He got the price of the watch, the one sold to the public, plus a few sniffs more, which of course means the pawnshop man had his suspicions. You can look it up, there are a few of them unaccounted for, the real ones I mean, lost to the black market. Anyway, with that money the three of them got a vacation rental back in town, I'll show it to you on the drive back, this beautiful deck on a hill, a hot tub cut into it, a front room that was all found windows, just surrounded by trees. He could have spent it on more doctors, whichever fashionable eastern medicine, but he said no. They had these big dinners, of course he couldn't really eat much, shaved truffles, oysters from Bodega Bay, I'll take you. He made the shopping lists and wrote out the coursing in the mornings. When he sensed it was getting to be time, the end of two months, he had the idea that he wanted a going-away party. A hundred people came, formal attire. Someone brought fifty of those paper lanterns you get in Chinatown and they rigged them in the trees somehow. He had this thrifted Nehru suit, peach, and an orchid boutonniere, and he just held court on the deck in his wheelchair, kissing everybody goodbye. Anyone who cried he sent away. He was in bed by ten and they all walked to the river and sent—tea candles—down it in plastic—boats. I'm sorry, it always gets me. Brandon, his name was Brandon. We're almost there. Isn't that the most beautiful story you've ever heard? You're not looking at me like that's the most beautiful story you've ever heard.

They are approaching the last sign to be seen for a while, a three-way stop known for its accidents, people turning against the glare onto the coast road built the century before for mules. There is a piece of a bumper, there are the shards of a clipped side mirror.

He should have— I'm sorry, the boy says, but he should have been in a hospital. I don't think it's a beautiful story. I don't care about the fucking tea candles. He shouldn't have been sick to begin with. I don't think it's a beautiful story. Who was his family? What about his friend? Are you saying his friend never.

I've heard it both ways. He came at the last minute, he didn't come. Had been in New York, disappeared to Mexico after, was sending back AZT, took a photo that mattered. You've seen it, that boy in a wheelchair who couldn't hold up his sign, it's half-curled in his lap, that protest down—

Here it is, superseding talk and feeling. It's the last color, someone told this boy at the party, and if he didn't believe it at the time, wanting to stay in his life and not imagine millions of others, if he didn't believe it, he does now: that our thinking fails when it comes to this, when it comes to borders, water and sky that are the edges—that blue is the last color, in every known language, to be named.

19.

Hands open to the heat she waits.

He is taking her for another flying lesson. In the pockets of her overalls there is always a pen, always some paper. She is a promising student, he doesn't need to tell her that. Like all other growth in her life, all other knowledge, this goes without document or ceremony. It is evident only in how she speaks and moves. A word that wasn't available to her before, a concept she turns over alone. The desert is her partner in this, a blankness where she sees new parts of her life and thinking printed.

Behind her in the Florida evening is the rocket, designed she knows by the German whose first destroyed cities. She forgets what life is like with the cushion of sleep. In her pockets there is nearly nothing. A dime, the book of matches. The people around her know her name. To her they are legs in denim, feet in woven leather sandals. They hold signs and banners, photos of lives cut short. Numbers of innocent dead, of dollars spent on launches such as this. She knows to get to the real inside of any message is like a trip to the center of the earth. It goes only one way.

In his truck they hardly speak. Sometimes it is like this, a kind of praise, a proxy for love, evident in how little needs to be explained. There are his two fingers on her ear, there is the air that whips from his window over his body and then over hers, comparing the interruptions of their shapes. When they reach the hangar, a structure that looks accidental in the flat of sand, he kills the truck and slips his hand past the rivets at her waist, beneath the cotton men's undershirt to the curve of her belly.

She is arranged in lotus posture, an exacting shape her body knows well. It is not supposed to come easily, she can remember reading. Do not sickle the ankle. Enlightenment is a thousand lives away. The tops of her feet are flush with the tops of her thighs. The soles look at the sky. Then a question appears in her body, somewhere in her molars or the juncture in the throat that allows water in. Where is her son?

Both their doors are open. He keeps his face on the view while he does this to her, as if his middle fingers moving in her underwear are dependent on the purpling chaparral or the smear of cirrus. That he has seen this part of her more closely than she ever will, how it changes given touch or heat, has not gone unconsidered in her mind. A mirror couldn't show her, a camera couldn't. This is part and parcel of the female, which is created, she begins to know, not by who lives it but by who watches it—a male invention, stunning, wicked. She imagines herself as separate from the body he acts upon. At a certain moment he loses precision and goes too fast and she cries out. When it is over he calls her Clyde. Are you ready, Clyde? She hops onto the dirt first. It is how she needs him to see her, a few feet ahead, a few minutes more prepared.

The question she treats as any other thought, a ripple in the surface. Where is my son? She allows it to pass. A thought is not a rule or fact. It cannot yell or conduct heat. A thought alone cannot open a door or turn off a light.

As she prepares for the flight, circling the plane, he keeps his hands flat on his knees where he sits inside it. With the strength of her calves she rolls the plane two feet back to test the tread of the tires. She enunciates her checks, every light that works, calling out what this man has taught her in secret. Now she sits next to him. Right aileron. Left. Oil temperature at seventy-one.

The oil in her hair feels cooler and lighter than she had imagined, when she let herself. Less like a change to her body and more like a change in the weather. The match she lights without seeing.

Hats on, he says, and they slip the headsets over their ears, although she only ever listens. To the control tower, the low auctioneer voices that yawp numbers, it is always just him in the plane. The figures he bleats about its weight are lies, her one hundred and ten erased. What does this make her once they're off the ground? She passes beyond being his secret into something else, a life so removed from its context it weighs nothing.

The question comes to her again and she realizes now it is not her mind feeding it to her but something outside of her. A sound, an advancing movement. Her eyes are just cracked, a tiny crescent of vision, but what she sees is enough. Crouching, he removes the match from her hand and holds it there, a little limp. He has only planned this far. She knows this about him, the way he is led by his mind, the path up but not down.

It's a kind of pain she likes, becoming nobody, being nowhere anyone knows. As a child she was drawn to guest quarters yet to be furnished. As a child what she wanted to be was an empty room. The plane, taxiing now, is a sound so complete as to ask what was there before, and to answer, in the down-tick, nothing. The blue swims through the glass and into her mouth.

It is not what she says that will make a difference, but the voice that she uses, the name. No one knows it but the two of them. In speaking it into his ear she asks his permission to go. When she can no longer hear him breathing she lights another.

There is a kind of understanding that occurs just after. If we are lucky, we catch it at the door on our way out, watch it enter the rooms we have left. It is not always possible to tell the exact moment you have separated from the earth. So much of what we know for certain is irrelevant by the time we know it.

A NOTE ON
SOURCES, RESEARCH, AND
HISTORICAL VERACITY

Alan Bean, who left this planet again in 2018, was deeply generous with what he saw on the moon. My phone calls with him, speaking about color and sound, as well as life after the Apollo program, were a highlight not only of my research, but my life.

Sam Fordyce, who worked as engineer at NASA Headquarters Office of Manned Space Flight during the Apollo program, gave me great insight into that environment and the personalities that ruled it. For this interview, and his grace in welcoming me in, I am indebted.

Roger Hobler, at the Petaluma Pilot Training Center, taught me what I know about flying.

In certain cases, primary sources have been positioned here as fiction. Because these materials have entered the public domain and because they are the voices of the people who lived through this moment in history, I opted not to bring my own twenty-first-century imagination to their paraphrasing. The transcript of the Apollo 1 launchpad fire that killed Gus Grissom, Ed White, and Roger Chaffee on January 27, 1967, is used here, verbatim, in ser-vice of the fire that kills the fictional astronaut Sam Bisson in the fictional Apollo 1. Likewise, the letter drafted by the review committee of that incident finds direct use here. Pieces of the transcript of the Apollo 11 mission were also used in service of the fictional Apollo 11 mission, though departures in that case are significant.

Touring the jungle with Remigio "Casi Guapo" Grefa, of the Napo Wildlife Center in Yasuni National Park, was an education.

The memoranda of the Weathermen—who became the Weather Underground—inspired the memoranda of the fictional political collective on these pages; certain elements of their practices, ideas and misfortunes correspond with those of Shelter. Though it will be obvious to anyone familiar with that group's history that their trajectory is not mirrored here, it feels important to clarify that mimesis of their actions was not my intention. The Weatherpeople's writings, as collected in *Sing a Battle Song,* edited by Bernardine Dohrn, Bill Ayers, and Jeff Jones, were deeply helpful in my early thinking about this project, as was the 1970 journalistic investigation into Diana Oughton's life and death by Lucinda Franks and Thomas Powers.

The fictional protest image Wright describes in a letter to Vincent is in tribute to Bernie Boston's 1967 photograph *Flower Power.*

Mention of a demonstration at the fictional Apollo 11 launch refers directly to that organized by the civil rights leader Ralph Abernathy against the launch of Apollo 11. Protesters also met Apollo 11 goodwill tour stops at the University of Brasilia in Brazil, and in Montevideo, Uruguay; during a GSO tour, a GI reportedly asked Neil Armstrong why the U.S. was "so interested in the moon instead of the conflict in Vietnam." These pieces of research, many drawn from James R. Hansen's *First Man,* allowed me to comfortably imagine factually divergent instances of dissent. In terms of the Mercury, Apollo, Gemini, and Space Shuttle programs, I have tried to remain generally faithful to the milestones and trajectories as they really happened, and when.

Other books that served me greatly during the years I spent

with this project include Andrew Chaikin's *A Man on the Moon;* Charles DeBenedetti's *An American Ordeal;* Randy Shilts's *And the Band Played On;* Gabriel Rotello's *Sexual Ecology;* Gloria Emerson's *Winners & Losers;* Frances FitzGerald's *The Fire in the Lake; The Sixties Papers,* edited by Judith Clavir Albert and Stewart Edward Albert; and, of course, the poems and letters in Daniel Berrigan's *America Is Hard to Find.*

Pancho Barnes's Happy Bottom Riding Club, which burned in 1953, served as inspiration for Charlie's bar.

Conversations with Dean McArthur, MSW, helped me write about gay male sex and culture.

Finally, the reportage, correspondence, and journals of my father, David Lee Alcott (1941–2004), were a crucial introduction to my writing about the era. The light coming off my mother, Carolyn Power Alcott (1953–2013), who escaped her cul-de-sac in a Volkswagen and a few lives after that in as spectacular a manner, is at the center of this novel. "I want to be expanding gas, not shrinking solid," my father wrote once—and so he and my mother became.

ACKNOWLEDGMENTS

Thanks to

Catherine Lacey
The Russian River
Charles Buchan
The Rio Upano
Megan Lynch
The Carnic Alps
Sara Birmingham
Alexandra Christie
The San Gabriel Mountains
Jessica Friedman
Jin Auh
The MacDowell Colony
Blake Tewksbury
Cindy Fallows
Alex Ross Perry
Sebastian Pardo
The Saco River
Hollis, Maine
Guerneville, California

The Rio Grande
Jonathan Lee
Petaluma, California
John Wray
Columbia University
Jason Porter and Shelly Gargus
The White Mountains
Barbara Henderson
Brian Smith
The Green Mountains
Bennington College
Anni and Peter Wünschmann
Clinton Avenue, Brooklyn
Friesach, Austria
Catapult
Dorla McIntosh
Macas, Ecuador
Daniel Kaufman
The Kaweah River